THE GIRLS AT THE HOTEL GRAND

THE GIRLS AT THE HOTEL GRAND

A Novel

Mark Schreiber

ISBN: 0997616717
ISBN 13: 9780997616712

cover design by Julius Tan

CONTENTS

CHAPTER 1

A WORKING GIRL RETIRES

On the gleaming terrace of her new home, high in the hills of Escazu, Laura Mendoza Flores was mixing strawberry margaritas, waiting for her guests to arrive. Porter, however, was already there. A skeletal Virginian fast approaching fifty, Porter was the kind of man who always arrives first. His mother, a bank clerk, had preached punctuality next to cleanliness and godliness, which served him well in the Boy Scouts and in his own career as a bank manager, but which contributed to the sorrows in his personal life. One afternoon he had come home early and surprised his wife in their bedroom with their lawyer.

"Our lawyer!" he had cried to Laura several years ago, the night they had first met. "What could I do? Beat him up? He'd sue me for assault."

"You couldn't beat an infant," Laura had replied, encircling his bony wrist with her thumb and finger. "I've never seen any man so thin! You have one foot in the grave already!"

They had been lying naked in the Irazu suite at the Hotel Grand, But Laura's penetrating dark eyes were too much for him. This was his first trip to Costa Rica, and the divorce was still fresh. He had never been with a prostitute before and imagined downcast eyes, prolonged silences, an automated kind of experience, like an express car wash. And yet here was this foreign woman looking him in the eye, encircling his wrist with her fingers, sincerely listening. So he told her everything, things he had never told anyone. Details about his marriage he was too embarrassed to share with his friends, not that he had many friends. Then he showed her the pictures of his sons that he kept in his wallet and a picture of his ex-wife fell out. Laura told him how handsome his sons were and that one day she hoped to have two children, a boy and a girl. But when she saw the picture of the ex-wife she snatched it before Porter could react and shamed him with it as he had not even been shamed by the judge in divorce court.

"What is this doing here?" she demanded.

"I...I..."

Porter was a bank manager old enough to be this woman's father, wealthier, better educated, more respected in society. Yet none of that seemed to matter in the Irazu suite at the Hotel Grand.

"Burn it!" she ordered, taking a lighter from her purse and shoving it, with the picture, into his trembling hands.

Tears welled in his eyes. "I...can't!"

"She is a witch! Believe me, I can always tell. What is the word for money that is not real?"

"Counterfeit," Porter answered automatically.

"You told me you work at a bank. So you know counterfeit money. Well I know counterfeit people. You had the misfortune to marry a witch, and as long as you carry her picture the eyes of a witch will follow you."

They sat on the bed facing each other, her eyes trained on him, his on the photo. She pushed an ashtray into his lap and impatiently waited.

He cried and cried that night. For Porter was that kind of man too. The kind who cries in the arms of a whore.

But it's not just the witches who make men cry. Laura, with her penetrating gaze and stark honesty, has plunged many men from a fit of boyish revelry into girlish tears. How many times had their rash sentimentality compelled her to say the four words they could least bear to hear: "She doesn't love you."

She didn't want to do so now, with Porter. After all, this was a party to celebrate her new home and retirement. She didn't want to augur it with bad news.

But Porter displayed remarkable indiscretion for a banker. "It's too bad Ginger couldn't come," he said, sampling a margarita.

Laura finished pouring the drinks and stepped into the kitchen to check on the hors d'ouevres in the oven.

"I know you don't like her..." Porter continued unwisely.

Laura returned to the terrace and took his free hand in hers. "I probably wouldn't have this house without your advice. What do I know about houses and banks? Well, Porter, you're just as ignorant with women as I am with mortgages."

"I know Ginger isn't attracted to me physically. I don't expect her to be. That doesn't make her a witch. She's had a hard life. Her mother is sick."

Laura let go of his hand and sighed, glancing at the lush vegetation on the hillside. "Oh Porter, don't make me tell you."

"Tell me what?"

"My God, how did you ever succeed as a banker? When people come to you for loans do you say, 'Yes, with pleasure, are you sure you don't need more'? Or do you check them out? Have you ever actually met her mother?"

"Of course. I went with Ginger to Limon a few times."

"And was she on her deathbed? I bet she thought *you* were the one with one foot in the grave."

"I met her before her heart condition."

"Heart condition!" Laura exclaimed. "You're the one with the heart condition! Did you go to the hospital? Did you talk to doctors, ask for records?"

"This is the woman I'm going to marry, not a bank applicant—" he began to protest.

But Laura cut him off, taking his arm this time. "She took the four thousand dollars you gave her for her mother's operation and got a nose job!"

Porter took another sip of his drink, then laughed. "There's nothing wrong with her nose."

"She had a long nose with a bump on it and now she has a tiny nose like a Japanese. I saw her yesterday."

Porter set his drink on the folding table. Laura hadn't bought patio furniture yet, so he leaned against the wall for support. "Where did you see her? She told me she went to Limon."

"She went to the supermercado, that's where she went. I didn't talk to her of course. She didn't see me."

"Then how do you know it was her?" Porter asked in a hopeful voice. "If her nose was different I'm sure it was a different person. If you wanted me to believe you why didn't you take a picture with your cell phone?"

"I'm not a spy! And what's the point? She has you in a spell."

"She's beautiful and young and brings out a side in me I've never been able to express. Do you think any women like that at home would look twice at me?"

"I don't know about the women at home, but here there are plenty of women who would appreciate you. I'm sure you could find someone who would love you, and if you would let me help, if you would consider someone older than twenty-five... But this witch will never marry you. She will take your money to change her nose and other parts of her body so she can trap a man who is richer and better looking, and that's who she will marry. She doesn't love you."

It was early evening and the sun was still bright in the cloudless sky. Porter slumped on the terrace wall. His eyes swept across the city below, coming to rest on the sea green facade of the Hotel Grand. He wondered if Ginger was in one of its rooms with another man and not in Limon with her mother. He was trying to think of something to say in his defense, in her defense, when the doorbell rang.

Paulo was Laura's driver. Not hers exclusively, of course, but he drove a gypsy cab and his rates were more favorable than the official red taxis that swarmed around the Hotel Grand. But Laura preferred Paulo as much for his discretion as for his prices and punctuality. He was a quiet tico in his early thirties with a wife and three children. Laura didn't know anything more about him, and he never asked questions of her or her clients. In appreciation she had invited him to join the select few who would bridge the life she was leaving behind with the life she had attained.

She led him by hand to the terrace, offered him a margarita, and introduced him to Porter. They shook hands cordially but Pablo was shy and Porter preoccupied. "Don't you think this is a lovely view of San Jose?" Laura said to stir the conversation. "Look, you can even see the hotel! I feel like I'm an angel here, looking down on it all..."

But the doorbell rang again and she had to leave them to each other. Colorado Bob was already standing in the foyer, gawking at the cathedral ceiling, a bottle of Chilean wine wrapped in one arm and a Panamanian girl in the other.

"Moving up in the world!" he roared, his cowboy hat grazing the glass chandelier that lit the entrance to her home. "I thought you'd gotten too good for me!"

"I've always been too good for you," Laura replied, not quite with a smile. "Can I take your hat?"

"You know I'm sensitive about my bald spot," Colorado Bob said, handing her the wine instead and bending far down to give her a kiss. He tried for the lips but Laura reacted with the instinctive grace of a gazelle eluding the pounce of an overweight leopard and she only felt his grizzly white beard sweep across her cheek.

"This is Isabel," Colorado Bob said, letting go of his companion and stepping into the living room, sparsely furnished with a brown leather couch, a glass coffee table and an entertainment center. He went to the stereo, which was playing classical music, and began thumbing through the CDs.

Laura forced a smile at Isabel, trying to remember if she had said anything about bringing guests. Her list had been selective, of course even if it included Colorado Bob. Her mother hadn't been invited, nor—excepting Carmen and Tita Moon—other working girls. But she couldn't recall explicitly pointing this out to Colorado. She wished at this moment she hadn't invited him at all. He was neither discreet nor polite not sensitive, but they had a long history. He lived in the affluent expat suburb of San Pedro and had become as much a fixture at the Red Volcano bar at the Hotel Grand as the marlin hanging above the entrance. Planted on one of the far bar stools like a grizzly bear on a fire hydrant, a cigar in his mouth and a bottle of Coors within reach, he instructed groups of men like a Dear Abby for whoremongers, or let girls entertain him by sitting on his lap and lighting his cigar.

Laura had once been one of those girls. But his lap had proved too small for her, and her wit too sharp for him. He hadn't retired to Costa Rica, he hadn't escaped from the cold women he'd lived with in the cold Rockies, to be challenged by a warm tica in the tropics, to be seen for the soft man he was. But the Red Volcano bar in the Hotel Grand was the scene in San Jose, and neither Colorado Bob, who had traveled the world, or Laura, who had slept with men from all over the world, would have settled anywhere else. So they had reached an uneasy alliance, like neighboring Central American countries, lacking the affinity for trade or the firepower for war.

She wished she hadn't invited him. He had brought a prostitute Laura had never seen before, without even having the courtesy to ask, as if this were one of his whoremonger barbecues. He would take center stage, get drunk if he weren't already, fill the house with cigar smoke. Even now he was changing the Schubert, which set just the right tone for her new life, with coarse merengue.

"Will you turn it down!"

But her reasons for inviting him had been sound. Although he was a notorious gossip, he was bound to hear about the party one way or another, and so it was wiser not to snub him. And the truth is he had done some kindnesses for her in the past. He was a big man, not a fighter, but the sort of man who excels at breaking up the fights of others, especially when those altercations threaten to spill his beer. He could also chase off a man with a few words, when a lot of words from a woman proved insufficient, and this he had done for Laura on one or two occasions. She had also invited him out of vanity and pride, as if to demonstrate that she and other women were *Homo sapiens* after all, like him. Or better. But even if these reasons hadn't persuaded her, she would have invited him anyway because she had to invite Dennis, and she couldn't expect her new employer to come without his best friend.

"Where's Dennis?" she asked, peering out the door. "Parking the car."

Laura turned her attention back to Isabel, who hadn't said a word or moved from the foyer. She was an average-looking girl of about twenty, dark skinned, with short, kinky hair, wide cheeks, a high forehead. Her eyes were demure but she stood with her back straight, her dark shoulders revealed in a strapless brown cotton dress. She wasn't wearing jewelry except for silver earrings. Her nails weren't painted and she was tall enough to get away with low heels.

Laura, on the other hand, had just had her shoulder-length hair permed and had gotten a French manicure and pedicure. She was wearing a sunflower print dress, gold loop earrings and high gold heels that brought her within reach of everyone but Colorado Bob.

"I haven't seen you before," she said, analyzing Isabel with her eyes.

"I'm new. Two weeks."

"Where are you from?"

"Panama City."

Laura forced a smile. At least she wasn't Colombian. And then she chided herself for being ungenerous. She was her guest, after all, and a member of the profession. It wasn't her fault she wasn't Costa Rican. If Laura had been Panamanian she would probably have come here to work as well.

"I'm studying at the university there," Isabel explained, making eye contact.

Laura flashed her eyes back at her. "Aren't we all."

Then, after an uncomfortable pause, "How much is he paying you?"

Isabel had never encountered such directness, not even in the men who approached her in the hotel, not even in Colorado Bob. She looked toward him, uncertain what to do, but he was still playing with the stereo.

"Eighty dollars."

"For last night?"

"Not all night."

Laura drew closer to her. "You know the price is a hundred, don't you?"

"I asked for a hundred."

"But you settled for eighty. That drives down business for all of us, don't you see?"

It took an effort from Isabel to again make eye contact.

Although Laura was only three years older, she felt as though she were speaking to a woman of her mother's generation. "Colorado told me you were retired."

"What's that have to do with it? *I'm* retired," Laura yelled a little too loudly. "But I have friends who are not. Costa Rican friends who are not studying at the university, who have children's mouths to feed. And when you go for eighty instead of a hundred that means they have to go for eighty and that twenty dollars they don't make is twenty dollars they don't have in their purses to pay the taxi or the nanny or the day care or the grocery!"

Isabel's back slumped and she looked down, as she had in high school when she'd received bad marks. She was about to cry.

"And what about today?" Laura pressed on.

"She's off the meter today," Colorado Bob answered, remembering his date and taking her hand protectively, or possessively.

Laura set the bottle of wine on the coffee table. "Give me your wallet!"

Colorado laughed. But he gave her his wallet, thick with credit cards and bills.

Laura took out a twenty. Colones were the official currency in Costa Rica, but dollars were liberally exchanged. "This is the balance for last night," she said, handing it to Isabel. She then gave her a crisp hundred dollar bill as well. "And this is for today. And if he keeps you all night two hundred more."

She pressed the thinner wallet against Colorado Bob's large belly and he accepted it back with a sigh. "Stiffest motherfucking cover charge in history," he muttered not too loudly.

Isabel held the bills out for a moment, glancing at Colorado, expecting the big man to snatch them back. When he stuffed his wallet into his jeans she gleefully placed the money in her vinyl pocketbook. A moment ago she was fighting tears. Now she had to suppress a grin of triumph. She had been wrong to compare Laura to her schoolteachers. No schoolteacher had ever taught her such a valuable lesson.

Laura took each of them by the arm. "Come on the terrace. Have a margarita."

She could no longer hear the doorbell because of the merengue. She wanted to greet all her guests at the door, like a proper hostess, but Dennis surprised her on the terrace.

"Thanks for inviting me," he said, giving her a warm hug, which she returned.

"You didn't bring a date too?" Laura asked, glancing behind him for a straggling companion.

"There was no room in the car. Colorado takes up the whole back seat."

"She could have sat on my lap," Colorado said, engulfing the younger man with his arm. "All work and no play."

Dennis had first come to Costa Rica for a whitewater rafting trip with some college buddies. Before going home he had not only discovered the girls at the Hotel Grand but the business opportunities just waiting for the right entrepreneur. Costa Rica was a democracy with ninety-four percent literacy. Good schools, free healthcare, a large gringo community, tax incentives for foreign investment. He had received an MBA from San Diego State and, after a couple years working for a retail corporation in California, he saw Costa Rica as his chance to start his own company.

Laura excused herself to check on the hors d'ouevres, and returned with a tray of Italian meatballs and breaded shrimp. She also brought out a wheel of gouda cheese. All this she set on the table beside the margaritas, with small paper plates toothpicks, and festive napkins.

"Please help yourself, everyone. There is more warming in the oven."

"Hot dogs I hope?" Colorado Bob teased, spearing one of the shrimp with a toothpick.

"In my country we do not serve hot dogs at cocktail parties," Laura informed him.

"You made these?" Dennis asked, tasting one.

"That depends whether you like them or not. Actually I have to confess I have a friend who is a chef. I just heated them."

"A male friend no doubt," Colorado Bob guessed. "And all men here," he added, glancing at the others. If I hadn't brought Isabel I would think this was a stag party. I thought you were retiring, not drumming up business."

"I would rather starve than have your business," Laura shot back. "Carmen and Tita are coming. And Raquel, from the travel desk."

"A civilian!" Colorado Bob exclaimed at the mention of Raquel. "Maybe she'll see this house and this view and join up! God knows I've tried to corrupt her. Maybe the way to a woman's pussy is through a three-bedroom villa in the hills!"

Nobody really ever laughed at Colorado's jokes, but he always laughed loudly enough that he wouldn't have heard them if they had. So it didn't really matter. Polite smiles from his friends and the women he paid for were enough for him.

Laura thought it strange that Dennis and Colorado had become friends. But she realized that if opposites can attract in love, why not in friendship? Dennis was much younger, more fit, intellectual, sensitive, industrious. He wore polo shirts and khakis and was always clean shaven, smelling of cologne. He preferred wine to beer, chess to cards, golf to football, and was too fastidious in his romantic tastes to take advantage of the variety of female accomplishment on hand at the Red Volcano. He had found a girl there once, but she had been too much to his liking and he inevitably fell in love with her. Laura, of course. She profited greatly from the experience, and he had gained as well. True, he lost his heart and his equanimity. But the best nights of his life were the nights he had spent with her. In time it became too messy. She didn't consider him boyfriend material, though she liked his company and wished all her clients treated her as respectfully. "Tell me how to turn you on," he had said during their only heated exchanged, after a session of lovemaking during which she had been particularly unresponsive. To which she had acridly replied, "Sometimes you can't even teach an MBA how to fuck!"

But a friendship had emerged at the other end of that tunnel, and now they were heading even farther afield, into business together.

Dennis would naturally have encountered Colorado Bob through his friendship with Laura, but they never would have become friends themselves had a fishing buddy of Colorado's not eloped with a Nicaraguan maid the night before they were scheduled on a Pacific charter. Colorado made an announcement in the bar and Dennis happened to be there. He had toyed the with idea of deep sea fishing. Even though San Jose sat in a valley surrounded by mountains, it was almost as hard not to think about game fishing at the Hotel Grand as it was not to think about women. There were fishing brochures at the travel desk, photos of famous catches on the wall behind reception, marlin place mats in the restaurant, enameled marlins on the tile surrounding the pool, marlins carved into the door of the Irazu Suite, and of course the marlin hanging over the bar.

So Dennis volunteered.

"Ever been deep sea fishing?" Colorado had asked, suspiciously eyeing Dennis's polo shirt and khakis.

"No, but I've done quite a lot of whitewater rafting. Usually we go too fast to catch much of anything," he added in a spirit of bravado that he had grown accustomed to hearing at the Hotel Grand but hadn't quite acquired himself.

Colorado Bob extended his hand. "That and two hundred dollars is good enough for me."

One would assume a man who has run Class IV rapids would find the lolling Pacific off Puntarenas hypnotic and might have to be shaken from time to time so he didn't fall asleep at his pole. But the vestibular canal, which signals motion to the brain, makes distinctions which can shock even the most rabid sportsman. Dennis threw up from one side of the bay to the other, leaving Colorado no choice but to drink the whitewater rafter's share of the beer. It was a story Colorado would mercilessly exploit to all who would listen.

"Level IV rapids my ass! This motherfucker gets on the boat with me and we've hardly weighed anchor, he starts puking his guts out. And it's a calm day! Ha, ha ha!"

But Colorado had taken pity on the Southern Californian, whom he'd nicknamed "Polo." Every whoremonger in Costa Rica needs a nickname, Colorado Bob had proclaimed, driving Dennis home and tucking him in bed.

Dennis was surprised to find that his weakness on the seas endeared him to the gringos at the Red Volcano. Colorado took a paternal interest in him, not having children of his own. He also realized Dennis was bright and ambitious and might be useful to him one day. Dennis, for his part, had never been a man's man and savored the slaps on the back, the barbecues, and the long nights hunched over poker chips.

"Hello, it's me! Where is everyone?" came a high-pitched voice from the living room. This was Tita Moon, trailed by Carmen. Tita Moon was a nickname her father had given her as a child, and since it was unique it was not wise to use it as her working name. But Tita Moon was not the most reflective of women, and was too proud to have a name given to her by her father not to show it off. Besides, her father was a fisherman in Puntarenas, so there wasn't much likelihood he would pop into the Hotel Grand at one o'clock in the morning. He did not share his daughter's passion for life, her vivacity and uninhibited curiosity, and they didn't have much to say to each other when she visited her parents, but Tita Moon took uncommon pride in this rather common man and spoke about him to her friends whenever the opportunity arose, for she was that rarest of girls at the Hotel Grand—a girl with a father.

She and Carmen were working tonight and would go directly from Laura's party to the hotel, so they were already dressed in combat attire—low-cut, tight designer jeans that accentuated their round asses, tight tops that revealed their navel studs, light makeup, thick hair gel, expensive perfume that preceded them to the terrace.

Laura made the introductions, Colorado Bob lit their cigarettes. He knew both girls but had never slept with them because they wouldn't come down from a hundred, even when there were twenty girls in the place for every guy, or at three o'clock in the morning when the bar was thinning out and prospects bleak.

"Look at this place!" Tita Moon exclaimed, spinning around like an ice skater. "Wow, it's amazing!"

She was short, like Laura, but more voluptuous, with a round ass, large natural breasts, and an adorable wide face with wide eyes. She had light brown skin and wore her kinky hair cut just below her ears, dyed a dark shade of orange.

Carmen had a similarly seductive body, but bronze skin, a smaller mouth, and long straight black hair, which she wore tonight in a ponytail. Both she and Tita were twenty-three, a year younger than their host, but they appeared even younger and were invariably asked for their ID's at clubs.

"I'll give you a tour," Laura offered. "A lot of blood and sweat went into this house."

"And cum!" Tita Moon added.

Unlike Colorado Bob, everyone laughed at Tita Moon's jokes. How could they not? Her devious grin, her full moon eyes were comical enough without her high-pitched gutter humor, and her own squealing laugh—unlike Colorado Bob's oppressive laugh—was often infectious. Although it must be admitted she also flustered many men by breaking out into laughter at precisely the wrong moment.

Raquel from the travel desk had yet to arrive, but Laura was too excited to wait. Leading guests through her own home was a dream she had entertained for years. As a teenager she had gazed up at the houses in the hills and imagined one of those houses as her own. Of course at that age her dream had been to marry a rich man. She could not imagine that a man—or one man—would be unnecessary to her reaching such a lofty height, that she could do it by herself, her name alone on the mortgage.

She grabbed the garage door opener from the kitchen counter and led the party outside, all the way to the wrought iron fence, so that they could view her house in full. Not that they had to walk very far. The yard was tiny, with untended flower beds flanking the steps to the door and a single palm tree which gave no shade. The house itself was single-story Spanish, the garage flush with the bright white stucco facade. Most of the windows were in the back, to take advantage of the view. From the front the only glazing was the window to the master bathroom and bezeled panes around the door.

"Can you believe I have my own palm tree!" she exclaimed, hugging it like a child. "I always hoped I would own a home but for some reason I never thought about trees. I am going to grow hibiscus here," she said, pointing to the flower beds.

She opened the garage. "Of course I don't have a car, but someday..."

"It's bigger than my apartment," Tita Moon said, stepping inside and looking around, although there was nothing to see.

"You could rent it out," Colorado Bob suggested.

Laura took this as one of Colorado's jokes. "I guess there are some people who would live in a garage."

"I mean for storage," he clarified.

Laura suddenly saw the gray concrete walls lined with green dollars. She made some quick calculations and realized the space might bring in five hundred dollars a year. And she began to think of what she could buy for five hundred dollars. Why did she need a garage anyway? If she ever did buy a car she could park it in the driveway.

"Do you know anyone who needs storage?"

"I can ask around. I might rent it myself."

Laura didn't know how to respond. She could certainly use the money, and it wasn't as though Colorado Bob would be living there, but he would be visiting often enough, rummaging around, piling up who knows what, old shoes and fishing poles, carcasses of animals. She looked at the garage door opener in her hand and realized she could never give it to someone like Colorado Bob. She would rent the garage to a retired couple or an affluent family or a gringo without dirt under his fingernails, but not to Colorado Bob for any price.

"This is the utility room," she said, leading them inside. "If anyone has an extra washing machine I'll be happy to take it off your hands."

She opened another door, which lead to a long hallway with three doors on the left. She invited them into a small bedroom, made to look more spacious because it was furnished only with a new twin bed and a white wooden nightstand with a plastic lamp on top. Laura had furnished the other guest room the same way, and had done so not only to attract lodgers but to attract the right kind of lodgers.

She had put yellow curtains on the large window, the room's best feature. But Tita Moon didn't care about the view. While the others peered out, she plopped down on the white duvet, as if to stake a claim.

"Get off, I'll have to clean it."

Tita Moon lay where she was and inhaled the rarefied air of Escazu. "Get out of my room! I'm trying to rest."

"How much are you asking?" Dennis said.

It wasn't as though her plans were a secret, she had talked about them often enough, at least in general terms. Renting the two rooms would pay her mortgage. Her job with Dennis would cover her other expenses, and she hoped she would even be able to save enough for a car, or for the university if she decided to take classes. And now that she was finished with the Hotel Grand and all the wrong men who frequented the Red Volcano, she had every reason to believe she would find the right man. And when that moment of destiny arrived she would be a woman of property, she wouldn't succumb to rash decisions caused by economic desperation. She could even get her own tourist visa to the U.S. without marrying a gringo or bribing a lawyer. She could join the class of people who traveled on planes larger than the thirty-two seaters that plied her small country. She might even meet the man of her dreams on such a vacation. It would be so ironic, with all the men coming to Costa Rica to find women, that she would travel to Florida or California or New York and find a man. And if she was still single in a year or two she might sell the house. Property values were soaring in Escazu and she was bound to make a large profit, which she could use to start her own business, just like Dennis was starting his own business. Why should it always be the gringos who got rich in Costa Rica?

"Three hundred dollars," she replied.

Tita Moon sat up and threw her tattered Mickey Mouse purse into Laura's arms. "Take what I have. I'll give you the rest in a day or two."

"Get off of the bed, you're wrinkling the sheets," Laura said, setting the unopened purse on the floor.

"I'm not joking," Tita Moon pursued, looking at Laura directly.

It was hard to say whose eyes were larger, or darker, but at this moment Tita Moon's were the more penetrating, and Laura glanced away in confusion, sensing this pretty little white room with yellow curtains, which had seemed so idyllic when she was picking out the furniture, might be a volcano that could explode at the slightest tremor.

"You already have an apartment," was all Laura could think to say.

"I live in the slums. My roof is made of tin and I have no windows and I lock my door with a padlock! I pay one hundred for that shit. What's two hundred more? This room is so light and clean and sweet."

"It's not a good idea to rent to friends."

"So we won't be friends anymore," Tita Moon declared with impeccable logic. She gave Laura a big squeeze. "Hello landlord!"

"No, Tita."

"Come on. I'm serious."

"It's impossible," Laura said, disentangling herself. She looked to the others for help, but they were pretending to admire the view. She was on the verge of soliciting their support when she realized they might instead side with her prospective lodger, so she simply retreated to the door.

"You don't want me because I'm a whore!" Tita Moon shouted.

All eyes turned to Laura, who was now standing in the hallway, as if acknowledging the room were no longer her own.

"Yes, I won't rent to you because you're a whore! This isn't the Hotel Grand."

"That's illegal. You can't discriminate against me. There are tenant laws."

"You watch too much TV! That's the U.S. maybe, not here. It's my house and I can do what I want."

"Oh please!" she begged, suddenly softening. "At least think about it. I won't bring men. I promise."

Laura didn't want to keep arguing, but neither did she want to give Tita Moon reason to hope she might change her mind. "It's bad luck to talk business at a party," she said instead. "Now to show you the rest of the house..."

But the next door was the second bedroom. Laura gripped the knob. What if Colorado Bob launched himself onto the bed? She would be run out of her own house.

"It's the same as the first bedroom," she said, opening the door only wide enough so they could peek inside to confirm her description, but not letting them enter.

"The guest bathroom. Nothing special." She flung the door open and moved on. "You've seen the living room," she continued, waving at the entertainment center. And the dining room. Someday I'll buy a table, but I don't need one right now. The island in the kitchen is good enough. Don't touch the oven, it's hot. Can I get anyone another drink? And the master bedroom," she said, slowing down to let them pass. After all, they couldn't lay claim to that, could they? Her clothes were already hanging in the walk-in closet and her slippers were on the floor.

"No twin bed here," Colorado Bob observed.

"I've never seen such a big closet," Carmen said, disappearing inside. "And look at all these shoes! Fuck!" And she began counting. "You have twenty-five pairs of shoes!"

"Twenty-seven," Laura corrected. "You forgot the slippers out here and the heels I'm wearing. Hey, no guys allowed!" she shouted, pulling Pablo away with one hand and Dennis with the other. When the girls stepped out she closed the closet door.

"And no testing the bed," she told Colorado Bob, who was bouncing on the edge. She pointed toward a rattan chair in the corner. "If you're tired you can sit there."

The window was larger than in the guest rooms but the view was the same, so it didn't attract much attention from her guests. Instead they glanced over the nightstands on either side of the bed, one with a lamp and alarm clock, the other with her cell phone charger, a dish filled with coins, and a small framed photograph turned face down. There wasn't much else to look at—a pink throw rug at the foot of the bed, a Monet print on the wall.

The master bathroom was big enough for all of them. Carmen turned on the vanity mirror and checked her makeup. Colorado

Bob salivated over the jacuzzi. "I've always wanted one of these, but I'm just a poor gringo."

Laura laughed. It was the first time she had ever laughed at one of Colorado Bob's jokes. But it was a compliment, after all. And at least he wasn't getting his fingerprints on the faucet.

"Let's go back on the terrace," she suggested, glancing over all of them, except Tita Moon, whose acquisitive eyes she avoided.

The sun was beginning to set in the valley. Scattered lights glimmered below. The hors d'oeuvres were a big hit and Laura served the second batch from a ceramic tray. The margarita pitcher was also empty and she slipped away to the kitchen to refill it. When she returned Porter was the first to take advantage. A minute later she spotted him in the corner of the terrace, leaning against the wall, talking into his cell phone.

"Don't be rude, Porter. Come mingle with the other guests."

She took his arm but he remained where he was. He wasn't having a conversation after all but just leaving a message. Laura heard him whisper "I love you," before putting the phone in his pocket.

"Why don't I get you some juice," Laura said, trying to take the glass.

But he raised it to his lips and drank distractedly. Laura had never seen him drunk. She didn't drink herself and avoided drunks whenever possible, although for a woman in her profession—or former profession—drunks were ubiquitous and it was simply impractical to refuse them. Sure, she would turn down men who were belligerent or offensive, however much they offered, the ones who pinched her ass too hard or tried to kiss her on the lips or called her "puta," a demeaning word for prostitute. But from a business point of view alcohol had its advantages. Drunk men tended to haggle less and fuck less. They fell asleep quickly and didn't wake her with a stiff cock at six o'clock in the morning. Still, she deplored the conversation of men who had drunk too much and their ceaseless insistence that she drink as well. These were men whose sole strategy for laying women was to ply them with alcohol to release their inhibitions. "But I am going to sleep with you," Laura had said on countless occasions. "Why do you care whether I drink or not?"

In the present situation, her concern wasn't that an inebriated Porter would ruin her party. How could she worry about something so trivial when she saw the sadness in his eyes? Rather she feared he might crash driving home or make some other desperate mistake.

"Ginger doesn't answer," he said, looking at Laura with his sad eyes. "Maybe I should go to Limon."

"You can't leave my party. I haven't even served the cake." She squeezed his arm. "Don't worry, Porter. She'll marry you."

"You think so?"

Laura didn't think so at all, but she said it to save his life, because she knew if he tried to drive to Limon tonight he would plunge into darkness from one of the steep mountain roads.

"Will you come to the wedding?"

It will be a witch wedding, Laura thought, but she nodded agreeably.

"Hey girl!" Raquel exclaimed, poking her in the back.

Laura spun around and saw the girl from the travel desk beaming affectionately, wearing a denim mini-skirt, a red blouse and flat shoes, and holding out a large gift adorned with a golden bow. She was tall enough and beautiful enough to be a model, but she walked with the lumbering, heavy gait of a man and had none of the pretensions that beautiful women have. She had straight blond-streaked hair, olive skin, high cheekbones and blue eyes. Many people thought she was European, and Italian blood probably flowed in her veins, but her parents and grandparents had all been born in Costa Rica.

"What's this?" Laura asked, taking the gift.

"A housewarming present. Open it."

Tears almost came to Laura's eyes. None of the other guests had brought gifts, nor had she expected any. The wine from Colorado and Dennis was for the party. It wasn't a traditional housewarming present.

"You didn't have to bring something," Laura protested, but she was already undoing the bow.

The others crowded around and Laura held up a set of crystal margarita glasses.

"Ayyy! They're beautiful," she shouted. "And we can use them right away. Since it's your gift you will have the honor or being served first." And Laura opened the package, washed out the glasses and handed Raquel a margarita.

"Did you just come from work?" Laura asked.

"Yeah. That's why I'm late. I hope you weren't waiting for me."

"Not at all. It's just a cocktail party, not a dinner party. But now that you're here we can have the cake."

Laura started to speak again but held her tongue. She was on the verge of asking Raquel about the hotel. In the past she would have pressed her for information. Was it busy? Who was there? Were there many girls? But she realized with a sense of relief that none of these statistics mattered. The place could be swarming with statuesque Colombian girls with fake tits. There could be a convention of cheap mongers with their Nicaraguan sweethearts. She would never know. She wasn't going to the hotel tonight.

"Have you seen the view?" she asked, leading Raquel to the low wall. "Look, there's the Grand. I don't have much of a backyard because of the hill. My property only goes to those magnolia bushes, but that's less that I have to take care of. Would you like to see the house?"

This time Laura went in the opposite direction, showing the master bedroom first. When they reached the second guest bedroom Laura closed the door behind them with a flash of inspiration, wondering why the thought had not crossed her mind before.

"Maybe you would be interested in renting this room?" she said in a hushed voice, as if Tita Moon might be listening outside. "You would be able to use the kitchen and living room when I'm not there, it would be like having your own house. I'm going to buy some patio furniture for the terrace. You could sit out there every night after you come home from work and sip a margarita."

Laura had placed ads in *La Nacion* and the *Tico Times* but had received no offers. Raquel might not be able to afford the rent, but it was worth asking. They had been friends for more than a year and, although they rarely socialized outside the hotel, Laura knew Raquel was just the kind of tenant she desired—quiet, clean, responsible, polite. Raquel was nineteen, had never been married, or even lived with a man. In Laura's eyes she was practically a virgin.

Raquel considered the offer carefully. She had a car, so the commute would not be a problem. And she believed Laura would be a fair landlord and a pleasant housemate. Normally she wouldn't want to associate with a prostitute, but Laura was different from the others, and besides she had retired.

The girls at the Hotel Grand were independent workers. They could come and go as they pleased as long as they showed their National Identity Card, proving they were over eighteen, and registered before going up to a room. The women who did work for the hotel, the maids and barmaids and waitresses and reception clerks and travel desk clerks were not on offer and could in fact lose their jobs if they went upstairs with a man. Even though these women were often young and pretty themselves, and regularly solicited by men who weren't satisfied with the hundred genuine prostitutes coursing through the hotel, an invisible barrier existed between them, a sort of moral apartheid. The employees tended to either scorn the putas or envy them, or both. They resented these girls who didn't have to work, who were spoiled by otherwise intelligent men and received more attention than they deserved, who threw away the equivalent of a clerk's monthly paycheck on shoes and perfume and cocaine. The prostitutes sensed this, of course, and kept their distance, not wishing to be judged. Anyway, who were these women to judge them? Punching time clocks for low wages, marrying working class ticos who would never buy them diamond pendants or long-stemmed roses or tickets to Miami.

But Raquel was a tolerant young woman, a psychology major who found the human and animal nature displayed in the hotel more instructive than text books. She had enough self-confidence not to worry that these people would corrupt her, and was not so insecure as to be intimidated by the opinions of others. Since she had begun to work at the hotel, Laura had often sat on the other side of the travel desk, holding the hand of a client who wished to take her to Tamarindo Beach or Manual Antonio National Preserve or Arenal Volcano for the weekend, or to any one of the full or half-day tours listed in the brochure. Laura didn't have any tattoos and only her ears were pierced. She dressed elegantly in dresses or skirts and blouses, was articulate, kind and funny, and no more judgmental than Raquel herself. On one occasion her client had gone back up to his room to get his credit card from the safe and this gave the two girls a few minutes to discover each other. Laura had noticed the psychology textbook and asked which year she was in and what she planned to do when she got her degree. "I bet I can teach you more about the psychology of men than that book!" she boasted. Which led Raquel to pull out a handwritten letter in English from her drawer, from a guest who had booked a canopy tour and now wanted her to visit him in Milwaukee.

"Are you in love?" Laura had asked.

"I don't really know him. He seems nice. We didn't go out when he was here. But now he's writing me letters."

Laura took the letter, but her client returned before she could read it. A couple weeks later she stopped by the travel desk after spending the night in the hotel, and asked about the man from Wisconsin.

Raquel shrugged. "Oh, I e-mailed him my phone number, but he didn't call, or write again," she said in a disappointed voice.

Laura leaned forward. "When he wrote you that letter he had probably been fighting with his wife or girlfriend, and now they are back together. It happens all the time."

She was about to go home, but when she saw the disappointment on Raquel's face she invited her to lunch. And although, due to their conflicting schedules, they hadn't often socialized outside the hotel since that time, Laura made a point to stop by the travel desk when she happened to be at the hotel during the day, and when Raquel for one reason or another had to work late, she searched for Laura in the bar before leaving, on the pretense of official business, and the two women, like enemy soldiers leaving their trenches during a Christmas truce, shared stories of the unending war between women and men.

"I would love to live here," Raquel said, fingering the curtain as if it were the finest silk. "But I'm sure I can't afford it."

"I'm asking three hundred a month. How much are you paying now?"

"A hundred and twenty."

"Hmmm. Is that with utilities?"

"No."

"Well I'll include utilities."

"Do you know what I make at the Grand? And a lot of that goes into my car. Just last month I had to repair an oil leak."

Laura wasn't willing to give up so easily. The thought of paying the full mortgage herself, even if only for a month, unsettled her. It would be prudent to secure one of the rooms, even if she had to slash the rent. She could make up some of the difference by renting the garage, as Colorado Bob suggested.

"If..." Laura proposed, with the air of a government agent announcing the winning bid for a highway contract. "If you would be willing to do some light housework, cleaning and whatever,

maybe, maybe, I can let you stay here for two hundred a month."
She looked straight at Raquel, and when her friend failed to respond, she did the math for her. "You're paying a hundred and twenty now. With utilities that's probably two hundred—"

"A hundred and fifty."

"OK, a hundred and fifty. And I'm offering you a home in Escazu for only fifty dollars more!"

Raquel hesitated a moment longer before letting out a shout and taking Laura in her arms. "How can I thank you?"

"Let's just not say anything about this to the others," Laura replied, as she opened the door. "It's bad luck to talk business at parties."

Tita Moon corralled her in the kitchen while she was taking the cake out of the box. "I know you're afraid I will eat your food," she said. "But I promise I won't even use your salt. I can even buy a small refrigerator and keep it in my room."

Laura counted out paper plates and plastic forks, ignoring her.

"I'll also do the cleaning! Not just my room, all the rooms. You won't have to hire a maid."

For a moment Laura wondered if Tita Moon *had* been listening in the hallway. "I'll need two maids to clean up after you! I've seen your apartment. It's filthy."

"I live in the slums. Why should I sweep a concrete floor? Here it will be different."

"If your heart is set on Escazu I'm sure there are plenty of other houses with rooms for rent."

"Is that what you say in your ad?"

Laura hated confrontation, especially on those rare occasions when her position wasn't supported by logic, compassion and fairness.

"You know me," Tita Moon pleaded.

"Yes, exactly."

"I thought we were friends. If you don't want me in your house why did you invite me to your party?"

"Because we are friends, Tita. And as a friend you are always welcome in my home. But to live here, it would be a big mistake. I've worked very hard to get out of that life, and even if you didn't bring men here—and I know you would bring men here, Tita. You can't help yourself. But even if you didn't, you would bring that world inside these walls just the same."

Tita Moon realized she wouldn't get any further tonight and had made a tactical error in offering to do the cleaning. "You'll feel different in a few weeks when the rooms are still empty. You'll be happy then to accept me as a tenant. But I won't do the cleaning. You're right, I hate to clean. I'd rather swallow cum than mop the floor!"

She stormed back out to the terrace, leaving Laura to carry the cake, plates, knife and forks herself. Laura was too modest to congratulate herself for her retirement or new home, so the cake simply read, "Pura Vida," a Costa Rican idiom that celebrated this slice of heaven squeezed between the ocean and the sea.

She handed out the cake, not overlooking Tita Moon, who diplomatically accepted.

Her guests raised their glasses in a toast and Colorado Bob yelled, "Speech!"

Laura set down her glass and looked at her friends, wiping a tear from her eye. "Thank you. Thank you all for coming. I've dreamed of this moment for a long time," she said with the impatience of youth. "Now God has answered my prayers, and you, my friends... Well, without you, I don't know where I would be."

Dennis caught her eye and thought her smile was for him alone, although it might have been the growing shadows that made the exchange appear more private than it was, or the three margaritas he'd drunk, which were two-and-a-half more than he could consume without ill effect. He had felt shamed when Raquel presented her gift. Why hadn't he brought a housewarming present? What an idiot he was, completely lacking in social graces. But he had a brainstorm now and, encouraged by the tequila, stepped forward to make his presentation.

It was too late to give a housewarming present, but this was also a retirement party, and the moment to honor that had not yet passed.

"Ah...excuse me, I'd like to make an announcement," he said.

Everyone stopped talking, somewhat surprised. Dennis was even less given to public speaking than Porter, and despite the months he had spent among these people, he did not feel socially comfortable among them.

"It's a custom in the U.S... I mean, it's an old custom, I don't know if they do it anymore, I think with people getting laid off before they're old enough to retire... What I'm trying to say, is that our custom was to present the retiree with a watch."

"Why does someone who retires need a watch? They should give the watch when they start the job, not when they finish," Laura declared.

This wasn't going as smoothly as Dennis had hoped. But it was a spontaneous gesture, he shouldn't expect perfection. "So I would like to give a watch."

Of course, since the idea had just occurred to him, he could only give his own watch. But it was a substantial gift, a stainless steel Tag Heuer with a calendar.

"You idiot, that's a man's watch!" Colorado Bob said. Dennis was mortified. His heavy Tag Heuer was unmistakably a man's watch. A woman could never wear it.

He reached to grab it back, but Laura had already taken possession and was holding it triumphantly in the air by the strap. She gave him a kiss on the cheek.

"Of course I'll replace it with a ladies' model," he said.

"I'll keep it on my nightstand," Laura told him.

Dennis beamed like a child. The idea of having something of his so close to her filled him with a sudden warmth.

The sun had set and the lights of the city shimmered below. Laura lit half a dozen candles and set them on the wall to illuminate the terrace. But even though the night was still early, the party was concluding. Pablo's cell phone rang and he had to excuse himself to take a fare. Laura asked him to drop Porter on his way. He was in no condition to drive and could get his car tomorrow. She was relieved that Porter acquiesced.

"Go to sleep," she advised him. "You have all day tomorrow to pine for your witch."

And it was time for Carmen and Tita Moon to go to work. Their day was just beginning.

"I'll be back," Tita Moon told Laura. "With my things. In a week or two when the rooms are still empty. And I won't clean a fucking thing!"

After they'd gone Laura took Raquel aside. "When can you move in?"

"I pay by the week and I don't have to give notice. So tomorrow."

"Tomorrow! Great. If you need any help I have a friend with a truck who won't charge much. And please don't mention this at the hotel. You know how the girls there gossip. Tita wants to live here, but I can't let her, you understand? She'll just cause trouble if she learns I'm renting to you, even though you're not a working girl."

"But she'll find out eventually."

"She doesn't have to know now. Maybe if enough time passes she'll have a new boyfriend, or she won't have the money. Or she'll have changed her mind for any one of a thousand reasons."

She walked Raquel out, then said goodbye to Colorado Bob and the girl from Panama, who whispered a heartfelt "mucho gracias" in her ear.

She thought they had all gone, but when she stepped back onto the terrace Dennis was pouring another margarita.

"Thanks again for the watch. That was very sweet."

He stepped toward her. Close enough so that she could smell his cologne and he could smell her shampoo. "I thought I could take you to dinner."

"I'm not going out."

"Then I can make something here."

"I'm not hungry. It's been a long day and I'm going to bed."

"But you never go to bed this early!"

"I have a new schedule now," she joked. "I will no longer go to sleep with the cocks. I will wake up with them."

Dennis wavered before her, his mouth open but not knowing what to say. She could smell the tequila on his breath. "Let Colorado drive," she said. "I thought he would be the problem and look who got drunk instead. Porter and you."

"I won't drive. I'm going to stay here."

"What are you talking about? I just said I'm going to sleep." "In my arms," he declared, taking her in his.

She pushed him away like a rag doll. "Are you crazy? The day of my retirement and you want to sleep with me?"

"I wasn't going to pay you."

"Get out. Out!"

She grabbed him by the hand and led him to the door and slammed it behind him. Then she opened it again and shouted down the street, with a hint of ironic disapproval, "I'll see you in the office Monday. Boss!"

Each girl at the Hotel Grand had arrived by her own path, but somehow those myriad roads were all the same. If you were a tica of eighteen or twenty or twenty two, or a Colombian or Panamanian or Nicaraguan or Dominican who could make her way to San Jose, if you been deserted by your husband or boyfriend, if you had young mouths to feed, if your family was unable to support you or even turned to you for support, if you had been neglected, beaten, raped, if the world had overlooked you except for the salacious looks of men, if you found yourself in urgent need of funds, if you had a taste for Versace or lobster or cocaine, if you were pretty or at least sexy and aggressive, and if you saw that you could make more money spreading your legs than you would ever make standing on them, as much money as a doctor with years of training might make, and all the training you would need would be a few words of wisdom from a girlfriend in the profession and a little practice with a box of condoms, and powerful men, men who knew the world, with university degrees or their own businesses, with pensions and investments, would cross the Atlantic or Pacific or Gulf of Mexico just to see you, would buy you gifts, would reveal secrets they did not even share with their wives, would ask your opinion as if you were the one who had gone to college, would patiently wait for you as if you were the chairman of a corporation—if you were such a young woman and suddenly spotted at the crossroads of your washed-out path, the alluring sea-green facade of the Hotel Grand, would you cross the threshold of the Red Volcano and take your place on one of the high stools at the bar?

Laura had done just that. And the volcano had not consumed her, as it consumed so many, but had thrust her up into the clouds of zzu, an unchaste angel. One of her dreams had been to buy a house. But a more urgent ambition, which had stirred within her ever since she began working at the hotel at the age of twenty, was to retire before she turned twenty-five. It was a young woman's game, no question. And while it could be a lucrative profession for a time, it should not be considered a career. She saw for herself the women who were twenty-eight, twenty-nine, she even knew one who was thirty-four. They were doomed, these women. Old before their time, they didn't know anything else. They couldn't do anything else. They'd taken too many punches, like boxers who couldn't leave the ring.

But this goal too she had achieved. She was twenty-four. She had months to spare.

Yet she gazed down at the Hotel Grand with fondness, the way a traveler after reaching a farther shore might glance back at the ship. These had been the best years of her life, and although she'd made mistakes and suffered loss and betrayal, she didn't regret one night of it. She had made true friends, traveled the country, enjoyed the finest restaurants and hotels, learned a great deal about business, about men, and often enough enjoyed the sex if not the company, or the company if not the sex. It wasn't a road she would want her future daughter to travel, but the fact that she had traversed it herself perhaps made that prospect less likely.

The Grand had made her grand. The Red Volcano had enameled her with its fire. Let other girls blossom meekly like flowers. She would erupt.

CHAPTER 2

THE HOTEL GRAND

The Hotel Grand had never been grand. It was old enough, having been built in the forties, and formidable in relation to its surroundings, covering half a city block, its eight stories still towering over the neighborhood of nightclubs, restaurants, small offices and tourist shops. But it had never known gilding, not even when the first coat of paint was fresh and the tile newly laid and the original carpet unscarred by cigarette burns. It had never known velvet banisters or crystal chandeliers or marble bathrooms. One would have looked in vain for liveried doormen or tuxedoed waiters or maids in French uniforms. There had never been a wine list in the restaurant, or cognac in the bar, or chocolates on the pillows. Unlike the grand hotels in the Brazilian Amazon, built during the rubber boom, or in Panama, with its canal, or in Venezuela with its oil, or in Colombia with its coffee, or in Cuba with its casinos, Costa Rica was a country that for most of the twentieth century had been ignored by the international business community and its attendant society. The hotel's immodest size was gamble enough for a city ten times smaller than Bogota or Caracas, and the ordinary materials with which it had been constructed and decorated, in a style that combined Art Deco with Spanish Colonial, were so costly for the local visionary who built it that he went bankrupt before its completion.

Unlike the Imperial Hotel in Manaus, which made European society feel at home in the jungle, the Hotel Grand never made an effort to attract business conventions, political congresses, aristocratic couples with trunks filled with starched clothes. Costa Rica, much more at that time than now, was a destination for travelers rather than tourists, naturalists and volcanologists, surfers and bird watchers and fisherman. The hotel offered a civilized way station for these single men before they ventured to the forest or the sea. Formality was the least of their concerns. Even now Costa Rica was a country without a dress code. What these men wanted was sanitary plumbing, hot food, cold beer, a knowledgeable English-speaking staff, a friendly casino, a bar where they could trade tales.

It hadn't been very profitable the first years, and in the summer, which was low season, it closed. But when Communism came to Cuba the gringo fisherman flocked to Costa Rica for sailfish, tuna and marlin. The hotel began selling out, for the first time in its history, and the Red Volcano became the most popular bar in the country.

Prostitution was technically illegal, then as now, but tolerated. Confined to a few seedy brothels and occasional street walkers who catered to the locals, it had never caused the citizenry much concern. But as more men visited from abroad, and some settled in the country for good, the demand for women grew. In the seventies an entrepreneurial expat opened a New York-style strip club across from the hotel. The dancers made good money, but they could make even more if they followed the men to their rooms. Soon the neighborhood succumbed to the detritus of debauchery—pickpockets prowling in the shadows, whores shoving each other beneath lamp posts, drunks smashing bottles in the gutter.

Had the club's owner been a tico with connections, he might have kept it open. But the city closed him down and a bulldozer razed the firetrap with Biblical overstatement. The photos in *La Nacion* reassured the population, and the neighborhood did regain a semblance of respectability. Soon a hardware store would rise in its place. But whores are no less tenacious than politicians and merely jumped like checker pieces across the street. Many of them were accustomed to hanging out in the Red Volcano, sleeping in the rooms upstairs. In retrospect the strip club seemed like an unnecessary middleman.

The owners of the Hotel Grand, now three brothers from the nearby town of Cartago, had not anticipated this development. Later it would be rumored they had been behind the club's demise, and perhaps they had, but this revolution in the history of prostitution, as with most revolutions, was not something they had planned.

In a sense not much had changed. After all, these women had been coming back to the guests' rooms before, drinking with them at the bar, hanging around their necks at the casino. There might be more of them now, and they circulated constantly, having nowhere else to go, but as the Grand rarely received bookings from families or couples or single women—the travel agents knew the hotel's reputation and steered them to bed and breakfasts or chains—and as the neighbors weren't complaining, why should the owners disturb the natural evolution of the trade? In fact it turned out to be a bigger boon for them than the Cuban embargo with its catch of North American fisherman. They wisely decided not to regulate the girls or take a cut of their earnings. They were running a hotel, not a brothel. Instead they adopted the policy of many respectable hotels and charged a nominal fee for additional room guests. They also raised, much more substantially, their prices at the bar. But no one complained about forking over twice as much for a beer as they would pay at the tico bars down the street, any more than they might complain about hot dog prices at Yankee Stadium.

The unique symbiosis that arose among the owners, the girls, the guests and the municipality, was no less extraordinary than the symbiosis among certain insects and plants in the Costa Rican rain forests. Without this delicate balance the police might have levied fines, or the girls scattered to other bars, or the owners recast the hotel as a traditional resort. But instead the Grand became a legend, put down roots, grew, so that in time it was unthinkable for anyone to imagine it as anything other than what it was. Prostitution thrived elsewhere, of course, in massage parlors and newer strip clubs, and in bars in other towns where working girls congregated. But the Hotel Grand, despite its success, never spawned competitors. It was unique in all the country. In all the world.

From the moment a guest enters through the unassuming glass doors, usually open to the balmy air, he knows he has come to a hotel unlike any he has ever visited. Sure, the trappings of a traditional hotel are all there—the familiar name on the sign, the tropical pastel paint scheme, the wicker sofas in the lobby, the long reception desk, the row of clocks showing times for different countries, the travel desk, placed just to the side of the entrance, covered with racks of brochures advertising fishing charters and rental cars, a placard displaying the restaurant's dinner menu. There are luggage trolleys heavy with suitcases being pulled to the elevator by casually attired bellhops, the rapid clicking of heels on the ocher tile floor by clerks rushing to find out why three people have been given the same room, the ringing of phones, the buzzing of printers, the sound of chips rattling in the casino beyond.

This is the scene in the daytime, when most guests check in and the casino and bar are relatively quiet. But even at this hour a newly arrived traveler would be unavoidably struck by certain peculiarities. He might notice, for instance, the absence of children, or older women. He might notice that all the guest are men, mostly middle-aged, dressed in florid shirts, and that the women who are present are much, much younger, and Latino. In fact there don't seem to be any women present over the age of thirty. Even the desk clerks are young. And then he would notice, he would certainly notice, the uncommon affection displayed among the couples, as if they were on their honeymoon. But then one of the women would kiss her man, hurry out the door and into a taxi. And what about that girl sitting on the wicker sofa, talking on a cell phone? What is she doing here? And what about those two young women who just walked in together? Why did a security guard ask to see their ID's? And why did they saunter to the casino, looking right and left as though they were crossing a street, and position themselves against the wall, as if they were...

Now it's night, it's Saturday night. Carmen and Tita Moon have been here a couple hours already after coming from Laura's, and the place is jumping. There are probably two girls for every guy, poor working conditions. Carmen and Tita Moon are among the prettiest, so they're bound to get attention, even against these odds. The problem is a lot of these girls will go for less than a hundred. As the night wears on, much less than a hundred. Some will do anal, which they don't. Or golden showers, or who knows what. Many have tit jobs, which they can't compete with. And one can never be sure of men's tastes. But they both speak English, a big advantage here, where most of the patrons are gringos with limited Spanish. They have lighter skin, also an advantage, except for those guys who think darker girls are better in bed. And although they aren't as aggressive as some of the girls here—they'll never roll their tongue at a man or grab his crotch *en passant*—they come to work. They don't waste time and money at the slot machines or loiter in the ladies' room or gossip with groups of other girls or hide themselves in the bars' shadows.

Besides, the scene is very fluid. There's a street entrance to the bar, for expats like Colorado Bob, or those staying at other hotels.

Many of the girls enter this way as well, flashing their ID cards to the bouncer. People also circulate through the bar's rear, to the casino, and to the side, where the puta receptionist sits in front of the freight elevator. So on a night like tonight, when there might be two hundred people in the bar, the majority of these don't behave like patrons in a typical bar, who come to relax, to drink, to socialize. Rather they flow like cells circulating from one organ to another in the body of the hotel.

So even though women might outnumber men two to one, this could change from hour to hour. The bar, of course, was open twenty-four hours. Not that there was much action after three, but if Carmen and Tita Moon arrived at ten, that was five hours in which to hook a client, or even two, or perhaps an all-nighter, or that biggest of fishes, the "boyfriend experience."

Both girls, like any of the girls here, like young women anywhere, occasionally visited normal clubs or bars to dance or drink or meet friends, and the way they prepared for those nights out—styling their hair, matching their clothes, stashing a toothbrush and a condom or two in their purse just in case, squinting over their makeup in a rearview mirror—was no different from their preparation for a night at the Hotel Grand. And catching their eye in the Red Volcano, a man might be forgiven for thinking he was participating in that most common of mating rituals, evident in bars all over the world.

It was only on closer inspection that the motivation of Carmen and Tita Moon distinguished itself at the Red Volcano from their behavior in civilian bars. For one thing, they stood. True, all the chairs and stools were occupied by at least one person, but they had been here for a couple hours already, and in that time several tables and stools had opened up, sometimes right in front of them. And yet they would let a group of gringo buddies most unchivalrously take the table rather than claim it themselves. Some of the women did sit, of course, but many were already with men, or sat beside men as a way to introduce themselves. Carmen and Tita Moon preferred standing. They could be better seen that way, and as they were among the best looking, this strategy suited them. Standing also allowed them to see the action better themselves, to make eye contact, to advertise their availability.

On closer inspection, one might notice they didn't drink either. The men never complained about the prices, reasonable enough by U.S. standards. But Carmen and Tita Moon were here to pay the bills and only drank when men bought them drinks, and even then drank cautiously, a beer or cocktail and then only water.

But certainly what all men who entered the Red Volcano noticed, even if they failed to observe the more subtle peculiarity of girls in the bar not sitting or drinking, was the attention. For every man who crossed the threshold of the Red Volcano was a matinee idol. As he strolled or pushed his way from one end of the bar to the other, scores of female eyes followed him. Sometimes hands and lips. Even women who were already claimed shot him a glance, because there was always tomorrow.

And this, perhaps even more than the prospect of ready sex, or even the natural beauty and charm of Costa Rican women, brought men back time and again from every corner of North America, even as far away as Europe, Asia, and Australia, to the Hotel Grand. There were brothels enough in Thailand, street walkers in Germany, window girls in Amsterdam. But where else in the world could an average guy walk into a bar, a hotel lobby, a casino, a restaurant, and all the women looked at him? All the women smiled? Where they always accepted an offer of a drink or a meal or a few colones for the slot machines? Where even the most reticent of men found patient listeners, could make conversation with a woman and look into her eyes and get to know her in what appeared a familiar setting, but charged with the certainty of consummation, absent the demon of rejection?

Carmen and Tita Moon stood on the raised platform of the bar, facing the entrance, with the acquired patience of their trade. Not much had happened in the last two hours. A lot of men had looked at them—well, all the men had looked at them. But only a couple had spoken, and then moved on. One young man wearing a Tommy Bahama's shirt, shorts and loafers had asked Carmen her price, quite directly, without any attempt at conversation. Even though she found him attractive and might have enjoyed sleeping with him, she disliked such impoliteness. When she answered "A hundred," he countered with, "Fifty," at which she disdainfully looked away and he moved on. She might have gone with him for eighty, especially as there were so many women tonight, but his abruptness left her in no mood for negotiation.

The bar was incredibly noisy, drowning out the music videos playing on the televisions above the bar, but conversation was still possible. Indeed, the cacophony resulted from so many conversations, in English and Spanish from one end of the bar to the other, and beyond to the casino, which even drowned out the traffic from the street, horns and car alarms that otherwise would have assaulted one's ears through the open door. Carmen and Tita Moon were mostly silent, but over the two hours they had talked briefly about Laura's house, and later about the guy in the Tommy Bahama's shirt.

"What a jerk," Carmen had said.

"He was cute."

"Not cute enough for fifty."

"I would have sucked him for fifty."

"You're crazy. Besides, he didn't ask you, he asked me."

"You should have at least asked him to buy us a drink."

"Guys like him don't buy drinks. He's probably staying at a hostel."

"He was wearing an expensive shirt. I'd go after him if I was you."

"Well I don't fuck for fifty dollars."

"I didn't say I would fuck him for fifty dollars. I said I would suck him. Besides, I'm sure he'll come up. And in the room, once you get his dick talking, I'm sure he'll pay a hundred. Your problem is you don't know how to play men."

"Oh yeah? Who's the one with the car and the house?"

"That's only because guys like your 'girl next door' smile. If I had that smile I'd own a house, a Mercedes and I'd have a visa."

"Okay superstar, I'll bet you ten dollars you can't get him to go higher than sixty."

At that point Tita Moon shot off to catch her prey, but she returned a minute later only to report that he'd was holding hands with a fat Nicaraguan deep in the shadows of the bar, who was notorious for doing all-nighters for seventy.

And there Carmen and Tita Moon stood, resuming their silent vigil, until at half past twelve when a boyish Latino approached them. He looked too young to be in a bar. Indeed, they had observed him being carded and his backpack searched by the bouncer, while older gringos passed unmolested. He wasn't good looking, his nose was too big and his face pockmarked, but he was sharply dressed, and his gold jewelry was not unnoted by the girls.

He addressed Carmen in Spanish without making eye contact, nervously shifting from one foot to the other.

"What's up?"

"Hello. I'm Carmen. This is Tita."

"So Carmen, you want to party with me?"

Sometimes when a man showed interest in Carmen she would suggest a *ménage à trois* with Tita Moon, and Tita Moon would do the same for her. It was a common strategy, and networks developed among the girls here not simply for social reasons or to alleviate the boredom, but because add-ons and referrals constituted a significant percentage of the business.

But Carmen's initial impression was that he couldn't afford them both and might in fact be the worst of Red Volcano patrons—a local. Locals weren't technically prohibited, but the prices kept them away. And there were enough cheap massage parlors to serve their needs. But occasionally a tico walked in, curious to see the scene for himself.

"Where are you staying?" she asked.

"I just got here. Where should we go?"

There was a place down the street that rented rooms by the hour, and girls sometimes took clients there if they weren't staying nearby. But it was too squalid for Carmen's tastes, and besides the kid needed to sleep somewhere.

"Why don't you stay here?" she suggested. "We can see if there's a room."

She took his hand and led him past the puta registration desk to reception, still wondering if he had any money. But then she smelled the marijuana on his breath, good marijuana, and knew at once, even before he pulled out his Colombian passport, that he was a narco. At least he wasn't armed, she thought. The bouncer had searched him for weapons, if not for drugs.

After he checked in she led him back to the puta registration desk and handed over her national identity card. Some men found this procedure embarrassing or objected to the "guest" fee and stayed at other hotels. But girls who caused trouble or stole from clients could be banned from the hotel, and this back door registration provided a measure of security not found elsewhere.

After the kid signed a receipt they rode the freight elevator to the fourth floor, both of them on edge. He was obviously high, and Carmen was always uncomfortable with narcos, although she was glad they were staying on the premises.

Ironically, she knew the room better than he did and helped him with the key and turned on the lights. He went immediately to the minibar and opened a beer and a pack of cigarettes. He offered the cigarettes to her, which she accepted, but still did not speak. He took a silver lighter from his pocket, but his hand was trembling.

"Can you pay me first?" she asked.

"Oh yeah." He set the backpack on the king-sized bed and fumbled inside, bringing out a thick roll of crisp twenty dollar bills. "How much?"

Many girls at this point would have clung to him like a strangler fig until the entire roll had been transferred from his possession to theirs. They would have stayed the night or weekend or dragged him to the casino until even the contents of the minibar had been depleted. But Carmen never took advantage of clients and in any case thought it prudent not to tangle with narcos, even one as naive as this kid.

"One hundred for an hour, three for all night," she answered, although if pressed she would stay two hours for a hundred and all night for double that.

He paid without negotiating or even asking what her fee included. Then he took a cellophane package from a hidden compartment in the backpack and went into the bathroom.

He left the door open. Carmen watched him bending over the sink, snorting a line of cocaine. He motioned her to join him but she shook her head.

"I thought you wanted to party," he said, sniffling.

"Not like that. Like this."

And she took his hand and led him like a child to the bedroom. She took his cigarette, and hers, and set them in the ashtray. She helped him take his clothes off and eased him back on the bed, pressing his cock through his underwear.

"Do you have a condom?"

"Don't you?"

She opened a pack from the minibar and set the condom on the bedspread. "Do you want the lights?"

Sometimes she liked the lights on, if her client was good looking or she found him friendly and wanted to see his eyes, or conversely if she distrusted him and wanted a clear view of everything. But she did not consider this kid a threat. In fact she was beginning to feel sorry for him. He wasn't at all like the other narcos she'd met. Dangerous men who flaunted their power, who talked too much rather than not at all, who tried to impress her as though she were Miss Universe. But when the kid had revealed his roll of cash and offered the high-grade coke it had been without pretense. He was naive and scared and acted as he did because he didn't know any other way.

After switching off the lights she sat back on the bed, still dressed herself, and ran her fingernails over his underwear, but he remained soft. She reached inside and squeezed him. He closed his eyes, as if making an effort.

"How long are you here for?"

"I'm supposed to meet someone tomorrow. Then I'm going to Mexico," he said.

"I've never been to Mexico. Is it your first trip?"

"I've never been out of Colombia," he admitted. "I've never even stayed at a hotel."

"Well don't expect all hotels to be like this one!" she told him.

She pulled his underwear off and stroked his balls with her fingernails. None of the girls fucked without condoms, but some gave bareback blow jobs. Carmen did not, but she would lick around the base and up and down the shaft before putting the condom on. She felt his body writhing, but it was probably more from the cocaine and nervous tension that from her efforts. She felt disappointed because she knew he didn't care, like some men, about keeping her for the whole hour. This kid was not interested in cuddling or talking or taking a shower together, or worried about getting his money's worth. If she could make him come in two minutes she knew she could leave and he would not complain. Other men might bring her to orgasm with their prowess or captivate her with their conversation or even become true friends, but it was the clients who only wanted to come as quickly as possible and then be done with it who made her profession seem the easiest in the world.

After two minutes, however, he still hadn't achieved even the semi-rigidity necessary to put on the condom.

"Too much cocaine," she said.

"Do you want to smoke a joint? It's good shit."

"I'm sure it is. But this is better."

And she pulled off her top and brushed her nipples over his mouth. He began to suck, then bite, and bit too hard. She cried out.

Worse, he was still soft. Carmen now knew she was stuck for the entire hour. That he might not come at all. Fortunately, he didn't seem the type who would ask for his money back. Not that she ever returned money to an impotent client. But she hated the arguments.

"Turn over. I'll give you a massage."

Massages were to a working girl's menu what bread was to an expensive meal. If the sirloin was scarce or the sea bass over-cooked, fill the diner on bread and he won't have as much appetite for the main courses. If a girl was stuck with a ravenous client, which was easier? Sucking him for twenty minutes and fucking for another forty, or kneading his back for half an hour, giving him a slow hand job with oil, and riding him to completion in the final minutes? There were numerous massage parlors in San Jose, open only during the day, some with genuine massage tables rather than beds. The girls there went for forty or sixty dollars and only kept half of that. But it was a more tranquil environment to work in, far less competitive, and some of the women actually had some training in massage.

Carmen was not trained, and her personality was too demur to dig the heels of her hands into a man's spine or karate chop his shoulder blades with authority. She concentrated on conversation, affection and sex, and only offered massage if these failed, or if her clients requested it. Some men were disappointed if she didn't know shiatsu or Turkish or Swedish massage. Some preferred erotic massage to actual sex and came without her having to completely disrobe. One client tried to teach her Thai massage, in which the man lies naked, first on his back, then on his stomach, while the woman, also completely naked, lies and sits on top of him and slides from his chest to his ankles in a glaze of oil. She made a hundred and fifty dollars as the student in this seminar on full body massage, which had to be performed on the bathroom floor, as they lacked the customary air mattress. But Carmen found it messy and exhausting and was glad none of her clients had requested it since.

"Relax," she told the kid, gently exploring the knots in his back.

"I can't."

"Be happy. All the guests here are happy. They call it Disney World for men."

But the kid squirmed around and grabbed for his cigarette and lighter. Carmen saw the burning tip slowly move around the room like a firefly. She sat where she was. It was painfully quiet. She could hear cars honking outside and the voices of taxi drivers soliciting fares.

"I made a mistake," she heard him say in a breaking voice, and she wondered if he was crying.

"Go back to Colombia then."

"That's impossible."

"You must have family?"

"That's why I'm here. My father's dead and I'm the only son. I thought this way I could take care of them."

"You're young and healthy. I'm sure there are other things you can do. Of course you won't make as much. But money isn't everything."

Carmen was so intent on the kid's turmoil she didn't even realize how often she had heard those same words spoken to her, by clients in these very rooms.

"I thought it would be easy, but I'm scared. I was trembling downstairs when he searched my bag. He wasn't even looking for money or drugs, only guns. What am I going to do in Mexico? What am I going to do when it's the real police?"

"But you haven't done anything yet. You're just starting. Go home."

"They'll kill me."

"But you're not betraying anyone."

"It's either the police, another gang, or my own gang."

She watched the burning ash move closer and saw his naked body sit on the edge of the bed, turned away from her. She heard him crying.

She wanted to console him, but she didn't move. She felt too uncomfortable herself to approach him.

"Tell them your sick. Think of a story."

"They've invested in me. They've spent time to train me. They've paid for my tickets and clothes."

"How much?"

The words were out before Carmen could think and she instantly regretted this attempt to become involved. She didn't even like the kid. He was a narco, probably an addict himself. She only felt sorry for him. Fortunately he didn't respond.

"Why don't I introduce you to my friend," she then said. "I think you'll like her. Forget about Mexico. Tonight you're in Costa Rica."

"Bring her up," he agreed, sniffling away the tears, or the cocaine.

"You have to come down to sign her out."

She put her top back on and brushed her hair and waited for him to dress and wash his face. Then she led him back downstairs to the bar. But Tita Moon was gone.

She took out her phone to call her, but then thought she must be with a client. Besides, she spotted Angela standing outside the ladies' room. Carmen didn't like the Colombian prostitutes any more than Laura did, but Angela was an exception, her one friend among the South Americans. Of course, she thought. He needs a Colombian. And she loves cocaine. She'll understand him better, he won't feel so homesick.

She made the introduction and watched them walk to the puta registration desk before resuming her former position in front of the bar.

While Carmen was with her narco, Tita Moon was down the hall with a middle-aged Chinese real estate agent from Vancouver.

"I only know of Hong Kong and Beijing," she had told him after he bought her a beer in the bar.

"Vancouver is in Canada," he informed her.

"Oh. Well that's why I'm a whore and not a professor," Tita Moon declared with her special brand of logic.

She had been with Japanese men before, and even an Indonesian, but not a Chinese. She assumed they all had small cocks, but his was normal size, and already hard when she began stroking it.

"You're my first Chinese," she told him. "But not my first Canadian." She let go of him to take off her top, exposing large natural breasts. "Do you like my tattoos?"

She had a butterfly on her left breast and a small dragon on her back right shoulder.

"Were you born in the Year of the Dragon?" he asked, as if discovering a kindred spirit.

But Tita Moon naively replied, "What's the year of the dragon?"

She shook her jeans and cotton panties off, revealing a third tattoo just above her shaved pussy: a stick figure pushing a lawn mower. Men always laughed at this one, but not the Chinese real estate agent, who was rather conservative and had chosen her despite her pierced tongue and naval, had chosen her for her round, inviting face, smooth complexion and mischievous eyes. The tongue stud, however, was a sign to him that she would be wild in bed, a real Latin lover, not like the fussy escort girls in Vancouver. As for the tattoos, a dragon was one thing, or a butterfly. But to make a permanent joke on one's skin was incredibly poor taste. Not that it diminished his desire.

Tita Moon unwrapped a condom from her purse and put it in her mouth, framing it with her lips. She then bent down over him and expertly rolled it on. He groaned deeply and she worried he might come, so after half a minute she rubbed some KY into her pussy, got on top of him and rolled her hips slowly in a circular motion. Like Carmen, she wanted her clients to come quickly, but she found that if they came too quickly, especially without fucking, they wanted a second round, and more often than not she had to comply, as she usually told them in the bar they could have her for two hours. If a man fucked hard for five minutes and came, especially an older man who could stand to lose a few pounds, he might be too exhausted to claim the remaining time. But if he was simply lying back while she sucked him off, well, his heart wasn't even pounding. And with all that time left on the meter, and the Viagra he had taken an hour before still assisting with the hydraulics like an engineer at an aging dam, it was a cigarette, a beer, and then back to business, and poor Tita Moon would really have to earn her wages.

After a couple minutes of grinding, she tapped him on his hairless chest, said, "You on top," and sprawled on the pillow beside him, spreading her legs wide.

He clumsily missed the mark, so she guided him in and put her hands on his chest to keep him upright. He grunted like an animal and thrust rapidly, but she hardly felt him at all, due to all the lubrication. After a minute, however, she did feel a jet of warm liquid speeding the wrong way.

"Shit!"

She swatted him off like a fly and grabbed his wilting cock. "Fuck, it broke!" she screamed, pulling the condom off and examining it beneath the light the way a cyclist might examine a flat bicycle tire.

Confirming the break, she threw it on the floor and strode into the bathroom, where she scrubbed herself vigorously in the shower. When she returned to the room the Chinese man was lying beneath the covers watching an action film on TV.

"You better hope I'm not pregnant!" she said, quickly dressing.

"It's not my fault," he replied, not looking away from the television.

"It's always the man's fault," she argued. "You're the one with the dick. You were too rough."

"It was your condom, not mine."

She stepped into her heels and walked into his line of vision, blocking the TV, just as his wife sometimes did. "What are you going to do?" she demanded.

This had never happened to her before, but she had heard stories from other girls. Some guys were assholes and did nothing. Others offered their phone numbers or e-mails, and promised to pay for the abortion if the pregnancy test was positive. Still others took fright and tried to settle the matter at once with a few hundred dollars.

The Chinese man didn't reply. He belonged to the assholes.

"I have high friends at this hotel," Tita Moon lied. "If I'm pregnant, they'll give me your name and address and I'll send the baby to your wife!"

She hoped this might scare him into making a settlement, but he regarded her with equanimity. "You won't get pregnant. I've had a vasectomy."

"Liar! I know you're lying. Swear—" But then she realized he probably wasn't Christian. What did Chinese swear to? She lowered her shoulder. "Swear on the dragon!"

But she immediately realized the absurdity of her request and rose. She knew nothing about Chinese, or Canadians. "Fucking bastard," she cursed, slamming the door.

She had no patience for the elevator, so she took the stairs. He was an asshole for certain, but she was mostly angry at herself. He hadn't been that rough, not more than most. The condom probably would have broken with any client. She should have checked it. The first few nights of her career she had filled the condoms with water in the bathroom sink to check for leaks, but that proved tedious. Then, for a couple weeks, she examined them by eye after putting them on. But this too became a chore, and in time she grew lax. Besides, condoms could tear from other stresses, like age or heat, so what was the point of checking for holes? She came to believe it was enough to buy the condoms herself, to monitor the expiration date and keep them out of the sun.

"You don't look very happy," Carmen observed.

Tita Moon made no effort to conceal her distress and flagged the nearest barmaid. "Rum and Coke."

But then she remembered pregnant women shouldn't drink. Yet when did that prohibition begin? Certainly not within an hour of conception. But why was she worrying about birth defects? She didn't plan to keep the baby. She had a child already she couldn't take care of. A three-year-old son from a worthless former boyfriend. The child lived with her mother, although Tita Moon did see him frequently and gave her mother a substantial percentage of her earnings. Her mother never asked where the money came from. Like many mothers who benefited materially from their prostitute daughters, she suspected, or knew. Tita Moon loved him, of course, and bought him presents, and played with him, but she was too wild and immature herself to be a good mother, and she had the sense, at least, to understand this. There were times she dreamt about taking him back, but she couldn't take him now. She would have to hire a nanny, and her present apartment was too small. She imagined a time in the future when she would be rich and retired, married to a sensitive gringo who couldn't have children of his own and would adore hers.

"I tried to set you up with my narco, but you were gone," Carmen said, joining Tita Moon at the bar, where they rested on empty stools. "He had some good cocaine."

"I need cocaine. I need a blizzard of cocaine."

"What happened to you? Why are you buying drinks?" Carmen stroked her friend's face. "Who were you with? Don't tell me he hit you?"

"Worse."

"He didn't pay you? You didn't get the money up front?"

"Worse."

"The condom broke?"

"Why me? Why me? All the rich women in the world who pay twenty thousand dollars to have their baby in a test tube and I get the defective condom. I should sue the company!"

"When did you finish your last period?"

"Two weeks ago."

"That's not good."

"Tell me, doctor."

She drank her rum and Coke. She had never had an abortion. Abortions were illegal in Costa Rica, which was overwhelmingly Catholic. Available, sure, if you knew the right people, but very expensive. Tita Moon hadn't considered an abortion the first time around. That was before she had started working at the Hotel Grand. She thought her boyfriend in Puntarenas would marry her. She looked forward to having a family. Instead he deserted her. Soon after giving birth she moved to San Jose, at the suggestion of a school mate. Tita Moon initially thought she would work just a few months, until she could save enough money to buy a decent apartment and food for her baby. But the Hotel Grand seduced her, just as she seduced her clients. She loved staying out all night, flirting with men, playing blackjack and dancing and getting high. The rich gringos treated her far better than her boyfriend ever had, and she'd never had girlfriends as solicitous as Carmen and Laura. Growing up poor, she couldn't afford to dream. Now men paid her to dream with them.

"Do you have the morning-after pill?" Carmen asked.

The morning-after pill was also illegal in Costa Rica. "Where am I supposed to get that?" Tita Moon asked irritably.

"Laura probably knows someone. You should call her tomorrow. You have seventy-two hours to take it."

The bar was beginning to thin out, and the ratio of women to men was now more or less even. A minority of the girls, like Carmen and Tita Moon, had already made money tonight and were hoping for a windfall. The remainder were restless with desperation, bouncing like pinballs from man to man, or lethargic from the long night, slumped in their bar stools or drinking coffee upstairs in the 24-hour restaurant.

Carmen had been anxious to tell Tita Moon about her narco and the plans that were swirling in her head. Crazy ideas, probably dangerous too, but what could she do? He was just a kid, more innocent than any of them. And fate had placed her in his path. For a reason. His sign... She hadn't even asked his sign. He must be a Libra, she told herself. Unbalanced by extremes.

She wanted her friend's advice, not because she respected Tita Moon's opinion but because she didn't want to carry the burden alone. But Tita Moon was in no condition to appreciate the unique despondency of narcos. The best she could do was offer Carmen a drink, and order another for herself.

"How long are you going to stay?" Tita Moon asked after a while. Normally she took a taxi home, but if Carmen was leaving at the same time she would ask her for a ride.

"You want to leave? Sure. It's been a bad night for both of us."

"Both of us? Oh, your narco."

"It's not what you think. I'll tell you about it in the car."

They finished their drinks and were about to leave when Ginger entered the bar and walked straight up to them. She was a voluptuous woman of twenty-five with dark skin and long frizzy hair, a small mouth and of course now a small nose, compliments of Porter. She had breast implants and gleaming white teeth, funded by various gringos like bricks on a memorial walkway, except their names had not been engraved in recognition of their donations.

"Giving up already?" Ginger asked them.

"We've made our hundred," Tita Moon told her with a scowl.

"Want another eighty? Not you," she added, glancing at Tita Moon. "I have a client at the Ambassador who wants a threesome. Interested?" she asked Carmen.

"Why didn't he take two girls to begin with?" Carmen wondered.

"I met him at the hotel. I talked him into it."

Carmen knew she must have an ulterior motive, she wasn't simply being kind. But eighty dollars was eighty dollars, and threesomes were usually easy, so she agreed.

She said good night to Tita Moon, with a reminder to call Laura in the morning, and followed Ginger to the Ambassador, three blocks away. Carmen had only met Porter that night and, although she knew he and Ginger were involved, she didn't know the nature of their relationship. It was their business anyway. Carmen never gossiped, as most of the girls did. She respected their privacy, and the privacy of men. But, more than that, she just didn't care. She wasn't a socialite like Laura or a night owl like Tita Moon. On her days off she cooked and cleaned, went shopping with her mother, watched television, went to bed early. She didn't consider Ginger a friend. She knew she was a gold digger and a liar, but probably no worse than many of the girls at the Hotel Grand. She wasn't going to turn down the chance to make eighty dollars.

As for Ginger, girls like her gravitated to girls like Carmen, passive and honest. Easy to ask a favor of. Safe to share a client with.

They didn't talk on the way, the client's name wasn't even mentioned. Carmen was still preoccupied with her narco, dreaming of ways to save him. Ginger nodded to the Ambassador's security guard and they walked through the empty lobby to the elevators.

"Why didn't he come himself?" Carmen asked as they rode up to his room.

"I told him I would bring him someone and he liked the idea of a surprise. If he came to the Volcano maybe he would pick someone else or want to stay and drink."

Her client was a stout American in his mid-thirties with thinning hair and a slight beard. He answered the door wrapped in a towel, a beer in one hand. Carmen heard the television in the background.

He smiled at her, obviously surprised at his good fortune, and spoke a few words in broken Spanish. Normally Carmen would have replied in English, but she didn't feel like conversation, so she let Ginger, who was also fluent in English, do the talking.

"Do you like my choice?" she asked, pinching his towel. "Don't you think she's beautiful?"

The man beamed at Carmen in assent. "Want a beer?"

Carmen pointed instead to the pack of cigarettes on the nightstand, and he gladly lit one for her, caressing her waist while she smoked.

Ginger hugged him from behind, kissing his back and stroking his broad chest. Without words, like an erotic ballet, the two girls began working him over. Ginger squeezed his cock until it was hard while Carmen let him kiss her breasts and neck. When he tried to kiss her on the lips she deftly moved away. Ginger had by now put the condom on. Carmen began sucking him while Ginger sat up and massaged his legs.

Carmen now clearly understood Ginger's motives. Getting work for another girl, as Carmen had done earlier for Angela, was considered a professional courtesy, and it was bad taste to expect a kickback. They were prostitutes, after all, not pimps. But Ginger had made the deal with her client beforehand for two hundred and would pay Carmen only eighty, a ploy which allowed her to take a twenty percent cut of Carmen's share without the appearance of doing so. Carmen would not complain, of course, as she could not prove it without asking the man what he'd paid, and that would be unseemly. But Carmen could tell by his behavior that he had paid two hundred. A man who would have tried to negotiate the price would also try to negotiate the performance. Instead of lying contentedly he would at this moment be engaged in a legal skirmish over what the Party of the First Part would be doing to or with the Party of the Second and Third Parts, and on and on. Bareback blow jobs, pussy eating, kissing, lesbian shows, all would be limited and defined like terms in a union contract.

For all Carmen knew, their client *was* a lawyer. But Ginger was a master negotiator herself, as evidenced by the pound of flesh she had extracted from her skeletal bank manager. She wasn't going to do any heavy lifting for a mere hundred. And if she could secure a pliant accomplice, such as Carmen, well, she would hardly have to do any work at all. Her client would be the last to complain. She had offered to fulfill his fantasy of two girls, and had brought him such a pretty one. He wouldn't last long enough for them both.

Which is exactly what happened. Ginger should have used her tongue for something more than salaciously licking her gleaming teeth. She should have been the first to fuck. Instead Carmen received him on top and from behind, while Ginger lay on her back and made a lame show of masturbating.

He shuddered into Carmen and collapsed between them. Ginger rose immediately and washed her hands, although it hardly seemed necessary.

"Maybe we can do this tomorrow night," she suggested as they took their leave, slipping four twenties into Carmen's palm.

"I wish, but I'm going home tomorrow. I mean, today."

"Have a nice flight."

Back on the street, Carmen thanked her, although she didn't feel grateful.

"You owe me one," Ginger said, and ran to hail a taxi.

Carmen walked back alone to the Hotel Grand. She had a hundred and eighty dollars in her purse, but this part of the city was not dangerous. The police kept it safe for the tourists. And there were still people out—taxi drivers, security guards, panhandlers, mongers and whores.

The Hotel Grand was a circus compared to the stolid Ambassador, but even here the night was winding down. It was four o'clock. In the Red Volcano the barmaids were cleaning empty tables. A few small groups of men and women remained, but they were quiet, like figures in a still life. For the first time all night one could hear the Latino music videos playing on the TV screens above the bar. In the casino the poker tables were empty. A lone gringo was playing blackjack with a distracted girl resting on his shoulder.

In the lobby there was only one clerk at the reception, cataloging the night's receipts. The security guard sat wearily by the entrance, his magnetic wand resting on the travel desk. A bottle blonde wearing a plaid skirt was sleeping in one of the wicker sofas, her bare feet resting on the green cushions. Nobody bothered her, or even noticed her, as if it were the most normal thing in the world for a prostitute to nap in a hotel lobby.

Carmen had not returned to the hotel to work. It was too late, and she'd had an excellent night. She hoped the narco might have come down for a drink, and she wanted to speak to him. But he wasn't here. He was sleeping, or still high from the cocaine. Perhaps he had taken Angela for the night. In any case she couldn't disturb him now.

She fumbled for her keys and drove home.

Carmen lived in a simple three-bedroom house in a middle-class neighborhood of San Jose. One of those bedrooms was occupied by her mother, the second by her two younger brothers. Carmen's room was actually the smallest of the three. She had given her mother the master bedroom, or her mother had commandeered it, Carmen could not recall the exact circumstances. And since her brothers had to share, she gave them the larger of the remaining two rooms. It had been built in the eighties in a South Florida style that showed its age, with turquoise walls that had never been repainted, Formica cabinets and shag carpeting. The matching leather couch and chair in the living room were new, however, as was the frost-free refrigerator and the microwave. Carmen had put ten thousand down on it and her mortgage was only half that of Laura's. It wasn't as good an investment, and she didn't have a view of the valley, but how many women her age in Costa Rica owned their own homes, supported their families and still had enough left over to invest in their savings accounts?

Everyone was asleep. Carmen took a quick shower, drank a glass of water, and collapsed into bed. She slept fitfully, her dreams centering on her plans for the narco. Her first plan was simply to bail him out.

"How much money do you need?" she asked in her first dream.

She said this at the Ambassador Hotel, while Ginger was rubbing his back.

"Twenty thousand dollars."

"Twenty thousand dollars!"

Carmen couldn't imagine why he needed so much. Now they were drinking rum and Cokes in the Red Volcano.

"All the gold and silver..." he explained.

So she took his lighter, his bracelets and everything else, including his clothes and piled them on the bar. Now he sat only in his underwear and she asked him, "How much do you owe them now?"

"A thousand dollars."

"That's better." And she opened her purse and gave him everything.

"This is only nine hundred," he said.

"Wait here." She saw the guy from the Ambassador. Surely he would give her a hundred. But then Ginger stepped in the way and led him off and when she turned around the narco was lying in a pool of blood and the pile of clothes and jewelry were gone.

Carmen's second idea was more complicated, but less costly. After all, if she gave him money to quit he would never be able to repay her, even if he wanted to. But in her second plan he would retire for health reasons, and it would cost her nothing. She would go to his room in the morning and, after persuading him that this was the only wise course, call for an ambulance. She would flush the cocaine, of course, but leave enough marijuana to interest the police. She would claim he had suffered a heart attack, it happened enough at the Hotel Grand. True, he was very young, but look at his pockmarked face. Hardly a picture of health. He would lie unconscious as she had instructed him to and the ambulance would take him to the hospital for a few days, after which the police, having found the quantity of marijuana too trivial to prosecute but too substantial to ignore, would deport him back to Colombia, where his record would make him useless to the cartel.

In her second dream, however, everything went wrong. No one answered when she called for the ambulance. The phone hadn't been turned on, as sometimes happened to a new guest in the hotel.

"Use your cell phone," he suggested.

"Good idea."

But instead of opening her purse she was rummaging through his backpack. And all she could find was package after package of cocaine. Soon the bed was covered with cellophane wrappers, and that's when the police stormed in.

In fact it was Carmen's mother, waking her. She had made coffee and was anxious for Carmen to get dressed so she could take her brothers shopping, as promised. Carmen shielded her eyes from the light. It was almost noon.

She lit a cigarette and took the coffee cup with her to the car, promising to return in an hour. She raced to the hotel, the nightmares still spinning through her mind. But of the two plans, which should she choose? Simply giving him money was less complicated, and she did have a thousand in the bank. But what would Laura say? What would her mother say? Well, who was going to tell them? Still, the figure of a thousand dollars was a product solely of her imagination. The sum might be quite higher or, worse, it might be something indefinite. What if she gave him a thousand dollars and he offered it to the cartel and they still refused to let him quit? No, the second plan seemed wiser. Better a few days in a Costa Rican hospital or jail than a brief and violent lifetime in a Colombian drug gang.

After a madcap night, the Hotel Grand was wide awake. Raquel was describing excursions to two guests at the travel desk. Suntanned gringos with tired smiles were dragging their luggage to waiting taxis. Others were checking in at the crowded reception desk. The girls who occupied the wicker chairs and sofas were not dozing but eager and alert, the day shift vying for the new arrivals.

Carmen pushed her way to the reception desk and asked one of the clerks to dial the kid's room. But he had already checked out.

CHAPTER 3

THAT WOMAN

For Laura, the worst part of her former profession was not that she had sex with strange men, or the risk of pregnancy, or assault or theft or even murder, or the late nights, or the tedious hours standing in the bar, or the unpredictable fluctuations in income; no, the worst part for Laura was the isolation it imposed on her life. The men with whom she had shared this concern, such as Dennis, did not understand how an elite working girl like Laura could complain of loneliness. They thought she wasn't lonely enough. Didn't affluent men pay to take her to dinner? Wasn't she surrounded by friends at the bar, at the hotel? Didn't she have connections throughout the country with taxi drivers and hotel clerks and waiters and hair stylists?

"But that's all work," Laura would answer. "What do you say when you go home and your neighbors ask you questions? Or you go to the grocery or video store and people make small talk and gossip as they always do? What do you tell your family? If you have a child how do you explain that you cannot be there when they have a bad dream and want to sleep in your bed? It is like being a spy. You have two lives and you must keep them separate. Clients want fantasy. They want a girl who is there just for them, who doesn't have children or boyfriends, who doesn't have periods or get colds. They want an actress who always smiles. And maybe that's easy enough for the client who just takes you for an hour. But what about the client that takes you to the beach for three days? You're supposed to be lying in the sun drinking cocktails but maybe your child has a fever or your boyfriend keeps calling or it's your mother's birthday. Sure, you could say no. But you need the money. And then you go home and everything you've been doing, all the men and the girls from the bar and the people who have seen you out with them, all that has to be pushed into the closet like a Christmas present that isn't wrapped. Everything that is simple for a normal person, like going to the park, is complicated and dangerous. Your secret can be exposed at any minute. And sometimes your head spins just trying to remember which side of your life people belong to, and which lies you have told them."

Dennis was one of the few she had allowed to cross the line. The only client she had ever introduced to that person she referred to, never without a preceding sigh, as "that woman."

Her mother. Donita to the world. At this moment she was pounding on the door, ignoring the buzzer. Laura had not gone to sleep immediately after the party but had watched TV until midnight, and slept late. She was only now brushing her teeth.

"Coming!"

This was not how she wanted to welcome her mother to her new home, in her pink terry robe with her hair still wet and a toothbrush in her mouth.

"You're early!"

"I am not early. You said eleven and it's a quarter past," her mother replied, pointing to her watch. Unlike her daughter, she wore lots of costume jewelry, heavy makeup and dyed her curly hair a brash shade of blonde. But Laura had inherited her lovely complexion from her mother, who at forty-three, still turned heads.

"I said noon. Noon!" Laura repeated. "Who has lunch at eleven on a Sunday? You never listen to me. I could write 'noon' with an airplane in the sky and you would still come at eleven because that's when you want to come. Maybe you think you will surprise me sleeping with the husband of one of your card playing friends."

Her mother stared at her like a general blocked at the gates of his own city. "Are you going to let me in?"

"No. I mean, please wait in your car for five minutes."

"You do have a man!"

"Of course not. I just don't want to greet you in my new home with toothpaste in my mouth. And there are still cups and towels that need to be put away. I haven't made the bed. You can't see it in this condition."

"Nonsense," her mother said, pushing past her into the foyer. I'll wait on the couch. Take your time."

Laura threw up her hands in frustration and returned to the bathroom. "Welcome to my fucking home."

She rinsed out the toothpaste and then rinsed her tearing eyes. Last night went so well. The working girl half of the welcome party. She knew the friends and family party would be the more difficult of the two. First, she had no civilian friends, which was the main reason she felt so lonely. She longed for normal friends, who didn't know she slept with men for money. But she hadn't had such a friend since school. As for family, it would have been nice if her aunts were in town and could have come. Not because she was close to them; she only saw them on holidays. But their presence would have created a buffer between her and her mother. That was her family. Sometimes she joked that she was an orphan, but as with many jokes, the statement contained an element of truth. In school she had envied those of her classmates who had extended families, dozens of cousins, living grandparents, siblings. Fathers. She had been born out of wedlock and had never known her father. Her mother had been married and divorced twice. The first husband, briefly, when she was a small child. The second husband she married when Laura was sixteen and divorced five years later. And in between, and since, there had been numerous men, none of whom mattered to Laura. They blurred together in her memory more than the faces of her own clients. Indeed, in her fantasized monologues she chastised her mother for being the real whore in the family. "And what do you get? They treat you like dirt, every time." Her mother was weak with men. Her otherwise indomitable personality collapsed when she fell in love. And like the child of an alcoholic who will never herself set foot in a bar, Laura vowed never to let her destiny be controlled by a man. Ironically it Laura who was the more cautious when it came to the opposite sex, and her mother's example, more than Laura's career, explained why at twenty-four she had never been married.

She made chicken and rice and served it on the terrace with mixed salad and lemonade. She had looked forward to giving her mother the grand tour, but her bed was unmade and, upon reconsideration, it was better not to give her the chance to pry. So instead she gave her a brief tour of the guest bedrooms and bathroom and kitchen and garage before leading her back to the living room and turning on the television for her while she returned to the kitchen and made lunch.

Her mother worked in the admission's office at the university. She had a college degree herself and still harbored hopes that Laura would one day enroll. Laura's grades in high school had been good enough, but she hated studying and there weren't any courses that interested her. "Now if they offered a degree in astrology…" she had said at the time. But this hid a still deeper reason. For most students university life was a liberating experience, but Laura viewed it as an extension of her mother's house.

The cute palm tree out front, the tiled floors, the matching guest bedrooms, the sparkling kitchen, even the view were lost on her mother, whose aesthetic sensibility was limited to a winning gin rummy hand. Instead she asked about interest rates and mortgages and insurance coverage. Not even Porter had asked her so many financial questions. The closest her mother came to a compliment was when she said it seemed like a good investment.

"It's a great investment!" Laura replied. "In five years this house will double, that's what a banker friend of mine says, and he should know. And with the money I make from the bedrooms, and the garage..."

"Have you found anyone yet?" her mother asked, picking the orange slices out of her salad.

"For one of the rooms. My friend Raquel, she's a travel agent. She also goes..." Laura was about to say, "to the university." But then her mother would ask for her full name and course of study and probably check her file first thing Monday morning.

"Mama, why don't you eat the oranges?"

"I don't like oranges."

"But they're fresh, and you need the vitamin C. You're always telling me I should eat things that are good for me that I don't like and I eat them just to please you."

"Green vegetables are different. I can get vitamin C from the lemonade."

"Suit yourself. But if you're not going to eat them at least give them to me," she said, and scooped the orange slices into her own bowl.

"Have you taken an ad in the paper?"

"Yes, but I haven't had any offers for the other room. I'm sure I will. It's just a matter of time."

"Maybe," her mother said, beginning on her chicken and rice. "But you can't be sure. I've been trying to rent your room for months, since my last lodger moved out, but I've had no takers."

Laura wanted to say, Yes, but you live in a small run-down house on a bad street in Guadalupe, not in a brand new spacious home in Escazu. But she only said, "You ask too much money. You really don't want to rent, you like to live alone, or with your boyfriends."

Even this edited opinion was sufficient to give offense, but Laura's mother was too deep in thought to take any. "If it weren't such a long commute I might sell my house and take that room myself," she said, spearing a cube of chicken. "My finances aren't what they once were."

For a moment Laura's heart stopped. The word "take" hung in the air like the proclamation of a conquistador. "It's much too far," Laura concurred at once. "You'd spend more money on gasoline than you make at the university. How is the chicken?"

"Not bad," her mother said, apparently letting the matter of the unrented bedroom rest.

"Actually I have two women scheduled to look at it tomorrow evening. Maybe three. I'm sure I'll have it rented by the end of the week," Laura added for good measure.

She looked out at the view. It was another clear day, except for the clouds that invariably hung over the mountains behind her, too distant to cast shadows. "I don't think I'll ever get tired of look-ing down at the city," she said, wishing she were down there now, shopping for vegetables in the central market and not fending off her mother. But this lunch was a duty, and to delay it would only invite suspicion. At such times she wondered why she maintained a connection with the woman, and such a close one at that. They spoke on the phone frequently and hardly a week went by that they didn't see each other. Whether it was guilt or memory or sympathy for her mother's loneliness, or weakness in the face of her mother's persistence, or the horoscopes that frequently mentioned "family," that kept her spinning tightly within her mother's orbit, Laura did not know.

"Has Dennis seen the house?" her mother asked.

"No," Laura lied, not wanting her mother to know about last night's party. "But he will. I start working for him tomorrow."

"That's so nice of him to give you a job. I'm sure it will be much better than the casino."

Laura had told her mother she worked as a blackjack dealer at the Hotel Grand. This served to explain her late hours, as well as her presence there, should she ever be spotted by one of her mother's friends. As for her finances, dealing was a well-paying job, and there were tips from high rollers. She had also made some investments with the money she had saved, or so she told her mother. And that was how, at the age of twenty-four, she was able to buy a house in Escazu.

Her mother was not naive, but neither was she overly familiar with the world her daughter lived in. To the gringo, prostitution in Costa Rica might seem ubiquitous, but in reality the trade in San Jose was confined to the Hotel Grand, a handful of upscale massage parlors and strip clubs, and a score of nondescript low market brothels for the working-class locals. As for the rest of the country, there were small brothels, as well as bars where prostitutes congregated, in the coastal cities, but nothing substantial enough to call a red light district and, strangely, no pornography. So a conservative woman such as Laura's mother could spend practically her entire life without knowingly encountering mongers and whores, just as a villager might build a house next to the forest and never see a jaguar.

Laura's mother knew about the Hotel Grand, of course. She had read about it in the newspaper, and often seen its distinctive facade at a distance from the road, and sometimes the women in her office mentioned it, usually when they required a metaphor for depravity, such as, "I'd wear that skirt if I were working at the Hotel Grand." And of course she did not condone her daughter's working in its casino, and never admitted this to her friends, telling them instead that she worked in the Grand Riviera Resort, the hotel where autographed photos of world leaders lined the entrance to the lobby. It had been a constant source of friction between them,

Laura weakly defending herself, gladly playing the game, thinking, if only she knew! Telling her mother to be patient, she would soon find a better job. And when that strategy failed reminding her mother of all the rich gringos who laid bets on her table, who might want to gamble on a tica wife. It happened often enough.

"But you know what those men come for," her mother would object.

"And I'm sure the professors at your sacred university don't look up their students' skirts," Laura rejoined. "I'm sure there's as much sex on campus as there is in the hotel." A statement which was not true, but was bold enough to give her mother pause, for she was more familiar with the sexual misconduct at the university than she was with the indiscretions at the Hotel Grand. "And just because they gamble at the hotel doesn't mean they stay there," Laura would add. "Some come with their friends or for jungle tours. If they wanted sex why would they sit at my table all night?"

Her mother could never approve, and as a rummy player she held simple games like blackjack and poker in contempt. But Laura's goal was deflection, and to this length she had succeeded for four years. If she were a prostitute and needed to lie about her work, why choose a profession guaranteed to displease her mother?

All these factors reassured her mother that Laura was not a fallen woman. But the main reason she believed her daughter's countless lies was that she herself could not conceive of circumstances in which she would sell her body. And if such a life were so far removed from her own—and she was not a saint after all, but a normal woman who enjoyed sex and the company of men—how could that underworld reach out and grab her daughter? No, it was not possible. Laura had been properly brought up, educated in a private school, sheltered in fact. Except for a youthful indiscretion or two, she'd been careful with men, perhaps too careful. After all, she was twenty-four and still not married, and this alarming fact, more than any vague suppositions about her daughter's morals, accounted for her maternal anxiety.

"Has Dennis asked you to marry him again?" her mother asked.

Again! Laura berated herself for ever telling her mother about the proposal. There had been many proposals, actually. The indirect ones mentioned casually between courses at dinner, such as, "Why don't you come live with me in the States?" To more explicit declamations, though of questionable seriousness, as when she was shampooing his hair in the shower and he said, with a laugh, "Let's get married tomorrow." But the occasion she told her mother about was during a recent trip when he actually said nothing after a candlelit dinner on the patio of the Hotel La Perla, but simply presented her with a ring. She had told her mother because she was proud of the gesture, and perhaps to contrast the gentlemen she refused with the scoundrels her mother accepted.

Yet her mother was impervious to that attack and only asked about the ring. But Laura couldn't say, and for once did not lie. "I closed the lid on the box and pushed it back. I didn't even look at it," she had confessed.

"Next time at least try it on," her mother had said, convinced there would be another time. "Anyone can see he loves you, and men like that don't give up easily."

Dennis was the only client Laura had ever introduced to her mother, and they got along much too well for Laura's purposes, so that she viewed the pair as conspirators in a scheme to get her married.

"I told you, I'm working for Dennis," Laura now said. "And everyone knows business and marriage go together like eggs and chocolate. But what about you?" she asked to deflect the conversation away from her personal life. "Why don't you start dating again? Maybe you'll get a proposal or two."

To Laura's knowledge, her mother had not gone out with a man for several months, since breaking up with her last boyfriend, an electrician from Cartago.

"I have started seeing someone," her mother informed her with the hint of a smile.

"Really? That's great! Why didn't you tell me?"

"We just started dating. Do I tell you every time I have coffee with a gentleman?"

"Yes! But it's never coffee with a gentleman. It's always tequila in a reggae bar that was raided the week before and you paid the tab."

When it came to her mother's love life, Laura was surprisingly squeamish. With her friends and clients she could talk about fisting and rimming and all manner of perversions, but if her mother so much as described the scrape of her boyfriend's beard on her cheek, Laura covered her ears.

"He's from Florida," her mother revealed, sipping her lemonade.

"A gringo! No way!" Her mother had never dated a gringo before. Maybe a man with money, finally. "What does he do?"

"He's a professor of biology. He came into the admissions office by mistake one day and we started talking and he invited me for coffee."

Laura's initial excitement on hearing the news that her mother was dating again and might have found a good match was supplanted by occupational paranoia. She did not know any biology professors, but that didn't lessen her fears.

"What's his name?"

"Lawrence."

Laura didn't know any Lawrences either. A Larry, but he was from California. "What's his full name?"

"Dr. Lawrence Martin," her mother answered proudly, lighting a cigarette and reaching for the ashtray.

Laura didn't know why she asked. She rarely knew last names, and many gringos, especially the regulars, like Colorado Bob, had nicknames. "What does he look like?"

"I don't know. He has light skin and is thin and most of his hair is gone," her mother attempted, lacking her daughter's verbal gifts.

A description that, except for the weight, could describe half the men at the Hotel Grand. "Do you have a photo?"

Her mother stared incredulously. "A photo? Why would I have a photo?"

"Oh, I don't know. To remember him, maybe. So you don't have to describe him when someone asks. Really Mama, you're always scraping the bottom of the barrel and now you have a gringo professor and all you can say is that most of his hair is gone?"

Her mother blew smoke toward the valley. "Why are you so interested?"

Why indeed? Laura's instinct had been to protect her identity. Since her mother had never dated gringos before she never had to worry that her boyfriends might also be patrons of the Hotel Grand. Not that it was likely they would blow her cover in any case, but one never knew. While drunk or during an argument, they might say anything. And Laura had heard enough men talk in their sleep not to trust them with secrets.

But during the pause that hung in the air like the smoke from her mother's cigarette, Laura remembered she was retired now. So why did it matter? If the professor knew her, he could prove nothing. A private investigator would not be able to find her consorting with men at the Hotel Grand because she would be working at Pan American Web Services.

Unfortunately this realization failed to relieve Laura's apprehension, which simply re-focused on her mother. Her mother dating a monger! It was too awful to think about. He might be married, he might be a fugitive. Sure, he was a professor, but what did that mean? Hadn't she read an article in *la Nación* recently about a gringo dentist who was arrested for soliciting children? If he was a professor with nothing to hide why wasn't he teaching at Harvard or some place like that?

All kinds of dark thoughts ran through Laura's mind. But it was no use trying to talk sense to her mother about men. Her mother would probably just think she was jealous. Besides, what if Laura was wrong? Some mongers, like Dennis and Porter, were as decent as they come. And some gringos weren't mongers at all.

"I'll have to have you both over for dinner one night soon," Laura said, surprised at the difference a day makes. In the past she never would have suggested such a risky first encounter.

"Yes, and you'll have to invite Dennis," her mother replied, looking back at her.

"Of course." Why not, if it would persuade her to come. And while Dennis and the professor were talking computers or biology, she could scour him like a map from the shadows of the terrace or the dining room.

The phone rang.

"Hey, I need to talk to you!"

Tita Moon.

"I'm not renting the room to you," Laura replied, and hung up.

"Who was that?" her mother said, and why won't you rent her the room? You told me you still had one available."

"She's a distant acquaintance," Laura improvised. "She takes drugs."

The phone rang again. Laura turned it off to avoid further indiscretions.

"Oh," her mother said approvingly. Another mother might have actually expressed approval in words rather than in a sound. But another mother might have taken comfort in her daughter's judgment rather than raised fresh concerns.

"Why are you friends with a drug addict?"

"Who said she was an addict?" Laura shouted. "And I said 'distant acquaintance,' not friend."

"Does she work at the hotel?"

"Yes," Laura answered, before she could think. Why hadn't she said they had been classmates instead?

"She's not one of those girls?" her mother wondered, stringing out the words like an Inquisitioner stretching a prisoner on the rack.

"Mother, it may surprise you, but even desk clerks take drugs. Even professors."

Now they had come full circle to the professor. It was time to clear the dishes.

Her mother offered to take her shopping. Well, to drive her anyway, to accompany her. She rarely bought her daughter anything. More often than not Laura bought her mother clothes or cosmetics when they went shopping together, and her mother was certainly more likely to accept her daughter's generosity now that she was living in a fancy house in Escazu. But Laura couldn't stand to play cards with her mother, who was too critical and competitive. And they had different tastes in movies, Laura preferring love stories and her mother crime dramas. And neither attended church regularly, and cooking was out of the question because a kitchen was too confining a space and there were too many knives lying around. So shopping was the only activity they could share in relative harmony.

They went to the mall and Laura bought her mother a pair of acrylic earrings. Then they went grocery shopping at the supermercado and Laura paid here as well. But she was thinking about furniture, not clothing or vegetables, for after coming in from the terrace after lunch they had passed through the empty dining room. Laura had initially thought buying a table could wait, but now it became essential. The folding table on the terrace was adequate for lunch with her mother or a cocktail party, but a dinner required a dining table, and Laura knew just the place. So after the supermercado she asked her mother to drive to the home of a former tico client who made furniture in his cluttered workshop.

Fortunately he was in, sitting at a lathe, wearing work pants, a tank top and thick goggles, which he promptly removed when Laura and her mother entered.

Ernesto, like the professor, had also lost most of his hair, and seemed on the surface quite innocuous, short and wiry, laconic and polite. But Laura knew better and so didn't bother to introduce him to her mother, whom he might try to seduce. He was married, with a teenage daughter, but had screwed Laura in the same chair where he had been sitting a moment ago, before the lathe, the air thick with sawdust.

"I'm looking for a dining table, nothing expensive," Laura said, sliding her hands along the polished sides of wooden desks and bookshelves.

Actually, nothing was very expensive here, despite the quality of the wood and workmanship, furniture being one of the best bargains in Costa Rica.

"This is very nice," Ernesto said, pulling a table without legs from a stack against the wall. "And you can have round legs or square as you wish."

He set it with some effort atop a desk, where they could see the checkerboard inlaid birch and mahogany.

"You could play chess," Laura said, caressing it with both hands.

"I don't think there are enough squares," Ernesto pointed out.

"How much is it? I just moved to a new place and don't have much money at the moment."

The furniture maker made sure to position himself between Laura and her mother. Then he winked.

Laura didn't know how to pantomime, "I'm retired." But it really was a gorgeous table, it would look perfect in her home. And she would be able to have that dinner without delay and perhaps save her mother from a fugitive. True, she had thrown a retirement party last night. But lots of workers had retirement parties and still worked for a week or two. It wasn't as though she were going back to the hotel. And Ernesto was no stranger.

"What about the chairs?" she asked.

When her mother dropped her off there was a silver Toyota parked in her driveway and boxes of clothes piled on the doorstep.

"I tried to call you," Raquel said, approaching from across the lawn, nodding to her mother, who was backing away.

"I turned my phone off. So these are all your things?"

"My whole life in five boxes," Raquel confessed. "I don't have twenty-seven pairs of shoes like you, only four. Two dresses, a few skirts, pajamas, makeup and jewelry, a couple photo albums, my music and school books and my Teddy bear, who's followed me everywhere."

"Well now you have a whole house," Laura said, inviting her inside. "And soon even a dining room table, although you won't believe what I'm doing to get it."

Raquel lugged one of the heavier boxes into the living room and set it down. "You dirty girl! I thought you were retired?"

Laura helped her with the other boxes and closed the door. "I played golf with a client once. Not really played, you know. I went with him and he let me hit a few balls. He told me if you start with a bad shot it doesn't count. Well, this is my shot that doesn't count."

"I see."

"Actually he would have given me the table for a straight fuck, but I wanted the chairs too and that's where it gets kinky. But enough about me. Did you come from the hotel?"

Normally, Raquel would have been more inquisitive, but she was too stressed about her own job to care much about Laura's and welcomed her friend's curiosity.

"Yes. I've worked eight days in a row because Maria has been sick. But why do I have to cover all the time? Why can't Nancy or Paula take her shift? It's because my boss has it in for me. And I have classes at night. I can't work seven days a week and go to school too. When am I supposed to study?"

Laura helped her carry the boxes into the guest bedroom nearest the kitchen and asked if she wanted any help unpacking.

"No, I think I'll unpack later. I just want to rest for a while."

She looked for her purse and gave Laura the first week's rent. It was the first time Laura had ever received money from a woman. When she had begun her career as a prostitute, that first hundred dollars set on the night table gave her a sense of empowerment she had never known before. Now she again felt that sense of having a voice in her destiny. Her new life might not be as profitable, but it was respectable. She wouldn't have to lie about it. Except to Tita Moon.

"You still seeing that guy?" Laura asked tentatively. Some months ago Raquel had asked her advice about a guy she was dating, but they hadn't discussed him since.

"Eduardo. Yeah. I don't know. He doesn't seem to want anything serious, but he's nice enough, I guess. And I have no one else."

Laura wasn't interested in boy talk, at least not now. She had asked the question for another reason. "I know you're a responsible person or I wouldn't have rented to you," she began with some hesitation, uncomfortable in her new role as landlord. "I don't know if I mentioned this yesterday, but I don't allow overnight guests."

Raquel sat down heavily on the bed and laughed. "Where would I put him? On the floor?"

Laura laughed as well, relieved that her friend respected her authority. "On a rug maybe."

"No, he does not deserve a rug!"

But just as Laura was beginning to feel comfortable in her role as landlord she realized she had forgotten an important detail. "Keys! I'll have to make a set of keys for you."

"Don't worry," Raquel said, pulling off her shoes and lying down on the bed. "I'm not going anywhere."

Laura hadn't set a time with the furniture maker. She didn't want to make arrangements with her mother present and assumed she could return later in the week. But after closing the door on Raquel and stepping out on the terrace for coffee she realized there were still many hours left in this day and she had no plans to fill them.

She called him to confirm, then she called her driver to pick her up and, while waiting, took a quick shower without washing her hair.

When she arrived at the workshop Ernesto too had showered, or at least he had washed, because he was no longer sweating and was wearing a clean t-shirt. He gleamed at Laura with anticipation and locked the entrance, as well as the door that connected to his house. His wife and mother-in-law were cooking inside, which only intensified his lust. He had not made love to her this morning because he had drunk too much the night before and by the time he woke she was already in the kitchen.

Laura noticed her table had been assembled in the middle of the workshop and she examined the legs.

"Do you like them?" he asked. "Sit down and see if the height is good for you. I can make it lower if you like."

Laura sat in one of the simple wooden chairs. The table was a little high, but she would buy cushions. "No, it's perfect."

"My wife and mother-in-law are cooking trout if you would like to stay for dinner," he said with a salacious grin.

Laura could smell nothing except the sawdust. "Maybe you'd like a foursome. But then you would have to give me a bookcase as well."

Ernesto put a finger to her mouth. He turned on the lathe. "Now you can talk dirty as much as you wish," he said, tearing off her clothes, then his own, down to their shoes.

"Let me see your big cock. I want you so much. Fuck me on the table."

The furniture maker couldn't risk head, the sight of Laura naked in his workshop so excited him. As soon as she put the condom on he lifted her onto the table and pounded her while standing on one of the chairs. As the lathe buzzed he groaned rapidly. Laura held tightly to the sides to keep from slipping and coughed from the sawdust.

At the last moment he pulled out, tore off the condom, and aimed at the table. Afterward, Laura balanced herself on her knees and slowly lowered her head, her tongue wagging like a pendulum, and licked it up.

Darkness was beginning to fall as the furniture maker drove her back to Escazu in his pickup. He set up the table in the dining room and scrutinized the varnish under the light, as if looking for traces of himself.

"Can we do it again?" he asked. "Not for a bookshelf, but I have a pair of small square tables that would look very nice in the corners. You could put plants on them."

"You don't want to keep your wife and mother-in-law waiting. Besides, I have a guest."

Ernesto, assuming she meant a man, walked quickly to the door. Laura kissed him on the cheek and waved goodbye.

She lingered in the doorway as he drove down the hill, reflecting on the fact that she was now officially retired. But the pickup had no sooner faded from view than a fresh reminder of her former life arrived in the form of Carmen's red Ford Fiesta. Laura would have been happy to see her, but she had not come alone.

"Why don't you answer your phone?" Tita Moon demanded.

"Come in if you want, but keep your voices down. Raquel is sleeping."

"Raquel?"

"She moved in today. And I've found someone for the other room," Laura lied, "so don't even ask me about it."

"I didn't come here about the room."

"You bought a table," Carmen interrupted. "Where did you get it? It's beautiful."

"A friend of mine makes furniture. I need to get cushions for the chairs."

"I think it's fine as it is," she said, sitting down. But then Carmen was taller than Laura. "I like the plain look of wood." She ran her hand over the table, and Laura couldn't help but smile. "It was expensive?"

"I got a good deal," Laura replied, not wishing to say more, especially in front of Tita Moon.

"Have you eaten yet? We can break it in. I can make soup and corn, and I think I have some salad left from lunch."

"Thanks, sure," Carmen said, while off to the side Tita Moon vigorously shook her head. "Do you need help?"

"I don't think so. But you can keep me company in the kitchen. How was work last night? Did you get anybody?"

"That's what we wanted to talk to you about. Tita had a guy and the condom broke. She needs the morning-after pill."

Laura had gone into the kitchen and turned on the stove. She threw a sympathetic glance at Tita Moon, who was leaning like a wilted plant against the wall in the dining room. Although this had never happened to Laura, broken condoms were an occupational hazard, and she knew Tita Moon was not at fault.

"I don't know where to get it. I've never been in that situation. Did you talk to the guy? Ask him to get it?"

"He's Chinese," Tita Moon answered, as if that explained why his help could not be solicited.

"I hope you at least got a couple hundred out of him?" Tita Moon wilted further.

"Tita, you're too soft! A Colombian would have shaken him down for a thousand. Well, why don't you wait? Maybe you're not pregnant."

"But I get pregnant easily," Tita Moon protested. "When I had my child the gynecologist said I was made to have babies."

"Then find someone who will give you an abortion, or take that stomach medicine." She was referring to an over-the-counter gastritis medication, contraindicated in pregnant woman because it could cause miscarriage.

"I would rather take the morning-after pill," Tita Moon insisted. "Won't you help me?"

She recounted the incident in detail over dinner and Laura agreed to do what she could, but asked to change the subject, she would think about it in an hour, there was no reason they couldn't enjoy supper.

Then Carmen talked about her experience with the narco, but she didn't mention her plans to help him.

"You both had a busy night," Laura said, mentally calculating what she might have made herself had she not retired. Why did I retire on a Saturday and not during the middle of the week? she asked herself. I could have another hundred or two hundred in my bank account, and in fact I didn't retire yesterday after all, but only today.

"It got busier," Carmen added. And she mentioned Ginger and the threesome.

Laura banged down her fork. "The witch! I knew it. How could you go with her?"

"Don't blame me. It was eighty dollars, easy."

"Nothing is easy with her. And it should have been a hundred."

"Hey, if I didn't do it someone else would."

"Poor Porter. Wait till I tell him! But he won't believe me. You have to tell him, Carmen."

"I don't even know him."

"Let him believe what he wants," Tita Moon offered. "You'll just bring him down."

"But she's bringing his bank account down. She's ruining him."

"He's a grown man," Tita Moon said. And then had a thought. "Maybe he knows how to get the morning-after pill?"

"If he doesn't believe you, who are his friend, why do you think he will believe me?" Carmen rationalized.

Laura bit her thumbnail. "That's true. Maybe next time you could take a photo."

"The guy left today. There won't be a next time."

"Sure there will. With someone else. She knows she can work with you. And if not you can just take a photo in the bar, showing her working."

"I can't take photos in the bar!"

"Use a cell phone," Laura said, recalling Porter's suggestion.

"Why is it so important to help this guy?" Carmen asked in all seriousness, forgetting that just that morning she had considered giving a thousand dollars to save a narco from a life of violence.

"Because he's my friend. And I hate to see putas like Ginger get away with their plots. It gives all of us a bad name." She pushed her salad away. "I mean all of you, since I'm retired."

Laura thought it painfully ironic that only a day after her announced retirement and a few hours after her functional retirement, she was flashing her ID to the guard at the Hotel Grand.

"I never thought I'd step foot in here again," she told Carmen as they walked through the crowded lobby. "I do this only because you're my friends. And if I don't see someone within thirty minutes I'm leaving. I'm not hanging out like I'm still working."

"I really appreciate it," Tita Moon said.

Laura glanced around, wishing she were wearing a mask, as if her retirement had been reported in the newspaper and everyone would infer from her presence here tonight that she was unable to lead a respectable life even for twenty-four hours.

But that wasn't the only reason she felt apprehensive. She really didn't have a plan for obtaining the morning-after pill. Her friends had talked her into coming, in the hope that she would make a connection with one of her acquaintances. But now that she was here she wondered who that connection could be. Carmen and Tita Moon had friends as well. Why were her chances any better?

She didn't see anyone she knew in the lobby and they walked on to the bar. Sundays were usually less crowded than the end of the week, at least on the male side, since many guests departed on Sunday. Still, all the bar stools were occupied, and most of the tables. Who did she want to see? Certainly not Colorado Bob, who was chatting with a barmaid at his usual coordinates, next to last bar stool in the back. He seemed to be drinking alone. Laura thought why not, she had to try something to placate her friends.

"Didn't we just throw you a retirement party?" Colorado Bob asked, rising to his feet to greet her. "Maybe you feel guilty about taking all that money from me."

"I didn't take money from you. I gave it to your companion."

He sat back down. She ignored the empty bar stool beside him and stood with her back straight, her hands clasped in front of her.

"Mortgage rates go up?"

"I came with Carmen and Tita," she replied, nodding to her friends, whom she had instructed to remain where they were. She was going to ask about the pill, but then another question occurred to her, one with more personal relevance.

"You don't know any biology professors at the university by any chance?"

Colorado Bob raised his bushy eyebrows. "Your boyfriend just about fulfills my intellectual quota," he answered, referring to Dennis. "But if you're wanting to learn biology I can tell you all the news that's fit to print, and one or two things that aren't fit for anybody."

Laura didn't even try to segue from one topic to the other but simply said, "Tita needs the morning-after pill."

Colorado Bob squinted across the bar at Tita Moon, who was looking the other way. "Her tits do look bigger," he remarked.

"Can you help or not?"

"Condom break?" He took a long drink and rubbed his beard, then smiled at Laura like Santa Claus. "I do have a buddy flying in tomorrow."

"Great. What's his price?"

"I think if I buy him a beer he'll be happy. The question is, what's my price?"

Laura's posture collapsed and she leaned against the bar. She shouldn't have felt angry, after all it wasn't her concern. But she was a generous person herself and didn't like when people tried to negotiate favors.

"How much can this pill cost? She'll buy him all the beer he wants. But you're not even doing anything."

"I'm making the phone call, I'm asking him to take a risk, and taking a risk myself by being an accessory."

"An accessory to what? What risk? It's legal."

"In the U.S. But what if they confiscate it at Customs?"

"It's one fucking pill. How are they going to find it?"

"But what if they do? It's my buddy's ass. And I won't expect him to take the rap for me, so that puts me at risk as well."

"I've never heard such nonsense. If Customs finds it, which of course they won't—but if they do, your buddy only has to say he bought it for his girlfriend at home, but it turned out she didn't need it and he forgot to throw it away."

"And in the meantime he's lost an hour or two fucking with officials at the airport instead of fucking with you beauties here. Not to mention the time I might lose if I'm called in for questioning.

"Yes, we know how valuable your time is. So what do you want?"

"I want Tita Moon."

"All right. I'll ask her."

"Sin condom."

"She won't do that."

"Why not? She'll have the pill tomorrow!"

Laura walked back to her friends, who were standing in their usual position, smoking cigarettes.

"Well?" Tita Moon asked expectantly.

"You're in luck. He has a friend coming tomorrow." "And he'll bring it?"

"Yes. And you won't have to give him anything. But Colorado wants a freebie."

Tita Moon waited for a barmaid to move out of the way and clear a view of the lumbering figure at the far end. He raised his glass in reply.

"Without a condom," Laura added.

"No way!"

"You're already pregnant," Laura said, surprised to find herself supporting Colorado's argument. But perhaps she wasn't pregnant. And what if Colorado Bob knocked her up instead and his friend forgot the pill or it didn't work? Not to mention STD's. Tita Moon wasn't known for making judicious decisions and Laura should have applauded her refusal. But she had made an effort to help her and didn't want to see it wasted.

"I'm not fucking without a condom! What if he has AIDS?" Tita Moon exclaimed, glaring not at Laura but toward Colorado Bob. But fortunately the barmaid blocked the view.

Laura walked back the length of the bar. "She'll give you a free-bie but only with a condom."

Colorado had always wanted Tita Moon, but she would never go down from a hundred for him. Colorado Bob was a man of few principles, but never paying a hundred for a piece of ass was one of them.

"What about a bareback blow job? And I come in her mouth?"

Laura was beginning to feel she should get something from this deal as well.

"Come in my mouth?" Tita Moon shouted when she heard the new offer. "Is he crazy? I never do that. Only for boyfriends."

"Oh, Saint Tita!" Laura said, exasperated. "Do you want the pill or not? Tell her, Carmen."

"I don't even swallow cum for boyfriends," Carmen confessed. "I always spit it out."

"The hell with you both," Laura said, and returned empty handed to the other party.

"Will she let me come on her face?" Colorado asked graciously.

This time Tita Moon considered the request. "Not on my eyes," she replied. "I got it in my eyes once and they were red for hours. And not in my hair "

"Where then? Up your nose?"

"On my cheek and lips."

Laura threw up her hands in frustration. "You won't let him come in your mouth but he can come on your lips?"

"I'll keep my lips closed and wipe it off right away."

"I can't believe I'm doing this! You can close the deal yourself. I'm going home."

Carmen drove Laura back to Escazu while Tita Moon went up-stairs with Colorado Bob. Colorado never stayed in the hotel. He had a home in San Pedro. But if he didn't have an all-nighter it was more convenient to fuck the girls here, and if the hotel wasn't booked and Edna or Rosalita were working the front desk, they would comp him a room for the duration and even waive the guest fee.

Tita Moon could barely squeeze into the elevator beside him. She took his enormous hand.

"This is your lucky night!"

"Yours too," Colorado said. "You've never looked upon a real man before."

"Just don't have a heart attack. I charge extra for CPR."

Tita Moon was glad it was only a blow job. What if he'd said yes to fucking with a condom and tried to get on top of her? Then she would be the one having a heart attack. Of course she never let fat men screw her that way, but sometimes they tried and it was unpleasant having to pinch them through all that fat. Sometimes she had to bite them to get the message through.

She had been working at the Hotel Grand for more than two years, five or six days a week, and gave no more thought to seeing a strange man naked than a nurse would in a hospital. But Colorado Bob was hardly a stranger. During the whole span of her career they had occupied opposite ends of the Red Volcano, she standing near the entrance and he sitting in the back. They looked at each other all the time, and sometimes nodded when they passed each other, and sometimes exchanged a few words. But Laura was always complaining about Colorado, and Carmen had heard a rumor there were lice in his beard, so Tita Moon kept her distance.

So it was unsettling, after all those night seeing him fully clothed in the bar, to suddenly find him lying naked on one of the hotel's king-sized beds. And what a body. White as a polar bear, covered with white hair. The mattress sagged to a depth Tita Moon had never observed. But his cock wasn't so big.

"Can you wash it first?" she asked.

"Why don't you wash it for me?"

She led him into the bathroom and positioned him in front of the sink.

"Don't burn it," he cautioned, as she turned on the faucets.

"Do you think I've never done this before?" But in fact it wasn't routine. Most men were fastidious enough to take showers beforehand, even when they were going to use a condom.

She worked the soap into a rich lather and stroked him with both hands until he was hard. Then she squeezed his balls and he nearly lost his balance.

"OK, I think it's clean," he murmured.

She laughed and tickled him frantically, so that he had to take her by the shoulders and lift her away.

"You wanted me to do it," she reminded him.

He took her in his wide arms and carried her into the bedroom. "Maybe you *are* worth a hundred!"

He set her on her feet and lay down on his back, relieved and proud that he was still hard, for the moment had caught him by surprise and he had not taken any vitamin V.

"What are you staring at?" he asked, seeing that Tita Moon's big eyes were focused on his chin.

"Is it true you have lice in your beard?"

"Is it true you have lice in your pussy?"

"I shave my pussy."

"Yes, I noticed. I like the tattoo. No, I assure you, I fumigate my beard twice a month. Roaul from Pest Control uses an industrial spray."

Tita Moon kept his cock hard in one hand and reached much more tentatively for his beard. She tried to run her fingers through it but they got tangled.

"Santa Claus," she said.

"And I have two gifts for you, my Moon Child. One, in pill form, you'll get to open tomorrow. The other, in liquid form, will arrive in about five minutes."

His reference to the morning-after pill reminded her why she was here. "Are you sure your friend will bring it?" she asked, as she began to lick him.

"I phoned him after Laura left. He said he would. That's good enough for me."

She knelt forward at the foot of the bed and looked up at him as she flicked her tongue along his cock. "What if he misses his plane?"

"What if there's an earthquake? I can't control everything."

"I just have to take it before Tuesday night. If he can't bring it you'll have to pay me."

"Just do your job and I'll do mine."

She began to suck him, hard for a moment, but then eased off. "What time does his plane get in?"

"Twelve-thirty."

"Maybe I should meet him at the airport?"

"And make his girlfriend jealous? He's coming straight to the hotel. You don't have to deal with him at all. I'll meet you in the bar at five, like I already told you."

"Why don't you want me to meet him?"

"I don't care whether you meet him or not," Colorado said, breathing heavily. "It's just not necessary."

"Maybe you're making him up," she accused him through narrowed eyes.

He clutched her thick black hair in one hand and stared at the ceiling, feeling the moment closing in. "Why would I make it up?"

"To get a free bareback blow job."

"I wanted a bareback fuck, remember? And it was your friend who came to me."

"Oh yeah."

"The time to be paranoid was last night before the condom broke."

Tita Moon laughed and relaxed. Colorado Bob was right, she was concerned about nothing. At least she should give him a chance. She would know by five tomorrow.

She rewarded Colorado Bob for having satisfactorily answered her questions by asking no more. As she increased the pace, his was the only voice to be heard, rising in pitch, surprising for a man so large.

Then suddenly he pushed himself up like a whale breaking the surface of the water and plunged Tita Moon's head against the pillow.

"Look at me! Open your eyes!" he gasped.

"No."

"Open your eyes bitch."

Tita Moon kept her eyes and lips tightly sealed and blindly searched for his balls with her left hand.

"I want to see your eyes. I won't blind you. Or do you want me to shove it down your throat?"

Tita Moon lifted her right eyelid just in time to see Colorado Bob oscillating over her in a state of intense labor, so at odds with his placid demeanor at the bar. But he was true to his word and gave it up on her nose, lips and chin.

She wiped it off with the back of her hand, then went to the bathroom and washed her face thoroughly with soap and hot water before daring to part her lips.

Fifteen minutes later they were both back in the bar, she smoking a cigarette near the front with Carmen—who was still waiting for a client—he at his customary stool in the back, where his unfinished beer awaited him, a few degrees warmer.

CHAPTER 4

PAN AMERICAN WEB SERVICES

For someone who was not used to waking before noon, Laura thought it was quite an achievement to get out of the door by ten. Unfortunately she was supposed to be at the office at nine, and she still had to wait for the bus. By the time she arrived at Pan American Web Services it was a quarter till eleven and her boss was not amused.

"I guess I should have given you an alarm clock instead of a watch," Dennis complained.

"We're on tico time. The world isn't going to come to an end if I'm a few minutes late," Laura said unapologetically.

She set her purse on the swivel chair in front of what she assumed to be her desk, which was bare except for the computer and phone.

"You're not a few minutes late. You're almost two hours late! Banks open at nine and Pan American Web Services opens at nine. If you're going to treat this office like the Hotel Grand you're not going to last very long."

"I'll come at nine tomorrow. Give me a break."

She ran her fingers over the computer—her computer. "How do you turn this thing on?"

Dennis had no more experience running a company and being a boss that Laura had being a landlord. But, unlike her, he conformed to the role easily. Perhaps because he had dreamed for so long of starting his own business.

Not that Pan American Web Services was in the same league as the Silicon Valley start-ups of some of his fellow alumni. Even by Costa Rican standards it was modest, almost anonymous—two rooms on the second floor of a low-rent building at the edge of town. A single window by Laura's desk looked onto the street. There was no air-conditioning or carpeting, just a creaking ceiling fan and a dusty area rug. Dennis's room lacked even these features, and was furnished only with an arm chair that needed upholstering and a coffee table, on which he had set his laptop.

But why waste money in the beginning? He could always upgrade later. He had even toyed with the idea of working from his apartment, but he was one of those people who liked the idea of having an office. The only essential requirement at this point was a high-speed connection for his computer.

And Laura.

Dennis was not exactly deceiving himself in this venture. After all, this had been his dream when he was still in school, long before he'd even heard of the Red Volcano. A trust fund, along with his own savings, now made it possible, and Costa Rica was a sensible choice for tech companies, since taxes and wages were much lower than in California, the country had good infrastructure, an educated workforce, and was closer to the U.S. than India or Ireland.

But although he had scrawled the name "Pan American Web Services" on a Post-It note long ago in his San Diego apartment, the idea to locate in Costa Rica had occurred only much later, during one of his sessions with Laura at the Hotel Grand. He had been fucking her doggy style, admiring her ass, when the inspiration took hold of him.

So a Costa Rican address and Laura's ass had been inextricably bound together in his business plan. Of course he told himself Laura was a practical choice to run the office. She was bright, sociable, spoke excellent English, and honest where it mattered. Where he was deceiving himself was in his belief that he could separate work from pleasure, that he was as much a professional in his field as she had been in hers, and that proposing the job was not a proxy for his unsuccessful proposals of marriage.

This hadn't happened overnight, of course. Dennis had told her during their first encounter about his plans to start an internet company, and was both flattered and impressed that Laura took a genuine interest. Months later, after his inspiration to locate in Costa Rica, she encouraged him. Which gave him the resolve during his next visit, while dancing at Club Valentino, to offer her the position of office manager.

They were both sweating and he had pulled her into a corner, away from the music, and taken both her hands in his and said, just like a marriage proposal, "Be my office manager."

He knew that she was looking for an exit strategy from the Hotel Grand. She hadn't made a secret of her wish to retire before twenty-five, and he realized her material prospects were limited, unless she wanted to marry. But she hadn't met the man of her dreams, and normal jobs, such as working in a bar or in the travel industry would have paid far less than she was making now and demanded longer hours.

At first she was hesitant, though she didn't ask about the money, an oversight he found extraordinary in a prostitute. Her concern was whether she could do the job, what it entailed.

He briefly described the duties. For most she was already capable and for the rest he was confident he could train her. The money wouldn't be what she was used to, of course, but he could offer her a higher salary than she would make working in a hotel or restaurant or club, and more flexible hours. At first it would just be the two of them. But if Pan American Web Services prospered he would give her a raise or even a stake in the company and would hire more staff, whom she would supervise.

She had shouted out her agreement and hugged him and the sex that night was even good for her. From that point on they dreamed together, and began planning in earnest. He rented an apartment in the city and stayed weeks at a time. She ran errands for him and offered advice based on her own knowledge of the business community.

More importantly for Dennis, she was a real partner. She might not have consented to be his wife or even his girlfriend, but no spouse could have been more supportive. She might disagree with him on minor matters, such as where to rent office space—she wanted a prestigious address in a brand new building, whereas he wanted to save money—but she never doubted his capability to run a company.

"I can tell you are destined for success," she would say, and this, even more than her language skills and knowledge of Costa Rica made her invaluable to him at this vulnerable stage in his career.

His business plan was deliberately vague, and while Laura knew how to navigate the internet and send e-mails, he didn't require her to have any technical knowledge. He anticipated that most of their business would come from overseas, and he could handle the e-mail queries himself. As for the phone, Laura's excellent English would reassure customers in the States that they were not dealing with foreigners. Dennis would offer an array of services, including hosting, web design and security consultation. His plan was to see what people wanted, to gain satisfied customers and then ask what else they needed. In this way he hoped to compete with larger enterprises which had big advertising budgets. Since his start-up costs were so low and his only big investments were Laura and the rental of a server at a data center, he could change course literally overnight, so that if he found a high demand for hosting he could upgrade his capacity, or if he received more queries for web design than he could handle himself, he could hire designers locally. In this way he hoped to maximize his opportunity while minimizing his risk. He also understood himself well enough to know he wasn't a wunderkind with dreams of global domination, willing to work eighteen hours a day. Dennis's goals were less ambitious, but more rounded. He wanted to build a successful company not for its own sake but to give him the freedom to pursue other pleasures and to support a family.

He tried not to think too far ahead, and the demands of moving to another country and starting a business kept him focused on the present. But his visions always included Laura.

"Is what I'm wearing all right?" she asked.

She was wearing a short red skirt, a bright print blouse and heels. Dennis didn't think her attire was any different from the outfits she wore at the Hotel Grand. "You look great," he said.

"I didn't know if you wanted me to wear stockings or white blouses, you know, more conservative."

"You can wear jeans if you like, I don't care."

Dennis himself was wearing khakis and a gray polo shirt. Although by Colorado Bob's standard he seemed buttoned up, in truth Dennis hated wearing suits and only owned one sports jacket.

"I just thought for clients."

"Our clients will never see you."

"I mean our Costa Rican clients."

Dennis shrugged. "That will come later. I'm sure you'll make a good impression."

He showed her how to turn the computer on.

Laura smiled. "Will you let me decorate the office?"

"Yes, but you'll be on a budget. I don't want any leather couches and expensive rugs."

Laura frowned. "How did you know that's what I wanted?"

"There are more important things to spend money on. And speaking of money, let me show you the accounting program."

He sat on the desk and motioned Laura to sit in the chair. He then led her through the software, which he had already set up, since he had to open a bank account and pay bills. He showed her the various categories of vendors and how to write checks. Once or twice, while looking down at her to answer one of her many questions, he found himself gazing into her eyes and lost his train of thought.

"You'll print the checks, but I'll sign them," he told her.

"Ah, you don't trust me."

"If I didn't trust you I wouldn't let you handle the books. But you're not an officer in the company."

"Yet," she teased.

"Yet. Besides, it's not sound business practice. A lot of celebrities have lost fortunes because they let their managers sign their checks."

"You're hardly a celebrity." She looked around. "Where's the printer?"

"In my office."

"Don't I get my own? How do I print?"

"It's on a wireless network."

"Cool. What about accounts receivable?"

He smiled in surprise. "How do you know about accounts receivable?"

"I'm not an idiot," she replied, slightly offended, forgetting that she had insulted him just a moment before. "My mother works at the university, so I grew up hearing all kinds of business language. When bedtime stories didn't work I asked her to read me test score statistics. Are we finished with the bank stuff? I think it's time for lunch, boss."

"For normal employees. Not those who come at eleven."

"The first thing I'm going to buy is a coffee machine. And can I buy a small refrigerator?"

"Do you plan to live here? I thought you just bought a house?"

"We could keep snacks. We won't have to go out so much."

"There are restaurants across the street."

"This is a shitty neighborhood, if you didn't notice. I'd rather eat here."

As if to prove to her that the neighborhood wasn't so bad, Dennis decided to take her to lunch. He let her decide, and she chose a soda after examining the zinc counter like a food inspector.

Sodas were typical Costa Rican fast food joints. Tiny restaurants, some with tables, some only with counters and stools, that served tortillas and gallo de pinto. They invariably looked fifty years old, were sparsely decorated with religious trinkets, soccer photos or outdated calendars, but they possessed a certain charm and satisfied Laura's craving for banana milkshakes.

"See, I'm saving you money by bringing you to a soda," she said after they ordered.

Dennis was about to make a remark about dating, but held his tongue. He was enjoying this day immensely. Except for being late, Laura had justified his confidence in her. She took the job seriously, despite her witticisms, and learned quickly. Whatever worries he might have had about her had been dispelled. Furthermore, he enjoyed her company. Having her to himself, knowing she was no longer for sale. Even if theirs was now purely a business relationship, he was the boss, and her sincere respect, the sight of her eyes watching him for instruction, gave him enormous pleasure. And it wasn't just a business relationship. They had been lovers, or something like lovers. And friends, definitely friends. She might say she didn't want to marry him, but she flirted with him nevertheless. He sensed that if he took her hand she would not pull it away. But he feared being proved wrong and restrained himself. Despite being her boss, he felt he was the one being evaluated.

And how to handle lunch? As business? It certainly would be efficient to use this time to talk about her responsibilities. But lunch could also demarcate where their professional lives ended and give him the opportunity to legitimately talk about personal matters. He was still inwardly debating how to handle this delicate situation when Laura decided for him.

"My mother came yesterday to see the house," she began, sipping on her banana shake. "I invited her. My God. I had to invite her, of course. But what a mistake. I mean I shouldn't have done it alone, I should have had other people there to cushion the blow. My aunts couldn't come. I should have just waited until they could come, and invited her then. Or invited you, but you came to the party and she would just embarrass us. Maybe she should work for you instead of me, she always comes early. I was brushing my teeth. And I had this grand dream to show her the house in exactly a certain way, but she came early and ruined everything. Sometimes I wish I could have a father instead of a mother. It has to be easier, right? There must be plenty of women who don't have mothers but have fathers. Tita Moon has a father. She has a mother too. But my point is she has a father she isn't close to. I'd love to trade my mother for her father. God, a father wouldn't drive me so crazy, don't you think? And she's so critical. I show her my new house and she doesn't say one kind word. I might as well have invited her to the opening of a prison, that's the kind of reaction I got. Do you think she noticed the view? We ate on the terrace and I swear, you know how insects see differently, like they can't see in color or their focus isn't so good? Well, I swear my mother has insect eyes. All she can say is it might be a good investment. Which would be like me saying about your business, which you've worked so hard to create, well, it might be a good business. I mean, who needs people like that in their lives?"

She took a breath and finished her milkshake, suddenly thirsty. "By the way, do you know any biology professors?"

Dennis was eating his hamburger, enjoying her monologue. "Biology professors?"

"My mom's dating a gringo professor. I want to check him out."

"Why don't you invite them both for dinner?"

"I did. You too. So keep your calendar open."

"I have no time for a social life right now," he told her. "Except for you."

Back at the office, he showed her scripts he had written for telephone queries. He expected most contact to come by e-mail, but there would be a few callers, and Dennis explained which subjects she could handle herself and when she should take messages.

"Now I'd like to show you the website," he said excitedly, turning back to the computer.

"What website?"

"Our website Platinum Web Services. What I've been working on for the last five months."

He hadn't shown it to her in its earlier stages because he wanted to impress her with the finished product.

"What's that?" Laura asked, squinting at the screen, pointing to a silver image below the company name on the home page.

"A satellite image."

"It's not very sexy."

"I'm not running an escort agency," Dennis said defensively. "Clients want to feel they're dealing with a solid, well-capitalized firm, like a bank."

"I've seen prettier banks."

Dennis should have let it go. Why did Laura's opinion of the home page matter? She hardly represented his target demographic of male, college educated, small business owners in the U.S. and Western Europe.

But he allowed her criticism to distract his long-anticipated presentation and surfed to a banking site.

"See, it's boring. Lots of text, no color. Small graphic of a safe."

"But there's a picture of a family. That's what you need. Someone's face, so we feel like we're dealing with a person."

"I don't know," Dennis considered, switching back to his home page. "I wanted to give an impression of size and strength. I don't want people to think it's one person working in a back room in a poor barrio in Central America."

"Two people," Laura corrected. "And soon more. In a big office with leather furniture. But even if you go to a big corporation you still want to see a human face."

"Maybe I should use your picture?"

"No, not me. You're the owner."

"I don't photograph well. But your picture will attract clients," Dennis realized, envisioning a pleasant photography session.

"But what kind of clients will my photo attract?" Laura said with a smile.

"Okay, back to business. Let me show you how to navigate the site."

He led her through the pages for "Hosting" and "Web Design" and "Security Consultation," explaining what these services meant. She didn't ask many questions, as she had about the accounting software, and simply nodded when he asked whether she understood something. He felt somewhat disappointed. Laura betrayed her enthusiasm at the slightest things. She would jump up and down and clap her hands if she won ten coins at a slot machine. Her cries when eating a hot fudge sundae would border on the orgasmic. And yet now, while scrolling through the culmination of his high-tech dreams, she was unresponsive.

"Let me show you the client site," he said, logging in to another screen.

This was where customers could access their account information, as well as viewing detailed demographics about their own sites. But Dennis recalled what Laura had said earlier about statistics putting her to sleep and decided to abbreviate his presentation.

"That's great," she said without enthusiasm.

He resisted the urge to win her over. She was supportive enough. Not everyone's heart raced at the sight of a well-designed website. Maybe as she became more familiar with the computing world she would come to appreciate his efforts.

He gave her some clerical tasks for the remainder of the afternoon and retreated to his office, feeling the same kind of disappointment that plagued him when he failed to arouse her during sex.

Shortly after five o'clock, Tita Moon entered the Red Volcano. At first she looked around, a bit disoriented, for she had never been at the hotel during the day. She couldn't believe how quiet, empty and light the place was and even wondered for a moment whether the bar might be closed. But then she spotted Colorado Bob sitting at his usual stool and nervously walked over.

He motioned to the barmaid. "What are you drinking?"

"I don't know. Orange juice."

"Good choice. It's too early for the hard stuff."

When her glass came he raised his beer mug in a toast. Tita Moon sat down and tentatively lifted her glass.

"Better to wash this down," Colorado said, placing something wrapped in clear plastic on an empty coaster.

Tita Moon unwrapped it and examined the two tiny white pills. She held the blister package up to the light, though she didn't know what she was looking for.

"Take one now and the second twelve hours later. Cheers!" Tita Moon carefully placed them in her purse.

"Thanks."

Colorado Bob put a hand on her bare shoulder. "Aren't you going to take it?"

"Not here."

She slid off the bar stool and walked out without saying goodbye. On the street taxi drivers called to her, but she ignored them.

When the light turned green she crossed the avenue, but she didn't know where she was going. For several minutes she walked aimlessly, her thoughts in turmoil. When she spotted a church she went inside.

It was an old Catholic church she had never entered before, although she had passed it countless times in the arms of clients, en route from the Red Volcano to other hotels.

It was dark inside, darker than a bar. A pair of old women were sitting in the front. A younger priest was tending to the altar.

Tita Moon did not want to draw their attention. She sat in the rear and bowed her head. She could hear the rush hour traffic outside, taxi drivers impatiently pushing their horns.

Tita Moon took out the pills from her jeans pocket, held them away from her like a profane object, and made her deal with God.

"Dear God," she said, following her own brand of logic. "If I promise not to take the morning-after pill, which I know is a sin, maybe not as bad as abortion, but still a sin, then please don't let me be pregnant."

She rose quickly and turned to go. There was a trash can near the entrance and she was about to discard the pills, but then she thought it unwise to leave a profane object in a house of God, and waited until she reached the corner to throw them away.

She started walking, unsure what to do. She usually didn't start working till after nine and it wasn't even six. But it didn't make sense to go back home. She could eat, but she didn't have an appetite. She called Carmen but got her voice mail. A few minutes later she found herself back at the hotel and decided to go in. She didn't want to stand in the bar, however, not this early. And she didn't want to see Colorado Bob because he would ask her about the pill and she would have to lie and tell him she took it and thank him again for his help.

So she sat in the lobby, on one of the wicker sofas. Raquel was not working at the travel desk, and she didn't know any of the other staff, so she absently watched the action in the casino and the men checking in.

She thought about her favorite soap opera, "Vale of Tears," and wondered what Cindy or Angelique would have done in her situation. Not that they were good role models. Everyone always came to a bad end on that show. Women were always getting pregnant, but they weren't prostitutes and they didn't take the morning-after pill. They got knocked up by a lover and then their husband beat them in a jealous rage, causing them to lose the baby. Or their car ran over a cliff in their ninth month and they were lucky to survive. But of course the baby could not be saved. Or they had a miscarriage after seeing the ghost of their dead father in the courtyard. Or they slashed their wrist in the bathtub.

But these were not practical options for Tita Moon. She had to find her own way in the world. When she had her first child she was as excited as any expectant mother. But the father left, and when the baby arrived Tita Moon fell into a deep depression. She was overwhelmed by the responsibility and horrified that she didn't feel as much of a connection with her child as she expected. A boy. "I only know how to take care of men," she would joke years later to Carmen. But in fact she felt very guilty. Her mother, in Puntarenas, agreed to take the baby, and Tita Moon assuaged her conscience by sending money and visiting on holidays. She rationalized that she was too much of a child herself to raise one. Yet every day on the streets of San Jose she saw women younger than herself carrying their babies or pushing them in strollers.

A man set a large backpack and a camera case in front of the couch and sat down next to her. He was wearing khaki shorts and an Orioles t-shirt. He had fair skin, wavy hair, a thin mustache and looked young for thirty-five.

He smiled at her awkwardly.

"Strange I have to wait for the maid to clean my room," he said after she smiled back. "You'd think by six o'clock I could check in."

Tita Moon shrugged.

He eagerly glanced around, trying to take everything in. But the hotel was pretty quiet at the moment. A couple day girls were standing by the casino, but there were no others in the lobby.

"Are you with someone?" he ventured after a minute.

"No."

He moved closer. "My name's Rick."

"Tita Moon," she answered, shaking his hand. He was much smaller and thinner than Colorado Bob, but his grip was firm.

She imagined he was probably good in bed, especially compared to the men she'd had lately.

He was thinking the same of her, drawn by her dark eyes, her youthful figure, the curve of her breasts in her tight-fitting top. He felt like he was in high school again, the first day of a new year.

"I just arrived," he said nervously.

"Yes, I can see." She waited for him to go on, but he just smiled. "It's your first time in Costa Rica? Where are you going?"

"To the rain forest. For a couple weeks."

"Which one?"

"Manuel Antonio. Maybe Corcovado. I haven't made reservations yet. I've been making plans my whole life. Now I just want to be spontaneous, get lost in the forest."

"And if you don't get lost will you come back here?" She wanted to know if he might be a return customer, although it didn't occur to her that he might invite her, or he might not go at all.

"I guess so. For my last night. What's your favorite forest?" he asked cheerfully.

"I don't know."

"Do you have any suggestions, any advice?"

"No."

She should have been more helpful. She liked him but she risked driving him away with her unenthusiastic answers. But while Tita Moon could lie well enough when she needed to, she had no talent for the finer art of artifice, and when something failed to interest her, such as the rain forest, she usually let it show.

"What's in there?" she asked, looking at the square metal case. "Something important of course!"

He unlatched the case on the sofa cushion between them and showed her his digital Nikon, its lenses, and a small video camera."

"You're a photographer?"

"I wouldn't call myself a pro, although I've done some work. Portraits, weddings, that sort of thing. But what I really do is manage a photo shop. I've always wanted to photograph the jungle."

"That jungle or this jungle?" Tita Moon joked.

He saw this as his opening. He had heard about the beauty and friendliness of Costa Rican women from a friend, and he had read about the Hotel Grand online, which is why he had booked it for his first night in the country. But he was still unsure how to read the situation and didn't want to offend her.

"Do the women here let people take their picture?" he asked in the most abstract of terms, as if Tita Moon were not herself one of those women.

"Not sex pictures. But normal photos, sure."

He wanted to ask if he could take her picture now, but thought this might be somehow inappropriate. Perhaps the hotel didn't want guest taking photos in the lobby. "Since I have to wait for my room," he said instead, "and I haven't eaten, would you like to have dinner with me?"

He left his backpack at the front desk, but kept the camera case with him. Tita Moon led him down the street to a small Italian restaurant.

They were shown to a round table in the corner. "I expected more of a local flavor," he said.

"I eat rice and beans all the time," Tita Moon replied, looking at the menu.

"I guess you're right. If someone visited me I wouldn't take them to eat hamburgers."

"Costa Rica is not famous for its food. But at least you won't get sick, like in Mexico."

"Have you been to Mexico."

"No. But I've heard so many stories. The same with Nicaragua and Honduras and Guatemala. A lot of men brush their teeth here with bottled water and I always laugh at them. I tell them, where do you think you are, Mexico?"

He smiled.

"I hate when people think we're a third world country," she said defensively. "There are even men who are surprised when they see me write my name in the hotel register. They say what pretty handwriting I have, as if they expect me to print like a child. What do they think all those years of school were for? I'm even going to university."

"You are?" he asked, trying not to sound surprised. "What are you studying?"

"Nursing," she lied. "Well, the truth is, I started but had to stop because my son was sick and he needed expensive medicine." But this was a lie as well. "I hope to get a degree some day," she concluded, which was closer to the truth than her previous statements, because she did sometimes dream of becoming a nurse.

They ordered spaghetti bolognese and a bottle of chianti.

Tita Moon normally looked men right in the eye, and she had been looking straight at Rick all this time, but now she nervously glanced away. She was talking nonsense, trying to impress him. Why did it matter to her whether he thought Costa Rica was a developed country or she a nursing student? She decided not to say anything more, to drink her wine.

Rick felt nervous as well. He had just come through a bitter divorce and hadn't dated much since the separation. He had kept to himself, working a lot, playing softball, drinking. He had not dated a woman as young as Tita Moon since he met his wife eight years ago.

He asked her for suggestions on where to go. She just shrugged. Their dinners came and she ate hurriedly, suddenly hungry.

"Is something wrong? You look like you haven't eaten all day," he observed.

"No."

"So you don't have advice?" he pursued. "It's such a small country, you must have seen most of it."

"I don't like the jungle," she replied. "I like the beach."

"So what's your favorite beach?"

"I like them all," she said. "Sand is sand."

He laughed, though he was unsure whether she was making a joke or not.

"Even Jaco? I've heard Jaco is dirty, crowded with bars and—" He was about to say cheap whores but caught himself at the last moment.

"If you want a clean beach and no people than Tamarindo and Guanacaste are better. But Jaco is not so expensive and I like the nightlife. If you go to the resorts there is nothing at night, or just some expensive shows for tourists."

"Well, I think I'll spend my time in the forest."

"Are you married?" she asked suddenly. She didn't know why she asked. She often asked clients if they were married. It was a common question for prostitutes to ask. And many, if not most men were married, whether they answered yes or not. But it surprised her that she asked it now, in the middle of a conversation about his Costa Rican itinerary.

The question caught him off guard as well. Tita Moon was looking at him again, her fork dangling spaghetti in front of her parted lips. Now it was he who turned away.

"I just got divorced. It took two years, even though we don't have kids. It just came through last week and I decided to come here to celebrate. Or to escape. I'm not sure which."

"So this is the honeymoon of your divorce," Tita Moon shrewdly remarked.

He was on the verge of melancholy, though he certainly didn't need to be reminded why he was here. But Tita Moon's comment and her mischievous smile and her large eyes fixed on him made him laugh and gave him courage.

"But you're supposed to have sex on your honeymoon," he responded.

"Of course you'll have sex," she told him, as if it were the most natural thing in the world.

His heart began to race. He knew it shouldn't be possible for a prostitute to flirt. Flirting was playful, or dangerous. It wasn't a sales pitch. And prostitutes were interested in racking up sales, not in the patient art of seduction.

But he was the one in a hurry. He paid the check and led her out, realizing only on the street that he was holding her hand. When had he taken it? Had she slipped her fingers into his? In that case his wallet was beyond saving should she wish to steal it. He thought of his dates since his separation. The personal ads and fix-ups. All had been women of similar backgrounds, and yet he felt more comfortable with this Costa Rican girl he'd met just an hour before, who probably knew nothing about photography or baseball or Baltimore. The women he knew were sophisticated and their vacation photos were of pristine beaches in the Caribbean. And he himself was no less guilty of such pretensions, whether it came to cameras or cars or designer beers. Hadn't he just been asking her to rank her country's forests and beaches? And she would have none of it. "Sand is sand," she had said, and it was the best advice anyone had given him in two unendurable years.

She led him to the Red Volcano, to a table in the front. It was still early and only half the tables were occupied. Tita Moon glanced around quickly for Carmen, but she knew her friend wouldn't be here yet.

Had Rick come here alone he would have observed the scene more closely. He would have gawked at the girls and let his fantasies run wild. After all, this was his reward to himself. A night of celebration before escaping into the jungle. But his eyes hardly strayed from Tita Moon, and he felt a sense of contentment he had not known since the early years of his marriage.

A barmaid came over and Rick thought she looked more the part of a whore in her vinyl miniskirt and fishnet stockings than did Tita Moon in her jeans. All his assumptions seemed challenged in this exotic country.

He decided to try the local beer, but Tita Moon grabbed his arm. "You have to drink a Red Volcano." She nodded to the barmaid. "And orange juice for me."

"What's in a Red Volcano?" he asked, as the barmaid sauntered off.

Tita Moon took his hand across the table. "Fire. What else?"

A minute later he was stunned to see an enormous conical glass set before him, smoke pouring from the small opening at the top. He could not tell whether the glass was painted blood red or whether that was the color of the liquid inside. But it was hot to the touch and hardly seemed drinkable. He had patronized numerous bars during vacations to Cancun and the Bahamas and had drunk his share of quaint and terrible cocktails. But this concoction appeared more suitable for a child's science fair than a licensed bar.

"Drink it all at once," Tita Moon urged.

"But it's boiling!"

"It's just warm. Don't be a baby."

Rick noticed the stares and smiles of those around him. Conversations seem to have ceased. Even the barmaid was watching, leaning her empty tray against a post.

"I can't possibly drink all this."

"It's mostly water," Tita Moon assured him, forgetting that a moment ago she had told him it was fire.

Suddenly he felt a comparable warmth in his groin. Tita Moon's hand squeezing him encouragingly under the table.

He was certainly in a new world. The rain forest, after this, would seem like civilization.

He heard male voices cheering him on, laughing, shouting lewd remarks. He had been drinking much too much these last two years. Perhaps this was just what he needed to moderate the habit. In any case, why would Tita Moon poison a potential client? Sure, sometimes prostitutes, or women posing as prostitutes, knocked men out and took their money. But they didn't do it conspicuously in bars with scores of witnesses.

He cupped the wide glass and held it briefly to his nose, wondering if that was sulfur he smelled. Then he tipped it into his mouth and let the liquid sear his throat until he could bear it no longer and set it down with a gasp.

He grabbed Tita Moon's orange juice and drank it all, struggling to catch his breath.

The barmaid took the Red Volcano and held it aloft, to applause and some boos. Only about one third had been consumed. A chant began for him to finish, but he grabbed Tita Moon's hand and fled unsteadily to the lobby.

Before he could go upstairs, he had to sign Tita Moon in at the puta registration desk. He seemed uncomfortable at first, but then wondered why he should care whether people saw him with a prostitute. All the men here were doing the same thing.

He felt dizzy in the elevator. "Have you ever had a Red Volcano?" he asked her.

"It's only for stupid gringos. And it cost twelve dollars."

She waited until he had unpacked before asking for the money.

"Are dollars okay? I haven't had a chance to change for colones."

"Of course. One hundred please."

She expected him to negotiate and was prepared to go for eighty since she liked him, but he gave her a hundred dollar bill, which she held up to the light.

"Don't you trust me?" he asked, and realized it was a stupid question.

"Once a Peruvian gave me a counterfeit bill," she answered matter-of-factly.

"But I'm not Peruvian," he said, wanting to distinguish himself from her other clients. At certain moments this evening he had almost forgotten she was a prostitute, but now it was all business, and that disappointed him.

"I guess you won't be offended if I use the safe," he said, locking up his cameras and passport.

"It's a good idea."

"So I shouldn't trust you either?" he said, approaching her closely.

"Of course not. I might steal your heart." And she gave him a quick bite on the neck and ran into the bathroom.

He tried to follow but she closed the door. He opened the window and peered out. A gentle breeze carried up the sounds from the street—taxis honking, vendors chanting "cigars," "roses," women laughing. Office buildings obscured the surrounding view, except for the mountains, visible beneath thick clouds in the distance.

He undressed to his boxers and turned the TV onto music videos, which he didn't care for but thought she might like and which would, in any case, drown out the sounds from the street.

When she emerged from the bathroom he took her in his arms, expecting to hug her. But she kissed him firmly on the lips and didn't let go. He opened his mouth and felt her tongue tickling him. How long had it been since anyone had kissed him like this?

"I should take a shower," he said, suddenly self-conscious, worried about his breath, wanting to be clean for her. "Will you join me?"

He felt uncomfortable asking her. Despite what he had read on the web, he didn't understand the rules these women followed, and he didn't want what had started as a magical encounter to descend into an argument over what was included and what was not, as though he were fighting again with his ex over household possessions.

But Tita Moon made it easy for him by undressing and leading him by the hand into the bathroom. She bent down and turned on the water, as if he were the guest in her room. She seemed to take a lot of time adjusting the temperature, but he took advantage of her position to run his hands along her back, down to the curves of her ass.

After she turned the shower on she slipped into the bedroom to pull her hair back. When she returned to the bathroom she left the door ajar and turned off the light. She knelt and pulled down his boxers and led him into the shower, not by the hand this time but by his stiff cock.

She pushed him under the hot water and kissed him passionately, as he reached down to feel her breasts. He began to squeeze her nipples, and they became hard. He wanted to kiss them, but before he could bend over she was sliding down his body, licking him as she went. When she reached his cock she took it all in her mouth, something she rarely did. Hadn't she refused Colorado Bob's request for a bareback blow job? But she felt hungry for this guy and the hot water made it feel more sanitary. She unwrapped the soap and pushed him away from the water, to lather him from behind. First she did his chest and back, massaging him as she went. Then she went up from his ankles to his thighs. Finally she lathered his cock and balls and began to stroke him mercilessly while tickling his balls with her fingernails. He didn't want to come yet and even tried to pull away, but it was too late.

Tita Moon laughed and lathered his cock again until he couldn't stand it. She pushed him under the water and rinsed him off. Then she opened the shampoo and massaged his scalp with both hands. When they emerged from the bathroom, wrapped in towels, his entire body tingled, simultaneously exhausted and invigorated. No one had ever touched him this way.

He expected Tita Moon to dress and leave, but she lit a cigarette and slid under the covers. His throat was still parched from the Red Volcano and he got himself a soda from the minibar and poured an orange juice for her. Then they sat silently for a few minutes in bed, watching music videos.

"You mentioned at dinner you had a child," he finally said. "Are you married?"

"No. My son lives with my parents. Do you have children?"

"No."

"Why not?"

"She had a career. She wasn't ready. I guess you weren't ready either?"

"I feel bad but what can I do? At least I didn't run away like the father. So you wanted children but your wife didn't?"

"I don't know what I wanted," he confessed, watching the close-up of a female Latino singer on TV. "I thought I was happy but now I don't know."

She ran her hand down his body and grabbed him so that he became hard again.

He kissed her and this time took a more active role, exploring her body. He caressed her shoulders and lightly stroked her arms. He had read that the way to make love to a woman was slowly, obliquely, avoiding her pussy until the last. But that was for wives or girlfriends. There weren't any texts for making love to a prostitute, and it seemed absurd to waste time on subtleties. Everyone knew prostitutes hated to be touched, they never came, they felt contempt for their clients. Still, he felt justified in making love to her. Whatever she felt or didn't feel, she seemed to understand what he needed. When he cleared aside the covers and began kissing between her legs she clutched his hair and guided him and moaned.

After a minute she rose and put a condom on him and straddled him. She slowly rocked back and forth, her eyes closed, rubbing away the tension of the last two days. Then she opened her eyes and placed her palms on his chest, thinking how different his firm chest was from Colorado Bob's, thinking that some men were so different from each other that they might as well belong to different species.

She stared at him intently and began to bounce up and down. She could see from his expression that her passion surprised him. But why shouldn't she enjoy herself? Why shouldn't she come if she felt the opportunity?

He lay in a state of sublime exhaustion. Only a few hours ago he had been in the United States, divorced, alone, miserable. For two years he had envied thousands of men, men he saw in the streets or in bars or in his shop, men with their arms around women, men being kissed, men wearing wedding rings. He had cursed God and pleaded with God, lost his faith and yearned for something to believe in. He never considered himself a model of virtue, but compared to most men he knew he was a modern Job. And, like Job, he was suffering beyond his ability to endure. He had drunk himself into oblivion. One night he had tried to kill himself with alcohol and pills.

But now he thought himself the luckiest of men. If only he had come to this place years ago. If only he had known. He would have saved all that money on lawyers, he would have given his wife what she wanted, and fled with the rest to this paradise.

Tita Moon quietly disposed of the condom. When he looked up he noticed the room was in a state of chaos, clothes strewn on the minibar, the blanket on the floor, cigarette ashes spilled on the telephone, but he might have been gazing at a Japanese garden, so rhythmic was his breathing.

Tita Moon emerged naked from the bathroom, looking radiant. He expected her to begin dressing with a speed he imagined necessary to her profession. But she came back to the bed, lay next to him, and smoked another cigarette.

"Did you really come?" he asked, wondering why it mattered to him, whether it was simply pride or something more.

She confronted him with her big eyes. "Did you?"

He laughed. "No, I always fake it."

And she laughed as well and put out her cigarette and silently began dressing.

He wanted her to stay, of course. He would have paid whatever she asked. But he was afraid of ruining the moment. He was too desperate to trust his instincts. Internet posts warned against falling in love with these girls. They were professionals. Some were married. Most had children. Hadn't she told him herself she had a son, even if he lived with her mother? Besides, his bus left for Quepos at 7:00 AM and he was tired from the flight.

He rose to walk her to the door but noticed the camera case and asked if she'd pose for a photo. When she nodded he quickly got his camera out of the safe, plugged in the external flash, and motioned her to stand toward the window. The lighting was poor and the wall dirty. He asked her to stand in front of the beige curtain, which he drew part way. But why was he playing the perfectionist? Did the lighting or background really matter when all he wanted was an aid to memory?

He was still fumbling when she walked out of the frame. He wouldn't have blamed her for leaving in a fit of impatience, but instead she reached into her purse and brushed her hair. When she returned she posed with a hand on her hip and smiled. "Let me see," she demanded, blinking from the flash.

"Nice, huh?" he said, pleased with the composition.

"Delete it. I look fat." And she stepped back to try again.

This time she was more satisfied. "You aren't going to put it on the internet?"

"Of course not. But maybe I'll print it and hang it in my shop."

"Really?" She thought for a moment and went back to her purse to re-apply her lipstick. "How do I look now?"

"Why don't you sit in that chair?" he suggested, pulling the chair out from the desk.

He crouched down and shot her face from below. Then he put the timer on and took one of them together, she sitting on his lap with her arms around his neck. After a few more photos they sat next to each other on the bed and he deleted the ones she disliked. But that still left half a dozen photos, which he knew he would always cherish.

He expected her to ask for money, but instead she kissed him on the lips, said, "Ciao," and left.

He might have accompanied her back to the bar had he been dressed, but by the time he put on his pants she was already in the elevator. He briefly considered going down to the bar and having a drink with her, but then he recalled his unfinished Red Volcano and thought better of it. The truth, though, was that he didn't want to dispel the illusion, however transparent, that she had given herself to him. He didn't want to watch her disappear in another client's arms.

Back downstairs things were picking up. Thankfully Colorado Bob wasn't at the bar. Tita Moon didn't want to have to talk to him and lacked the energy even to exchange smiles with the man. But Carmen had just arrived and proved more draining.

"So, did you get it?"

"Did I get what?"

Carmen dug at her arm. "Come on, crazy. The morning-after pill."

"Oh. Yeah."

"Whew! That's great."

"I didn't take it."

Tita Moon looked away, wondering why she had confessed this fact to her friend, who was sweet and sensitive and supportive and no doubt a better Christian than herself, but would surely not understand.

"Don't put it off. You only have seventy-two hours."

"I threw it away."

Now Carmen grabbed both of her arms and nearly shook her. "What are you saying!"

"God will look over me."

"You better hope so! He wasn't looking very closely when the condom broke. Fuck, Tita, you could have given it to me. What if I need it one day?"

"You take birth control pills."

"Birth control pills aren't a hundred percent effective. You had a perfectly good morning-after pill and you just threw it away! You sucked Colorado Bob for nothing."

Tita Moon shrugged. "I don't care. I already had a client today. I think he's in love with me."

"How long is he staying? Maybe he wants a threesome?"

"I just said he's in love and you want me to ask if he wants a threesome? Besides, he's going to the jungle tomorrow."

"So why doesn't he take you with him? If he's in love?" Carmen shook her head in disbelief. "You didn't ask him, did you? You didn't even ask if he wanted to take you?"

Such an obvious and common strategy had not occurred to Tita Moon and she looked away sheepishly like a wife who had gone to the grocery and forgotten to buy bread.

"If he really likes you, do you know how much money you could make? What if he's going for a week? Go back upstairs and ask him."

"I don't know his room number."

"Call him from reception."

"I don't know his last name. Anyway, I hate the jungle," she added, an afterthought that failed to serve as justification, even to herself.

"You are a disgrace to prostitutes," Carmen said coldly. "This is why after all these years you still live in the slums while I have a house and a car. Your name should be Tonto Moon. Stupid Moon!"

"Stupid but rich!" she retorted, dangling the hundred dollar bill in front of her friend's disapproving eyes.

CHAPTER 5

THE TRAVEL DESK

No sooner had Raquel opened the travel desk the next morning and begun sorting through the e-mail and telephone messages than a man entered the hotel soaking wet, carrying a large backpack and a metal camera case, and plopped down in the chair across in a posture of one who has lost his battle with Nature.

Raquel jotted down the last of the phone messages and decided to let the remaining e-mails wait. She turned to the man with a smile. "Lousy weather this morning. Where are you coming from?"

"Here! I'm coming from here," Rick said in a voice a little too loud, drawing attention from the clerks and guests at the reception counter across the lobby. "I'm supposed to go to Quepos but the taxi driver took me to the wrong station and I missed my bus."

"So you want to know the next bus?" Raquel asked, reaching into her drawer for a bus schedule.

"To hell with the bus. Can you get me a car with a driver?"

"Sure, but it's expensive. Or you can rent a car or fly. But if you don't mind paying I think taking a taxi is the best way. The roads aren't good and you could get lost if you drive yourself. And it's only four hours, so I wouldn't take a plane."

As Rick looked at Raquel's reassuring smile his frustration melted away, and for a moment he considered checking back in to the hotel. Everyone was so nice here. He had just spent one of the best nights of his life within these walls. Why venture back out to the cruel and unpredictable elements? He could see Tita Moon again...

But for all his talk of spontaneity, he remained determined to see the forest. He could always see Tita Moon when he returned to San Jose, he told himself. To become a willing prisoner of the hotel, and of her, was a risk he was unwilling to take. Happiness in immoderation was no less perilous than despair. Just witness the case of unsupervised children who eat too much ice cream. No, he thought, wearing his wet clothes like a badge of honor, the outdoors will be good for me. And I have the photos of her to look at when I'm alone in my cabin at night, and when I come back and see her again it will be like the first time.

"Maybe you could suggest a place to stay," he added. "I want something basic, in the forest."

"Well you can't stay in Manuel Antonio National Park itself," Raquel told him, unfolding a map of the area. "But I can book you into a tent hotel just outside, and you can take guided tours, or pay the entrance fee and go on your own. Although I suggest a guide because it can be hard to see the birds if you don't know where to look."

"I was also thinking about going to Corcovado."

"Yes, you could do that. It's larger and more remote, so there aren't as many tourists. Of course the roads aren't so good, but you could take a plane from Quepos."

In the end Rick decided to book the tent hotel near the beach outside Manuel Antonio for three days and once he was there he would decide where to go next. Raquel gave him her card and told him she could book the rest of the trip for him or he could call her if he had any questions. She also arranged for a driver.

He wanted to tip her but didn't know if that was acceptable. He was about to ask if she wanted him to bring her something, but thought she might perceive this as an attempt to pick her up. He felt uncomfortable enough with the implied guilt of having stayed at the hotel and assumed she must hold him in low regard.

Then he wondered why he cared what she thought. Hadn't he come here to escape social conventions?

"I hope the weather's better down there," he said instead in parting.

"For the beach, yes, but I like the rain in the forest."

"I guess that's why they call it a rain forest," he realized, feeling like an idiot.

"But it's not bad when it rains there. Sometimes you don't even feel the drops because the trees are so close together."

"Of course."

He felt so awkward he didn't even think to change into dry clothes in the lobby rest room but immediately walked out with the driver.

Raquel had just finished the paperwork on his hotel reservation when a pair of young men in shorts and t-shirts, one wearing a baseball cap, the other orange tinted sunglasses, sat down across the desk and began looking through the brochures.

"We want to go whitewater rafting, honey," the man wearing glasses said.

"Well it's too late today. I can book you tomorrow."

"Then what the hell did we get up for?" his friend complained. "Look, it says in the brochure 'noon departure.'"

"But that one doesn't run this time of year. The trips we have pick up from here at five."

"Five in the morning? You gotta be kidding?"

"You could stay up all night and sleep on the bus. It takes a couple hours to get to the river. Not that I suggest that. You need to be alert on the raft. If you fall asleep there you may never wake up," she said with a slightly sadistic grin. She had liked the last client, but she could tell these guys were typical assholes, the kind who would throw beer cans in the river if they had their way.

"Anyway, it's raining today. You're better off doing something indoors."

"Got any ideas, honey?" the guy with the glasses said, resting his elbows on the desk.

"There's the butterfly farm," she suggested. "That tour leaves at noon."

"With all the butterflies flying around in here?"

"I'm surprised you can see anything with those glasses," she countered. "Why are you wearing them inside on a rainy morning? Do you have something to hide?"

"Doesn't everyone here have something to hide?"

"Not me," Raquel said, looking at him with a guiltless expression. She liked to play with her customers. It was harmless enough and she often got the best tips from the men she had teased. Perhaps they admired her strength, or her innocence. In any case, whether it was flirting or sarcasm, such exchanges made her day go faster.

"So which river do you suggest?" the other man asked, reading the descriptions on the brochures.

"Have you been rafting before? No? Then I suggest the Class III. It's good for beginners."

"Well fuck that!" the man with the sunglasses said. "Give us some rapids. Ain't that right, Jim?"

Jim's eyes were on the photos in the brochure. One photo showed a group of eight adventurers smiling on a rubber raft as it floated along a calm stretch of water. That was the Class III. The photo below pictured a raft plunging over a liquid abyss, the faces of those on board taut with fear and concentration.

"Sign us up for the Class IV," the man with sunglasses said, tossing down his credit card as though he were calling a high stakes bet in a poker game.

Raquel regarded his companion with sympathy. This was how men died, she thought. When in the presence of a young woman, even one they had never met before and might never meet again, something in their hormones or DNA committed them to choose the most dangerous alternative. Her psychology textbook put it down to mate selection, but she didn't see how men who killed themselves in an effort to impress women were in a better position to pass on their genes. She certainly preferred a more sensible man, one who wouldn't make her a widow and single mother. She thought the phenomenon had less to do with biology than with action films.

"Have you done this trip yourself?" Jim asked, setting down the brochure and reluctantly taking out his wallet.

"Yes, once. It was great. I loved it."

"I just don't like cold water," he said, not wishing to admit to the less manly fear of drowning.

"Oh, it wasn't cold at all when I fell in."

"You fell in?" they both asked at once.

Raquel smiled. Of course she hadn't fallen in, but she couldn't resist. "They rescued me almost immediately."

"They rescued you?"

"Now Class V, that's another thing. *That's* dangerous," she taunted, knowing that prior experience was necessary for that level.

"We'll take Class IV," Jim said, placing his credit card next to his friend's.

She took their money, called the agency and handed them vouchers.

"So what are you boys going to do today?"

"Go back to sleep," Jim said.

"What time do you get off?" the man wearing sunglasses asked.

"I just started."

"Well maybe we can go out to dinner?"

It never ceased to amaze Raquel that despite all the women on offer at the Hotel Grand, men constantly asked her out. She attributed this less to her looks or personality, however, than to her perceived unavailability, for she knew the receptionists, waitresses, barmaids and dealers were propositioned as well.

"Next thing you'll say I'm the prettiest one here."

"Well you are!"

"Maybe you should take off your glasses."

He accepted her challenge and gazed at her with bloodshot blue eyes. "Damn, you're gorgeous! You'd never fall out of my boat. I wouldn't let go of you."

She laughed, wondering how she could feel genuinely flattered by such morons. But she liked it when men noticed her. Her boyfriend never called her gorgeous.

"Have a good nap, gentlemen. Don't forget to give your vouchers to the driver in the morning."

It seemed to be a good day. The rain subsided and by lunch she had booked a canopy tour and a day trip to Arenal Volcano. She bought a tuna sandwich and cup of coffee at the restaurant upstairs and ate at her desk while reviewing her psychology textbook.

Her boss, Mr. Escudero from accounting, looked down at her. He was a humorless man whose shiny black toupee always seemed to hang at a strange angle. The girls at reception and the travel desk loved to make jokes about him behind his back, but he seemed as oblivious to their insubordination as he was to the hotel's pageantry. Always dressed in a dark suit, appearing in the lobby only when necessary and never sitting down when he did emerge from his green vinyl chair in the back office, Raquel could only conclude that he had been hypnotized earlier in life by a sadistic magician to think he worked at a five star hotel somewhere in the mountains of Europe.

"I need you to work Thursday evening," he said abruptly when Raquel glanced up.

"I can't. I have a test."

"Then you'll have to make a choice."

Raquel set her book down. "What does that mean?" she challenged him in a louder voice. She knew this moment was coming, she had been expecting it for days. Nevertheless, his words surprised her and her hands began to tremble.

"I've worked nine of the last ten days and twice I worked double shifts," she went on, rising to her feet so that she didn't have to look up at him. In fact she was taller than him, much taller in the heels she was wearing, and menaced him with a furrowed brow. She had always been complaisant and it had gotten her nowhere.

For the last week she had complied with his requests and controlled her temper. She was a good judge of character and knew if she continued in this manner he would continue to take advantage of her, and in the end would probably fire her just the same. Rumor had it he wanted the job for his niece.

"What about Nancy or Paula?" she asked. "I'm sure one of them can work then."

"Nancy will be on vacation and Paula is working the day shift."

"So ask her to work a double. I've done two doubles the last week."

But her boss was not one to be swayed by logic or drawn into emotional arguments. He simply turned on his heels and disappeared into his back office behind the casino.

A guest approached her with a question about volcano tours. But then he noticed the unfinished sandwich on her desk and apologized for interrupting her lunch. Raquel was still standing, trembling. She felt as if the entire hotel had witnessed the encounter, but not even the security guard at the front entrance had overheard their brief exchange. The phone rang but she couldn't answer it. The man who had booked the tent hotel said he was going to the jungle to escape. She sympathized with him complete-ly and wished the car she had booked for him had not already left.

She walked out, leaving her lunch and textbook on the desk, and crossed the street to Tico Souvenirs. She distractedly picked up a carved wooden mixing bowl from a long shelf filled with local handcrafts, trying to settle her nerves.

Mrs. Santos, the proprietress, welcomed her with a hug. "Raquel, where have you been?"

Raquel tried breathe steadily. "I've been very busy."

"You work too hard! You need to take a break," her friend said presciently.

At this Raquel let go of the bowl and burst into tears.

There were no customers in the shop. Not that Mrs. Santos would have acted differently had her shop been filled with tour-ists. Raquel referred many clients to her shop. And she reminded Mrs. Santos of her eldest daughter, now in her thirties, married to a Brazilian and living in Sao Paulo.

Mrs. Santos took her by the arm to a semi-private cubicle, parti-tioned from the rest of the store by a blue curtain, sat her down on the only chair and poured her a large cup of coffee. When Raquel finally caught her breath she told her story. The older woman had never heard of this Mr. Escudero and asked if he was the owner. Raquel explained that he was in charge of the business office.

"Then you must go to the owner. You've worked there for almost a year, yes? And you haven't had any complaints from customers?"

"No."

"Or from anyone else but this Mr. Escudero?"

"That doesn't matter. He's my supervisor. The owners aren't going to interfere. And if they did he would make my job a night-mare. He wants the travel desk for his niece," Raquel explained, wiping her eyes.

"I see." Mrs. Santos thought for a moment. "You could work here part time, if you like."

Raquel thanked her profusely but declined. She knew her friend couldn't pay her as much as the hotel, and a few hours would hardly pay for the commute from Escazu.

"Well I can ask my friends if they know of any jobs," Mrs. Santos said. "I'm sure with your qualifications you'll have no trouble finding a better position. Personally, I think it's a blessing to be out of that hotel of sin."

Raquel was about to remark that her friend's shop was across the street from this hotel of sin and relied on the gringos who stayed there for her business. But instead she politely finished her coffee and hugged her goodbye.

She wanted to go to her car, which she could no longer afford, and drive as recklessly as possible to her new room in Escazu, which she could no longer afford. She wanted never to have to set foot in the Hotel Grand again. But her car keys were in her purse, and her purse was in her desk drawer. Well, it was still her desk. She might as well derive some advantage from the fact.

She found the same guest who was there before, interested in the volcano tour. He asked about the half-day tour to Irazu, but Raquel knew she could persuade him to take the more expensive full day trip to Arenal. But why should she put more colones in the pockets of these scoundrels?

She had an idea. She asked the man to wait for a minute, cleared her lunch, and made the long journey across the quiet casino and knocked on the door marked "office."

She opened it without waiting for a reply and found Mr. Escudero sitting in his green vinyl chair behind stacks of invoices, typing on his computer keyboard. He looked up without speaking, which made Raquel feel nervous again. The resolve she had felt a moment earlier vanished. She looked at the cluttered desk of his assistant, who was out, and at the empty chair before her. She remained standing but closed the door for privacy.

"I would like my paycheck please."

"You know that payday is Friday."

"I won't be here Friday, since you insist on firing me. And I want a reference."

Mr. Escudero seemed flustered by her demands. "How can I give you a reference when you won't work when needed?"

"I can leave this minute and you will lose half a day's commissions. Or you can give me my check for the rest of the day and a reference and I'll stay until four. I have a client at this very moment who wants to book Arenal."

"So go, go!" Mr. Escudero screamed, rising to his feet, more distraught by the vision of an unserved client than by the prospect of conceding to his employee's demands.

Raquel stood firm. "As soon as I have my pay check and reference."

"I can't do it now! You'll have them by the end of the day."

Raquel hesitated a moment, wondering whether she could trust him. Trying to think it through psychologically, she had won and should leave before Mr. Escudero changed his mind. But all she had won was a promise, while she was agreeing to work. What if the end of the day came and he didn't give her her pay check and reference? She concluded that he would, because if he wanted the job for his niece it was in his best interest to get rid of her with as little fuss as possible. Of course, people didn't always act in their best interest. In that event, she decided, she had nothing to lose and would wrench off his toupee and hang it over the bar in the Red Volcano.

She hadn't noticed before, but her client was somewhat good looking. Tall, clean shaven, wearing one of those flop hats with a chin strap. It didn't take much effort to sell him on the Arenal tour, but then she added, to her great surprise, "You want to take me with you?"

He laughed, as surprised as she was by the proposition. Too surprised to take it seriously. And although upon reflection it wasn't serious, at the moment the words came out Raquel was thinking,

Take me to Arenal, take me all the way back to Texas or wherever it is you come from. Why should the putas have all the fun?

"Is this job just an assignment for your class?" he asked, fingering her psychology text book. "I can't think of a better place to study human nature."

"Not anymore," she answered, handing him his voucher. "You're probably my last client."

"Really?" he wondered with growing interest. "Then you are free tomorrow?"

Normally she would have flirted with such a man, but she was in no mood for pleasantries and cut him off quickly. "I have a boyfriend."

"Oh. Lucky guy."

Raquel watched him walk to the elevators. They didn't always leave so easily. Some she had to push away. But whenever she confessed to having a boyfriend, men invariably remarked, "lucky guy." They couldn't all be bullshitting, could they? she asked herself. How come the whole male world was aware of this fact except the one for whom such knowledge mattered? The chapter in her text book that she was currently studying was titled "Identity." What was her identity? She was a young woman, a student—now an unemployed student—admired by gringos who paid other women to sleep with them, whose worldly possessions didn't fill six boxes, as well as a car that still leaked oil after she had given Alajuelita Motors seventy dollars to fix it, and a boyfriend oblivious to his good fortune.

Raquel sometimes envied the working girls their clothes and jewelry, but more often she pitied them. Most didn't have fathers. Many had children, drug addictions, low self-esteem. Raquel had been a virgin until her eighteenth year, had never smoked a cigarette, and valued herself highly.

And look where it's gotten me! she told herself, while she waited for her final day at the travel desk to end.

CHAPTER 6

THE PROFESSOR

She drove directly from the hotel to the University of Costa Rica. Besides her psychology class, she had a class on Latin American history. Normally she enjoyed school, even when she was tired after work. The classes were small, with no more than thirty students, in clean, modern rooms whose open windows looked onto lawns covered with subtropical vegetation. She had become friends with several of her fellow students and enjoyed her exchanges with the professors.

But this afternoon she was understandably preoccupied. She had hoped to put the consequences of unemployment out of her mind, but all she could think about was how would she pay for the next semester. Rather than being encouraged by the dream of a degree in psychology, she was frustrated by the many years it would take her to graduate and the impossibility of continuing without an income. What am I doing here? she asked herself. I will never get a degree. I am fated to work in a hotel or a restaurant for heartless bosses like Mr. Escudero.

Walking to her car after Twentieth Century Latin American History, she remembered to check her cell phone. Another thing I will have to give up, she thought, checking a message from her boyfriend, Eduardo. She had forgotten they had a date tonight. Not a formal date exactly. Rather, he had phoned her Sunday and said, "Maybe we can see a movie Tuesday night."

She had met him last year at the university, but he had since dropped out. He lived with his parents, the youngest in a large family, and took advantage of their generosity to find his place in the world. At the moment he wasn't looking very hard, or very far, not having a car, and seemed content to play video games with friends and dance with Raquel at discos which catered to university students.

Raquel had not dated much in high school, being a good student whose friends were not part of the popular crowd. Besides, she had a fear of getting pregnant and, having a strong personality, turned off a lot of boys who were otherwise attracted by her classic features and long legs. Eduardo had been her first real boyfriend, the one who had taken her virginity. She liked his curly hair and subdued personality. He wasn't one of those ticos who flirted with girls or played drinking games or got into fights. And she liked his family, which accepted her as one of their own. In the beginning she liked that he didn't pressure her to get married and have children, as she wanted to get a degree and embark on her career before having a family of her own. But now their relationship had stagnated and she realized she had outgrown him. He was an adult child and she didn't want to fall into the trap that so many women fell into with such men—of merely replacing their mothers. But she also liked having a boyfriend, someone to dance with and hold hands with at the movies and make her feel loved, even if he never said the words. So she tolerated his limitations and was careful to take her birth control pills.

She picked him up at his house and they drove to the mall at San Pedro and stood in front of the ticket desk, looking at the list of starting times. When he asked her what she wanted to see it was the first thing he had said to her since mumbling *"Buenos noches,"* when she came to his door. Had he asked about her day, which he never did, she might have told him, but instead she turned the radio up in her car and they listened in silence.

She picked a vampire film, knowing he liked horror movies and hoping to be scared out of her depression. I've only lost my job, she told herself. It could be worse. Look at this poor girl being chased by vampires. This strategy failed to work, however, because she couldn't overlook the fact that the victim was in reality a wealthy actress who doubtlessly drove a car that didn't leak oil and had a boyfriend who could pay for movie tickets.

They kissed a little and for a few moments Eduardo put a hand between her legs, but he was too absorbed by the events onscreen to try anything further.

Eduardo's parents were home and a visiting cousin was sharing his room, so after the movie he asked her to park on a secluded street nearby. Raquel turned off the lights and engine, except for the radio, which was playing love songs from Latin idol Jaime Primero. Now was the time to tell him that she'd lost her job, to cry a little and let him console and reassure her. But when he pressed his lips to hers she just let him kiss her. He untucked her shirt and artlessly caressed her breasts through her bra before settling back in his seat and unzipping his jeans.

Raquel unwrapped a butterscotch candy, which helped with the taste, before bending down and taking his cock in her mouth. He moaned quietly and kept his eyes open for passers-by. Raquel neither liked nor disliked giving head, but thought it part of the cost of having a boyfriend. As for doing it in her car, she considered this an unfortunate necessity, since he didn't have a place of his own and Laura didn't want her to bring men to the house. She wouldn't have taken him to Escaza in any case because it was too far to drive him back and forth, and she wouldn't want him to spend the night, even if she had a double bed, because then he might not leave and when she finally found the strength to break up he would feel too comfortable to go willingly.

Although she worked at a hotel dedicated to the sex trade, Raquel knew surprisingly little about sex. It wasn't in any of her textbooks and her high school friends were equally naive. Nor was her boyfriend particularly knowledgeable. But he never complained, so Raquel did what she thought she should do and left it at that.

She closed her eyes and began planning her schedule for tomorrow, her first day of unemployment, which ironically would be a busier day than when she had worked. She would have to wake early and buy a newspaper and call about jobs. She would go to an internet cafe and search for jobs online as well. She also needed to update her resume. And she still had to study for her psychology test. She became so overwhelmed that she forgot where she was and when Eduardo came she swallowed the butterscotch and sat up coughing.

"Are you okay?" her boyfriend asked, suddenly concerned.

By the time Raquel's throat was clear and she could talk she realized the futility of responding and drove him home in silence, as Jaime Primero sang something about farewell kisses and broken hearts.

On her way to Escazu Raquel remembered she didn't have a house key and called Laura on her cell to make sure she was home. Laura greeted her at the door with a margarita and they sat in the living room while a soap opera played on TV.

Unlike her taciturn boyfriend, Laura immediately asked about Raquel's day, both as a matter of politeness and because, despite her retirement, she had a lingering curiosity about the hotel, much as an Egyptologist now living in a cold climate might inquire from a former colleague about developments at Luxor.

Laura shouted out in shock at the news her friend had been fired, although she was disappointed with herself to find her genuine sympathy corrupted by self interest, for her initial thought was that her lodger would no longer be able to pay the rent. She compensated for this by expressing the exact opposite of what she felt, assuring Raquel that it was quite all right if she was a few days late with next week's rent.

Although Laura didn't know Mr. Escudero, she cursed him without mercy and urged Raquel to threaten a lawsuit. "All you have to do is say he sexually assaulted you and he will be the one who will be fired, or he will take you back to save his job. His niece would not seem so important then."

Raquel laughed at the idea of her former boss, with his crooked toupee and dark suits, making salacious advances. "No one would believe it," she replied. "Besides, I couldn't falsely accuse someone. Even Mr. Escudero. But I'm going to buy the paper tomorrow and update my resume and talk to anyone who will interview me," she added, not wanting her homeowning friend to view her as a student unable to make a living, as Raquel had viewed her boyfriend before he lost even his student status.

"I'm sure Dennis will help you with your resume," Laura offered. "He's very busy with the business, but I'm sure he'll make time if I ask."

"That's very kind," Raquel replied, touched by her friend's generosity. "But with the resume it's only a matter of adding the travel desk. But maybe you could ask him if he knows anyone who is hiring. Maybe one of his gringo friends needs a secretary or something. By the way, how are things going with you? Do you like your..." She was about to say 'new job,' but since that indelicately alluded to her 'old job,' she simply said, "job?"

"Yes, it's great. I mean it's hard to tell, I've only worked two days and everything is new. The hardest part is learning the computer. But Dennis is real laid back and has so much confidence in me it makes my job easier. And of course I like the hours, except for getting up so early. But it's such a relief not to be out all night. Like tonight, it's midnight. I never used to be home at this time. Only when I was on my period or taking a day off. God, when I think about the hotel it seems like a lifetime ago, but it's only been, what, four days? I feel like that was another person, you know what I mean? I fell sorry for girls like Carmen and Tita who still have to go back there and stand in that awful bar instead of relaxing at home. Well, actually Carmen doesn't have to work there, I mean she has her own house, not like mine, but how many girls our age have houses? If it weren't for her lazy family spending all her money... And even Tita, I have no idea where her money goes. She's one of the most popular girls and she lives in the slums. Ah, well, we can't live other people's lives."

And with that the two women, neither of whom expected to ever see the inside of the Hotel Grand again, turned their gazes to the weeping figures onscreen, whose improbable suffering helped them forget their own.

The following Thursday Laura spent her lunch hour grocery shopping, and that night roasted two chickens stuffed with rice and peppers, declining Dennis's offer to assist, fearing he would hinder more than help her, and that she would have to beat off his advances with the baster. Still, she was glad he arrived before her mother and, after letting him kiss her casually on the lips, asked him to help her set the table.

"What table?"

Then he walked into the dining room. "You said you didn't need any more furniture right now and you preferred to eat on the deck!"

Laura lit a tall candle and placed it in the middle of the table. "Don't you think it's beautiful?"

Dennis was used to Laura's capriciousness, but was nevertheless puzzled. "I thought you said you didn't have the money for dining room table?" he remarked, knowing he had no right to ask, but unable to suppress his curiosity.

"I got it in trade," Laura answered matter-of-factly, setting out cloth napkins. "Are you going to help or not?"

Dennis carried out the ceramic plates, almost dropping them in his distracted state.

"What do you mean, in trade?"

"The guy who made it is a former client."

"Oh. So when did you arrange this?"

"Sunday."

She had handed him the silverware, but all he did was drop it in a heap on the table, which he now viewed not only as wages of sin but as an inanimate rival.

"But you retired!" he reminded her, trying not to shout, but shouting nevertheless.

"Well it was only the next day."

Laura had characterized her boss as laid back, but that was only because Dennis repressed his more violent emotions. He had never paid for sex before coming to Costa Rica and was still not comfortable with prostitution, despite having fallen in love with a member of the profession. He justified this inconsistency to himself in any number of ongoing internal arguments, but the truth was he lacked the insouciance common to the patrons of the Hotel Grand, who were too busy enjoying their incredibly good fortune at having discovered this singular paradise. Dennis, on the other hand, felt cursed to have discovered his soulmate in that lurid place. In this he even differed from Porter, who was not particularly possessive and would easily enough fall in love with another tica were Ginger to ultimately prove unattainable. For Dennis, there were no other ticas, and he would have renounced Costa Rica altogether if it weren't for the desire with which Laura's attention infected him.

And at moments like these Dennis felt as if it were an infection, some mental affliction he had to battle to keep his sanity. He helped himself to a beer, as if it were an antibiotic, and watched the sports channel slumped on the couch.

The professor brought a bottle of Australian wine and a bouquet of flowers. Laura accepted them with a smile, but this polite gesture didn't diminish her suspicion. He was wearing loafers without socks, khakis, a white dress shirt and a gray blazer. But there were plenty of mongers who dressed well. He was thin, pale and balding, as her mother had described, but he wore a thin beard and round glasses, which gave him a distinguished look, and spoke excellent Spanish in a quiet, easygoing voice that set others at ease. Laura, however, was far from being charmed. Her initial impression was that had she met him at the Hotel Grand she would have been glad to go upstairs with him, a notion she immediately banished from her mind. This unpleasant hypothetical thought was followed by the realization that, in fact, she had never been with him. Well, that was the first answered prayer, she thought, looking at him so hard that she ignored her mother, who was asking her daughter's opinion of her new dress.

"Yes, Ma, it's lovely," she said, hardly taking her eyes from the professor. "Oh, and this is...Dennis." She was going to say "my boss," but thought that sounded too cold. Then she was going to say "my friend," but women always used "friend" as a euphemism for "boyfriend," and she didn't want to give that impression. So she just said "Dennis," and went into the kitchen to open the wine.

"Why don't you show Dr. Martin the house," her mother called to her, after giving Dennis a warm kiss.

So it's going to be "Dr. Martin," Laura thought, pouring the wine. He gets to call me by my first name but I have to call him doctor. And he doesn't even perform operations.

But the professor cleared another hurdle by saying, "Please call me Larry. This is a beautiful home. I admire your taste."

"What's your taste like?" Laura asked a little too harshly, handing him a glass.

"I'm happy if my socks match," he replied modestly.

But Laura didn't let him off the hook. "You aren't wearing socks."

"Yes, well that's the easiest solution," he answered with a laugh.

"Come, look at the house," her mother said, taking his arm, and impatiently led him off as if it were her own house she was showing. "Laura has made a very good investment here, don't you think?" And turning her head back to glance at her daughter. "Dr. Martin has a very nice apartment near the university. All the walls are covered with books." And turning back to the professor. "Laura read many books in school, but I'm afraid she doesn't read now."

"Oh come on, Ma, you don't read either."

"I read *la Nación* every morning."

"That's a newspaper, not a book."

Dennis listened to their voices trailing away into the unrented guest bedroom. He remained in the dining room, brooding over the table like a jilted lover.

They had just sat down to dinner when Raquel walked in. Laura invited her to join them, but her friend declined, saying she had to write a paper.

"Raquel is studying psychology at the university," Laura informed her mother. And then to Raquel, "But don't tell my mother your last name or she'll look up your file."

"There's nothing in my file but poor grades," Raquel said with a sigh.

"But you did well on your psychology test."

"I passed, that's all."

"You know Dennis from the party. And this is my mother's... friend. He likes to be called Larry, but he's a professor of biology at the university. Maybe you've seen each other."

"I'm afraid not," the professor replied, shaking her hand.

"What level is your course? I need more science classes. Maybe I can take it next semester, if it's not too hard."

And they stood talking for a moment, while the others stood politely around the table, listening. Except Laura, who didn't pay attention at all to the professor's description of his class. Instead she was scrutinizing his body language, as the professor himself might scrutinize the mating behavior of a male quetzal in the forest. Laura had seen enough mongers to know how they looked at women, how they leaned over them or into them, how they touched their shoulder, seemingly by accident, but forgot to let go. The professor wasn't touching Raquel's shoulder, but there was certainly lust in his eyes.

The professor was explaining that although some students found his class challenging, he recommended it for psychology majors because there was much that could be learned about human behavior by observing animal behavior.

The only word Laura heard of this was "animal." In her imagination the professor was saying something completely different. He was looking at Raquel with lust in his eyes over cocktails at the Red Volcano and saying, "Maybe you can wear a plaid skirt?" He wasn't the kind to quibble at a hundred, and he would take her to a fancy restaurant and impress her by referring to the vines on the terrace by their Latin name. But in bed he would take a long time to come and Raquel would have earned her money and more. That was the kind of monger he was.

Out him! Out him now! the devil on Laura's shoulder urged. Send him packing back down to the Red Volcano, where he belongs.

But the angel on her other shoulder said, Why shouldn't he have lust in his eyes? Raquel's beautiful and young, you lust after her yourself and you're not even bisexual. If you're going to see mongers behind every tree why did you retire?

When Raquel finally excused herself they sat back down to eat. Laura asked Dennis to cut the chicken, and he took the carving knife with a firm grip. Normally he would have been proud to have been given the husband's role. He would have felt himself a host, not a guest.

But all he could see was the inlaid wood peering out around the cloth placemats, and as he tore into the chicken he raged at himself, She fucked a carpenter! For a fucking worthless table!

He filled everyone's plates and strode to the refrigerator for another beer.

Dennis might have been consumed with jealousy and Laura with suspicion, but the professor seemed cheerful enough, and her mother had rarely appeared more relaxed. They didn't feel the tension across the table for a moment, but Mrs. Flores did observe the bottle of Imperial.

"I didn't think you drank beer, Dennis?" she asked, as if simply making conversation and not a moral judgment.

"Why are you drinking beer?" Laura asked as well, only now noticing. She had bought a six pack in case the professor liked beer, and just to have for visitors. But she didn't drink beer herself, and didn't expect Dennis to take one, let alone two. "He's stressed from work," she then answered, still looking at him, before he could think of anything to say. "Poor guy's been working sixteen hour days," she said, ruffling his blow dried hair.

"Donita tells me you're in business together. A computer start-up," the professor said, looking at them both.

Laura wanted no more credit than she deserved. "It's not my business. It's Dennis's. I'm just an employee."

As she looked at the professor her smile faded. Obviously her mother, in describing her daughter to her boyfriend, had exaggerated as usual. Laura regretted she hadn't previously discussed this with her mother so she could tow the party line. And now she saw the wheels spinning behind the professor's round glasses, as he asked himself how a mere employee, at such a young age, could afford a house in Escazu. If Laura didn't answer fast, the wheels would stop spinning, having come to rest on the word 'puta.'

"You're probably wondering how I could afford this house," she said hurriedly. "Actually I saved money from my last job and made some good investments. When you don't have children to feed or a car to feed it's amazing how much money you can save. And Dennis advised me on the investments. Isn't that right, Dennis?"

Dennis shrugged.

The professor then asked Dennis about his plans for his company. Normally Dennis would have answered enthusiastically, if not eloquently, boring everyone but himself. He was shy in groups, but could be garrulous in a more intimate settings, especially if the subject was business or computers. But tonight he answered the professor's questions evasively, his thoughts far from Pan American Web Services.

When Laura felt any suspicions on the professor's part had been diverted she resumed trying to satisfy her own.

"How long have you lived in Costa Rica?" she interrupted.

The conversation at the table stopped. Mrs. Flores was much less talkative than usual, allowing the professor and Dennis to speak about business and technical things as men like to do, enjoying their company, though not necessarily paying close attention, for the subject did not interest her. She threw a sharp look at her daughter for interrupting and might have reproached her if the professor hadn't quickly and graciously replied.

"I've been at the university three years," he answered. "But I first came to Costa Rica many years ago to study turtles."

"Where did you stay?"

"In Tortuguero."

"And where did you stay when you were in San Jose?"

"At that time I was only in San Jose for a day or two."

"But where did you stay?"

Thankfully, the professor showed no signs of suspicion or annoyance at Laura's unusual line of question. He was used to being asked unusual questions in this country and was willing to humor her as a matter of politeness.

He slowly swallowed a piece of chicken, trying to remember. "I don't know."

Gotcha! Laura thought. Turtles, my ass!

But then the professor raised his fork in triumph. "The Radisson. Why do you ask?"

"Laura used to work at a hotel," her mother said, unknowingly coming to her daughter's rescue, and for once Laura appreciated her interjection. "She was at the Riviera."

"The Grand Riviera, yes," the professor said. "Unfortunately our budget was more modest. But the Radisson was fine, and it was only for a day or two." Then he had a thought and turned to Laura's mother. "Maybe next time we can all go to the Riviera for dinner. I've never been there but I hear they have a French restaurant."

"That's a great idea," Laura's mother agreed. "And I'm sure Laura still knows people there. She can get us a discount."

A possible complication, but nothing to be concerned with now. She remained intent on her main objective.

"Why didn't you teach in the States?"

"I did. I was an associate professor at Penn State."

Associate professor, Laura thought with contempt, having no knowledge of the nomenclature of academic titles, thinking he must have failed some test or, more probably, been caught in a scandal and demoted.

"So why did you come here?" she pursued.

"A Costa Rican researcher I knew urged me to apply for an open position. I loved the country and was looking for a change and thought, why not?" He smiled and took Donita's hand.

A change, Laura mused. "Were you married?" she asked aloud. "Once."

He said it without shame, almost as it were an achievement that a man his age had been married only once and not several times.

"Are you divorced?"

"Of course he's divorced!" her mother replied.

The professor laughed and took another bite of chicken. He didn't feel offended at all by Laura's line of questioning but thought it rather touching, a modern reversal of roles in which the daughter interrogated her mother's date at the dinner table. He was glad in a way to see her take such an interest. Donita had told him her daughter was flighty, irresponsible, unambitious, and that for these reasons they sometimes didn't get along. But he could see her mother, like most parents, tended to exaggerate their children's faults, just as they exaggerated their abilities. Surely it attested to the closeness of their relationship that Laura took such an interest in assessing her mother's boyfriend.

"Why of course?" Laura wanted to know. "Plenty of men are separated but not divorced. Divorces can take a long time." And if anyone knew, it was Laura, for countless men had complained to her of their obstructionist wives and endless legal bills. And she was such a patient and sympathetic listener that over the last five years she had she learned more about American divorce law than most paralegals.

"Think, Laura, he's been here three years."

"So? I knew a man whose divorce took six years. I mean, I heard about it," she added quickly. "Not that it matters to me. Do you have any children?"

"I have a son in college."

Great, Laura thought. The son could be a monger too. Does he come to Costa Rica?"

"No," the professor confessed. "He took his mother's side and we haven't seen much of each other since the divorce."

That's a relief, Laura thought. And she decided that was enough of the résumé questions, time to explore his personality. He was a biologist. "What's your favorite animal?" was the first question that came to mind. "Turtles?"

The professor laughed. "Actually, I have to admit I grew kind of tired of turtles. I think I like faster animals."

"Like women?"

It just came out. It was the kind of quip she was accustomed to making with her monger friends, and it surprised herself no less than the others.

Dennis, who was seeing the checkerboard pattern of the table spinning beneath him and hadn't really been following the conversation, snorted righteously. Women were fast, that was a fact. And Laura, the woman he loved, was one of the fastest. No turtle she.

The professor laughed, thinking it a good joke, but her mother sighed. "Laura!" And she turned to the professor apologetically. "I warned you my daughter can be very ill mannered. Sometimes you just have to ignore her." And she looked sternly at Laura. "You should apologize, darling."

And for once Laura thought her mother was right, and she would have apologized, but the professor spoke first.

"What's your favorite animal?"

Laura answered immediately. "Polar bears."

The professor was startled, and impressed. "I've never heard anyone say polar bear before! Most people say dogs or horses. Maybe *you* should be a biologist!"

This time Laura had the sense to hold her tongue. She wanted to say, Believe me, I've done more field work than you.

The professor leaned toward her with growing curiosity. "May I ask why you didn't go to the university?"

"Maybe I will someday. I just don't have the patience for it."

"Laura's very independent. She doesn't want to follow after me," her mother clarified.

"Oh, right, like you're an honor student or something. You have a B.A. in accounting, don't make it sound like more than it is. Dennis has an M.B.A. and you don't hear him bragging."

Normally the professor would have taken this as a cue to ask Dennis about his education, but at the moment he was more interested in Laura and wanted her to answer some of the same questions she had asked him.

"And do *you* want children?" he continued.

"I want a boy and a girl. Someday."

Her mother smiled across the table at the two young people, thinking they looked like a very happy couple, although they were both preoccupied with very different concerns and weren't even looking at each other.

On another night Dennis might have taken this answer as encouraging, knowing that if he attended enough of these dinners, and if enough guests viewed him and Laura as a couple, she eventually would too, and those kids would be his. But now he could only think of the progeny of her latest coupling and he indignantly thought, You could marry the carpenter and have a wooden boy, a wooden girl.

Laura decided to resume her interrogation with the question that mattered most, the question that always mattered to her when she met someone she liked or who might play an important role in her life.

"What's your sign?"

And she stared at him like a clairvoyant about to pronounce his future.

Unlike many academics, who consider a stimulating argument no less essential to a good dinner than a robust wine, the professor had thus far behaved agreeably, disputing nothing, praising the house and the meal. But he was a scientist, after all, and people in Costa Rica were always asking him his sign.

"I don't believe in that nonsense," he replied, with a smile that hardly eased the sting of the statement.

Laura held firm. "What's your birthday? You believe in birthdays, don't you?"

The professor should probably have done the polite thing and humored his hostess. Despite the inherent awkwardness of meeting your new girlfriend's adult daughter and the supposed friction between the two women, the evening had taken a surprisingly pleasant course. But suddenly they had reached a hairpin curve and the otherwise cautious professor decided to push the throttle. He might have laughed it off and tried to change the subject, but Laura's unusual question intrigued him and he reverted to his role as a teacher.

"Well, what is a birthday after all?"

"It's the day you're born," Laura replied with a shrug.

"Exactly. But what is a day?"

"Everyone knows what a day is. It's twenty-four hours."

"Yes, but more precisely, it's the time it takes the earth to rotate about its axis. And what is a year? A year is the time it takes the earth to rotate around the sun. But why should the earth's orbit around the sun matter to human affairs?"

"Because it's how the planets and stars are aligned with the earth at that point in time," she answered, thinking he took her for a fool.

"Which planets, which stars? The universe has billions of stars. All moving away from us because the universe is expanding. As for their gravitational effect, this table has more influence on us!" And he pounded his hand on the smooth wood for effect.

Dennis raised his head at the sound. He couldn't have agreed more.

Laura would have argued with him all night, but her mother interrupted with a question for Dennis. Laura had been too preoccupied with the professor to appreciate her mother's good behavior. Except for a couple remarks, she had not embarrassed her daughter, and had kept quiet for most of the evening. She had even complimented Laura once or twice and, indeed, felt proud of her daughter for reflecting well on her upbringing. Even if she hadn't gone to college and wasn't married, she now had a good job and a nice house and she and Dennis made such a handsome couple.

Laura noticed the empty plates and realized her role as interrogator had supplanted her role as hostess. "Does everyone want coffee?"

She cleared the plates and served coffee, thinking he must be a Taurus. Dennis grabbed another beer, his third. And he had drunk a glass of wine too. Laura knew he wouldn't be able to drive home if he drank this beer, but she couldn't say anything to him in front of her mother and the professor. And she couldn't very well ask them to drive him. How could Pan American Web Services conquer the world if its CEO got smashed at dinner parties and had to be driven home?

She would have to wait until after they left and call Pablo to chauffeur him. She only hoped he would remain quiet until then and that her mother and the professor wouldn't notice his intoxication.

They pushed their chairs back and the women smoked cigarettes and they all drank their coffee, full from the meal and relaxed, except for Dennis, whose hand was grasping his third Imperial and whose head was spinning. Laura felt a creeping admiration for the professor, despite his contempt for the stars and the probability that he was a Taurus. She still had her reservations, but she couldn't pronounce him guilty without evidence. As for the professor himself, he was pleasantly surprised. From the way Donita complained about her daughter he was prepared for anything except what he found—a bright, independent, capable young woman. The way Donita had talked he wouldn't have been shocked to find a drug addict within these walls, or a stripper, even a prostitute.

Now that the two were no longer interrogating each other, Laura's mother filled the void, complaining about potholes, as if the roads in Costa Rica hadn't been built with potholes already formed, then complaining about something the President had done, then complaining about new regulations at the university.

She had behaved so well tonight that Laura didn't mind her rambling now and she let her talk. Not that she was listening. She had retreated into her own world, as she had grown accustomed to do during her years standing in the Red Volcano. The place could be packed with hundreds of mongers and whores, the music blaring, waitresses banging the edges of wet trays against her ribs as they struggled to squeeze back to the bar. And she would be looking for houses with a real estate agent, or mentally shopping for clothes, or lying on the beach at night with an imaginary boyfriend, looking up at the stars.

Now she was reflecting on the night, though it was not yet over, proud to have pulled it off. Her first real dinner party in her own home. The chicken had been a success and everyone was having a good time. She didn't account for Dennis, whose shyness was well known, and whose drinking she assumed was related to work. He was just kicking back. A magnificent evening.

She was startled from this daydream of domestic accord by the doorbell. Very startled. Who would be calling at this time? She realized it must be one of Raquel's friends, or her boyfriend come to pick her up.

But Carmen stepped inside. And there was a man attached, a tico, older but not too old, good looking, dressed in a tailored suit. Carmen looked elegant as well, her hair styled, her eyes made up, a gold necklace shimmering against her bronze skin, though she wore her usual casual uniform of halter top and low cut jeans.

Laura would have barred her admittance, but they were already inside the door. A quick glance assured her that she did not know the man and she leaned toward Carmen's ear.

"What are you doing here!" She said it less as a question than an expression of anger.

Her mother turned around in her chair. "Is that Carmen?"

"Hello, Mrs. Flores."

"Invite them in, Laura," her mother said. "We were just having coffee."

Carmen grasped the situation and looked at Laura apologetically. "I didn't know you had company."

She turned to go but Laura could hardly let her leave now and reluctantly grabbed her arm. "Yes, please stay for coffee." She shot another glance at the man, wondering if he was a client or a date.

She led them into the dining room and hurried to the terrace to get more chairs. She didn't want to leave the pair alone, but she couldn't just let them stand. She should have stood watch and asked Dennis to do it, but she had forgotten about Dennis. When she came back her mother had an arm wrapped around Carmen, who was standing beside her.

"Carmen worked with Laura at the Riviera," she informed the professor.

Oh my God, Laura thought. This was one of those times when the tapestry of lies necessary to a prostitute's existence threatened to come unraveled by a single gentle tug. It was like being a spy and passing through customs for years with forged documents and convincing your neighbors you worked for the post office and raising children who believed your hobby of stamp collecting accounted for your trips to Albania and Kyrgyzstan, and then, after you've finally decided to retire and are hosting a quiet dinner party, your old colleague barges in and blows your cover while you stand helplessly holding a pair of folding chairs.

Laura had excluded Tita Moon and other working girls from her private life, particularly from meeting her mother. But Carmen was not only her best friend, she was quiet, discreet, educated. Laura was confident Carmen would not betray her, raise suspicions or otherwise reflect poorly on her. On the contrary, as with Dennis, Carmen endeared herself to Laura's mother. She had invited her to dinner, they had all gone shopping on occasion, and Mrs. Flores even had Carmen's phone number in her address book. She liked Carmen so much that more than once during an argument she had compared her daughter unfavorably to her apparently virtuous friend.

Laura had told her mother Carmen was also a dealer at the casino, and Mrs. Flores translated one lie into another by telling her friends Carmen worked with her daughter at the Riviera. Laura didn't mind this when her mother was playing cards with her friends, but in situations where she and Carmen were present it made her quite uncomfortable.

"What if the person you're introducing us to works at the Riviera?" she would say.

But her mother would shrug and reply, "What are the chances? Besides, it's a big hotel."

"If you are ashamed that I work as a dealer in a casino then don't tell them anything. You are bad when it comes to lying. People like you should not tell lies."

Laura now hurriedly introduced the professor and Dennis before her mother could say anything more. Dennis nodded from across the table. The professor stood to greet them.

"This is Javiar," Carmen said belatedly.

Her companion gave the professor a firm handshake, then reached over to Dennis, then kissed Mrs. Flores on the both cheeks. When Laura came over with the chairs he kissed her as well, though she tried to back away.

"This is such a surprise!" Laura said, failing to bring a pitch of cheerfulness to her voice. "You are the first night time visitors to my new home. I mean, the first unannounced visitors. I mean, the first visitors I did not expect."

She sighed in frustration. The evening had gone so well, without scenes or tension. And now a dangerous silence hung over them all and Laura, like an actress with stage fright, forgot her lines.

"What brings you out this way?" her mother filled in for her.

"Yes, what brings you here?" Laura echoed. That was it. That's what she wanted to know.

"Javiar lives up the hill," Carmen explained, leaning forward in her chair. "We were on our way to his house and I said, 'This is the road to Laura's. Why don't we stop by and say hello?'"

"Oh, so you're neighbors?" Mrs. Flores concluded, looking approvingly at Javiar. Approvingly because his clothes and address marked him as a member of the affluent class.

"Not exactly neighbors," Javiar replied with a smile. "I live about a half a kilometer further up, and not on this road. But I'm close enough that should you need to borrow sugar..."

"Speaking of sugar," Laura interrupted. "Could you help me with the coffee, Carmen?"

Laura didn't want to leave Javiar, whoever he was, alone for a moment with her mother, but she had no choice. She pulled Carmen up to the cabinets in the kitchen.

"You could have called!" she whispered.

"I'm sorry. But we were just driving and I recognized—"

"Never mind. Are you working?" she whispered in an even lower voice.

Carmen nodded.

Laura peered into the dining room. Javiar and her mother were talking about the housing market in Escazu.

"Who is he?"

"I don't know. A lawyer or something."

"He came to the hotel?"

Carmen shook her head. "Ginger gave him to me."

Laura stepped back but maintained her hushed tone. "Ginger! You're doing another three way with her?"

"No. She called me and said one of her regulars wanted her but she couldn't do it. She's in Limon or somewhere."

"Well I guess sometimes she really does have to be in Limon," Laura realized. "How much of a commission are you giving her?"

"She didn't ask for money."

Laura raised her eyebrows. "You're joking? She hands you a rich client and doesn't ask for anything?"

"I didn't say she didn't ask for anything."

"Ahh!" Laura said, with a sense of vindication.

"She wants me to be a witness at her wedding."

Laura had picked up the coffee maker, but at the word "wedding" she set it back down.

"'That whore is getting married?"

Now it was Carmen's turn to be surprised. "You should know. He's your friend."

"Porter!"

She was no longer whispering. Everyone in the dining room could hear the name. Fortunately there wasn't anything incriminatory in the exclamation.

"I can't believe she said yes," Laura mused, reverting to a hushed tone, glancing up at the ceiling as if for an explanation. "I was sure she was just stringing him along. You know what this means!" she realized, looking forcefully into Carmen's eyes. "It means she has a greater plan. Something really terrible."

Carmen was no saint. She could lie and steal when she needed to and swear as strongly as any sailor. But she lacked Laura's cynicism and tended to think the best of people, even those who had taken advantage of her.

"I don't know," she said. "Maybe Ginger loves him."

Laura stared with utter disbelief, as though her friend had suggested the moon were a giant tortilla.

"Ginger only loves Ginger. What a tragedy. I have to stop it. It will be a witch wedding."

But stopping Porter's marriage to Ginger would have to go on the back burner. Coffee was on the front burner, and the first crisis Laura needed to avert was brewing in the dining room.

She forced herself not to be distracted by this alarming news and quickly served the coffee, with a plea in Carmen's ear to take their leave as soon as possible. Javiar was obviously not interested in committing indiscretions, and to Laura's relief the conversation never strayed from the safe subjects of business, soccer and cinema.

She shooed them out with a silent prayer and then gave farewell hugs to her mother and the professor, who also decided it was time to go. She closed the door with a thud and leaned against it, exhausted.

Of course, Dennis was still there. Was that a fourth Imperial in his hand?

"No you don't!" she commanded, taking it away from him. "What's the matter with you? Why are you drinking like a monger?"

"I am a monger," he said in a slurred voice, no longer hiding his inebriation.

She took some dishes into the kitchen. He followed and put his arms around her waist as she bent over the sink.

"If you want to help, help," she said, pushing him away. "Otherwise go watch TV."

Her eye caught something on the shelf above the sink. Dennis's camera.

"Shit!" she screamed. "Shit, I don't believe it! How can I be such an idiot?"

She grabbed the camera with the thought to run after them, but of course they were already gone. She slammed it down on the counter with another exclamation.

She had asked to borrow Dennis's digital camera and had put it on the shelf above the sink while she was cooking. The whole reason for the dinner, of course, had been to take the professor's picture so she could show it around the hotel to prove whether he was a monger. This had been the one thing on her mind, and she had forgotten it.

"Fucking Carmen," she breathed to herself. "Fucking Ginger. Get your hands off me!" she yelled to the only person conveniently present to abuse.

"I want to fuck you," Dennis said, undeterred.

"What? What!"

"Pretend I'm a carpenter. Here, I'll show you my ruler."

Laura had no idea what he was talking about. He was drunk and Laura knew drunks were always in some combination horny or quiet or loud or violent or completely incomprehensible. Her thoughts were so far away from his own that she never made the connection between his mood and the dining room table.

"I'll do it in trade," he persisted, picking up the camera. "Here, I'll give you my camera."

Laura was accustomed to dealing with drunks. Of course if they were violent you had to fight back or flee. But otherwise she dealt with them as she might deal with a small child, not taking their insults personally, reacting with a maturity and authority they lacked.

"It's a cheap camera," she pointed out. "And why should I want you to give it to me when I can borrow it any time I ask?"

Dennis put his arms around her neck. She could smell the beer on his normally odorless breath.

"I'll give you a computer!" he said in a sing-song voice. "A laptop?"

Laura came to her senses and released herself from his grasp. He was unsteady on his feet and it was easy enough for her to lead him into the living room and push him onto the sofa.

"Let me clean the dishes. Then I'll call Pablo and he'll pick you up."

"If you let me stay you won't have to take the bus to work," he said enticingly.

"I like to take the bus." And she carried the plates into the kitchen.

But when she returned to the living room, Dennis was not there. For a moment she worried he had gone to her bedroom. But he wouldn't do that. He wasn't that disrespectful, not even drunk. He was probably sick in the bathroom.

But the guest bathroom was empty. Then Laura noticed a figure in the unrented guest bedroom. Dennis was lying across the twin bed, fully dressed. She took a step forward with the intention of undressing him and sliding him under the covers, but she stopped herself and simply closed the door.

"Act like a dog, sleep like a dog," she grumbled.

CHAPTER 7

TITA MOON RISING

Laura was awakened early the next morning by the doorbell. She threw on her robe and hurried to answer it, thinking it must be Carmen stopping by on her way home after a wild night of sex with Ginger's client. But she hadn't been very pleased to see Carmen last night, and Carmen was both sensitive to others and to herself. It didn't make sense for her to reappear at seven-thirty the next morning.

Laura shielded her eyes from the light. A large woman her mother's age, wearing a blue dress that reached her thick calves, scrutinized her.

"Hello. May I help you?" Laura asked.

"I'm here about the room," the woman said, raising a folded newspaper in her hand.

The words jolted Laura more than a double expresso. The room. Of course! The room. I'm such an idiot! Laura reproached herself. I really do need to write things down and keep a calendar.

The woman had called Wednesday about renting the room. They had talked for a few minutes, long enough for Laura to conclude she would be an ideal tenant. Middle-aged, reserved, employed at an insurance company. The woman liked the location and said the rent was within her budget. Laura wanted her to come right away, but the soonest she could manage was Friday morning before work. Laura realized if she waited for the weekend the woman might find something else. Besides, she had to wake up early for work herself. What was an hour earlier?

But of course with the dinner last night she had completely forgotten, and despite her continued reminders to herself to make lists, take notes, keep calendars, she never did.

"Oh, hello! Thanks for coming! I'm so glad to meet you. Welcome to my home. And maybe your home too!" And she practically pulled her in.

"We did say seven-thirty?" the woman asked, looking at Laura's robe.

"Yes, I'm sorry. My alarm is broken. Have a seat on the sofa. I'll be right back. Would you like some coffee?"

The woman shook her head and sat on the sofa with her hands in her lap. Laura turned on the lights and dashed into her room and threw on whatever was at hand and ran a brush through her tangled hair. Then she darted into the bathroom to wash her face and clean her teeth.

When she returned her prospective lodger was sitting on the sofa exactly as she'd left her, a good sign. How many people would have wandered into the kitchen by now and started opening the cabinets? This was a tenant who wouldn't pry.

The woman stood and looked past Laura to the dining room, where the chairs, including the folding chairs from the terrace, were scattered in disarray and the dirty placemats and coffee cups still on the table.

"I had a dinner party last night and didn't have a chance to finish cleaning," Laura explained, leading her past the dining room and into the kitchen. She had washed the plates, but not the silverware. "I'm usually a very clean person," she decided to say. "I don't want you to think there are going to be dirty dishes lying around. Last night was an exception."

The woman said nothing. She didn't even look in the refrigerator. Very polite and modest, Laura thought.

Laura decided to save the terrace and its magical view for last. That would close the deal, she thought. And there was no reason to show her own room. So she led her to the guest bathroom

"This would be your bathroom," she said, pulling back the shower curtain.

The woman looked at the female toiletries covering the sink.

"Oh, those are Raquel's, my other lodger," Laura explained. "You would be sharing the bathroom with her. Of course once you move in she will move her things. I assure you she is not normally a messy person, either. It's just—"

"Is someone crying?" the woman interjected, backing into the hallway.

"Oh, that's Raquel. She lost her job and I think she's also PMSing."

Laura knocked on the door and opened it slightly, so that only she could peer inside. Raquel was sitting on the edge of her bed, still in her nightgown, sobbing. Her unemployed status and hormonal activity these last couple days had thrown her into crying fits, especially in the morning. She would be better after a cup of coffee.

"Are you okay?"

Raquel nodded and Laura closed the door. She began to open the next door when her eye caught a glimpse of a male shoe hanging at an odd angle over the bed.

Dennis!

She'd forgotten about Dennis. She slammed the door shut and turned to her prospective tenant with a look of panic. A successful prostitute had to be a quick thinker. Strange faces, strange places, dangers petty and perilous, one had to stay on top of situations in order not to end up in police custody, or with an empty purse. But this was a scenario Laura had no experience with. Had this been the familiar scene of so many soap operas of the jealous wife returning home early, she could have hidden Dennis in the closet. But the woman would undoubtedly want to look in the closet. She might plead for time and hide him somewhere else, but she was giving a tour of the house. And if it was quiet enough to hear sobbing from behind a closed door, the woman would certainly hear Dennis's shoes click against the tiles.

She might divert the woman's attention and push Dennis out the door. This was the second thought that came to mind in the dizzying whirl of alternatives that flashed through her scattered brain. Yes, show her the terrace and then, while she's lingering over the view, wake Dennis and thrust him out the front door. But what if she couldn't wake him? And how could she explain the delay? The woman would certainly be suspicious when the half-opened door to her future room was suddenly closed and she was told to admire the terrace instead. Laura might say the room was dirty and she wanted to tidy things up. But the woman might wonder why she hadn't done so already, especially after Laura made a point of what a clean person she was. How does an empty room get dirty anyway? And what if the woman says she doesn't mind viewing the room in its present condition?

Why would someone need to turn away from a room she wanted to enter? This was the question Laura needed to ask, and it immediately brought to mind countless hotel rooms from which she had been denied entry.

"It has been fumigated and it still smells," Laura said, wrinkling her nose. A stroke of genius, she told herself. But she hadn't thought it all the way through. "I'll show you Raquel's room. They're exactly alike."

She asked Raquel if they could come in. Raquel blew her nose, threw the blanket over the bed and hurried past them into the shower.

"I furnished the two rooms exactly alike," Laura said. "As you can see, the view is beautiful." And she parted the curtains to let in the light.

The woman shielded her eyes with her hand. "Fumigated?"

"And there's a large closet over there."

"Do you have an insect problem?"

"Oh no. It's just a precaution you take. With this being a new house, you know."

"But why just that room?"

It was a cruel question. She should have gone with painted. She had almost said, "The room has just been painted." But she rejected this because a prospective tenant would not balk at smelling paint.

"Well...well...the man came last week but he got a call, an emergency, and at the time he had fumigated all the rooms but yours." And she said "yours" forcefully, in a tone of desperation.

"So you haven't actually seen any bugs?" the woman persisted.

"I swear on the lives of my future children," Laura said a little too dramatically.

The woman said nothing more, and remained quiet while Laura led her out to the terrace. Obviously she had a phobia of insects.

Laura heard the faucet in the kitchen and assumed it must be Raquel making coffee. But it was followed by a male voice. "Fuck, do I have a hangover!" Dennis shouted.

And he looked at Laura and her former prospective tenant.

The following day, Saturday, another woman was scheduled to see the house. Laura spent the whole morning cleaning, but the woman didn't show.

"Renting a spare room in your own home can be problematic," Porter said later that afternoon at the Conquistador on the outskirts of town. He had phoned Laura to meet him for a drink, and Laura knew the reason, but didn't want to reproach him on the phone. So she agreed to meet, and when he began the conversation by asking if she had rented her rooms, she unburdened herself.

He had ordered wine for both of them, which they drank in the courtyard outside the restaurant. He was wearing a blazer with his shirt unbuttoned at the top and Laura realized he had not invited her to dinner because he was meeting someone for dinner, and she knew who.

"It can take months," Porter continued, sipping his wine.

"Months!"

"A cousin of mine in Virginia wanted to rent a room in her house. After six months she gave up and turned it into a bed and breakfast."

"Well I don't want my home to be a bed and breakfast. I don't want to cook for people, and I don't want mongers. You told me my location was perfect," she said, though not meaning to blame him for her empty room.

"It is a good location. But you don't want to rent to a man, so you're limiting yourself to half the potential market."

"Are you saying I should rent to a man?"

"Not at all. Maybe you should lower your price."

Laura said nothing. She was hoping for better advice, but what could he do? She hadn't come here to talk about her business anyway. She drank her wine and waited patiently for him to proceed.

"You're probably wondering why I asked you here," he finally said, regarding her through his thick glasses.

Laura resisted the urge to reply.

"I know you don't like Ginger," he began. "I know your concerns and I appreciate the interest you take in my welfare. I don't expect you to be pleased by my news, or to congratulate me, but... but she has accepted my proposal of marriage."

Laura felt flustered. She had prepared all kinds of speeches on the taxi ride over. She would squeeze his bony wrist and lecture him like a parent. She would use charts and graphs if she needed to. He had been a banker. She would make a presentation so forceful he would have to agree. No profit, she would say. You cannot profit from Ginger. She will drive you bankrupt. Financially and spiritually. On the taxi ride Laura had thought of all the banking terms she knew.

But Porter's self-effacing remarks weakened her resolve. Here was a man declaiming his engagement to perhaps the only friend he had in Costa Rica, acknowledging the likelihood that he wouldn't receive congratulations. Marrying a witch was tragic enough. Receiving no congratulations would only compound the sadness.

So Laura rose and gave her skeletal friend a long hug and said, "Of course I will congratulate you. I hope you will be very happy." And she went on and on, saying the opposite of what she knew in her heart to be true.

And then she sat down and they toasted the announcement with their wine glasses.

"I suppose you're wondering why I wanted to meet you, why I didn't just tell you on the phone," Porter then said.

But Laura wasn't wondering that at all. With all the recent shocks in her life, she didn't have room in her thoughts to wonder about anything more.

"We're going to have a simple, civil wedding," Porter explained. "Here at the Conquistador. No guests or reception. Just the ceremony here in the courtyard, and dinner. I'd like you to be my witness."

Laura nearly gagged on her wine. It shouldn't have been such a surprise. If they were going to be married, it seemed obvious

Porter would invite her, and since he had no close male friends in Costa Rica to serve as best man, it made sense he would offer this role to Laura.

Nevertheless, Laura felt she were the victim of a practical joke. She glanced around, half expecting the crowd from the Red Volcano to pop out from behind the potted trees and laugh at her expense. But the seconds passed in silence, Porter's gaze intent on her, waiting for an answer.

"That's very flattering," she finally stammered. "But I'm sure you have friends and relatives in the States who you would rather have stand beside you at this important time."

"I don't want to make a fuss," Porter replied. "Yes, I have family and friends, but once you go down that road, somebody's going to be left out and get offended. And there's the expense of coming here, and I told you it's going to be a simple ceremony. Five minutes, that's all. Besides," he added upon reflection, fingering the stem of his glass, "I've made a new life for myself here and you're as much a part of that as anybody. Excepting Ginger, naturally. And naturally, if you feel ill at ease with accepting what you view to be an old man's foolish—"

"No!" Laura interrupted, not wanting him to say another self-deprecating word. "Of course I accept. I'll be proud to be your witness!"

Porter smiled and sat back with obvious satisfaction. "I'm glad to hear it. You won't have any duties, per se. And you can wear what you wish. A nice dress. If you want to pick something out I will pay for it. And you can invite a guest to the dinner. Maybe that friend of yours from the party, Dennis. Or someone else. As I said, it will be very informal. No rehearsal or anything like that."

"Have you picked a date for the wedding?" Laura asked, hoping Porter was one of those men who preferred long engagements.

"Next Saturday at five o'clock," her friend answered.

Laura was afraid of that. She had only a week to stop this poor old train from chugging into the mouth of a volcano.

"Ginger's meeting me for dinner," he went on, looking at his watch. "You're welcome to join us."

Laura rose abruptly. She had given a stellar performance, but her acting abilities weren't refined enough to face Ginger graciously.

Porter pulled out his wallet to pay for her taxi, but Laura pushed both the money and Porter away, and hurried toward the lobby alone, as if she had just remembered she left the oven on.

Back home Raquel was dressing to go out to dinner with her boyfriend. "How do I look?" she asked, modeling a leopard print skirt with a canary blouse and open-toed sandals.

"You'd look better in heels," Laura suggested.

"I know. But these are more comfortable. And my boyfriend is shorter."

"Well, you look great anyway. Too good for him," Laura added, although she had never actually met Eduardo. But she had heard enough to about him to know the type, and she knew Raquel deserved better. "I hope he's buying you dinner."

"He better. I have no money." She bit her lip. That wasn't the kind of admission to make to your landlord. "But don't worry. I'll have the rent Monday."

Laura was glad Raquel was living here. Despite her crying the last couple days, Laura found her presence congenial, and she liked her better the more she got to know her. She thought of her less as a tenant than as a friend. And wasn't that one of her dreams, to have a friend who wasn't in the business?

"Don't worry," Laura assured her. "You can pay at the end of the month if you like."

"Really?"

"Why not. I trust you. Besides, there's a favor you can do me."

She led Raquel into the kitchen, where Dennis's camera still sat on the shelf above the sink. "Do you have school this week?"

"I have classes Tuesday evening."

Laura gave her the camera. "I forgot to take a picture of my mom's boyfriend the other night. Maybe you can do it."

Raquel took the camera and turned it over as if it were a meteorite. "What am I supposed to do with this?"

"Just find out where his class is and take his picture."

"But why do you want his picture?"

"Just his face," Laura clarified. "As close as possible. Use the zoom. The button is here."

It was a simple digital camera and Raquel understood how it worked well enough. It was the request which made no sense.

"But what do I tell him when he asks why I want his picture?"

"Oh, don't let him see you take it," Laura added, having forgotten this important detail.

This was not a favor Raquel felt comfortable performing, but she could hardly refuse Laura after her generous offer to let her pay the rent at the end of the month. Still, the thought made her laugh. "You want me to spy!" she realized.

"It's the first time my mom's dated a gringo. I want to make sure he's okay."

"You're going to show his picture to the police?"

"No. To the crowd at the Hotel Grand."

"Ahhh! Now I see. Well, I'll try, but I can't promise anything. I'm not talented as a spy."

"How do you know?" Laura challenged. "Have you ever tried? I might have said the same thing a few weeks ago about being an office manager. You never know until you try."

Raquel laughed again, her spirits lifted by Laura's optimism. "Yes. Maybe if I pull this off I'll apply for a job as a spy. Although I don't know who Costa Rica spies on. We don't have any enemies."

"You don't need enemies to spy. You don't even need to have an army. I'm sure we have spies in our government. Take the camera tonight and practice on your date. See if you can take people's photos without their knowing. And while you're looking around for subjects maybe you'll see some cool single guy to take the place of your loser boyfriend."

After Raquel left, Laura enjoyed the quiet evening alone, or at least she tried to enjoy it, with all that was on her mind. She heated left-over chicken for herself, then watched soap operas on TV. Despite a certain inner agitation over recent events, she felt remarkably calm. It was Saturday night. Saturday night was the busiest night at the Hotel Grand, and Laura had always worked on Saturday. Even when she had a cold she forced herself to go. Even when she was menstruating she sometimes went, offering erotic massages and blowjobs instead of straight sex. But now it was Saturday night and the house was quiet and her phone was turned off and she could lie on the sofa in her pink terry robe and watch her favorite programs and she didn't have to look at the clock or shower and dress or wonder if any of her regulars were there or if so-and-so who said he was coming this week had actually arrived. She didn't have to think about her bills and how much money she needed to make and how much or how little she had made yesterday or in the last week or month. She didn't have to worry about quarrels with Colombians or long taxi rides or blisters from standing too long in the wrong heels.

This is how the rest of the world must feel on Saturday night, she imagined.

She slept late. Raquel had already put the coffee on and left to visit her family and scan the newspaper for jobs. Laura made herself a fried egg with toast and drank a large cup of coffee before turning her cell phone on and reluctantly pressing one of the speed dial buttons.

"Hi Tita. You still want the room?"

Had Tita Moon been a shrewd woman she would have heard the tone of desperation in Laura's voice and answered equivocally, aiming to negotiate. But Tita Moon was not shrewd and she screamed like a twelve year old at a pop concert.

An hour later she knocked on the door.

Laura served her coffee. "Not that you should think being served coffee will become a habit," she admonished, and set before her a hand written letter of agreement to sign.

Of course there had been no agreement with Raquel. But Laura trusted Raquel. She didn't trust Tita. Not that this agreement, which she had penned while eating breakfast, would mean anything in court. But at least it would clarify Laura's position and put their relationship on a more formal footing.

The agreement stated that seventy-five dollars or its equivalent in colones would be due at the beginning of each week, with the last two weeks of the year exempt. Or she could pay three hundred dollars at the beginning of each month, with the first month's rent due today. She was letting Raquel, on the other hand, pay two hundred a month and lapse a month behind. Tita Moon was expected to keep to the common rooms clean and not leave food out or do anything that might attract insects—the inspiration for this clause being Laura's experience with the prospective tenant Friday morning. She was to label her own food and not use anyone else's, or share shampoo or other toiletries in the guest bathroom. She could borrow cups and dishes but must wash them and replace them as soon as she was finished. She could used the washing machine—Laura had finally bought one—but must buy her own detergent, and hang her clothes on the line immediately after the spin cycle. She must not smoke marijuana in the house, even on the terrace, and must not keep cocaine on the premises. She must not play the radio loudly or otherwise disturb the tranquility of the house. She must under no circumstances entertain men or give them this address, and no working girls were allowed to visit except Carmen. She was welcome to use the living room, dining room, kitchen and terrace, except when Laura was entertaining, at which times she was expected to make herself scarce. And she was not to enter Laura's bedroom under any circumstances, or use her jacuzzi bath.

"My God!" Tita Moon said after reading the document carefully at the dining room table. "You'd think I was entering a convent!"

"Well, if you keep that in mind we won't have any problems."

Tita Moon regarded Laura with her special brand of logic. "How will you know if I keep cocaine?"

"I'll know if I see mirrors in the guest bathroom that didn't come with the house," Laura replied in as rational a tone. "I'll know if I see white powder and no bottle of talc nearby."

"What if it's just in my purse?" Tita Moon challenged. "You have no right to search my purse."

"Are you going to law school this week?" Laura said caustically. "I thought you were still in nursing school?"

"Are you going to police school? Is this a convent and a prison?"

"Of all the things I put in this agreement, I thought you might argue about sharing the detergent or being able to play the radio loudly sometimes or having guests. I thought not keeping narcotics was the one thing you would understand!"

"What if I keep a joint in my purse and don't smoke it? That's not narcotics."

"Fuck, Tita, you've been here ten minutes and you're already driving me crazy!" Laura shouted. "Sign the agreement or get out!"

Tita Moon picked up the pen and signed in a florid script she was particularly proud of and which took her many seconds to finish. Sometimes she used this signature at the puta registration, to her self-conscious clients' dismay.

"It's not a constitution, Tita," Laura remarked, as her new tenant underlined her name with a flourish.

Tita Moon set down the pen and hugged her favorite landlord. "You won't even know I'm here!"

This softened Laura, who almost cried at the gesture. But she remembered she was a landlord and had to take care of business.

"Can you give me the money now please?"

Tita Moon had both cocaine and marijuana in her purse, so she opened it with her back turned and handed Laura three crisp one hundred dollar bills.

"I bet you've never gotten hundred dollar bills from a woman before," Tita Moon said.

She was right. Raquel had paid weekly, and in colones. "Well I hope it won't be the last time," Laura replied.

"What are you staring at?" Tita Moon asked.

For they were standing closer now and Tita Moon's round face was in the light and Laura was momentarily speechless at her discovery.

"You look pregnant."

Tita Moon laughed, but the statement shocked her, and she stared back in equal amazement.

"That's crazy!"

"No, I'm serious. There's more color in your cheeks."

"That's just rouge." But then Tita Moon remembered she wasn't wearing rouge.

"No, I can always tell," Laura went on. "There's just something, I can't describe it."

"But that's impossible."

"Why? The morning-after pill doesn't always work." Laura, of course, didn't know that she hadn't taken the pill, and Tita Moon wasn't about to admit to literally having thrown the result of her friend's good efforts in the trash. "Have you had your period since the condom broke?"

"No."

"Well then."

Tita Moon ran to the guest bathroom and looked in the mirror. All she saw was a nervous, frightened young woman who didn't know how to be a mother.

"But I'm not due till this week."

"I wouldn't wait if I were you. What's it been? Two weeks since the condom broke? Take a pregnancy test. Poor thing. Now you'll have to go to Mexico to get an abortion."

And this time it was Laura who hugged Tita Moon, who in her anxiety on this first day of her tenancy violated a clause in her agreement, by taking one of Raquel's tissues to wipe her tearing eyes.

CHAPTER 8

LAURA'S SECRET SERVICE

M onday morning Laura used the company credit card to go shopping, not for herself but to furnish the office. Business had not yet picked up at Pan American Web Services. When the phone rang it was either a telemarketer or a wrong number. Dennis had told her that it would take three to six months for them to start seeing any real activity, but that she could use this time to learn the accounting software and familiarize herself with other business practices. Laura was more interested in decorating, however, and shopping distracted her for a few hours from the Porters, professors and Tita Moons of this world.

Her heart raced when she entered an office furniture store that sold filing cabinets in designer colors. She had already bought a glass and steel table the week before to replace her crumbling wooden desk, and a floral area rug to cover the limp beige carpet. She had the delivery boy set the filing cabinet next to her desk, within her field of vision.

When Dennis returned from an appointment, Laura's latest acquisition so startled him he nearly tripped over the area rug.

"Where the hell did you find a pink filing cabinet?"

"It's fuchsia, not pink."

"Well take it back. It's awful."

Laura stood between him and the cabinet, as if he might remove it by force. "You said I could buy what I wanted as long as it was practical and within budget. You said we needed a filing cabinet."

"Not a pink one!"

"It's fuchsia. They didn't have pink."

"Who's going to want to do business with us when they come in here and see a pink, or fuchsia, or whatever you want to call it, filing cabinet? No one will take us seriously."

"First of all," Laura responded in a firm but very patient tone, "you said yourself most of our business will come from overseas through the internet. Next, we will get some business by phone. Only the smallest part, you said, will come from people visiting our office. But of those who do come to our office, I can't imagine anyone will be so offended by a color that they will not want to deal with us just for that reason. And I can tell you as a woman that women will be comforted by this filing cabinet. They will choose us because we have a fuchsia filing cabinet. If you were smart you would realize that women make up half the world but that all the web service companies are run by geeks like you who don't know the first thing about what a woman wants."

"Don't tell me I don't know what women want!" Dennis shouted, taking her comment a little too personally, still upset from last week.

"If you were smart you would put a photo of the filing cabinet on our website." Her eyes lit up at her inspiration. "A big photo, filling the page. And you could be leaning against one side, and I against the other. And the labels on the drawers would be the menu items for the site."

But Dennis dismissed her with a sigh. "You're crazy. I hope at least you didn't get it in trade?"

"No, I used this," she answered, handing back his credit card. "And I almost stayed within budget."

Dennis didn't say another word but walked past her to his office, another battle lost, and spent the rest of the day on his laptop.

Laura sorted through storage boxes that Dennis had stacked against the far wall, looking for documents worth filing. When she came across a micro-cassette recorder, however, her thoughts switched tracks. She took it to her desk and practiced using it, praising herself for this stroke of genius.

Unlike Raquel, Tita Moon's life filled more than six boxes. Tita Moon was the kind of person who never threw anything away, and she and Carmen spent the day toting boxes to her new place of residence. Boxes that should have gone to a landfill, crammed with broken costume jewelry, old magazines, outgrown or out of style clothes, empty lipstick containers, chipped ceramic plates, drained batteries and a beer-stained Bible.

When Laura arrived home some of the boxes were still stacked in the hallway, waiting to be sorted, while Tita Moon and Carmen rested on the sofa watching "Vale of Tears." Technically this was a violation of the agreement, but Laura was so pleased to see Carmen she overlooked the infraction and make dinner for them all.

After dinner she pulled Carmen onto the terrace and placed the micro cassette recorder in the palm of her hand.

"Dear Carmen, sweet Carmen, lovely Carmen," Laura began in her most seductive voice, a voice usually reserved for men. "I want you to do me a big, big favor."

Carmen looked down at the dubious gift. "You're giving me a recorder?"

"Not to keep. Just for tonight. Or whenever you see Ginger."

"Ginger?"

"Oh Carmen, you'll be saving a good man from ruin. God will forgive you many sins for this good deed."

It was still light outside, so Carmen could peer into Laura's penetrating eyes and see that her friend was speaking quite earnestly.

"It will be fun," Laura told her. "You will be my spy."

At the word "spy" Carmen loosened her grip on the recorder so that it almost fell to the ground. "You want me to record Ginger?"

Laura paced from one side of the terrace to the other, as though she were a private detective trying to solve a puzzling case. "I was sure she would not marry him," she finally said, turning back to Carmen and speaking in a louder voice. "Why? Why now? She's been stringing him along all this time, spending his money, ignoring his proposals."

"Maybe she wants to retire, like you," Carmen offered in all innocence.

"Don't ever compare that witch to me!" Laura exclaimed with a raised finger. "Putas like her never retire. Even if they get married, even if they stop fucking altogether. The Gingers of the world are putas from cradle to grave!"

She took a breath and resumed her pacing.

"But why marry the poor guy?"

"Because he's not poor. For his money," Carmen timidly suggested, hoping Laura would not take offense at such a rational conclusion.

"But he's given her thousands. She doesn't have to marry him for that. Besides, Porter is not rich. He is well off because he lives simply and has invested well, except for his investment in her. But if he stays with her another year, married or not, he will have to go back to work."

"Then she's doing it because she wants to live in the States."

"But Porter's told me many times he doesn't want to go back home. And I'm sure he's told her."

"But if she's so manipulative she can make him change his mind."

"True," Laura conceded. "But it doesn't make sense. If that was her intention, why wait until now? There has to be a deeper reason."

Carmen couldn't think what it might be. Nor did she particularly care. Occasionally, as with the narco, her overactive imagination carried her away, and sometimes got her into trouble. But those were situations where she felt sympathy for the person, or responsibility. Otherwise she tried to mind her own business and avoided gossip and speculation into the affairs of people on the periphery of her life.

"Why don't you ask her?" she wondered.

"Because we hate each other. The last thing she will do is talk to me. But you will be the witness at her wedding," Laura pointed out. "Or I should say her planned wedding. Because if things go the way I hope, there will be no wedding. All you have to do is talk to her casually, like you are just making conversation. It's the most natural thing in the world for the witness to ask the bride why she is getting married."

Carmen looked down at her hand. "But why do I need to record her?"

"Because Porter is in deep, deep denial. When I told him I had seen Ginger at the supermercado when she was supposed to be at the bedside of her supposedly dying mother in Limon, he did not believe me. He asked why I didn't take a photo with my cell phone. Can you believe that? But that's how men can think when they are under a spell. And that witch Ginger has put him under a spell. If I tell him her reasons he will just blame me for trying to break up their relationship. He will only believe it if he hears her scheming in her own voice. Only that will break the spell."

Carmen turned the recorder over in her hand, not unlike the way Raquel had examined the digital camera a couple days earlier.

"Here, I'll show you how to use it," Laura said. "It's very simple. I have everything set up. All you have to do is put it in your purse, here, in the outside pouch, but don't zip it shut, and press the record button."

"But I'm not a spy."

"If you can be a prostitute you can be a spy," Laura stated, having thought often of the similarities between the two professions. But until this moment she had forgotten she had also asked Raquel to spy for her. True, Raquel was not a prostitute, but she had worked at the Hotel Grand and knew the environment.

Laura laughed at the coincidence, and imagined that she might make a career for herself taking working girls and training them as spies. What if all the girls at the Hotel Grand were recruited to spy for Costa Rica? Costa Rica would learn all the world's secrets and could blackmail anyone it wished. Laura would be the general of this underground army, leading her tiny country into the ranks of the great powers.

Carmen stood anxiously in front of the bar at the Red Volcano, beside Tita Moon, compulsively fingering the recorder in the unzipped outer pouch of her red vinyl purse as if it were a pack of cigarettes and she had just decided to quit smoking.

Upon entering the hotel she had glanced around for Ginger, but only long enough to appease her conscience, and was relieved not to see her. Maybe she won't come tonight, she thought, reminding herself that in recent weeks Ginger had appeared only occasionally at the hotel. She would let the recorder lie in the bottom of her purse for a night or two before handing it to Tita Moon to give back to Laura with her apologies. Certainly Laura could ask nothing more of her, with the wedding fast approaching. She might be Ginger's witness, she imagined telling Laura afterwards, but that didn't mean they were close friends.

Two college-age steroid freaks swaggered over to them and started making small talk. They drank their own beers without offering to buy Carmen and Tita Moon drinks, but then a lot of the men were neglectful like that. It was their first trip to Costa Rica, they were sharing a room upstairs and were ready for action.

But when Tita Moon said a hundred each, the one who was wearing a tank top offered sixty, while his buddy, who was wearing a Dallas Cowboys t-shirt, stroked Carmen's arm.

Tita Moon, however, appeared uninterested in negotiating, and the gringo in the tank top, who seemed to know more about the scene than his roommate, pulled his friend away.

"Aren't you proud of me?" Tita Moon asked when they were gone. "See, I know what I'm doing."

"Yes, but it's early. If we did them now we might get two tonight."

"So you want to go for sixty?"

"I didn't say sixty. Maybe eighty. They weren't bad looking."

"Who cares what they look like? What kind of whore are you?" Tita Moon challenged, unable to pass up the chance to rebuke her friend with the same phrases Carmen had used on her a few days before. "You're the disgrace to prostitutes!"

Carmen could not tell her friend that the reason for her sudden affordability was that she wanted to get out of the bar in case Ginger came, in which case it would be worth it to her to shave twenty or even forty dollars from her regular fee.

"I was just testing you," she said instead. "I wanted to make sure if we did a foursome you wouldn't cave in to their demands."

"Oh right. Like we've never done a foursome before."

"That's what I mean. The last time we went together the guys asked for a lesbian show and you agreed just like that. It should be extra."

"Maybe I just like when you eat my pussy," Tita Moon said with a flick of her tongue.

"Then you should pay me too," Carmen snapped irritably, in no mood for jokes.

But Tita Moon had worries of her own. "Do I look any different to you?" she asked hesitantly.

Carmen looked at her face in the bar's hazy light, wondering if she was wearing different makeup. "No."

176

"You don't think I look pregnant?"

"How long has it been?"

"Two weeks."

"Two weeks! Ask me in two months. Maybe I can tell you then."

"Laura says I look pregnant. She can see it in my face. And she didn't even know that I threw away the pill."

"Did you take a pregnancy test?"

"No."

"So pee on the test strip. Then you won't have to ask me to be a clairvoyant."

"I'm afraid," Tita Moon confessed.

"That doesn't make sense! If you're pregnant, you're pregnant. If you're not, you're not. Or do you think taking the test will make you pregnant?"

"I'm superstitious."

"My God. Have you missed your period?"

"It's not due yet."

"Then wait."

"But I can't stop thinking about it."

"Your problem, Tita, isn't thinking too much. It's not thinking at all!"

Their conversation might have continued in this vein for some time, without resolution, but the steroid freaks returned, their beers finished, and offered eighty.

Carmen accepted before Tita Moon could respond and possessively grabbed the hand of the guy wearing the tank top and led him toward the puta registration.

His name was John and he claimed to know all about the hotel from his research on the internet. His buddy was Terry. Other than that they didn't say much.

Their room had two queen beds instead of a king, but they threw their clothes on the far bed and took the girls onto the near one. Carmen wondered if they were bisexual, but they were simply following the roles they had seen in porn films, where two couples share the same bed.

"Can you pay us first?" Tita Moon asked, as Terry, having undressed himself, began to kiss her neck.

"We'll pay you after," John, replied, caressing Carmen through her shirt.

"No. We always get the money first," Tita Moon demanded, drawing away from Terry.

Terry started for the safe, but John was adamant. "We'll pay you after, that's they way it is."

"You've never even been here before," Tita Moon logically pointed out. "How do you know anything about it?"

"All the guys on the internet say to pay afterwards," he answered. "That's the rule."

"Well it's not our rule. Maybe you can do that with some crack head, but not with us!"

She reached for her shoes, but Carmen stopped her. "It's okay," she said.

Tita Moon shot her a look but held her tongue. Carmen normally would have agreed with her, but Tita Moon didn't have a monopoly on capriciousness, and Carmen was in no mood at the moment to risk easy money. These guys were young, good looking, guests of the hotel. She thought the chances of not getting paid were low, and with Ginger lurking in the back of her mind, she was in no mood for confrontation.

Tita moved her man to the other bed and began to suck him, but he pulled her off. "Why don't you girls do a show for us first to get us in the mood?"

"You're already in the mood," Tita Moon said. "But if you want, it's fifty extra."

"Fuck that!" John shouted from the other bed. "We're not paying extra."

"Fifty each or fifty total?" Terry asked.

"Fifty total," Tita Moon said. "In advance."

"I'll pay for it," Terry decided. And while his friend tried to object, he opened the safe and handed Tita Moon fifty dollars.

"You asshole," John said. "You're just letting them hustle us."

"Here, take your money back, go find someone from the internet," Tita Moon said indignantly, thrusting the money at John.

But Terry placed himself between them and managed to placate her. While the two men sat on the edge of John's bed, Carmen and Tita Moon spread out between them and began to lick and kiss each other. Then Carmen crept between Tita Moon's legs and began to lick her.

Carmen preferred to be on the giving end and only performed shows with Tita Moon and a couple other girls, including, once or twice in the past, Laura. Tita Moon was less discriminating and, though she didn't consider herself bisexual, often enjoyed the experience.

But tonight her moans of pleasure were fabricated. Her thoughts instead were tracing a path to an all night pharmacy where she could purchase a pregnancy test. Carmen, meanwhile, was imagining an encounter with Ginger, who was certain to be in the bar when they returned downstairs. Carmen imagined interviewing her as Laura had suggested, but a barmaid knocked her purse over and the recorder fell out. She reached for it, but Ginger grabbed it first and accused her of spying. Then Ginger began to strangle her, and she fought to breathe. But no one in the bar came to her aid, thinking it a joke, and she suffocated in their midst.

"Man, she's really going at it," Terry exclaimed to his friend. "She's gasping for air!"

Carmen rose and wiped her mouth with her arm. She hurried into the bathroom and washed her face thoroughly with cold water.

When she returned Terry was already fucking Tita Moon on his bed, and Carmen barely had time to open the condom before John grabbed her roughly and turned her over. She echoed

Tita Moon's exaggerated groans, thinking that these jerks probably believed they were really giving them pleasure. Carmen preferred younger men and was more willing to negotiate if her client was good looking. But older men tended to be more appreciative, gentle and skilled. These steroid freaks doubtless thought they were doing them a favor, and as the beds alternately squeaked in rising frequency, Carmen realized they probably wouldn't get paid what they had asked. She had been wrong and would have to face not only Ginger's wrath when she discovered the recorder, but Tita Moon's reproaches for breaking a cardinal rule.

But it was too late. Her man was already crossing the finish line. Tita Moon's followed a minute later. The two girls ran into the bathroom together.

"Hey, we're just starting," John shouted through the door when he heard the sound of running water.

The girls came out wrapped in towels.

"No problem," Tita Moon said. "You got more condoms?" She was addressing Terry, but John drew her onto his bed and pulled off the towel.

"Hey, what are you doing?"

"It's my turn with you."

Tita Moon scrambled to her feet. "What the fuck! You don't get me."

John grabbed her by the wrist. "Hell, I paid for you."

"You paid for her!" Tita Moon clarified. "You want to change, it's eighty more."

John let her go in disgust. "I can't believe this shit!" He looked angrily at Terry. "I told you we should have taken the Dominicans!"

"In that case we won't pay you anything!" Terry threatened, more concerned with saving face with his friend than getting his way, for what he really wanted was another round with Tita Moon.

"You come here for the first time and think you know everything!" Tita Moon shouted back. "You should read the internet more carefully!"

Carmen felt some money was better than none and was too intimidated by all their bulging muscles to make threats of her own. "Let them have their way," she said. And, looking at them, "But this is all you get. Nothing more."

They traded beds, but this time desisted from moaning, in protest. Not that their clients seemed disappointed by their joint silence. The sound of the squeaking beds sufficiently aroused them.

Afterward the girls quickly dressed, not bothering to shower. John, who had put on his underwear and tank top, went to the safe and gave Carmen several bills. She counted them out. "This is only seventy. We agreed to eighty."

"And what about mine?" Tita Moon asked, looking at Terry, who was sitting, still naked, on the edge of the bed.

But John had closed the safe.

"That's for both of you," he told them.

"What the hell?" Tita Moon exclaimed.

"My buddy gave you fifty, this makes one-twenty, total. Which is all you whores deserve."

Tita Moon looked for an object to strike him with and picked up an empty ashtray. But the steroid freak easily grabbed it away.

"You can't do this!" she complained, fearlessly scowling up at him. "We'll tell the manager. They'll throw you out. They'll—"

"Beat it or we'll have you banned from the hotel."

"Try it!" she urged him.

Carmen, in the meantime, had stashed the money in her purse and retreated toward the door. "Come on Tita. Let's go."

Tita Moon drew in her breath and looked at Terry, who she felt might be more sympathetic to her cause. "Your friend reads the internet too much," she said, and followed Carmen out the door.

If prostitution was the world's oldest profession, then the world's oldest business practice was pay in advance. Sex for pay existed in many variations, from the overly polite bar girls in Bangkok to the aggressive streetwalkers in Hamburg's infamous Reeperbahn to the high-priced escorts in Miami who came to hotels with credit card readers stashed in their handbags. But all of these women, or their brokers, demanded the money up front. Yet for some unknown reason, many ticas ignored this policy, sometimes at great cost. And many mongers, having learned of this exception, proudly proclaimed that they never paid until the service was rendered, reserving the right to pay less than the agreed upon amount if the woman tried to leave earlier than agreed, or kept answering her cell phone, or performed unenthusiastically, or smelled bad, or for any of a thousand other reasons. In other parts of the world men paid what they had to and were grateful for what they got. Or, if not, were too embarrassed or intimidated to complain. But in the Hotel Grand a unique power play arose between monger and whore to determine into whose camp the risk of financial or sexual disappointment would fall.

In the elevator Carmen gave Tita Moon ten dollars to make up the difference, but her friend angrily pushed it away. Carmen offered another twenty, to make it the original offer of eighty.

"And what about my half of the lesbian?" Tita Moon asked sharply, taking the money.

Carmen slipped her another twenty. "I owe you five dollars," she said sheepishly.

"How could you?" Tita Moon asked. "After all the times you criticized me!"

The elevator door opened and Tita Moon stormed out without waiting for a reply. But Carmen did not want to go back to the bar. So she pressed the second floor and went up to the restaurant.

The Canopy Diner was most inaptly named, not only because of its less than lofty location on the second floor and its view not of the rain forest but of the line of taxis on the street below, but also because there were no plants or other decor to give one the impression of being in the jungle. Not that any of its patrons seemed to care. It was open twenty-four hours, had a six page menu featuring monger staples such as cheeseburgers, fish sandwiches, fries and pecan pie, and was staffed by attentive young waitresses whose mini-skirts appeared more whorish than those worn by the actual whores, who devoured club sandwiches while holding hands with their clients, or sat on their laps drinking milkshakes.

Carmen took a small table by the window and ordered coffee and a caesar salad. About a third of the tables were occupied by gringos, alone or in groups, with or without girls. Despite the sound of laughter and clattering plates, the restaurant was much more serene than the bar and, despite the strong coffee she was drinking, Carmen began to relax.

That is, until Ginger approached. She was wearing a strapless black dress as though she had just come from a ballroom and her long black hair fell in ringlets on her dark shoulders. She gave a cry of surprise when she saw Carmen, flashing her expensive teeth, and sat down without waiting to be invited.

Carmen had set her purse on the table and nearly knocked it to the floor in her anxiety. She felt as if Ginger could see right through the outer pouch, as if it were transparent.

"How was Enrico the other night?" Ginger asked, not having spoken to Carmen since hooking her up with her client.

"Nice," Carmen said, not knowing what to say.

Ginger pulled on a passing waitress's skirt and ordered a tenderloin steak and a glass of Chilean wine. "I hope you don't mind buying me dinner," she said to her cowering witness. "It's the least you can do, don't you think? You yourself would be starving without me."

"Well I'll have you know I already had a client tonight," Carmen replied weakly, trying to stand up for herself.

"Congratulations. Was he as sophisticated as my Enrico? How much did he pay? Why didn't he buy you dinner first?"

Carmen realized she could not answer these questions to her credit, so she changed the subject. "Is that a new dress? I see you got your hair done. Is it for the wedding?"

As she listened, or failed to listen, to Ginger describe her self-beautification crusade, she inwardly struggled with Laura's request. It would be easy enough not to turn the recorder on, to explain that it just wasn't possible to fool such a clever demon as Ginger beneath the fluorescent lights of the Canopy Diner. Or she could simply lie and say she hadn't seen Ginger. After all, honesty was not one of the first traits that came to mind when her friends thought of Carmen. But Laura was not a client or a prying relation, she was a good friend who deserved her assistance. And she also considered Porter, whom she only knew vaguely but whom she could imagine well enough, prey to the black widow crouching across from her.

When Ginger excused herself to go to the bathroom, Carmen felt she had no choice but to turn the recorder on. She didn't dare take it out from its pouch for fear Ginger would return. She hoped it would run silently, but she could hear it whirring, so she put it on the floor by her feet.

Ginger's steak arrived and Carmen let her eat for a minute in silence, not wanting to arouse her suspicion by appearing too eager to ask about her marriage. Finally she asked, as if just trying to make conversation, if she was looking forward to her wedding.

"Why not?" Ginger answered evasively.

"But do you love him?"

Ginger looked at her with raised eyebrows but said nothing.

"So you don't love him?"

Apparently Ginger thought the question too absurd to require a spoken response.

"So why are you marrying him, if you don't love him?"

Ginger was busy cutting the rest of her steak into tiny pieces. "You'll never guess."

"Money?"

"I have money now."

This was what Laura said.

"You want to live in the U.S.?"

"I want to live here."

"Well are you going to tell me the reason or not?" Carmen asked, growing flustered. The tape would not run forever and she realized that when it stopped it would probably make a loud click. So everything had to be settled by then. She had to get the answer and pay the check or excuse herself and turn the recorder off in the safety of the rest room.

Ginger set down her knife and learned forward. "I'm not Costa Rican!" she whispered softly, not out of fear or necessity, but dramatically, with a smile on her lips.

"You're not Costa Rican!" Carmen shouted.

"Why don't you tell the whole fucking world?" Ginger said, though her friend's indiscretion didn't seem to cause her alarm and her gaze remained fixed.

"I'm Nicaraguan," she whispered in a still softer voice, and immediately put a manicured finger to her lips.

Carmen stared in genuine surprise. She had only known Ginger for a couple years, and they had never socialized outside of work. But their profession involved such intimacy it often led Carmen to believe she knew her colleagues more completely than she knew her own family, who dressed behind closed doors.

"Many years ago when I came here I bought a fake identity card. But it's about to expire and the government is cracking down on illegals."

Carmen tried to show her shock or disapproval. Obviously Ginger trusted her and she did not want to give her the impression she might betray her confidence, even though she had. Poor Porter, she thought. Certainly he had a right to know the truth. But then again, if marriage was what he wanted, what difference did it make? People married for all sorts or reasons. Who was she to judge? In any case, it wasn't her business. She had fulfilled her mission.

The waitress came and she paid the check, but since Ginger lingered at the table to smoke a cigarette, Carmen excused herself and hurried to the bathroom.

A couple girls were primping by the mirror, so Carmen simply reached into the pouch and switched off the recorder. She wanted to play it back, but she didn't dare take it out in front of these other girls, whom she did not know. Besides, what if Ginger walked in?

Better to forget about it. Turning away from the girls, she transferred it from the outer pouch to the zippered pocket, where there was no chance of it falling out. Then Tita Moon walked in and diverted her attention from a probable witch wedding to a possible Moon child.

She held up the pregnancy kit in a trembling hand, her breath short.

"What are we waiting for?" Carmen asked, and they rushed into a stall together and shut the door.

Where else but in the ladies room of the Hotel Grand could two young women lock themselves in a stall and draw not even a look of interest from the other girls?

"I can't pee!" Tita Moon exclaimed, as the swinging door to the rest room opened and closed, and working girls came and went.

"Just relax," Carmen suggested.

"Can we watch?" a voice said from outside, and they heard laughter.

"Go fuck yourselves!" Tita Moon yelled.

"Too bad you didn't take that advice, new mama!" the voice said, and there was more laughter.

Carmen peeked out and gave them a menacing glare.

Tita Moon finally peed and they held up the strip. After a few minutes they read the result: "Pregnant."

"Oh my God."

Where else but in the ladies' room of the Hotel Grand could those three mournful words signify one thing and one thing only, understood at once by all those present, the way an adverse outcome on the operating table would have been understood by the nurses had that phrase been uttered by a surgeon? Yet it was not Death that played this trick of fate, but Life.

Carmen and Tita Moon went back to work, the way a surgeon would go back to work after a failed operation. But neither got another client that night, and at three o'clock Carmen drove her friend home in silence and tucked her in bed.

She had almost forgotten the recorder, but she took it out of her purse now and hesitated whether to leave it on the dining room table or wake Laura. She decided on the latter course and tapped lightly on Laura's door.

"It's me, Carmen."

Laura was accustomed to going to sleep at this hour, not waking up. But her friend's voice roused her with a sense of mission and she sat up with her legs crossed, feeling more alert than she looked.

She turned on the bedside lamp, turned the framed photo face down, and motioned Carmen to sit next to her.

"Tita is pregnant."

Laura rubbed her eyes. "She'll have to go to Mexico."

"She's going to have it. The baby I mean."

"But she already has one baby she can't take care of."

"I know. It doesn't make sense, but that's Tita."

"Poor thing."

And then the devil on Laura's shoulder whispered she would have to move out, she couldn't expect to have her baby here. True, she had failed to stipulate that in the agreement, unless it fell under the clause excluding overnight guests, but it was out of the question. She hadn't moved to Escazu to hear a baby crying every night. She was about to express her firm intention aloud, but then remembered Carmen was Tita Moon's best friend and it would seem ungenerous to speak about eviction at this moment.

So instead Laura took both of Carmen's hands in her own. "Where is she?"

"Sleeping."

Now the angel on her other shoulder rushed in breathlessly. "Well if there's anything she needs. Anything at all..."

"I'm sure. But I didn't come to tell you about that. Here," Carmen said, and handed over the recorder as if it were a smoking gun.

Laura instantly switched tracks from Tita Moon to Porter. "See, I told you you could do it! It wasn't hard, was it? What did she say?"

"Play the tape."

"I can't wait for the tape!" Laura said with mounting excitement. "Tell me."

"Guess."

"Porter has a terminal illness and she can only get the life insurance if she's his wife?"

"Nope."

"She has a secret child and wants Porter to adopt him?"

"No. You'll never guess."

"Well if I'll never guess quit telling me to guess!" Laura shouted irritably, scrunching her tousled hair behind her head.

"She's a Nica!" Carmen said with the sense of pleasure that comes from divulging secret information to the person who most wants to hear it.

Laura bounced on the bed. "I knew it! I knew she wasn't Costa Rican!" she exclaimed, although she had never actually suspected this. "I knew such a witch had to be a foreigner." And her mind began creating false trails of suspicion that led back to the time they had first met.

"She doesn't want a Green Card. She wants our card! Her fake national identity card is expiring. But if she marries a gringo everyone will be thinking about the paperwork for U.S. immigration. No one will worry if she doesn't have all the documents to renew her ID here."

"The witch! The clever witch! I knew it had to be something like this!" she exclaimed, although she hadn't suspected anything of the sort. "But we've got her ass nailed to the wall! We'll not only stop the wedding. We'll get her Nica ass deported!"

And she rewound the tape and pressed "play."

"We were in the diner," Carmen commented, as she and Laura listened to the sounds of clattering silverware.

Laura listened to the beginning of their conversation, then fast forwarded it at Carmen's urging.

"Well are you going to tell me the reason or not?" they both listened to Carmen say.

They pressed their ears to the recorder. But there was only silence.

Then Carmen's voice again. "You're not Costa Rican!"

"I can't hear anything," Laura said.

Carmen backed away. She should have listened to the tape herself before showing it to Laura. She had failed as a spy.

"Ginger was whispering," Carmen explained. "And my purse was on the floor."

"You idiot! Why didn't you move your purse closer? What was it doing on the floor?"

"I got the reason out of her, that's what you wanted."

"I wanted it in her own voice. I told you, Porter won't believe anything I say. He's under a spell."

Laura threw the recorder down in disgust. "You woke me up for this?"

Carmen walked out to her car in tears. Laura despised her because she had put her purse on the floor instead of on the table. Tita Moon was pregnant and in a few weeks would have to stop working. Carmen realized with a sense of foreboding that soon her only friend left at the hotel would be a Nicaraguan witch.

CHAPTER 9

VALE OF TEARS

The following evening Raquel went to the university early, before her own classes, on her covert mission to photograph Professor Martin. It was easy enough to find his course listing online, and she waited at the end of the corridor outside his classroom, camera in hand, hoping he would come out.

She dreaded this task no less than Carmen had dreaded hers, but what could she do? Laura wasn't just her friend, she was her landlord. And a beneficent landlord at that.

Raquel tried to calm herself by reading the notices on the bulletin board. She had told herself this was an easy job, with no risk, even if she was discovered. But how did she know the professor didn't have a violent temper? What if he complained to the administration? And what of the ramifications for Laura? What if he stopped dating her mother on account of her snooping? She would be breaking up a perfectly happy couple.

These were the thoughts running through her mind when the door opened and a loud stream of students emerged into the hallway. Raquel checked one last time that the zoom was pushed forward and the flash off. She stood facing the bulletin board, looking over her shoulder.

When the professor appeared there were still enough students between them that she felt getting a clear shot posed a greater challenge than remaining unobserved. She raised the camera, framed it quickly, and pressed the shutter. She quickly checked the viewfinder, only to see a blur of heads.

She tried again. Better, but still too distant. When she looked up from the viewfinder, ready to snap again, the professor was standing ominously before her.

"What are you doing?"

Raquel backed into the bulletin board. "I was just photographing the building for a class project," she stammered.

"You were photographing me."

"I was trying to get a group of students in the hallway..." And her voice trailed off as she noticed the look of recognition in the professor's eyes.

"Do I know you?"

He scratched his chin, scrutinizing her unabashedly. "You're not in my class, but I swear I've seen you."

"Maybe on campus."

"You're the room mate!"

Raquel decided to face him, knowing she could no longer hide. "I'm not actually her room mate. I'm her tenant."

"Why are you taking my picture? She put you up to this!" Now he leaned against the bulletin board, folded his arms and laughed. "She's being a mother to her mother. What does she think, I'm a child molester?" And he laughed again.

"Nothing that bad. She thinks you might be a monger."

"What's a monger? A fish monger? A...a whoremonger!"

"She wants a picture she can show around the Hotel Grand, to see if you were a patron," Raquel explained, forgetting that reticence was a critical quality for a successful spy. "I didn't want to do it. I'm sorry. I hope you won't tell her mother. They fight enough as it is."

The professor straightened up. "Well you better take my picture then."

"Really?"

"The girls at the Hotel Grand are too expensive for a professor's salary. I only visit the local bordellos."

And this time Raquel laughed with him. Who but an innocent professor would use a term like "bordello" in a country where there were only independent working girls, strip clubs and massage parlors?

Raquel turned on the flash this time and took his photo with a sense of relief. "I hope you'll still let me take your class," she said.

Raquel had not laughed often lately, but at least she wasn't crying as much, either. She'd been out of work for two weeks, but although her desperation was growing, so was her resolve. Her bank account was empty, her credit card was maxed out, she had to give up her cell phone, and her boyfriend no longer called her since she could not pay for their dates. She had asked her parents for money, but they were used to receiving help from her. Her father had given her twenty dollars last week, but she couldn't expect any more from them. As for jobs, she had been looking every day without success. One of her cousins knew a restaurant that needed a waitress, but it was too far away and the hours conflicted with school. Another restaurant, in town, had offered her a job, only to call back to say they didn't need her after all. She had grown so desperate she was now willing to consider sodas or third shift at convenience stores, anything at all. Well, almost anything. A massage parlor had an opening for a receptionist who spoke English, but the place had been raided by the police last month and the pay wasn't even what she had been making at the travel desk. Reluctantly, she said no.

But as it was getting harder to say no, her inner strength was growing. She had ample confidence in herself and had triumphed over the self-pity that had initially taken hold of her. This is only a temporary setback, she assured herself. Look at Laura and her friends, they do all right. I'm as smart as they are, or smarter. I'm as strong and resourceful.

As she drove home after class these thoughts were supported by her success in taking the professor's photo. True, she hadn't been as indiscreet as desired, but Laura didn't have to know that the favor would square her with her landlord, or maybe even put Laura in her debt. Enough for a free meal or two.

Raquel chastised herself for such thoughts. You're becoming like a wild dog, she thought. Keeping such accounts was beneath her, and ungenerous to Laura, who would undoubtedly invite her to meals under any circumstances.

But what she needed more than food was gasoline. The needle was on empty. She had never let it get this low in the past and was thinking she would have to put in a thousand colones first thing in the morning when the engine began to sputter. She barely had time to pull to the curb before it gave out completely.

"Fucking car!" she shouted, slamming the steering wheel with her fist. "You're only on *E*. Where's your reserve! You're supposed to have eight liters left! What am I supposed to do now?"

She felt completely stranded. She was miles from Escazu, without even a fifty colones coin in her purse. And she no longer had her cell phone.

The tears returned, but she wiped them away with anger at the world of machines for being so unkind to her. First the camera had given her away, now her faithless car. Use your brain, she told herself. It's all you have left.

The neighborhood was dark, but not unfamiliar. The Hotel Grand was a few blocks away. Her nemesis, Mr. Escudero, would have gone home by now, and if Clarissa was working the front desk she could borrow a thousand colones from her.

She reapplied her eye shadow in the rear view mirror and brushed her hair, not wanting her old colleagues to think she had fallen on hard times.

As she walked to the hotel a beggar approached and she realized with a twinge of self-pity that she was more destitute than he. For a moment she toyed with the idea of offering to sell him something from her purse, or the purse itself, but she hadn't sunk that low yet and moved on.

Her friend wasn't working at reception, so she continued past the puta registration to the Red Volcano, where she knew some of the barmaids.

The place was already packed, and before she could squeeze her way to the bar a hand grabbed her arm. A woman's hand.

"Hola!" Tita Moon shouted over the commotion. "I thought you quit?"

"I did. But my car ran out of gas and I came in here to see if I could borrow a thousand colones to get me home."

"Carmen's here somewhere. I'm sure she'd take you home. Or you can wait and come with me if I don't get taken for the night."

"Thanks. That's sweet, but I'm illegally parked and the last thing I need is a ticket. I thought I'd get a taxi to take me to a gas station and buy a couple liters."

Tita Moon reached into her purse and pulled out one of the ten dollar bills from the night before.

"Is this enough?"

Raquel almost refused the money, but she realized she was in no position to refuse money, even from a working girl. And why did it matter if it came from a reception clerk or a barmaid or a prostitute? But Raquel hardly knew Tita Moon. They lived in adjoining rooms but their schedules had kept them apart and Raquel did not consider her a friend. Until now.

"I don't know what to say," she said, brushing away tears. "I'll pay you back tomorrow, I promise."

Tita Moon hadn't given it to her as a loan. "Whatever."

Raquel hugged her goodbye and turned to go. As she maneuvered back through the crowd a tall gringo made eye contact with her.

"What's your name, honey?"

Raquel looked at him for a long moment, but not really seeing him at all. Rather seeing herself as he saw her. Then she shrugged and moved on.

Not much later Tita Moon spotted Rick, fresh—or not so fresh—from his outdoor adventures. He had not shaved for several days, his clothes hung loosely as if they had been pulled a thousand different ways and his face and arms were sunburned. He hadn't even gone up to his room, for he wore his backpack, which made it almost impossible for him to maneuver through the crowd.

He can't wait to see me, Tita Moon thought, feeling a pang of guilt for not having thought about him these last two weeks. But with her move to Laura's and her pregnancy, she might be forgiven this oversight. She hoped the time had passed for him less dramatically, and that he had found the tranquility he had been looking for.

But what if he hadn't been thinking of me, either? she suddenly wondered. What if he was squeezing through the working girls not because he couldn't wait to see her but simply out of curiosity, or to get from one end to the other? What if he chose another girl?

Tita Moon decided to take no chances and descended on him like a lava flow. She nearly knocked him over with her hugs, and it was all he could do to hang on to his camera case.

"Remember me?" she asked, with a grope down below.

"I never had a welcome like this!" he exclaimed.

"Do you want a drink? Or do you want to eat my pussy first?"

Images of Red Volcanoes flashed before his eyes and he took Tita Moon's hand and led her to the puta registration.

"Do you like when I talk dirty to you, or do you want me to be natural?" she asked in the freight elevator.

"What is natural for you?"

"I am shy."

"I don't believe it," he said with a smile, and put his hand between her legs. Then he noticed the security camera.

"We better behave in here."

"No they like it. Why do you think they work that job?"

It occurred to him that it might in fact be possible to have sex in the freight elevator. What wasn't possible in this place? Elevator sex had never been a fantasy of his, but where else would he have this opportunity? However, before he could decide anything the doors opened and Tita Moon pulled him out.

They entered the room together, as if it were *their* room.

"I need to get cleaned up," he said, setting his camera case in the closet and taking his toiletry bag from his backpack. "I'm surprised you can stand to be near me."

But all of Tita Moon's senses found him agreeable. "I'll give you a bath with my tongue!" she proposed.

He was going to take a shower, but she ran the bath and poured in a generous amount of shampoo. She lay in the tub next to him and kissed him gently but didn't touch his cock at all, preferring to take it slowly this time.

She realized she was really glad to see him. Perhaps too glad. She recalled Carmen's advice from two weeks ago, after their first encounter, and tried to calculate how much money she might have made if she had asked him to take her to the forest.

"When do you go home?" she wondered, determined not to make that mistake again.

But he told her he was leaving in the morning.

"Oh. Then maybe you want me all night?"

She was prepared for negotiations, but he simply kissed her and said nothing more.

"It's three hundred dollars," she informed him, although she would have accepted two.

"Do you want it now?"

She felt bad for having mentioned the money and wondered if he thought worse of her for it. Then she wondered why she cared what he thought. "It can wait," she said in a sweeter voice.

"It's good to be back," he told her. "I was afraid I wouldn't see you again."

"Did you get lost in the jungle?"

"Yes and no. Did I escape from civilization? Yes. Did I forget about my marriage? More than I ever thought. Did I forget about women...?"

"You didn't forget about me?"

"I felt you at my side every moment."

"Then I should charge you for it!"

He had made such a heartfelt admission, and she had been genuinely touched by it. She didn't know why she replied with such a crass remark. It just came out.

She bit her lip in disgust, but he merely laughed, so she let herself laugh with him. He must really love me, she thought.

She dried him off and led him to the bed, but still they didn't have sex. There was no hurry. She was there for the night, and he was glad to relax from his bumpy four-hour taxi ride from Quepos.

"Can I watch TV?" she asked, grabbing the remote.

It was time for "Vale of Tears." Cynthia was being wheeled into the operating room for her lung transplant.

"What did you do in the jungle?" she asked, lying on his shoulder, only her head peeking out from under the covers. "Did you have a lot of adventures?"

"I took the canopy tour. And a couple guided hikes. But I wasn't really interested in activities, or being around people. So I spent most of the time on my own."

"With me at your side."

"We have a saying, 'You can't see the forest for the trees.' It means you can't see the big picture—what's really important—because you're focusing on the details. Well, I went to the forest and I didn't see the trees."

This metaphor was lost on Tita Moon, but she smiled agreeably because she sensed it had something to do with her.

A parallel suddenly struck him, with the jungle called the Hotel Grand. Everyone came here and saw only the whores, dense as trees. But he had come back and seen only her.

He decided not to share this revelation. She might not understand it. She might understand it too well. So instead he talked about sleeping in bungalows without electricity, walking on the deserted beach at dawn, watching the slow progress of a sloth on a treetop, trying to follow the whirl of a hummingbird's wings. Yet he had stayed away too long. As he stroked her hair he wondered why he had left at all. All these days and nights he could have been holding her.

"I won't ask you what you did while I was away," he then said, as a corrective for allowing himself to lapse into romantic fantasy.

"I thought of you," she lied.

He hadn't expected this response and felt both touched and suspicious." Did you really?"

"I wondered if you would come back."

"Then you're glad to see me?"

He cursed himself for asking such a naive question. He was a client, after all, he represented money to her. Easier money than most, he imagined.

"After I watch Cynthia's operation you will find out how glad I am," she promised.

He let her watch her show in silence, but when it paused for commercial he decided to ask her about her son. She had told him last time she had a child, but had only mentioned it in passing, and he had been wondering about her home life while he was away. During the long nights alone he couldn't help fantasizing about taking her away from this life and living together with her, either in Costa Rica or Baltimore. He didn't mind that she had a young son, but what if she was still married to the father? Anything was possible with these women.

Tita Moon didn't want to tell him too much, specifically that her son lived with her parents. So for an answer she simply took a small picture out of her purse of a cherubic boy with large dark eyes.

"His name is Roberto," she said. "He's three."

"He has your eyes," Rick observed. "And the father?"

"There is no father."

"So you aren't married?"

"I was never married," she confessed.

"I see," he said diplomatically, and asked nothing more.

Tita Moon looked at the photo herself for a moment before replacing it in her purse.

The habit among tica working girls to show photos of their children to their clients was a rare, if not unique, custom in the world of prostitution. Often the girls at the Hotel Grand showed photos of their children without even being asked, almost as part of their own introductions. A hand shake. "My name is Vanessa." Then, flashing a birthday photo, "And this is my son."

"He's very handsome," the client would say. But what could he say? He had come to Costa Rica to escape from his wife and family, and now intruding on his fantasy of a young available woman was her child, mute witness to their dual adultery. But a few men, like Rick, were touched by these photos. These were men who longed for more than a fleeting illusion, who craved authenticity. And being shown a photo was like being invited into her home. It shattered the glass curtain that normally separated prostitutes from their clients, as if to say, "I only have a broken family, but this is who we are."

"I almost forgot!" Rick then said, and opened his backpack. "I had our photos printed while I was gone."

And he laid them out on the table and studied Tita Moon while she picked up each in turn and looked at it carefully.

"Can I have some?" she asked, obviously pleased by how they turned out.

"You can have them all. I made doubles."

She hugged him, carefully put the photos in her purse, and went into the bathroom and closed the door.

What she did next would afterwards surprise even her, although she would try to put it out of her mind. But at the time she had a perfectly good reason for her action according to her own special brand of logic. Actually there were several reasons, swirling together, several devils on her shoulder telling her to put a hole in the condom, and no angel pleading restraint.

She ran the water in the sink and, opening a safety pin, poked a hole in a condom while it was still in the package. When she emerged she turned the lights off but made a show of opening the condom and then put it on him in her usual style, rolling it down with her mouth, so there was no way he could have seen the tiny hole in the tip. As she began to suck him she used her free hand to surreptitiously stash the telltale wrapper in her purse.

Not that Rick would have noticed in any case. He was back in the jungle, but this time with her. Making love on the beach at dawn or lying together on the cool forest floor, dry despite the rain tapping against the leaves far above. He didn't mind that she had a child, not at all. It was a family ready-made, without the usual North American complications of ex-husbands and custody battles. She needed somebody, that was clear. And the child was still young enough to become his own.

"Do you want me on top?" Tita Moon asked.

Rick was tired, and dreaming, so he gladly let her take control. But Tita Moon was not tired at all and transferred all her frustration, disappointment and fear like an electrical charge through her body into his, and even on through the bed and the floor, deep into the bowels of the Hotel Grand, where it grounded like a lightning bolt in the indifferent earth.

This time Rick didn't have to ask if she came because her juices rained all over him, like the shower after a lightning burst. But he had no time to bask in the afterglow of his own orgasm because she immediately shot up and cried, "Fuck, the condom broke!"

She made a show of holding out the damaged prophylactic as evidence, like a catcher showing the ball in his glove after a collision at the plate, and then ran into the bathroom to wash.

Why? Why? Why had she done this? She would never tell anyone, ever. Not even Carmen. Especially Carmen, although Carmen had planted the seed for her treacherous decision. As she threw the damned thing in the toilet and jumped in the shower she could hear her friend's sharp words from two weeks ago, after her first encounter with Rick: "You are a disgrace to prostitutes!" And Carmen's disappointment that she had not shaken down the Chinese guy, had let him get away like a sailfish on the line, as a result of which she had to suck Colorado Bob for the morning-after pill, and then to throw it away, not even to give it to Carmen or sell it, and the positive pregnancy test, how much money she had lost or not extorted, and at the end of the day to be pregnant just the same!

She saw herself as an actress with a second chance to get her lines right after forgetting them on the first take. A better performance would not change the result of the pregnancy test, that was true, but it would erase the bitter memory of that scoundrel from Vancouver, wherever that was, watching an action movie and telling her not to worry, he'd had a vasectomy. And it might put a couple hundred dollars in her pocket, money she would be glad to have in a couple months when she was no longer able to work.

But there was another reason that urged her to action, that related specifically to Rick. He was a decent guy, but it was precisely because he appeared so nice that she made this preemptive strike against future disappointment. For while she had been too preoccupied these past two weeks to think about him, she now found herself thinking about him too much. It might be forgivable for a client to forget he was with a prostitute, but not for a prostitute to forget she was with a client. Yet in the bathtub she had sunk a little too deeply into his arms, and when he had spread out the photos on the table, the picture she most wanted to keep was not a close-up of her face but the photo they had taken together.

So puncturing the condom had literally been a stab at revising history, as well as an acid test for the virtue of men. She might hate herself a little, but she would feel less victimized. And if Rick, beneath his soft skin, was no less an asshole than the Chinese guy, or the father of her first baby, or the steroid freaks who had shortchanged them the night before, then it was best to know now, before she put his picture on her wall.

When she had finished her shower, Rick took his. But they did not touch as they passed each other and did not exchange words.

"You're still here," Rick said, toweling himself off, somewhat surprised to find her lying under the covers. Then he remembered he hadn't paid her. He took three hundred dollar bills from his wallet and handed them to her.

She put them in her purse.

"You aren't going to count it?" he asked, recalling that last time she had held the bills up to the light.

He moved closer and took her hand. She was standing naked beside the bed, her face blank, avoiding his eyes.

He found it ironic that after all his efforts with his ex-wife to have a child, their consultations with doctors and visits to fertility clinics, that he was suddenly confronted here, in this place, with the possibility of becoming a father, with a woman he hardly knew.

"What do we do now?" he asked.

Tita Moon shrugged. "I don't know. We could watch TV. Or if you're hungry—"

"I mean about this," Rick clarified, running a finger across her flat stomach.

Tita Moon wasn't feeling very good at the moment, but she knew she couldn't let this opportunity pass. She looked at him closely and spoke her lines like a veteran actress on "Vale of Tears."

"It's been two weeks since my last period, so this is the worst time. My gynecologist says I am a baby factory."

Rick let this information sink in. "You don't take birth control pills?"

"An abortion costs five hundred dollars."

Rick's efforts with his wife had been to conceive a child, not prevent one. He didn't know about the morning-after pill. Not that he was in any condition to think clearly now. His head was spinning and he just wanted to put this behind them, to make everything right.

"I don't have five hundred dollars with me."

"Whatever."

"I'll have to go to the ATM."

Tita Moon watched him with her mouth hanging open as he dressed and hurried out the door. Fifteen minutes later he returned and handed her five hundred dollars.

She stared at him with wide eyes, resisting the urge to hug him, to smile.

For his part he knew he was being rash. What if she wasn't pregnant? Shouldn't he wait and send her the money? But he wanted to put it behind him, and to reassure her. He knew most men lied in these situations and if he promised to send money if the pregnancy test was positive she would not believe him.

"Do you want to get something to eat?" she said.

"You mean you're staying?"

They ordered room service and ate in silence while watching a horror movie on TV, but they sat close to each other and exchanged smiles when their eyes met.

Later, holding her in bed, he said he was sorry.

Tita Moon nearly said it wasn't his fault. But she couldn't say that, could she? Five hundred dollars. She would not blow it on drugs or clothes. She would put it in the bank or give it to Laura against her future rent. She could relax, just a little.

As Rick was drifting off to sleep he thought he heard her say, "I wouldn't mind to have your baby."

In the morning he wondered if it had been a dream. But he hadn't the courage to ask.

She offered to ride with him to the airport. He told her he didn't want to go. That he would stay if he could, but he needed to get back to the shop. He hoped she would be all right.

She couldn't give him Laura's address because she didn't know it. Strangely, there were no addresses in Costa Rica. Letters were addressed in the form of: Reunion Street, third house on the left, one hundred meters east of the church, San Pedro. Some residents had post office boxes, but not Tita Moon. So she gave him her cell phone number and e-mail and told him she hoped he would come back soon.

"As soon as I can," he promised. "Maybe next time I can meet your son."

He still didn't know she wasn't raising her son herself but had pawned him off on her mother. But there was time to sort that through. If he ever came back. Maybe he would reconcile with his wife, or meet a female photographer. Any of a thousand incidents could prevent them from ever meeting again. And, despite their heartfelt pledges and optimistic smiles, they both knew this.

Has there ever been a scene, even on "Vale of Tears," to compare in its dramatic improbability with the almost daily phenomenon of a prostitute and her client standing beside an open taxi door on the sunlit curb of Juan Santamaria International Airport, their hearts pounding plaintively, their clouded eyes staring desperately, one moment longer, each into the other's?

CHAPTER 10

OH MY GOD, IT'S JAIME PRIMERO!

Two nights later Laura entered the Hotel Grand, armed with Dennis's camera. She didn't feel embarrassed, as she had her last visit here, because this time she was on a mission of filial duty, to vet her mother's boyfriend. So she didn't feel like a working girl, she felt like a daughter, and she expected everyone to view her that way as well, despite the fact that she was wearing a tightfitting white t-shirt with a heart outlined in red glitter, a pleated mini-skirt, and red stilettos. What am I supposed to wear? she would have said to anyone who challenged the intentions of her ensemble? All my clothes are sexy, and my jeans are in the wash. Dennis had learned this the hard way, of course, and her efforts to dress in a business-like manner only exacerbated his lust.

"I can wear stockings if you want," she had offered that first week.

"Not stockings!" he protested, having a weakness for nylon. Fortunately for him Laura, like most young ticas, wore skirts without panty hose.

She didn't see anyone she knew at reception and circled through the casino. The casino where her mother believed she was employed. But then she realized security might not appreciate her operating a camera at their tables.

Security! She went back to the security guard at the entrance. She knew him by sight only, but he didn't scowl at the girls when he checked their ID's, so that was a good sign.

"Excuse me," she said, turning on the camera. "Can you tell me if you have ever seen this man here?" And she held up the image of the professor on the LCD screen.

"Is he your boyfriend?"

"Don't be silly. My mother is going out with him and I want to make sure he is not a player."

"I only look at the chicas," the security guard said with a grin, as if he was a player himself.

"I'm sure you do. But come on, you haven't even looked. I'm sure if he was a regular you would recognize him."

The security guard took the camera and looked at the photo for several seconds. "Sorry. I don't know him. Why don't you ask Manuel?"

"You should be sorry if you did recognize him. Thanks."

She went to the puta registration and showed the camera to Manuel, whom she did know.

"An Italian guy, right?"

"Does he look Italian? He's a gringo."

"You want me to check the records?"

"Could you do that?"

He typed the professor's name into the computer and scrolled through several screens. "No, he hasn't stayed here, at least in the last year. That's as far back as these records go."

Laura gave him a tip in gratitude for his unexpected help. But this only meant the professor hadn't stayed at the hotel. But why should he, when he lived in San Jose? It was more likely he would have taken girls back to his apartment.

The bar was crowded, but Colorado Bob's stool was empty, and she didn't see any of the other regulars of her acquaintance. Nor did she see Tita Moon. But Carmen was standing patiently in her usual spot facing the front tables, her hands crossed over her pierced navel.

Laura nodded hello but went to the bar to show the photo to the barmaids. None of them recognized him. She also held the camera out to a couple of the working girls she knew. They shrugged and walked away.

She felt a weight had been lifted from her shoulder, a granite devil of suspicion. This wasn't definitive proof, of course, but she also had the supportive opinion of Raquel, who told her that based on her chat with him at the party and her furtive surveillance at the university she was certain he had nothing to hide. And Raquel was a psychology major. That counted for something.

She put away the camera and walked over to Carmen.

"You haven't seen Ginger?"

Carmen shook her head. "Not since the other night."

"I wanted to bring Porter up here, just in case. So he could see with his own eyes. But he won't come."

"Maybe he knows and doesn't want to see her here."

"No, I think he's in denial. I told him about the identity card, that Ginger's Nicaraguan. He thinks I'm the one whose lying! He thinks I'm so desperate to stop the wedding that I would tell him a lie."

"Well you are desperate."

"If only you had been a better spy!"

"Maybe it's his destiny," Carmen mused philosophically. "Maybe you're right. Maybe I should just let him get married," Laura said, as though she were Porter's mother.

"What does his horoscope say?"

"I don't know. That's a good idea. I'll read it tomorrow. What?"

Laura was puzzled because her friend's face had suddenly frozen in astonishment, looking past her.

Carmen learned close and whispered, "Oh my God, it's Jaime Primero!"

Now the Hotel Grand was a place where every gringo was treated like a matinee idol, where bald accountants and badly dressed contractors had to literally push their way through a gauntlet of young women on their way to the bar and couldn't sit in one of the lobby's wicker chairs for ten minutes without some salacious Latina with tits out to here sliding her fingernails down his arm. So what exactly happened when a real matinee idol crossed its threshold?

An expectant hush fell upon the Red Volcano. Conversations ceased. The merengue music issuing from the ceiling speakers filled the void. Clinking glasses could be heard at the bar, a sound never audible at this hour.

The gringos didn't know what was happening, only that their companions, who had been showering them with attention only a moment before, were no longer listening to their fish stories and ex-wife litanies, and had turned their eyes in unison to the door.

Laura too turned around. The first thing she saw was the security guard for the street entrance, holding his magnetic wand uncertainly in the air. And before him an enormous Mexican in a black trench coat waving him away, creating space for a smaller, but similarly dressed man, and behind him...

Laura's stilettos weren't high enough. She craned her neck to see the sublime figure behind the bodyguards. And there he was, only a few steps away, a miracle of leather and gold and pomade, capped teeth and Acapulco sunlight, Jaime Primero.

She almost lost her balance and fell over the ledge onto the table below. But the bodyguards parted and she no longer had to maneuver for a glimpse. In fact she could have sworn he was looking straight at her. Her face froze. She didn't know whether she was smiling or gasping, but she thought she must look like a clown. Of course, it was impossible to know the exact object of his gaze since he wore thick gold-rimmed sunglasses. But at least she had a direct view for a moment or two. The bar was too dark for bright reflections, but she could have sworn he gleamed from all the gold, from his sunglasses and gold earrings to a thick gold crucifix he wore outside his black silk shirt, to his gold belt buckle—and she dared not look lower.

But then the moment passed and he stepped forward, not toward her, but down along the bar, and of course now she had to look at his ass, and her eyes filled with wonder and she thought, this is what it must be like when men see a sexy woman's ass as she walks past. There is simply nothing else the eyes can do but follow its swagger.

"He looks just like in his music videos!" Carmen whispered breathlessly.

"Better," Laura replied. "He looks like he did in *Midnight Deception,* when he walked into that bar to find the man who murdered his wife."

Leaving his bodyguards behind, Jaime Primero slowly, deliberately walked the length of the bar, turned around and walked back.

And how did the girls of the Hotel Grand react to his approach? As much as they wanted to throw themselves at him, they could not, and it wasn't the gold crucifix that warded them off. They were terrified of this collusion of sensuality and fame. They were sexy women used to flattery and attention, yet here was a man who outshone them all. They were fearful of his disapproval, a step back, a frown, a caustic smile. So they stood like wallflowers, perhaps for the first time in their life. Certainly it was the first time in the history of the Hotel Grand that a man walked from one end of the Red Volcano to the other on a busy night without so much as brushing a woman's shoulder or hand or breast.

He returned to the front and sat at a table by the door, where he could see everything yet make a quick escape if necessary. Not long ago, in Mexico, he had been involved in an altercation with a mariachi singer.

His bodyguards sat on either side of him and signaled for a drink. Three barmaids competed to reach the table first, but Gloria, who had played basketball in high school, took advantage of her longer stride to win the race. She strode back to the bar with their order and filled it herself, pulling the draft beer handle with a suffocating grasp, as if it were the singer's virility itself.

"He's going to take someone!" Carmen whispered even lower than before, bending to Laura's ear but keeping her eyes on the star, unconsciously fingering a curl in her hair. "Maybe he will take me!"

"Don't be silly," Laura shot back, also still staring at the singer, who was now drinking his beer. "He isn't even looking at anyone."

"Then why did he come here?" Carmen demanded. "Why does any man come here?"

"First, he's not any man. Jaime Primero does not need a working girl. Second, he probably came because the hotel is famous and he was curious to see it."

"Then why did he walk up and down?"

"I told you. He's just curious. Maybe he was looking for the bathroom."

Now that he had settled in, conversations resumed, although in more respectful tones, as if the wearer of the gold crucifix were a bishop and not a sex symbol. Many of the women were now explaining to their companions who this special visitor was, perhaps using the opportunity to persuade them to buy tickets for tomorrow's concert. Few of the girls had tickets, as the show had sold out almost immediately. But they were available at a premium from brokers.

"Poor Tita," Carmen said. "Of all the times to be upstairs."

"Tita doesn't even like his music," Laura said. "She only listens to reggae and heavy metal." Laura didn't know why she suddenly felt competitive, but she began arguing with Carmen over which of them was the greater fan, naming albums, movies, soap operas, even commercials he had starred in.

"When Delerio soap came out I bought it because he was in the advertisement," Laura admitted shamelessly.

"I don't remember seeing his CDs in your collection," Carmen retaliated.

"I have them all, but I lent them to my mother."

"Please!"

Primero had a reputation as a hard drinker and he finished his beer before the girls had finished their accounting. They saw him whisper to the enormous bodyguard, who pushed himself to his feet.

The crowd did not part as readily for the singer's giant shadow, and he had to pause a moment of two before reaching Laura. He was standing below the platform, but he met her eyes. If he said something, she didn't hear. All she knew was that she was following him back to the table, like an audience member at a game show invited to spin the big wheel.

Actually, Jaime Primero was no longer sitting at the table. The table was empty. The bodyguard led her outside, where a black Hummer was parked on the curb. He opened the door and helped lift her inside. The last thing she wanted was to appear clumsy, but stilettos had not been designed with Costa Rican curbs or Hummers in mind and, despite the bodyguard's assistance, she stumbled from one to the other.

Fortunately Jaime Primero did not see this because he was sitting in front. The smaller bodyguard was driving. The bigger bodyguard sat beside her, almost making the back seat feel small.

For a moment she wondered if she had been selected not for the star, but for his bodyguard. But stars aren't known for accompanying bodyguards on such missions. But why was he sitting in front? Laura decided that acting unpredictably was one of the benefits of being a star.

In any case the sound system was playing too loudly for her to offer her greetings or ask where she was being taken. Dance music. A minute later she smelled smoke and he casually handed the joint back to her.

She took it, she had to take it, but didn't even get the pleasure of touching his hand in return for her politeness. She pretended to take a drag and passed it to the bodyguard, wondering if cocaine would be next. Clients were always asking her to get high with them, and she always said no. But how would she say no to Jaime Primero?

The Hummer pulled up to the entrance of the Grand Riviera Resort and two liveried doormen ushered them inside. The singer walked ahead and Laura followed him down the long corridor filled with autographed photographs of heads of state and movie stars. This wasn't unfamiliar territory to her. She had been here many times over the years with clients, but never anyone famous.

He noticed she was lingering over the photos and stopped, turning to speak to her for the first time.

"Have you not been here before?"

She was so intent in her search she forgot to look at him. "I have been here many times. I was looking for your picture."

He seemed pleased by this and smiled. "Well this is my first time. I'll have to give them one, of course."

And he stepped back and took her hand, as naturally as she took the hands of men whose hearts throbbed for her. He probably didn't even know he had taken it. He probably didn't even feel anything. But she felt a tightness in her throat and focused on the photograph of a media tycoon to calm her nerves.

"Where do you think they should hang it?" he asked her.

"Not with the politicians and business leaders," Laura said assuredly, walking along the corridor. "Here, beside this princess." And she pointed to a young, radiant member of some European court.

"You think I'm royalty?" he asked, laughing.

Now, finally, she looked at him. "We all do. I mean, in Costa Rica. I think it's terrible the way the press treats you in Mexico. That story about the mariachi singer for instance..."

"It's not just Mexico, it's everywhere," he added, leading her on, but still holding her hand.

"Not in Costa Rica," she said proudly. "You should spend more time here, you will see."

"We may shoot my next movie here, who knows? Are you coming to the concert?"

"I couldn't get tickets."

"Then I'll have to give you some."

He opened the door to his suite and let her go in first, suddenly acting the part of the gracious host. The bodyguards disappeared through the connecting door and she found herself alone with him.

Before she could even look around he had pressed his lips to hers. She could taste the marijuana smoke on his tongue and smell the beer on his breath but that didn't matter at all, as it did with other men. She closed her eyes and let him explore her.

But a moment later he turned on a table lamp and went into the bathroom. "Help yourself to the bar," he said, closing the door.

She heard the sound of running water and went over to the bar, a real bar, not a minibar. The smoke had made her throat dry and she was going to drink water. But then she saw an open bottle of German white wine and thought, why not?

It was soothingly quiet, after the excitement at the Red Volcano and the blaring dance music in the Hummer. She set her purse on the glass coffee table and sat down to wait for him in one of the leather chairs.

The room was very clean, the bed made, the closet doors shut, no suitcases or personal items lying in view. Maybe he had just checked in today. Or maybe he just slept here, and used the adjoining room to store his clothes and belongings. Laura would have liked some evidence of his personal life, some clues to the real Jaime Primero. She would have to settle for the bathroom, where she could discover if he actually used Delerio soap himself, and maybe steal his toothbrush as a souvenir.

He emerged wrapped in a towel, his face washed but every hair still held rigidly in place with pomade. It occurred to Laura with the force of a shock that this was the mirror image of a scene she had acted out countless times during her career. How many clients had sat expectantly on the edge of a chair or the bed, uncertainly, still clothed, while she emerged from the bathroom wearing only a towel?

Perhaps this reminder of her past, as well as a sudden urge to stop drooling like a teeny-bopper and behave like the sophisticated, intelligent woman she was, inspired her to stand and ask, in a steady voice, if he could pay her first.

"In the morning," he replied, walking toward her.

"Does that mean you want me all night?"

He put his arms around her gently, and seductively whispered in her ear, "I want you forever, my Laura!"

My Laura? How did he know her name? Had the bodyguard told him? Had the bodyguard asked her name when he signaled to her in the bar? She couldn't remember. But the sound of her own name sung from the lips of Jaime Primero directly into the folds of her ear was almost too much. Had he asked her at that moment to pay *him,* she would have agreed to any amount.

But he left her to drink a shot of tequila at the bar and she regained her strength. "Then it's three hundred dollars, and it's my policy always to get paid in advance," she asserted.

The singer turned on the stereo, soft love songs this time, and disappeared into the adjoining room. He returned with about fifty dollars' worth of Mexican pesos in crumpled notes. From anyone else she would have been offended and walked out, but she couldn't walk out, could she?

"You'll get the rest in the morning," he said, as if the balance had nothing to do with him and might fall from the sky for all he knew.

What kind of operation was this? Laura wondered. But then she recalled reading magazine articles about the rich and famous, that they were insulated by their handlers from the realities of life, like having to go to the post office or do laundry or carry money. Besides, hadn't he offered to give her tickets to the concert?

Why had she asked for money in the first place? Wasn't she retired? It would have been so easy and affirming for her to say that she was not a working girl at all but a businesswoman who had come into the bar to vet her mother's boyfriend. Perhaps then the singer would have placed her in the category of respectable women he had dated, and indeed it would be a date instead of a business transaction. But instead her status as a prostitute dashed any aspirations either might have for a real relationship. Even if he fell in love with her, his manager and sponsors would not sanction an official union, and he would inevitably marry an actress or singer or model, a woman with baggage enough, perhaps divorces, addictions, eating disorders, but at least not a whore.

And had she caught his eye anywhere else, in the mall or a disco, she would have come with him for free. He wouldn't have had to buy her a drink or offer tickets to his concert to get her into bed. She would have turned down the sheets herself.

But he hadn't found her in the mall. He found her in the Hotel Grand, where he had specifically come to choose a prostitute. He wanted to pay, even if he could only scrounge up a few peso notes, and the women he surveyed were there because they had rents due and mouths to feed. However innocently, Laura had been standing among them, and she felt a solidarity with her former colleagues. She was with the singer as a representative of the trade, and to proclaim her retirement now would betray a false sense of shame, which would only foster the negative images of a profession which had been good to her.

He turned off the lamp, but the room was faintly lit from a night light in the bathroom. He took her in his arms and began to dance with her, around the coffee table, accompanying the music with his own sweltering voice.

He was singing just for her! Her own private concert. As he drew her closer she could feel his erection beneath the towel and, for all the romantic satisfaction she felt from the dance, she had to resist the urge to snap the towel off and devour him then and there.

He danced her through another song, pushing her to the breaking point, before dancing her to the edge of the bed and falling on top of her. He kissed her and bit her neck, running his hand under her shirt and caressing her breasts. Then he knelt on the floor with her legs supported on his naked shoulders and kissed along her thighs.

She lifted her skirt for a better view, then let her head fall back and closed her eyes, moaning with pleasure. A few minutes later she sat up, panting for breath. She noticed her panties on the floor, although she was still wearing her stilettos. He pulled her shirt off and bit her nipples before pushing her down again and lying on top of her.

"Wait!" she cried. "The condom."

But he was already inside her. "I'll take it out in time."

"No. We have to use—"

"I promise. Trust me."

And he so charmed her with his fixed gaze and pop star smile that she offered no further resistance. As he bit her neck she felt herself coming again. And then she felt him come. She tried to push him off, but he was wrapped around her like a wrestler, shuddering to the last.

"You said you'd take it out!" she shouted when he rolled over, sweating with exhaustion.

"We could have such a beautiful baby together," he sighed, closing his eyes.

Laura raced to the bathroom and jumped in the shower. She didn't notice if the soap was Delerio or some other brand. She forgot to steal the toothbrush.

She returned to the room and began to dress. But she had only put on her panties and shirt when she paused. Jaime Primero was sprawled naked before her, the gold crucifix nestled in the black hairs on his bronze chest, sleeping like an angel. How could she leave now, with so many hours yet before dawn? He was hers alone for those hours.

So she straightened his legs and put a pillow under his head and pulled the covers over him and then crawled in herself and rested her head on his shoulder and squeezed his waist with her hand. He had tricked her, yes. But he was a man, after all, and men were programmed from the beginning of time to swim through all obstacles into the wombs of women and make themselves immortal. Yet Jaime Primero was already a god. What made him worse than normal men was that he knew women could not resist him, not even an ex-professional like Laura, who never in her four-year career had let a naked cock possess her.

Did he really think they could make a beautiful baby together, or was that something he said to all the girls? The wistful voice of Julio Iglesias emanated from the stereo, filling the dark room with soft reminders that men and women were destined for love. For a handful of hours she did not have to let go. For a handful of hours she could dream.

"Hey baby, time to check out."

She opened her eyes from a bottomless sleep and saw Jaime Primero standing above her, already dressed, smoking a joint.

She declined his offer to share it and shielded her eyes from the light. Normally she slept lightly when she slept with men, but last night she had lain awake for hours before giving in to unconscious dreams, committing his body to memory, daydreaming like a schoolgirl.

She threw on her skirt, somewhat embarrassed by her lack of professionalism. She no longer heard sweet love songs playing on the stereo, but the frantic voice of a sports announcer on TV.

Still barefoot, she took her purse into the bathroom to brush her teeth and comb her hair, but rushed out when she saw he was about to leave.

"Are you coming back?" she asked.

He gave her a quick kiss. "Be good now."

"Wait! What about the tickets? And the rest of my money," she added, trying not to sound too mercenary.

He shrugged like a cherub. "I'll tell my guys to leave them at reception."

Laura's eye caught Dennis's digital camera lying in her open purse. "Can I have a picture before you go?"

Where were the bodyguards now that she needed them? she wondered, showing him the camera. She wanted a picture of the two of them together, a romantic pose, on the chair perhaps, she sitting on his knee. But if the bodyguards weren't around there was still the self-timer. But would he have the patience for it?

A devilish grin played on the face of the singer, who had other ideas. "I will give you something special to remember me by," he promised, stepping back over to the bed and examining the camera's controls.

"It has a timer, here," Laura pointed out.

But he was only interested in the telephoto and the shutter. Before Laura understood what was happening he had lowered his trousers and pulled his shirttail beneath his chin.

"Oh my God!" Laura gasped, as he shot a close up of his cock.

He briefly examined the LCD screen to make sure there was no incriminating evidence which might tie the object in the photo to himself, before handing the camera back to Laura, buttoning his pants and rushing away.

Laura sat on the edge of the bed, trying to assimilate it all. A maid peeked inside, and Laura motioned her to enter. Jaime Primero had checked out, and after the concert he would fly with his enormous bodyguard and the not so enormous bodyguard and whoever else was in his entourage to the next country on the tour. But before that she would hear him sing, to thousands this time, not just to her. And maybe he would leave her a backstage pass, and maybe he would even invite her to come to the next city...

She went to the reception and informed the concierge that she was expecting concert tickets and money from Senior Primero and would return later to collect them. She made no attempt to hide the nature of their relationship. Prostitutes walked these marble corridors every night, and she was not ashamed that Jaime Primero had wanted to pay for her company.

But he hadn't actually paid her yet. And no taxi driver would take pesos. She had to pay for the ride home herself.

But it was worth it, she thought, as she rode blissfully up to Escazu, imagining the stares that would engulf her when she went back to the Red Volcano, and how she would tell the story of last night over and over, to friends and strangers, ticas and Nicas and Colombians and gringos, the greatest fish story of them all. But then she remembered she wasn't going back. For the first time since her retirement she missed the florid society of the hotel. Ever since her first night in that place four years ago she had dreamed of the day she would leave it forever. But now she realized it would be hard, if not impossible, to ever discover another environment that so lent itself to the competitive camaraderie and passionate encounters found every night at the Hotel Grand.

Work! It was Friday, after all, and she had completely forgotten about Pan American Web Services. Jaime Primero was not an early riser and by the time she got home it was almost two o'clock. She had turned her cell phone off, and now she listened to three messages from Dennis, in escalating tones of concern and dismay, as well as excited inquiries from Carmen and a reminder from Porter about the wedding. The wedding! It was scheduled for tomorrow.

But she couldn't deal with any of that now, so she turned the phone back off She made herself a cup of coffee, but it failed to revive her, so she collapsed in the comfort of her own bed, setting the alarm for 6:00 PM.

As soon as she awoke she dialed the Riviera and asked about the tickets. They weren't there. She asked to speak to the concierge, then the manager. Nothing had been left for her. Maybe the name was wrong? No, nothing had been left by the Primero party, for her or for anyone. She asked for the singer's phone number, his manager's phone number, or the bodyguard's. But the hotel could not release phone numbers. "Then please call them yourself!" she had pleaded, adding the offer of a generous tip. The hotel manager said something noncommittal, and Laura hung up in despair.

He has the concert on his mind, she thought. He probably forgot. She briefly considered going to the concert anyway. Maybe someone would sell her a ticket, or she could hang around. Maybe one of the bodyguards would see her and let her backstage.

But she knew these were just fantasies, and by the time she had finished dinner it was too late to embark on such a project. The concert had already started, and she would have to wash her hair and call her driver. Even if she showered in record time and Pablo could pick her up, it would take them an hour to drive to the arena. Jaime Primero would already be gone.

She might have asked Raquel to drive her, or even solicited Tita Moon's advice, but she had come home to an empty house, and she was alone in it still.

But soon Carmen and Tita Moon arrived and the tranquility of the last few hours was shattered by girlish screams. Laura resisted their rushed questions until she had made coffee and served it in the dining room. She closed the window, lest all of Escazu hear about her X-rated adventure with the pop singer and began relating her magical night, starting from the approach of the bodyguard in the Red Volcano.

"What did his bodyguard say to you?" Carmen interrupted. "I couldn't hear a thing."

"I don't know. I was in a daze. He must have asked my name, though, because Jaime—"

"She calls him Jaime!" Tita Moon exclaimed, nudging Carmen with her elbow.

"Because Jaime whispered it in my ear when we were dancing in his room."

"When you were dancing in his room?" Carmen shouted.

"He whispered in your ear?" Tita Moon squealed jealously.

"If you keep interrupting we will be here all night. Do you want to hear what happened or not?"

"Why didn't you ask if he wanted a threesome?" Carmen wondered, a question that had been on her mind all night and all day.

"Or a foursome," Tita Moon added. "I came down five minutes later."

"I told you, I was in a daze. I couldn't even breathe," Laura answered defensively, offended by the implication that she had forsaken her friends. "Besides, he's a romantic. He wouldn't have wanted a threesome."

"Oh no, he just wanted you," Carmen said. "Only you were good enough for him."

"He's a playboy, not a romantic," Tita Moon stated.

"I just told you he danced with me. In the dark with soft music," Laura explained, exasperated. "Was he going to dance with all of us?"

"Wow," Tita Moon sighed. "You are the luckiest woman in Costa Rica."

Laura slammed the table with her hand. "I know! I know!" she agreed, excited again. "But that's just part of it. Look."

And she pulled her hair back so her friends could see the bite marks on her neck.

"Oh my God!" Carmen screamed. "Can I feel them?" And she ran her fingers over the hickey with rapture.

A key turned in the door and Raquel entered, just back from having dinner with her parents, exhausted after another tiring day searching for work.

She noticed the state of excitement in the dining room. "What's going on? Did someone win the lottery?"

"Laura won the Jaime Primero lottery! Look how he bit her neck!" Tita Moon shouted.

Raquel forgot all about her own miserable affairs and basked in the glow of Laura's conquest.

Laura poured her a cup of coffee and began again from the beginning. Actually since before the beginning, since Raquel didn't know of the singer's visit to the bar and Laura had to explain why she herself was there.

"So you owe me a debt of gratitude," Raquel realized. "If I hadn't taken the photo of Professor Martin..."

"Yes, thank you, my friend," Laura said, giving her a kiss. "It was destiny pure and simple."

And she continued her narrative, with many impassioned interruptions from her rapt audience, vividly relating every detail but two—the fact that she had not made him wear a condom and that he had shortchanged her with pesos—details she found too professionally embarrassing to confess, especially after all the criticisms she had leveled at her former coworkers over the years.

But she did mention his broken promise.

"Maybe someone at the hotel stole the tickets," Carmen imagined.

But Tita Moon would have none of it. "He had a show and he just forgot, or he didn't care," she said. "You always think the best of people, Carmen."

"I don't think the best of the staff at the Riviera," she pointed out.

"I would like to believe you," Laura said. "But Tita is right. He forgot."

"You should have gotten his phone number," Tita Moon scolded. "I would have gotten everything, phone, address, e-mail. And I would have stolen something important so he would have to see me again."

"There was nothing to steal," Laura replied, not that she would have stolen anything more valuable than a toothbrush. And maybe he doesn't even have a phone. He doesn't keep—" She was about to say "money," but stopped herself.

"His manager has a phone."

"I never saw his manager."

"Well his bodyguards then," Tita Moon persisted. "Someone. I would have blown the bodyguards while he was sleeping. Then they would have taken you with them in the Hummer and you would still be with them now."

A thought just occurred to Carmen. "Maybe he'll come back to the Grand tonight!"

"No, he checked out, remember."

"People like that don't have long-term relationships anyway," Raquel observed. "But you had him to yourself for a whole night. That's enough to remember him by."

Laura was dying to mention that she might have his child to remember him by as well but held her tongue.

"You should have at least taken a photo," Carmen said. "And you had the camera with you!"

Raquel recalled. Laura's eyes widened, having completely for-gotten. "Ladies, brace yourself," she said, and retrieved the camera from her purse.

The three women looked at the image as though they had nev-er seen a cock before, as though it looked any different from a thousand other cocks.

"Oh my God!" Carmen cried.

Tita Moon licked the LCD screen with her tongue.

"Stop it!" Laura screamed, grabbing the camera away.

She was glad to have her friends stand witness to Jaime Primero's salacious act, and she glanced at the image once again herself, but she could hardly let it remain on Dennis's camera. She scrolled back to the photo of the professor, the only other image on the memory card, selected "delete," then selected "yes" and turned the camera off. But there were two options: "delete this image" and "delete all images" and, being habitually careless in matters of this sort, she had only deleted the image of the professor.

"You should come with us to the hotel tonight," Tita Moon said. "Everyone will want to hear your story!"

"Everyone was talking about you after you left," Carmen in-formed her. "In the bathroom and the casino and the bar, that's all I heard: 'Who was that girl Jaime Primero took?' 'Is she Venezuelan?' 'No, she's local: 'Lucky chica.' 'What did he see in her?' 'Is she your friend?' 'I thought she retired?'"

"Well I have retired," Laura reminded them, begging off Although in her heart she was dying to go, especially to brag to the tall Colombians with tit jobs who thought they were God's gift to men.

CHAPTER 11

A WITCH WEDDING

Laura slept late Saturday morning, having spent much of the night lying awake in her jacuzzi bath by candle light, listening over and over to a Jaime Primero CD she found by accident in one of the kitchen drawers, the only one in her collection she had not lent to her mother. She overlooked the singer's oversights, he was a star, after all, and one had to allow for a degree of personal irresponsibility commensurate with his responsibility to his public. What do I know of that life? Laura told herself. It must be hard being an international star with fan clubs and sponsors and producers, so many people depending on you for their livelihood and entertainment. And being a singer you have to worry about your voice, what if you catch cold or get hoarse? For me or someone else it's just a minor inconvenience, but for someone like him it means a fortune lost and all those unfortunate people who bought tickets and stood in line... No wonder he drinks and smokes.

Of course, she overlooked the incompatibility of marijuana smoke and a smooth larynx, but she was in an expansive mood that took no note of contradictions. As he sang to her from the CD player she was back in his arms and he was singing her name in her ear. Someday he would have to marry. Why not her? She was retired again, and saw no reason why anyone had to know about her past. Certainly much more damaging facts were covered up by publicists every day for celebrities and politicians. And it wasn't like he was running for office. He had dated beauty queens after all, who, some of them, were little more than whores themselves. He might be a playboy, but when faced with his paternity he would do the right thing and marry her. By the time the candle burned out their son was already in his teens.

But daylight forced a more imminent and tragic union to her attention. In just a few hours, unless she took drastic action or a miracle happened, she would stand witness to a witch wedding.

After washing her hair and having coffee and oatmeal for breakfast, she recalled Carmen's advice to check Porter's horoscope. She didn't subscribe to a newspaper, but there was a telephone line she sometimes used which gave horoscopes, and she called this now. Fortunately she knew Porter's sign, as she knew most of her friends' signs. But when the recorded voice of Senora Toledo welcomed her she couldn't resist listening to her own horoscope first:

"If you have just embarked on a new relationship, beware! Despite areas of common interest, this is not a person who will play a role in your future, and if you blind yourself to their defects—"

Laura pressed "nine" to return to the main menu. This was the horoscope she wished for Porter, not for her. She held her breath and listened to the day's prediction for Cancer, her friend's sign:

"Long-awaited dreams are about to come true. Now is not the time to change your plans! Stay the course, brave warrior, and victory will be yours!"

"Damn! Damn!" Laura cried. "He's doomed."

And with an air of dejection she shuffled into her bedroom to select her clothes.

Dennis picked her up early, afraid he wouldn't find her home at all. He was wearing his only suit, which he'd had pressed, and his only tie, but he looked like someone who always dressed this way. His discomfort stemmed not from his clothes but from his concern over Laura's whereabouts.

He was obviously relieved when she opened the door, and the sight of her in a full-length pink dress with matching heels and a white rose gracing the gentle curls in her brown hair took his breath away.

But a moment later he was yelling at her. "Where have you been? Why didn't you return my calls? I thought something happened to you!"

"Something did happen to me," she replied, kissing him on the cheek. "My, don't you look nice. I've never seen you in a suit before."

But her flattery failed to mollify him. "Did you forget we have a business to run? Clients depending on us?"

"No one's depending on us yet," Laura replied, retreating into the kitchen.

"Well if you're going to take that attitude I might as well find someone else!"

"Look, I'm sorry. What do you want me to say? I know I should have called. I'll work extra to make it up. It won't happen again."

"It better not," Dennis admonished, using the most threatening tone possible because he knew she could probably act in whatever manner she wanted and he would still employ her. His only hope lay in her own sense of professional duty, which he hoped to shame or frighten her into remembering.

"I'm counting on you," he reminded her. "But you just don't care."

"Of course I care about the business. And I'm grateful for your confidence in me. Why do you think I invited you to the wedding?"

This was not what Dennis wanted to hear. He preferred to think she invited him as a date, as the man in her life. Not as compensation for having hired her.

Actually, Laura's motives were complex. The thought to invite Dennis had first been suggested by Porter, and she couldn't think of anyone she would rather have accompany her. So she told him the situation—that she had been asked to be a witness to a wedding she opposed. But if it did take place, she wanted him to be her guest. She also assumed Dennis would have a sobering effect on her own blustery emotions, despite his recent drunkenness at the dinner for her mother and the professor, and that his calming influence would prevent her from doing something rash, such as stabbing Ginger with the cake knife.

"Promise you won't miss another day," Dennis said in a softer voice, holding out his hand. "And that if you're sick you'll call before nine."

Laura shook his hand firmly. "Do you want some coffee? Something to eat?"

"I think we should be going," Dennis advised, glancing at his watch, a cheap watch he had bought from a street vendor, having given his former watch to Laura as a retirement gift.

"So what happened that prevented you from answering your phone or coming to work?" he asked as they walked to his RAV4. "From your smile, it must have been something good."

"Something extraordinary," Laura told him, unable to prevent a grin from creeping across her face. But first things first, she thought. "I'll tell you later," she promised, her face clouding over with presentiments of disaster. "I have only a few minutes to think of a way to save my friend from burning at the stake at his witch wedding."

In the car she described several fantastic scenarios for rescuing her skeletal friend, one of which involved swinging from a chandelier, but as they entered the long manicured drive to the Conquistador Resort, Dennis had had enough.

"You're not going to do anything of the sort. He trusts you and you have to uphold that trust, whatever your personal feelings.

Maybe you're right, but he's a grown man. Have a little faith in him. Maybe he's not as foolish or weak as you imagine. And you know I hate scenes. So if you think you might do something violent, I'll drop you off, and you can call me from the police station."

Laura relented and took his offered arm into the plush lobby. There was a loud cocktail party in progress for a group of pharmaceutical representatives, who served as unanticipated spectators to the wedding preparations in the courtyard below.

Laura spotted Porter first, who was supervising the floral arrangements. There were no chairs or podium. The ceremony would be brief enough that the guests were expected to stand.

Porter was wearing a navy suit with a red carnation in his lapel and contacts lenses. It was the first time Laura had seen him without his thick glasses and he looked even more skeletal with his deep eye sockets uncovered.

"You remember Dennis," she said, as the two shook hands. "Congratulations," Dennis said. "Maybe someday I'll be lucky enough to marry a Costa Rican woman too."

"She's not Costa Rican," Laura whispered in his ear, ignoring Dennis's allusion to his dream for a future with her.

Next they saw Carmen, dressed in a sequined gown and black stockings, accompanied not by a date but by the oldest of her two younger brothers, a shy sixteen year old with acne.

Then Porter introduced them to the judge, who would conduct the civil ceremony.

"This is very nice," Laura found herself saying, although she herself dreamed of a church wedding. But a witch couldn't get married in a church, could she? The courtyard at the Conquistador was the best she could hope for, and more than she deserved.

"By the way, where *is* the bride?" Laura asked, somewhat maliciously, hoping Ginger had nabbed a bigger fish, or fled home to Nicaragua.

But she was in the rest room, attending to her lipstick and hair. When she emerged Laura greeted her with a brief hug and had to admit to herself she looked radiant, if you liked the sort of style which favored lots of hairspray, aquamarine eye shadow, and dangling bracelets. She was wearing a low cut marigold dress Porter had bought her for the occasion, which made her bare legs look even darker, and white heels.

Without formality they gathered before the judge, while the hotel photographer began snapping photos and pharmaceutical reps gazed on from above.

It was a brief civil ceremony in Spanish, with Laura and Dennis standing behind Porter and Carmen and her brother behind Ginger. The judge did not offer the opportunity for witnesses to offer objections, but Laura doubted she would have had the courage to raise her voice in any case. At some point she felt Dennis's hand around hers and pulled away. The judge's words, "Now let us bring together...this solemn ceremony...everlasting..." were like the ticks of a clock counting down to a catastrophe. Laura's mind was blank with frustration. What could she do? What could she do?

Although it was a civil ceremony, the name of God was mentioned several times, and this reminded Laura that if He did not intervene, after being invoked these several times, then this unfortunate union must be part of a higher plan beyond her comprehension.

And then she saw the sunlight refracted off a large diamond, which Laura quickly estimated as worth at least two thousand dollars. Perhaps not exorbitant by gringa standards, but certain to draw admiring stares in Costa Rica, and considering that Porter was retired and had already spent thousands on jewelry, clothes and cosmetic surgery for his bride, it was a most generous expression of his love.

I hope it burns your finger! Laura thought spitefully as the married couple kissed. But a moment later she was kissing Ginger herself and wishing her happiness.

Applause descended from the heavens, but it was only the pharmaceutical reps, who would have thrown rice had there been any. The judge led them to a table to sign the marriage license, which Laura did hurriedly, as if the pen were on fire. The judge then shook their hands and departed, and the wedding party was led to a private room in the restaurant and seated at a large round table.

"Do you think it was wise to bring your brother?" Laura whispered to Carmen, who was sitting to her left.

"It's a free meal," her friend replied.

"It will be an expensive meal if Ginger decides to talk about the hotel," Laura pointed out.

"Why would she mention the hotel? She's retired now."

"Don't believe it."

But Laura could understand Carmen's motivation, even if she did not agree with it, for unlike most of the girls at the Hotel Grand, Carmen was frugal. She dressed well, but bought her clothes second hand, and the jewelry she owned had been given to her by clients. She never ate out when not working and rarely went to movies or clubs unless someone else was paying. Her sole luxury was cigarettes, and every other month she made an effort to quit. The restaurant at the Conquistador was among the best in the country and, not having a boyfriend at the moment, Carmen could not resist the offer to bring a member of her family as her guest. She would have brought her mother, but she wasn't feeling well. Her brother actually didn't want to come, being shy and at an age that preferred McDonald's to gourmet dining. Carmen actually had to bribe him with a video game, negating the value of the free meal. But Laura was sure she would take home enough leftovers to last a week, and steal a bottle of wine as well.

But before the wine was served, the waiter opened a bottle of chilled champagne. Porter stood and first toasted his bride and then their witnesses and guests.

"We didn't even have to come," Laura then said, trying to make it sound like a joke. "You had all the hotel as witnesses!"

"Yes, wasn't that nice? They work for a drug company, you know. Maybe they can give us some samples for a wedding present!" Porter said with a wink, his ineffective attempt at humor, for among the company's products was a pill for erectile dysfunction.

Maybe they have a drug for the spell you are under, Laura thought, staring at Ginger over the lip of her champagne glass.

A trio of waiters served French onion soup, Caesar salad, shrimp cocktail and roast lamb in quick succession. Carmen managed to stuff several rolls in her purse before the over attentive staff plucked the bread baskets away.

Ginger ate silently, as if she were suddenly as shy as Carmen's brother. Laura surmised the bride felt uncomfortable in such company, although she was obviously enjoying the champagne. Laura wondered what she and Porter talked about when they were alone together. They were so different, in age, in culture, in education. Laura could understand such relationships working when love was involved. But when there was love on only one side, and convenience on the other, she concluded they could only be strangers to each other, despite sharing a home and a bed.

A mariachi band swayed into the room, compensating for the lack of conversation. Laura was reminded of Jaime Primero's altercation with a mariachi band in Mexico. According to reports, the band was singing one of his songs at another table, but the star, who had been drinking heavily, believed they were parodying him and smashed one of their guitars. Someone at the table had the presence of mind to take a photo, and the picture made all the papers in Latin America.

Coincidentally, Dennis decided now was the moment to ask her what happened Thursday night that had kept her from coming to work on Friday.

"I'll tell you later."

But Dennis had been thinking of little else and wanted to know the worst before his jealous imagination tormented him further. "Tell me now."

Laura leaned over to whisper in his ear: "I spent the night with Jaime Primero!"

Actually, Dennis had been thinking of one other thing as well. He had been thinking of using this wedding to engender his own. Perhaps Laura would be in a sentimental mood. Perhaps the approval of her friends would influence her to say yes. He was waiting for the right moment to propose.

He put down his fork and sat stunned, looking across the table at the happy groom. How could she tell him such a brazen fact? Did she think he was her hair stylist and not her date? Not the man who had slept with her himself so many times and loved her so deeply that he didn't even go with other women and had remained celibate since employing her? Didn't her woman's intuition tell her he was waiting for the right moment to propose?

"Who is Jaime Primero?" was all he could finally manage to say.

"One of the biggest Latino stars. He was here for a concert."

"A rock star?" Dennis said, dismayed.

"No. He sings love songs. I am sure you would recognize some of his hits if you heard them."

"Love songs?" And Dennis sat back in his chair, completely demoralized.

Carmen's cell phone rang and she excused herself for a few minutes. When she returned she whispered to Laura that a regular client of hers was coming in a couple weeks and wanted to take her to Arenal Volcano for a few days. "I don't like to be with him," she confessed. "He's fat and rude, but he's rich, and he'll pay me nine hundred for three days."

"Why don't you take your brother along?" Laura suggested with a tinge of jealousy. Now that she was retired, it would take her a month to earn that much working for Dennis, and he was paying her a good salary. Laura suddenly understood the resentment which much of the staff of the hotel felt for the working girls, and had no patience for Carmen's complaints. "For nine hundred dollars you can accept all the rudeness in the world," she said, forgetting that she had often made similar complaints herself, and occasionally rejected lucrative offers due to a client's past behavior.

When the mariachi band finished, Laura requested a song by Jaime Primero. "Listen," she said, nudging Dennis.

But the last thing Dennis wanted to hear were the words of his new and unsuspected rival. He had taken comfort these part weeks in his deepening friendship with Laura and the knowledge that if she was not in love with him, at least there was no one else.

"It was just a one night stand, right?" he asked hesitantly, grasping at this life raft of probability.

"Yeah. Unless I have his baby."

Before Dennis could respond to what he prayed was a joke, a waiter wheeled the cake in and the photographer took pictures of the couple feeding each other a slice.

"Oh, I forgot, here's your camera," Laura said, applauding politely. "But don't take any pictures of me. It's bad luck to take pictures at a witch wedding."

But the last thing on Dennis's mind was photographing his faithless soul mate, and he slipped the camera into his pocket.

"You went to his concert?" he asked after the bride and groom sat down and the waiters poured more champagne.

"No."

"Then where did you meet him?"

"At the hotel."

Dennis didn't understand any of this. It would have made more sense to wait until they were alone in the car instead of exchanging whispered phrases, but he could not wait. He felt a sense of vertigo, as though he were dangling from a wire on a canopy tour.

"Which hotel?"

"The Grand."

He looked at the piece of wedding cake that was placed before him as if it were the only wedding cake he would ever taste, for certainly no woman would marry such a loser as Dennis Rhodes, especially not Laura Mendoza Flores, who attracted the eye of international pop stars.

"You were at the Grand?"

Laura's thoughts were on the wedding, of course, her sympathy focused on Porter, with none to spare for Dennis. Had she realized the pain she was causing him she would have held her tongue, but she viewed Dennis as strong and logical, and believed him when he said he accepted that the bounds of their relationship were drawn at friendship and business, despite his occasional efforts to kiss her or hold her hand.

"I thought you were retired!" Dennis said a little too loudly.

"Will you be quiet!" Laura warned him through clenched teeth, with a jab in the ribs." I was there to show the professor's photo, and Jaime Primero walked in and selected me."

"What do you mean he selected you? Were you working or not?"

"No. But he's Jaime Primero! I would have gone with him for free."

"What do you mean 'would have'? Did you go with him or not?"

"I'll tell you later," Laura said, alarmed by Dennis's tone, but thinking the champagne and wine might be more to blame for his unpleasant attitude than the actual circumstances she was relating.

"Did he pay you or not?" Dennis pursued in as quiet a voice as he could. But what difference did it make? It was bad news either way.

Laura was not going to indulge him with an answer, and Dennis was too agitated to wait for one. Without paying his respects to the bride and groom, as if he and Laura had been dining alone, he rose with his eyes downcast and, as the mariachi band finished another love ballad by his exalted rival, fled the room.

"I think the combination of wine and champagne has made him ill," Laura explained.

Porter, who had witnessed Dennis's rapid intoxication at Laura's retirement party, accepted this excuse without further explanation, and proposed a final toast, to the future happiness of all.

Laura drained her glass with a fatalistic sigh. A man had deserted the wedding after all. But not the man she wished.

CHAPTER 12

CHINESE EYES

T ita Moon was standing in the Red Volcano the following
Saturday night when she thought she saw a ghost. But ghosts
were dead and Rick was still alive, as far as she knew. So what did
she behold? A vision, a hallucination, a product of her tormented
mind, or maybe it was just some other gringo with a thin mustache
who reminded her of the photography store manager?

"Buenas noches!"

"Ah, you're learning Spanish now," Tita Moon replied with a
beaming smile. "I thought you were a ghost, but ghosts are dead,
and I hope you are not dead."

"Feel me," Rick suggested, holding out his arm.

But Tita Moon reached lower. "Ah! So you came back for me?"
she asked with a hopeful grin.

"Why else?"

"There are a lot of girls in Costa Rica. Or maybe you forgot
your cameras?" Then she noticed this time he was unburdened by
luggage. "But where are your bags?"

"I checked in already. I decided not to run the gauntlet with
my backpack."

He also wanted to shower and change clothes, to look nice for her.

Tita Moon had taken both his hands and had not let go, although she was craning her neck toward the bar. "Carmen!"

Carmen was talking with some other girls and after a moment stepped over. She smiled at Rick and grinned at Tita Moon.

"So this is your new novio?" And to Rick. "She's told me all about you."

"Good things, I hope."

"She showed me your picture."

"This is my best friend, Carmen," Tita said. "Isn't she pretty?"

Rick wasn't used to being asked this question by a woman and wondered if it were a trap. "Not as pretty as you."

But this was not the answer Tita Moon was looking for. "You could have us both tonight."

Normally she used this line for her friend's benefit, to get her work, but this time was different. She was thinking of Rick, and saw her offer as a way to repay the pleasure he had given her by returning.

But Rick had no idea how to respond to this unusual suggestion. Could it be another trap, to test his devotion? More likely it was just a professional convention. However, Rick found his own motives as difficult to decipher as Tita Moon's. Carmen was certainly pretty, and he had often fantasized about a *menage a trois*. What man hadn't? But this wasn't the time.

"Do I have to drink another Red Volcano?" he asked. The two women laughed.

He exchanged an uneasy smile with Carmen before turning back to Tita Moon. What was the etiquette in such cases? How does one turn down the best friend?

"Maybe another time," he answered evasively. "But I'd really like to be alone with you. Have you eaten?"

Carmen kissed him on the cheek and gracefully departed. Tita Moon squeezed his hands. "I am hungry for you!"

Rick wanted to kiss her now, in front of everyone, but his natural timidity restrained him. First things first, he thought. He wanted to take her to a romantic restaurant, but he had arrived on the late flight, so they simply marched upstairs to the Canopy Diner and sat at a back table.

These weren't the surroundings Rick had wished for, with working girls sitting on customers' laps a few tables away and bright fluorescent lights highlighting stains on the table. But at least Tita Moon was here and not upstairs with a client or away on an excursion.

"I tried to call you but could never get through," he explained after they ordered.

Tita Moon shrugged. "I lost my mobile. I am always losing phones."

"And I e-mailed you..."

"I don't have a computer and haven't gone to the internet cafe since you left."

"So I just bought a ticket back. I thought I was being impulsive the first time I came to Costa Rica! I've changed a lot. Do you still recognize me?"

"I still recognize you." But only now did Tita Moon realize he was wearing an ironed white shirt and a navy blazer. "But you are not dressed for the jungle this time," she observed.

"I'm not going to the jungle this time," he replied. "Maybe the beach. If you'll come with me."

She patted his hand. "I'll rub lotion on your back," she promised. "I think you burn easily."

Not anymore, he thought, reflecting not on beaches but on his divorce. He had always done the right thing where women were concerned. Dated within his social milieu, married promptly, worked diligently, gone to the in-laws for Thanksgiving and Christmas, remembered anniversaries. And where had it gotten him? His family and friends and coworkers might not accept Tita Moon as readily as they had accepted his ex. She might be a round peg in the square holes of his life. Why did it matter?

"Do you have any news yet?" he asked with a sudden sense of urgency. It was the first of the two questions that had brought him back to Costa Rica.

"About what?" Tita Moon said. And she really didn't know.

"You're so cute. Are you going to torture me?"

Tita Moon rolled her eyes. Then she slapped her cheek with understanding. Lies can be so complicated, and she had forgotten what he didn't know.

"I know it hasn't even been two weeks," Rick went on. "But I thought maybe you had your period or maybe..."

Tita Moon gazed back at him intently. She wanted to tell him the truth, but she also wanted him to take her to the beach. She wanted to spend these days with him, and not simply for the money. She was so happy to see him it frightened her. In fact she had been thinking about him since he left, showing his picture to Carmen and Laura, dreaming of this very moment.

"What do you want?" she whispered.

Rick had wrestled with that question since his plane took off last Wednesday, and he still did not know. Part of him wanted to be a father, but was it practical, was he ready? And what of her other child? Starting a family was complicated enough without going abroad, without falling in love with a prostitute. In the end all he knew was that he didn't want to stand on that curb at the airport again, saying goodbye.

"I want everything."

Tita Moon squeezed his hands. She could tell him the truth then, or at least start down that path. "I took a pregnancy test," she said. And she nodded.

Rick smiled proudly, joyfully. The waitress brought the wine he had ordered and he toasted their baby, looking into her eyes. And Tita Moon looked back, shamefully, although her own eyes were tearful.

Rick would have liked to do something special or creative. He realized he didn't even have a camera to capture the moment. But what did it matter? He took the small felt box out of his pocket and simply handed it to her.

"What's this?" She opened the lid and was genuinely surprised. "Is it a real diamond?" she asked, not daring to touch it yet.

"I hope so. Try it on."

But she held it up to the light instead.

"When I got home I felt homesick," Rick confessed. "For you. My home didn't feel like home anymore. I examined my life and realized I had never been as happy as I had been those two nights with you. Maybe I was crazy. Maybe it wouldn't work. I know we hardly know each other. But I've lost so much in my life, why shouldn't I take the chance?"

"No one's ever given me a diamond before."

Rick had played out this scene in his mind countless times over the past ten days and had no patience to wait for an answer. "Well?" he said anxiously.

"Well what?"

He thought she was being coy, but she really didn't know. She thought he had given her a present. Working girls received presents all the time, even diamond jewelry. Engagement rings were much rarer, despite Ginger's recent ascension to the throne of marriage, and Tita Moon had never viewed herself as the kind of woman whom men might regard as anything more than fun.

"Will you marry me?" Rick asked, exasperated.

"Really?"

Now Tita Moon allowed herself to be swept away and modeled the ring for him. "What is your last name?"

"Lindsey."

"Tita Sanchez Lindsey," she attempted.

The waitress brought their dinners and Tita Moon proudly held the ring out to her. It was not as lustrous as the ring Porter had given Ginger, but it was impressive nonetheless.

"I bet you don't see many engagement rings in the Canopy Diner," Tita Moon quipped to her.

"Congratulations. Do you need anything else?"

But they were sufficient unto themselves.

They made love like a couple, like newlyweds, with the lights off and the curtains drawn, with soft music from the radio drowning out the sounds from the street. He came faster not having to wear a condom, but she did not let herself go at all, was unusually quiet and passive, too overwhelmed by love to concentrate on sex. And in the back of her mind was the lie and its consequences, but she pushed it away, she told herself everything would work out. This was life, after all, not a soap opera where every triumph is followed by disaster. She bit his lip when they kissed to keep from crying and then she cried in his arms, and said "Thank you," as though he had rescued her. And he had.

They were both tired and slept. They didn't discuss the practicalities of their future life together until they were in the taxi the following morning en route to Laura's house, where the immediate plan was for Tita to pack beachwear and then catch a bus for Puntarenas on the Pacific coast, for a few days in the sun and a side trip to meet Tita Moon's parents and son.

Tita Moon didn't ask how her son figured in their plans. In fact, she didn't ask anything, she was so intoxicated by the proposal. Rick had earned her trust and whatever he decided was good enough for her.

As for him, he decided to wait until he met her son and her parents before making any decisions in that regard. Maybe her parents wanted to keep the child. Maybe the boy wanted to stay. There were enough pressing matters otherwise, and he chose to raise these instead.

"I want you to live with me in the U.S.," he told her, holding her hand in the back of the taxi as it wound its way out of downtown San Jose. He deliberately phrased his intention as a wish and not a command. But although he loved Costa Rica, he was not emotionally or financially prepared to relocate here. "My ex got our house, but I was planning to buy another. We could buy it together. I think you'd like that. And your English is good enough so that you won't feel isolated, and you can take classes if you want. The winters are cold, and you'll have to learn to drive—"

"I don't care!" she interrupted, throwing her arms around him. "I'll do whatever you say. I know I'll be happy."

He was unprepared for this; it seemed too good to be true. To have made someone so happy, to have someone trust him so completely. He wondered if he deserved it, if he might fail her in some unintended way.

"And of course we can visit Costa Rica," he added, as if that were a concern for his new fiancée.

But she just smiled at him like a child who had been lost and now was back in her room with her dolls and toys.

It was early Sunday morning and the house was quiet. Laura was still sleeping and Raquel had spent the night at her parents'. Rick decided not to ask the driver to wait because they were going to have breakfast before leaving for the bus station. He helped Tita Moon in the kitchen and they talked about their plans over pinto de gallo and coffee.

Laura heard a strange voice and emerged in her pink bathrobe. But before she could remind Tita Moon of her prohibition against male guests, Tita Moon explained that they had just stopped at the house on their way to the beach.

And Tita Moon rose with such suddenness that she nearly knocked over her chair, and held out her finger. "Look!"

Laura wiped the sleep from her eyes and examined the diamond with a gaping mouth. For several moments she could not speak at all. She looked at Rick sympathetically, as if she knew him well, though they had not met before. But Laura had seen his picture and listened to Tita Moon rave about him. She hadn't been exaggerating, Laura thought. He was even better than boyfriend experience. He was husband experience. A good man like Porter, but better looking. And less pathetic. Or maybe not.

When Laura finally recovered her voice she grabbed Tita Moon firmly by the arm. "Can I talk to you?" And to Rick, looking over her shoulder as she dragged Tita Moon to her room: "Excuse us a minute."

She pushed her friend and lodger inside and closed the door. She looked at the half-packed suitcase lying open on the bed.

"What are you thinking, for God's sake?" she screamed.

Tita Moon's first reaction was to fight back, although she felt very little strength for this battle. "What business is it of yours? Maybe you're just jealous."

Laura made an effort to lower her voice. "Last week I was witness to a witch wedding and I said nothing. But you are in my house and you are my friend and he is a good man who does not deserve the catastrophe that is about to befall him."

What could Tita Moon say to this? "But he loves me, he's happy," she answered feebly, unconsciously twisting the ring, as if unsure whether to push it on more tightly or take it off.

Laura looked at the ring. "Tell me you are not married already?"

"Of course not. He just came back last night."

Laura sighed. "Thank God! I thought maybe you had just come from the ceremony."

"It wasn't my idea," Tita Moon explained.

Laura stared at her with her penetrating eyes, and Tita Moon felt like she was standing in an X-ray machine.

"You have to give it back, Tita."

"No! I can't."

"You must!"

"He'll never have to know," Tita Moon whispered.

"Of course he'll know!"

"I won't tell him."

"Do you think he needs words to discover the truth? What will he think when he looks at the baby he believes is his own and Chinese eyes look back?"

Tita Moon felt her legs growing weak beneath her. "Maybe the baby will take after me."

"Tita, you got knocked up by an Asian. A Chinese! I hope you choose a good hospital to give birth because your husband will have a heart attack at once! And if this doesn't kill him he will probably kill you in a jealous rage. So either way at least one of you will be destroyed by your lie and the Chinese kid will be given up for adoption to responsible parents!"

Tita Moon collapsed under the weight of this tragic premonition. She sat on the bed and sobbed with her face in her hands.

"You have to tell him, Tita."

"I can't! I can't!"

"You have to tell him now. Not at the beach. Not at your wedding."

Tita Moon looked up, her wide eyes obscured by tears. "You do it!"

"I can't tell him!"

Tita Moon grabbed Laura's hand and almost pulled her down. "Please!"

Laura regarded her troubling and troubled friend, her lodger, her former colleague. She knew this wasn't her affair or responsibility, but her heart softened at Tita Moon's genuine contrition, and she herself still felt guilty for not preventing Porter's ill-advised marriage.

She took very short steps back to the dining room, as if to give Rick a few more seconds to figure everything out for himself and retreat with honor. But he was still sitting at the table, drinking coffee, a horrible look of contentment on his face.

"I hope nothing's wrong?" he said.

"Do you want a beer? I think I still have some."

Rick laughed. "It's a little early, don't you think?"

"No."

"Well, actually I have a drinking problem, so I think I'll stick to coffee."

Laura poured him another cup. "Come see the terrace," she said, and led him out. "What do you think of my view?"

"Where's Tita? Is she okay?"

"Look—there's the Hotel Grand."

"Oh yeah."

They were standing next to each other by the waist-high terrace wall. Laura suddenly thought this was the wrong place to have brought him, but then realized the slope wasn't very steep and the magnolia bushes would break his fall.

While he was still looking down Laura gently took his hand and placed the ring in his palm.

He stared at it, comprehending in an instant more than he wanted to admit to himself.

"She asked me to give it back. She feels very badly."

"I don't understand."

"Try not to hate her. She's a good person. But she's young and impulsive. And don't be too hard on yourself. It happens all the time here. Decent guys like you fall in love..."

"But in the hotel last night, and in the taxi she said—"

"It's not your baby."

Rick unconsciously put the ring in his pocket and stared at Laura. He leaned back against the wall for support. As Laura's words hung in the air he realized that of course Tita Moon was a prostitute, so naturally the father could be another client, or a secret boyfriend. But then they would need DNA evidence to determine paternity. How could her friend speak those devastating words with such authority?

"I don't understand."

"Shortly before she met you she had a client and the condom broke. She was already pregnant..."

He didn't know what to say. Questions cluttered his mind, but the answers imposed themselves just as quickly. He understood too well.

Indignation and embarrassment rose within him, from his gut to his throat. But he did not move or speak. He had been conned. But he also knew his own fantasies were as much to blame as her devious pragmatism. Who visits Disney World expecting to sleep in Cinderella's castle?

Laura gazed at him with the helpless sympathy one feels when a player has been injured on the soccer field.

"Thanks for the coffee," he finally said, realizing he still held his cup in his other hand and setting it down on the wall.

He walked back into the house and, without looking for Tita Moon, picked up his backpack from the foyer and walked out. It was just as well he had sent the taxi away because he needed to burn off the energy simmering within him. The bright sky, the lush foliage, the painted houses mocked his despair, but the descent into the city mirrored his fall from grace.

He walked all the way back to the Hotel Grand. His intention, what was left of it, was to book the next flight home, and medicate himself with tequila for his remaining hours in this faithless country.

But a brochure caught his eye as he passed the travel desk. A nine day mountain bike journey across the central valley, from one coast to the other. Another woman was working there, not the pretty one he had booked the tent lodge with. But this girl spoke

English too, and was pleasant enough. She told him the next departure was in two weeks. He said he couldn't wait. She explained there was one that left that morning, but it was too late. He asked if it was possible to join them if he hired a taxi to the meeting point and left immediately. It was only noon. She made some calls and swiped his credit card and wished him bon voyage. He hurried off, desperate to channel his linear grief into the circular comfort of a bicycle pedal. If he drowned this time it would be in the ocean and not in a woman's arms.

CHAPTER 13

VOLCANOES AND OTHER ERUPTIONS

It was true that Lester Russell was fat and rude, as Carmen had told Laura at Porter's wedding. But if Carmen refused all men who were overweight or ill mannered she wouldn't own her own home or be able to support her mother and two brothers. She had been with him twice before, but never on excursions. During his first stay at the Hotel Grand he took her for an hour. During his second he took her all night and asked for her phone number. Carmen did not enjoy his company at all. He was old enough to be her father. But then many of her clients were old enough to be her father. He was obese, with rolls of fat that shuddered whenever he moved. But then the barstools of the Red Volcano groaned nightly under the weight of rotund asses. He was sharp tempered, never smiled, or said please or thank you. But again, that might describe many of the hotel's patrons. True, he was worse than most, but not as bad as some. Laura was right to be annoyed at Carmen's complaining. She wasn't being paid to enjoy herself, and nine hundred dollars for three days' work was a bonanza.

Still, Carmen's intuition warned her against Lester, so much so that she had hesitated when he called to her to go away with him. Actually, he hadn't asked at all, but simply told her the dates and destination. When she named her price he scoffed, but she held firm and he agreed. He didn't conclude with the normal pleasantries, such as, "I've missed you these months," or "Can't wait to see you," or even "Goodbye," but simply hung up the phone as if she had refused him.

She had been surprised by the call. The first time he had taken her she thought he was disappointed. He came, but it wasn't easy, and he didn't seem to enjoy the experience any more than she. He paid her a hundred but didn't speak in parting, so that when she saw him in the bar a few months later she was surprised he approached her. Again, he fucked her as if he were shoveling snow. They didn't talk, he snored all night. She cursed herself for not having demanded payment in advance, but in the morning he paid her in full and even asked for her number.

"Why do you want my number?" she wondered.

"Maybe next time we can go away for a few days."

She didn't think anything of it at the time and had quite forgotten about him in the intervening months. But the commanding voice was familiar and she knew no one else named Lester, so when he called, despite her astonishment that he had been serious in wanting to see her again, she knew immediately who it was.

Their excursion hadn't even started, yet she was already in a bad mood. It was much too early for her, nine o'clock in the morning and traffic was horrible as she drove to the hotel. He wants his money's worth, she thought bitterly. What if he isn't even there? Then I have interrupted my sleep and come to the hotel for nothing.

But her phone rang as she waited at a light.

"Where are you?" he demanded without saying hello or introducing himself.

"I'm in my car, stuck in traffic. You said nine o'clock." "It's nine fifteen."

She cursed under her breath. "I'll be there."

He clicked off and she slammed the phone on the passenger's seat. She was tempted to turn around and drive back home to her comfortable bed. But nine hundred dollars was nine hundred dollars, and she knew there were women in this country who sewed underwear in factories for ten dollars a day. Still, why couldn't she get the decent men? Look at Porter, or Dennis, or poor Rick, that wonderful guy Tita Moon treated so shamelessly. Why couldn't she be going to Arenal Volcano with any one of them? Why did she always get the Lester Russells of the world? Laura always told her she was too meek, too sweet, the sort of woman men love to take advantage of. Maybe it was true. At least they paid her, she told herself.

He was waiting in the lobby, dressed in khaki shorts and an extra large Tommy Bahama's shirt and sporting a straw hat.

"Aren't you going to give me a hug?" he asked, standing before her.

No, she wanted to say. Hug me if you want. But why should I hug you? You didn't even say hello.

But she threw her arms around as much of him as she could. He tried to kiss her on the lips and she drew away, embarrassed even here in the Hotel Grand.

"I didn't know you had a car," he said. "That's great. We can drive."

"But I don't want to take my car. I don't want to drive."

"Then I'll drive."

"Let's take a taxi."

"That's ridiculous. Why should I pay two hundred dollars for a taxi when you have a car?"

"I don't like to take my car out of the city. The roads are bad."

"Well I'm not paying for a taxi! We'll take the bus."

"Fine!"

Their next argument erupted a few moments later when Carmen refused to drive to the bus station in her car.

"We'll be gone for three days," she explained. "I have my car in a safe lot whose owner I know. If I drive to the bus station I will have to park in a strange lot, and it's a dangerous neighborhood."

Lester grudgingly accepted the solicitation of a taxi driver and opened the door for her. "I'm deducting this fare from your fee."

"Fine!"

As soon as they were seated in the bus, Lester took her hand. Carmen let him hold it, nothing wrong with that. But when he tried to kiss her she pulled away. She took her iPod out of her bag and put the headphones on.

"Don't listen to that," he said.

"Why not?"

"I can't talk to you."

Carmen was nonplussed. "But you never talk to me."

"Maybe I want to talk, okay? It's antisocial to listen to that thing when I'm paying for your company. And I don't want you using your cell phone while we're together."

Carmen stashed the iPod back in her bag and reclined in her seat.

"If you didn't want to be with me you should have said so," he then stated, no longer holding her hand.

"I'm sorry."

"That's better. Give us a kiss."

She pecked him on the cheek.

"You call that a kiss? My dog gives better kisses."

"We're on a bus," Carmen said nervously. "Wait till we get to the hotel."

"You just don't want to be with me," he complained.

Few girls would have lasted this long with such a client, but it was true that Carmen was meek and forgiving. Still, even she was nearing her breaking point.

"How can you say that?" she asked indignantly, looking at him. "I woke up early for you and all you can say is that I'm late. You don't say 'hello' or 'you look nice' or smile one time. I think you are the one who doesn't want to be with me!"

"Maybe we should just go back," he threatened.

"Maybe we should!"

But the bus rolled on and they stayed in their seats.

It was late afternoon when they arrived at the Grand Arenal Resort, which was rather more modest than the name might suggest, for although it was a five star hotel with attentive staff, there were only forty rooms, and the pool and restaurant were what one might have expected at a bed and breakfast. Guests came for the view, the unique sight of an active volcano less than three miles away. Arenal sprang imperiously from the Cordillera de Tilaran, smoke visibly rising from its mouth when not obscured by clouds, and at night, fire leaping against the black sky and lava ominously descending in rivulets like streaks of blood.

This furious display of nature attracted lovers as well as naturalists, perhaps for the same reason Niagara Falls attracted honeymooners. And there was a natural hot springs below to soothe muscles sore from hiking. People could not climb the volcano itself, of course, and there was always the chance of a deadly eruption, but guests tended to worry more about clouds than the possibility of being mummified in ash like the residents of Pompeii.

After tipping the bellhop, Lester pulled aside the curtain and stepped out onto the balcony. "Come here," he said. "Look at this!"

He put he arm around Carmen and they admired the volcano for a minute in silence. They were fortunate with the weather. A plume of light gray smoke rose silently from its peak.

Lester finally turned toward Carmen and kissed her on the mouth. His breath was terrible from the long ride and, besides, they were on the balcony where anybody could see them. She gently pushed him away.

"I want to fuck you here."

"Are you crazy?"

Carmen had been to Arenal several times with clients and she enjoyed the view, the hotels, the thermal spring. But she had never gotten such a request and would not have agreed to have sex on this balcony even with the man of her dreams.

"I've been fantasizing about this ever since I decided to come back," he confessed.

"Well find another fantasy," she told him. "Anyone can see us on this balcony, not to mention the sounds."

"Bullshit," he argued.

The truth was somewhere between, for the second floor balcony was neither private nor as open to view as Carmen believed. The hill sloped down beneath them and there was nothing between them and the volcano. However, they were exposed to the adjoining balconies and to some degree to those diagonally above on the third floor.

"Why do you care?" he asked. "You shouldn't be modest in your line of work."

"Families come here," she reminded him.

And as if to punctuate her claim a young boy stepped out onto the balcony to their right. Lester had no choice but to withdraw.

"We'll do it tonight," he said. "When it's dark and the kids are in bed, okay?"

Carmen said nothing, glad for the reprieve. Maybe she would be saved from embarrassment by a large eruption and they would all be burned to a crisp. Clients were always surprised that she was vulnerable to such emotions. You're a whore, they reminded her, as if that fact precluded self-consciousness and civility.

He undressed and lay down on the bed, waiting for her.

"Don't you want to have dinner first?" she asked.

"I'm not hungry. For food."

How can such a fat man not be hungry? she thought, feeling rumblings in her own stomach.

She closed the curtains and turned out the lights so she wouldn't have to look at the rolls of fat. Most girls would have asked him to brush his teeth, but she didn't have the courage. And she didn't want to suggest a shower because he would insist she take it with him and soap his back. It wouldn't be so bad if he were nice, she told herself. But to be ugly *and* unpleasant, that was too much.

But he was paying her a lot of money, after all, so she let him kiss her and she massaged his shoulders and gradually worked her way down to his cock. His breathing deepened but her squeezing and tickling failed to make him hard enough to put the condom on.

"It's not working," she finally said.

"Use your tongue," he snapped.

"You know I don't give blowjobs without condom," she reminded him.

"Fine. Then just do what you were doing."

She began to stroke him with her other hand. "Why don't you take Viagra?"

"I don't need that stuff!" he exclaimed defensively.

She sighed and continued her efforts. But after another minute she heard snoring. She stopped. He was sound asleep. Tired, no doubt, from the long bus ride. She was tired too, but also in need of fresh air.

She put on her bikini, took the key, and tiptoed out to the pool. The sun had slipped behind the volcano but the air was still warm and the pool was heated. Carmen had it to herself and splashed around like a child. It was too small to swim laps, and she wasn't much of a swimmer anyway. But it felt good to uncoil the pent-up stress from this long day and frolic unobserved.

Well, almost unobserved. "Would you like a drink, Senora?" the pool attendant asked, setting a towel on her chair.

Carmen looked up to see the god Vulcan himself, but in a youthful incarnation, younger than herself, bronze, muscular, wearing only a pair of tight white shorts and a blue shirt, unbuttoned.

"Senorita," she corrected, feeling like an old maid in his presence. "A piña colada, please."

When he returned he set it on the table but she asked him to bring it to her in the water and when he bent down to hand it to her their eyes met. The glass nearly slipped through her hands and she set it carefully on the pool deck.

"Would you like anything else, Senorita?"

You, she thought. Look at that firm stomach, that chest. In two minutes he has smiled at me more and has been more polite than that rhinoceros! I'm sure he doesn't have bad breath. I'm sure his fantasy is something more romantic than fucking while looking at a stupid volcano.

"I'm starving," she said aloud. "Could you please bring me chips or something?"

"You're not allowed to eat at the pool," he replied. But then he looked around, as if they were engaging in a vast conspiracy, and said, "Just a moment."

He brought her a bag of potato chips that he bought at the vending machine with his own money.

"I'm sorry I don't have any colones with me. I'll have to pay you later," she said after thanking him. The piña colada she had signed to her room.

"Don't worry about it," the pool attendant said, pulling up a chair and watching her as she stood at the pool's edge, devouring the chips. "If you're so hungry why don't you eat dinner?"

"That's a very good question! I'm waiting for my...uncle. He's sleeping."

The pool attendant smiled as though he'd already made the conquest. "So that's who you came with? He's not your boyfriend?"

"God, no," Carmen answered, wondering if the attendant had some kind of poison on hand, something he used to kill the scum in the pool. Something she could apply to Lester, not to kill him of course, just to prolong his sleep for two more days.

"Where are you from?" he asked.

"San Jose." Then she thought of Lester, white as a sail, and added, "But my father is Norteamericano, and my uncle also lives in the States."

Did she have to create an entire genealogy for a three-day affair? "My name is Carmen," she said to avoid further questions.

He took her wet but warm hand in his own, squatting on his powerful legs, and smiled into her eyes. "I'm Romeo."

No way! she thought. But she knew it must be true.

She and her "uncle" sat in the intimate dining room, surrounded by honeymooners and families, including the child whose appearance on the neighboring balcony had saved her from, or at least postponed, the most embarrassing moment of her life.

Her developing tryst with Romeo had been interrupted when an older couple appeared at the pool. She had guiltily stuffed the rest of the chips in her mouth, so that she could not even say goodbye when he left to take their order. Now she half wished he would be their waiter so she could see him again, while the other half felt being seen with Lester would be humiliating. Already he was holding her hand. How would she explain that? She pretended the wooden menu was so heavy she needed both hands to hold it.

But she needn't have worried. Their waiter was a woman. Still, she felt embarrassed to be with Lester in such conservative company. Why couldn't he have taken her somewhere where there were fewer people, or more people? At least she would finally get to eat.

The special of the day was surf and turf. Carmen ordered it eagerly, but Lester intervened.

"It's forty dollars!" he said. "I don't pay that much for dinner at home."

"Then you can afford it here."

"Why do you have to pick the most expensive thing on the menu? Everything else is ten, fifteen dollars."

"That's what I want. Medium rare," she added to the waitress.

"I'll deduct it from your fee."

"Will you watch it!" she whispered, leaning toward him. "What if she understands you?" She turned back up to the waitress with an air of resignation. "Just the twelve dollar steak then. I already have a monster with claws!"

Back in the room he took a shower and didn't even ask her to join him. She watched "Vale of Tears," wondering what Martina or Anna would do if faced with balcony sex in front of a volcano, with the possibility of human witnesses as well.

She was the only guest in the hotel who prayed for rain, but it was the kind of sparkling night that campers patiently wait days for and which brings out all the cameras with their tripods and telephoto lenses. Carmen wondered how many of those lenses would stray to their balcony and expose her forever in the flaccid arms of Lester Russell.

"You're in one of the most spectacular places in the world and you're watching TV!" he chided her when he emerged from the bathroom, wrapped in a towel which nevertheless failed to cover much of his body.

"I'm afraid of active volcanoes."

"Nonsense." And he slid open the balcony door and stepped out, inhaling deeply. "Come on, my chiquita," he said, addressing her for the first time in an affectionate tone. "The children are in bed, it's very dark, no one will recognize you even if they look this way. But I promise you everyone is looking at Arenal."

Nine hundred dollars, she thought. And then she realized he would probably want to do this all three nights. Suddenly those women who sewed underwear in factories for ten dollars a day didn't seem so wretched.

But she wasn't going to be naked. She put on her bikini, still damp from the pool, grabbed a condom, and marched to war.

He was leaning against the iron railing, admiring the view. She crawled in front of him and sat with her back to the railing, with a glance at the balconies diagonally above to make sure no one was looking. He let the towel fall at her feet.

"This is better!" she whispered, finding him hard at once. Now that she was here there was no point being unpleasant.

She put the condom on and sucked him intently. He moaned so enthusiastically she hoped he would come and she wouldn't have to fuck him. But as if reading her mind he rocked back, pulled her up, and turned her around. For a moment he fumbled in the darkness to draw her bikini aside and, with one hand on her ass for direction, pushed himself inside her.

"Oh God!" he moaned. "Oh please!"

Carmen gripped the cold rail. So this was what she had to do to get him to say please! Well, it just wasn't worth it.

She looked at the volcano. It really was breathtaking. Its slope outlined against the dark sky, incendiary nuggets from the bowels of the earth rising out of the crater, thick lava trailing over the rim in thin convoluted lines. She heard a low, steady rumble, but not the terrifying roar one might expect from an active volcano. The only terrifying roar was to her rear.

"Talk to me girl," he roared into her ear, thrusting harder.

Carmen felt the railing vibrate beneath her hands. They were only on the second floor, but people died falling from stepladders. If the railing gave way they would tumble down the hill. If the fall didn't kill her, his weight would surely crush her, just like being run over by a bus. She pictured them rolling down the hill in this obscene embrace. Could any death be more horrific?

"Not so hard," she cautioned. "The railing."

But he paid no attention. His eyes were fixed on the volcano, he was almost there. "Tell me I'm a volcano," he urged her.

"What?"

"Tell me I'm a volcano."

"Oh baby, you're my volcano. Yes..."

"Tell me you want to feel my hot lava. Tell me you want me to erupt inside you."

It never ceased to amaze Carmen that men failed to see the humor in their lovemaking. On the contrary, they were always so serious, squinting and grunting, as if they were carting heavy stones up a hill, when they should have been laughing the way babies laugh after they make some silly noise.

"Erupt in me!" she whispered.

He swore a few more times, shuddered, and threw his arms around her. The railing was no longer vibrating and she eased her grip.

"You're amazing baby!"

It was the first nice thing he had said to her all day. If that's what it takes to get a compliment, I prefer rudeness, Carmen thought. What had she done anyway? She hadn't done anything but hold tight to the rail. It saddened her to think of the way men estimated women. A woman could cook and clean, give birth, raise children, work at a shop or factory, and the man would think nothing of this. But let her bend over and grab a rail, suddenly her talents were prodigious.

She slept surprisingly well, perhaps due to fatigue from the arduous day. Perhaps because she dreamt of Romeo. In one dream she was drowning in the pool and he rescued her by holding out the straw of her piña colada, enlarged beyond phallic proportions. And then they were riding away on a black horse, past the angry volcano, and he shielded her from raining magma by holding a beach towel over her head. And then he was driving her in a BMW down the gravel drive to a grand estate, and he wasn't a pool attendant after all but the owner of a lobster farm. And there, swimming among the countless crustaceans in the enormous tank with his claws tied, was Lester Russell.

Alas, it was only a dream, and in the morning she shuffled behind him at the buffet breakfast, where he fortified himself for the day by eating pancakes, bacon, sausage, toast and a Western omelette. The weather was uniformly overcast, with stratus clouds hanging over Arenal like a duvet on a woman's tit. At least that's the image that came to Lester's mind. Carmen didn't care one way or the other, as long as it was warm enough to go to the pool.

However, Lester wanted to go to the hot springs. Carmen tried to talk him out if it.

"We can't have sex there. It's too public."

"Who said anything about sex?"

"Well you can go. I'll use the pool here."

"Why go to a regular pool when there's a hot springs ten minutes away? If I wanted to go alone I would have come here alone."

So they went to the hot springs and soaked in the steaming sulfur for an hour. He groped her a few times beneath the murky water, but otherwise behaved himself. They ate lunch in a cafeteria before returning to the hotel.

It was only mid-afternoon. Carmen felt this was one of the slowest days of her life. But now the sun was peeking through the clouds and Lester wanted to take a nap to rest up for another fantasy-filled night. Maybe this day wouldn't be so bad after all. Carmen changed into her bikini and hurried outside.

The pool again was empty. She had just spent an hour in the thermal springs, so she laid on one of the longue chairs to soak up the intermittent sun, and to display herself for Romeo. But when he hadn't appeared after ten minutes she decided to close her eyes and imagine herself somewhere far away.

When she felt something cold on her stomach she nearly screamed. And when she opened her eyes she wondered if she were still dreaming, for Romeo was laughing above her, holding out a piña colada, which he had just touched to her flesh.

"Maybe I want a margarita this time," she said, fingering the straw.

"I would be glad to get you a margarita too. Just don't swim drunk in the pool. Then I will have to rescue you."

"It's a very small pool. Do you rescue many people?"

"Only the pretty senoritas," he said with a gleaming smile.

She forgave him his macho jokes. After being with Lester for one-and-a-half days she was glad for the chance to flirt.

"Where is your uncle?" he asked.

"Sleeping. We went to the hot springs and it made him tired."

"The springs are good for your skin."

"It makes my skin dry."

He took this as an invitation to stroke her arm. "Your skin is very soft."

Carmen could have continued like this all afternoon, free from Lester, drinking coladas, absorbing the rays of the sun and the compliments of a solicitous pool attendant named Romeo. But the pool suddenly grew busy and he had to hand out towels and take drink orders.

Hungry again, but not wanting to ask favors, Carmen went to the vending machines to buy chips. But before she could insert the coins a shadow fell across the glass and she saw Romeo's reflection.

He pushed her against the machine and kissed her passionately. She did not resist. Then, out of the corner of her eye, she saw Lester at the pool gate. He stared at her for a moment like a cuckolded husband, then turned on his heels.

"Oh my God!" Carmen exclaimed, pushing Romeo away.

She had no time for words but ran after Lester. But she stopped on the grass. Why should she run after him? Why should she apologize? She wasn't guilty of anything, so why should she act guilty?

Still there was the practical manner of the nine hundred dollars and the fact she hadn't asked for payment in advance. She waited a few moments to compose herself before returning to the room, as if nothing had happened.

Lester was packing her bag.

"Hey, what are you doing?"

He turned to her with his lips pressed together in anger. "You're not a girlfriend experience. You're an ex-wife experience!"

"Let go of my things!"

He threw her bag down and turned to her, his jowls shaking with rage. "How dare you cheat on me!"

"I didn't cheat on you."

"I saw you plain as day making out with that...that boy!"

Carmen stared back at him with her hands on her hips. "How can I cheat on you? You're not my husband."

Lester took out his wallet and threw several bills down on the bed. "Here's $300 dollars for yesterday."

Carmen didn't look at the money. "How could I cheat on you? I'm a working girl."

"Don't remind me!"

"Well don't say I cheated on you. That's impossible."

"You're on my time."

"You were sleeping!"

"You have no right to fuck other guys when I'm paying you."

"It was only a kiss. And I can do whatever I want. You don't own me twenty-four hours. If you're sleeping and I'm not in your room I don't think it's any of your business what I do."

"I thought you were special," he said in a disillusioned tone.

"What are you talking about? You never said one nice word to me." She picked up the money and waved it in his face. "Three hundred dollars isn't enough for a day with you! I would rather sew underwear in a factory than spend another minute in your company!"

And she zipped up her bag and stormed out, still dressed only in her bikini. The short stone path to the left led to reception, the path to the right to the pool. She thought for a moment about going back to see Romeo, about getting her own room and investing Lester's money in this budding romance. But embarrassment and common sense dissuaded her. Romeo probably suspected by now that Lester wasn't her uncle. And if she stayed there was no telling what Lester might do out of jealousy and malice. Besides, her dreams of the black stallion and coffee plantation were only dreams. Romeo was hardly more than a boy, a couple years younger than she. He probably still lived with his parents and already had a girlfriend or two. She concluded there was no more future with a pool attendant named Romeo than with a fledgling Colombian narco.

So she pulled a pair of jeans and a top over her bikini and took the path to reception. She had to run to catch the last bus to San Jose. She was thankful it wasn't crowded and sat in the back and pulled the curtain over the window so she wouldn't have to see that damned volcano a moment longer and cried quietly, thinking how shameful the last day and a half had been. There wasn't enough money in the world to make her want to suffer such indignities again. She had chosen the world's most odious profession. Laura was smart to retire, and she would retire as well. She imagined throwing her own retirement party, and fantasized about someone like Porter but younger and handsome giving her a big diamond and saying "I do" in the courtyard of the Conquistador.

During the eight hour ride back to San Jose she fantasized a hundred different futures in which the Hotel Grand and gringos with double chins and requests involving balconies and mountains that spewed fire did not figure. But she knew the following night she would be standing on the raised platform behind the front tables at the Red Volcano.

CHAPTER 14

TITA MOON FALLING

When Tita Moon came out of her room that morning it was so quiet and still she felt as though she were the last person on earth. Raquel was out, Laura was taking a shower, and most importantly, Rick was gone.

She sat down listlessly, set her head against the table, closed her eyes and cried. Only a short time ago he had shared this table with her. Only a short time ago they had been a couple, she with a ring on her finger. She had found a husband without even looking, a father for her bastard sons, the best man she would ever know. And now he was probably at the airport waiting for the next flight home. He would burn her pictures. She would look at his picture every night for the rest of her life.

She felt a hand on her shoulder and for a moment she dreamed it was Rick. He'd come back, full of forgiveness. But it was Laura fresh from the shower.

"He's gone," Laura said.

Tita Moon nodded, wiping her eyes.

Laura knew her friend had brought this on herself, that she didn't deserve such a decent man. But she felt a pain in her stomach nevertheless and felt a tear trickle down her cheek. "I wish I could say something to cheer you up. You'll find someone else."

"Not like him."

"No, not like him," Laura agreed, forgetting her intention of a moment before to comfort her friend. "A man like him, who is good looking and healthy and faithful and kind, who will ignore your profession and see the goodness in your heart, who will raise another man's child as his own—such a man you are lucky to meet once in a lifetime."

But Laura's words of praise made Tita Moon burst into tears again. "What did he do with the ring?" she asked.

"He put it in his pocket."

"He'll give it to someone else. Someone not as bad."

"I'm sure he's not thinking of anyone else right now."

"What did he say?" Tita Moon wondered, looking up at Laura with her wide, clouded eyes, as though she might draw comfort from her former fiancé's final words.

"He didn't say anything."

"He didn't curse me?"

"No."

"He didn't swear? He didn't hit anything? Throw a glass?"

"He put on his backpack and left."

Tita Moon hurried to the door and opened it, as if Rick might simply be sobbing on the porch steps. But she knew he was gone. She knew she would never see him again.

"Why don't you go after him?" Laura suddenly suggested.

"Where?"

"I don't know. Try the hotel. The airport."

If Tita Moon had any confidence in herself she would have sprung into action. She would have called the hotel to see if he had checked back in. She would have taken a taxi to the airport. She would have applied for a visa and bought a ticket to Baltimore and searched every photography store in the city. But she had never felt so unworthy of happiness.

"I don't deserve him," she said, and closed the door.

She could not go to work. How could she? Not today. Not tomorrow. Maybe never again. Carmen was at Arenal. Laura was on her way out. Tita Moon would be alone in the house during the very hours she was supposed to be at the beach with Rick. How could she survive these days, and the days after that?

"The worst thing you can do is lie around feeling sorry for yourself," Laura told her before leaving. "Go to work. I know it's early, but it's Saturday. You may get someone just arriving. And you won't be alone."

"I can't go there now!"

Laura considered her situation. "Then go home. Visit your parents, and your son."

Tita Moon knew this was the best advice, as hard as it was to repack her bag, to take the same bus they would have taken together, to sit alone for the two-hour ride to Puntarenas. But where else could she go?

Puntarenas was a port city on the Pacific coast with a population of one hundred thousand. It didn't attract many tourists because the beaches were cleaner and more deserted across the Gulf of Nicoya, and to the south around Manual Antonio. But Tita Moon found the sea air invigorating and the people more friendly than in the capital. Except today. It was raining and the weather mirrored her bleak prospects. She felt lost, even in her hometown with its narrow streets and simple brick homes.

Tita Moon's parents lived in a single-story, two-bedroom house with peeling yellow paint and a broken drainpipe that leaked rainwater over the porch. It was the home she had been raised in, but she felt no particular affection for it. Usually places from one's childhood feel smaller when one is grown, but Tita Moon was the youngest of six brothers and sisters, and the house seemed more spacious now that her siblings were gone. As a child the house was always in a state of chaos and there was no privacy. Yet because she was ten years younger than the fifth child, she was never close with her brothers and sisters, who had since married and moved to other parts of the country. She rarely thought about them and only saw them now on holidays.

But Tita Moon was the kind of person who craved excitement and lived in the present. She hadn't thought of Rick after he went away the first time, even though she had begun to fall in love with him. Nor did she ever think about the father of her son, although she had once loved him with a passion. As for her parents, she was prouder of her father than of anyone in the world. The laconic fisherman almost old enough to be her grandfather, the man who had given her her cherished nickname. So few of her peers had fathers, and those who did complained of their alcoholism and other vices. But Tita Moon's father was a decent man who neither drank nor smoked, who woke before dawn, who had never mistreated her. Not that they were close or ever had much to say to each other, or even understood each other. It was the negative experience of her friends rather than any positive experience of her own that made her imagine her relationship with her father in almost idyllic terms.

She was actually much closer to her mother, who shared her ebullient personality, her hatred of housework, and some of her vices, such as smoking and swearing. She was twelve years younger than her father, and though she had given birth to six children and lived a hard, if not impoverished life, she wore her years lightly and was in excellent health. She was overweight but quick on her feet, dressed in colorful cotton frocks she sewed herself, wore her long hair in a thick braid and gazed at the world through childlike eyes, much like her youngest daughter.

Tita Moon's father was playing checkers at a restaurant down the street. Her mother was alone at home, cooking in the tiny kitchen.

"Good, you're here. You can help me peel these potatoes."

"Aren't you going to kiss me first?"

Her mother gave her a quick hug and kiss. She was expecting her daughter, but didn't know which day she would arrive. "Where is your boyfriend?"

"There is no boyfriend," Tita Moon replied. "I came alone."

She bent down to kiss the dog, a ragged-haired mongrel that had run in from the backyard at the sound of her voice. "How are you, Sunny? Have you been a good dog while I've been gone? Or are you still chasing the chickens?"

Her parents kept a couple chickens in a backyard coop for eggs.

She took out over two hundred dollars and quietly set the bills on the counter. Her mother waited until Tita Moon was peeling the potatoes to furtively stash them away. The issue of money was so awkward they never spoke about it, except for those times her mother explicitly asked her to send something. Otherwise, guilt prevented each of them from discussing it. Tita Moon felt guilty for not taking care of her son, and for lying to her parents about the source of her income. She told them she was a waitress at a top restaurant and make excellent tips. Whether they believed her she could never be certain, but she took comfort in the fact that they never visited San Jose and had probably never heard of the Hotel Grand. Her mother, on the other hand, felt guilty for taking advantage of her daughter's generosity, and for using some of the money on cigarettes or cosmetics or material for her dresses. Tita Moon would not have cared, of course, and would have given her parents money even if they weren't raising her son, but her mother did not know that. Her mother's guilt was compounded by her disappointment, which she tried to overcome but simply could not. Why couldn't her youngest daughter grow up like all the rest? Why couldn't she get married and be a mother to her own child? This disappointment often erupted into accusations and arguments when Tita Moon visited, requiring her father's intervention, the only time he entered their conversations. And today there was the bad news about Rick.

"What happened with your new boyfriend?" her mother asked, lighting the oven. "You sounded so happy on the phone. I thought you were engaged?"

Tita Moon had made the mistake of calling her mother last night to tell her the news and to expect them to visit in the next few days. Her mother immediately invited them for Sunday dinner, but Tita Moon demurred. They wanted to go to the beach first. She didn't want to make plans. They would just stop by.

"It was a mistake," was all Tita Moon could say. Fortunately her pregnancy was not showing and her mother's powers of perception were not as acute as Laura's. Tita Moon couldn't imagine what her mother would say when she found out. Or rather she knew exactly what she would say. First, Who is the father? Then, I hope you don't expect me to raise this one too.

"No, I don't," Tita Moon said aloud, imagining the conversation in her mind.

"What?"

Tita Moon finished peeling the last potato. "Where's Roberto?"

"He's across the street."

Tita Moon went to the neighbor's to get him. The rain had stopped and the sun had broken through, and for a few minutes Tita Moon's mood brightened as well, as she took her three-year-old son in her arms and twirled him around in her neighbor's front yard. She had last seen him a month ago and he seemed to have grown several inches.

"My you're so big!" she exclaimed, pinching his wide cheeks. "I hardly recognize you!"

Then she said hello to the neighbor's daughter, with whom he often played.

"We were coloring, Aunt Tita," her son said. Do you want to see?"

"Of course."

He was too young to know she was his real mother. Some day he would have to be told, or he would figure it out on his own. But by that time he would be so accustomed to calling the woman he lived with "mother" and Tita Moon "aunt" that he would probably always call them that.

She knelt down to look at their drawings and praised them lavishly. His was a picture of the neighbor's cat. "Can I have it?" she asked.

"Yes. Did you bring me candy?" He knew her as the woman who always gave him candy.

"No, I'm afraid I forgot." She watched the disappointment show on his face. Then she opened a purse. "But you can have a brush," she said, pulling out her brush.

Her son hardly had enough hair to brush. His grandfather took him to his own barber, who cut it like a soldier.

"Or I have lipstick," she said.

"I want the lipstick," the girl said.

Tita Moon hadn't expected this. She wanted to give the girl her lipstick, but realized the girl's parents would complain. Another black mark against her. "You're too young for lipstick." She put it back in her purse. "But maybe you can share a tissue?" And she waved a tissue in front of their faces.

They began to grow impatient, looking away. It was then that she said, "What is this? How did this get in my purse?" And she pulled out a bag of licorice.

"Candy!" he son shouted.

"Be sure to share," Tita Moon said, putting her son's drawing in her purse. "Do you want to come to the park?"

She played with them on the swings and the slide. If only motherhood were a matter of buying candy and swinging on swings, she would be a perfect mother. But all such moments had to end, and then she was lost. Before walking back to her parents' house a crazy thought came to her and she pulled her son over by the fence.

"Tell me, Roberto, would you like to live with me?"

His face lit up. "Sure!"

Tita Moon beamed. "Really?"

"Would Mama and Papa come too?"

Tita's face clouded over. "They would have to stay here. It would just be you and me."

"Oh."

"But we could visit them all the time."

"Can I go down the slide again?"

Tita Moon let go of his tiny hands and felt she was letting go forever, as though he were already a grown man, about to sail on a long voyage from which he might never return.

She greeted her father with a strong hug and a few tears before helping her mother set the table. Her father was a small man, much darker than her mother and herself from a lifetime spent in the sun, with deep wrinkles and rotting teeth. Still, he was healthy for his age and would even have looked handsome if not for his teeth. More than once Tita Moon had offered to pay to have them fixed, but he refused to go to a dentist.

"Just go for a consultation," Tita had urged him. "He won't touch you at all the first visit. Just talk. Then you can decide."

But her father refused even this compromise, complaining about the costs. His friends would tease him, he said, if he got his teeth crowned or replaced with dentures. They would say he was too good for them and should retire to St. Theresa with the rich people. But his real reason for refusing had nothing to do with putting on airs but rather was due to a lifelong fear of dentists.

He sat at the head of the unfinished wooden table, which had looked old when Tita Moon was a child. Her mother sat at the other end and Tita Moon and her son sat on opposite sides, her son in a high chair.

"Are you happy to see me, Papa?"

Her father smiled as her mother served him.

"Your daughter is not engaged after all," her mother told him in a sharp voice. "Tell your father what happened."

"There is nothing to tell," Tita Moon replied. "Let's talk about other things. Tell me about Roberto. He's grown so much! And his drawing!" She showed them the picture of the cat.

"Yes, he's been coloring a lot," her mother said.

"Why don't you hang them up? You must let me see them. Hey, Roberto, will you show me your drawings after dinner?"

Her mother said something noncommittal because his other drawings were portraits featuring himself and his grandparents, their dog, and even his friend across the street. But Tita Moon was never represented.

Her mother asked how things were in San Jose and in the restaurant where she supposedly worked. Tita responded vaguely, as she always did to such questions. But she did tell her parents about her new apartment with its wonderful view of the city.

"It must be expensive," her mother said. "How can you afford it?"

"Laura is my friend. She gives me a special price," Tita Moon answered evasively.

"You should be living with a husband and not two women," her mother remarked. "You're twenty-three years old. Your sisters were all married before they were twenty."

"In the United States a lot of women don't marry until they are in their thirties," Tita Moon countered. "These are successful women with careers. It is the way things are done now."

But the sight of her son across the table reminded her that she was not one of these women and she let her argument expire.

Her mother then began talking about her five other children, in Liberia and Guanacaste and on the Caribbean coast. About their families and how well they were doing and how proud she was of them.

But do any of them bring you two hundred dollars when they visit? Tita Moon wanted to say in defense. But she knew she could not raise the issue of money because it would invariably lead to her sin of having a child out of wedlock. This was hardly a rare occurrence in Costa Rica, of course, but Tita Moon's parents were conservative and religious. There were wooden crucifixes on the walls and a painting of Jesus above the bed. They had taken Tita Moon to church every Sunday and had expected her to turn out like their other children, quiet, serious, responsible. Instead, to their dismay, they discovered she was too fond of boys, started making the wrong kind of girlfriends, never came home on time and finally, after a thousand arguments, moved out of the house when she was seventeen to live in a squalid apartment with her worthless boyfriend. After giving birth she would abandon her family for the capital, to waste her time working in a restaurant instead of taking care of her child and looking for a proper husband. Of course, the real story was quite different. Tita Moon had heard from a girlfriend about the massage parlors in San Jose where a woman could earn twenty dollars a customer. So she moved to a tiny flat in the slums where the doors were locked with padlocks and took the bus each morning to Candy's Sauna, where she sucked and fucked clients on high, narrow massage tables that creaked under the weight. But she argued almost daily with the proprietress and was thinking of leaving for another establishment when a client secretly paid her to spend the night at his hotel. She had heard of the Hotel Grand by now, it was only a few blocks away. She knew the women there made up to a hundred dollars a client and kept all their earnings. What's more, they could work at night, whereas the massage parlors closed at eight. But her colleagues at Candy's told her it was packed wall to wall with working girls, and a woman could starve if she wasn't beautiful and willing to hustle. Tita Moon assumed she wasn't pretty enough, but her client assured her otherwise and she made the move.

"Did you go to church this morning?" her mother asked.

"I didn't have time."

Tita, of course, did not correct her parents' assumption that she still went to church every week, but she didn't feel she could lie when asked about particulars.

"You had time for this man you aren't engaged to," her mother snapped.

Tita Moon burst into tears, crying helplessly over her plate.

"What are you doing? Leave her alone!" her father shouted, interjecting in his daughter's behalf, as he always did in such moments, but always too late.

Roberto came around the table and pulled at her shirt. Tita Moon grabbed him so tightly she frightened both of them and fled into the bathroom to compose herself.

The rest of the meal passed in silence, and she helped her mother wash the dishes without a glance passing between them. Then she took her bags and kissed them all goodbye.

"But I thought you were staying," her mother said in a disappointed voice, as though they had passed the afternoon in a state of unremitting pleasantness.

"I can't stay," was all Tita could answer as she kissed her son a final time, tears raining on her cheeks.

She didn't know, of course, as she took the bus back to San Jose, that she was going to kill herself. She lived too much in the present to make such a plan, even if its execution was only a few hours away. Rather she reacted to the sense of isolation and loss she felt by fleeing home. For the moment it was all she could do to breathe, to sit quietly and not to cry.

A light was on in the living room but the dining room was dark and the table cleared. She didn't see Laura or Raquel, and that was just as well. She gulped down a bottle of water in the dark kitchen before going into the bathroom. It was only when she saw her pink razor on the bathtub that she recognized the solution to all her problems.

She ran the water, checking that the temperature was warm, then went into her room a final time and sat for a minute on the bed. She looked at the clock. It was 10:36. She stared at the photo of her and Rick, which she had taped to the wall. She pulled out her son's drawing from her purse and held it in both hands.

Back in the bathroom, she did not lock the door. She realized Laura would be angry enough that she killed herself in her new house without forcing her to break the door. She turned out the light and lit a scented candle on the sink. It belonged to Raquel, but it seemed a nice touch and she had no candles of her own. Although it was a violation of her rental agreement, she assumed Raquel would forgive her the use of her candle. As for her suicide itself, she had so much to feel guilty for already, she was not overly concerned about the effect this might have on Laura. She would try not to make a mess of it. What else could she do?

She undressed and sank into the water, her heart beating rapidly. She kept the water running but removed the plug so the blood would drain. This was how she had seen it done on "Vale of Tears." The warm water enveloping her body felt like a blanket and her mind was calm, although her hands were trembling as she broke the plastic handle and removed the razor. She did not think. There was nothing to think about. Only a final prayer.

With her eyes closed, she drew the razor across her left wrist in a rapid but instinctively cautious motion. Then she leapt up and screamed. It stung like the world's worst paper cut and she shivered uncontrollably, in mental and physical shock. This is not how it happened on "Vale of Tears," which was practically an advertisement for suicide, where tormented characters escaped their misery in silence and peace, with radiant expressions.

Then Tita Moon saw the blood and screamed even louder, jumping up and down in the tub. She grabbed her wrist but blood was spattering everywhere, on the walls and tile floor and sink.

A moment later Laura flung open the door and screamed in terror, putting her hands to her face. For a second or two she did nothing, paralyzed with the horror of the scene. But then instinct took over and she grabbed a towel and made a tourniquet around Tita's wrist and laid her on the floor and held the wrist aloft.

All this happened in a matter of seconds. Tita Moon was no longer screaming. Her lids were heavy.

"Hold the towel here, can you do that?" Laura asked, placing Tita's right hand around her left wrist. "Hold tight, I'll be back in a second."

She rushed to get her cell phone and called for an ambulance as Tita Moon lost consciousness.

When she woke she saw the troubled but comforting faces of her two best friends hovering above her.

"Am I in heaven?"

"I don't think they have IV's in heaven," Carmen pointed out.

Tita Moon looked at the IV in her arm and realized she was in a hospital. "True."

She had been taken to a public hospital, stabilized, then transferred to the maternity ward, thanks to Laura informing the doctor she was pregnant. Only a few hours had passed. It was still night, and most of the women on the ward were sleeping.

Carmen pulled a curtain around the bed for privacy and squeezed her friend's hand. "I'm so glad you're alive!" she cried.

Tita Moon reflected for a moment. "I thought you went to Arenal?"

"I came back early. But I was almost too late. Why didn't you call me when Rick left you?"

Tita Moon didn't have an answer. She looked at Laura instead. "I'm sorry about everything. I'll move out as soon—"

"Of course you won't move out," Laura told her. "Who will look after you? You are not my tenant, you are my friend."

This brought tears to Tita's eyes, but tears of gratitude.

The nurse on duty saw that her patient was awake and asked her friends to leave. She took her pulse and looked into her eyes. "You're going to be fine," the old nurse said with a sympathetic smile. "You lost some blood but it could have been worse. Just try to rest."

Tita Moon had cut her wrist not to harm her baby but to extinguish her own life. But now she realized that her rash action was a blessing in disguise and that she had solved the problem of her unwanted pregnancy without recourse to abortion.

"Thank you. It's too bad about the baby, though."

The old nurse looked at her with a puzzled expression. "What do you mean? The baby's fine. You're going to be a mother!"

Tita Moon did not understand. This never happened on Vale of Tears. On "Vale of Tears" they always lost the baby.

She leaned her head back on the pillow and gazed up at the white ceiling. "Oh my God! Give me a noose this time!"

CHAPTER 15

RAQUEL'S RECORD NIGHT

When Raquel came home late that Sunday night from her parents' house she set her purse on the dining room table and went into the bathroom. When she turned on the light she screamed louder than Tita Moon and Laura combined. She grabbed her purse and ran outside, fearing that the attacker or attackers might still be in the house. She dashed into the car, locked the door and called the police, telling them in a breathless voice that blood was spattered all over the guest bathroom and that while she didn't see any bodies, she feared either her roommate or landlord or both had been murdered or kidnapped.

She was told to stay where she was, but she felt like a target, even in her locked car. She wanted to drive away but knew she couldn't leave the scene of a crime when her friends might still be alive and in peril. So she ran to the neighbor's and banged on the door.

When Laura returned from the hospital she found the entire neighborhood awake, in a state of agitation, standing in clusters on their lawns or in the street, dressed in their night clothes. Four patrol cars were parked outside her house, and when she entered she found an officer in her closet, waving one of her dresses under the nose of a bloodhound.

"Why didn't you just call me?" she screamed at Raquel after explaining the mistake to the police and herding them out.

"I saw all the blood! I thought you were dead!" Raquel screamed back, hugging her friend with relief.

They cried on each other's shoulder. "It's my fault," Laura realized. "I should have called you from the hospital to warn you. But I wasn't thinking either."

Laura led her back inside by the hand, almost forcibly, and made chamomile tea to soothe their nerves. She closed the bathroom door.

I will clean everything tomorrow, and buy you new things. Tonight you will use my bathroom."

Raquel had been unemployed for nearly four weeks. During that time she had searched for work every day and submitted to so many interviews she could not remember them all. Three times she had even been hired, only to lose the job within a day or two for one reason or another beyond her control. She struggled to keep up her studies, but she was in a state of ceaseless distraction. She had broken up with her boyfriend because money had been the glue that kept them together and without it they drifted apart. She sought comfort and financial help from her family, but about all they could offer her now were free meals on Sundays. If she didn't find something in another week she would have to sell her car and move back home.

It was Monday night, and Raquel was still shaken from the events of the early morning. Yet the gory evidence of Tita Moon's desperation illuminated the jagged shoals of her own life like a beacon from a lighthouse. If she continued along this course and gave in to a sense of helplessness and self-pity, next week it could just as easily be her own blood on the wall.

She walked into a pharmacy as though she were going to buy shampoo or aspirin. But instead she stopped in front of the condoms. She had never bought condoms before. She used birth control pills and her former boyfriend was the only man she had ever slept with.

The choices confounded her. Colors and textures, lubricated and not. She should call Laura, but she was too embarrassed. Yet if she could not even talk about the act with her friend, how could she possibly go through with it with strangers? She tried to think. This wasn't university material. First she would suck, so lubrication was a bad idea. But then she would want lubrication inside her. She never used anything with her boyfriend, but then she was usually aroused and he came pretty quickly anyway. What if she got someone who took a long time or had a big cock? She didn't want her first client to put her out of commission.

Only then did she notice the row of lubricants on the shelf above. This was easy, after all. If only safe sex weren't so expensive. She spent the last of her colones on this small investment and avoided eye contact with the clerk as she made her purchase.

To be a psychologist requires years of study, she thought as she left the pharmacy. You have to buy textbooks for your classes and then after you graduate you need an office and receptionist and phones and shelves for files. But to be a prostitute all you need is a box of condoms.

This was an oversimplification, of course, which Raquel understood viscerally as she tentatively entered the Hotel Grand. A prostitute might not need years of study and an office, but she must have a shameless fortitude no amount of training can prepare one for. It was like touching your nose with your tongue, she concluded. You could either do it or you could not. And now was her chance to discover into which demographic she fell.

A mousy girl she had never seen before was finishing up at the travel desk. Probably Mr. Escudero's niece. This only solidified Raquel's resolve and she strode on to the Red Volcano.

She had deliberately come early, before the crowd. She would lean against the bar and chat with the female bartenders, whom she knew. Anyone might think she was there on hotel business and not to pick up men. She was still a respectable young woman, who wore a denim skirt and flat shoes. Certainly not the costume of a working girl. Her blue eyes were made up and she wore lipstick, but she had no jewelry or tattoos, not even earrings. Her only accessory was a simple denim purse with a box of condoms and a small bottle of lubricant inside.

She was still a psychology student and this evening's exercise might be nothing more than that—an exercise. If no one approached her she would leave the hotel as a woman who was still not far removed from her virginity, and she could go to sleep no richer than the night before, but secure in the knowledge she had tried this avenue of last resort before selling her car, abandoning her studies and moving back home.

Gloria, the bartender who had played basketball in high school, gave her a beer on the house, and the two chatted for some time. Raquel realized Gloria would be a good resource but she wasn't ready to show her hand. Of course there was also Carmen, whom Raquel had met a few times, but she wouldn't arrive until later. So she leaned against the bar and listened to Gloria gossip about hotel staff, many of whom were familiar to Raquel, and patiently sipped her beer.

"Hello beautiful!"

It was Colorado Bob lumbering toward her. How had she not seen him? He must have just come from the casino. They had known each other long before Laura's retirement party. In fact, Colorado was one of her first clients at the travel desk, where he often booked fishing charters. He never failed to invite her and occasionally made salacious comments. "There's a premium on blue eyes here," he would tell her. "You could buy a lot of textbooks if you stood on the other side."

"And how much would you pay me for my blue eyes?" she would banter back with a smile that was as intimidating as it was seductive.

"For you I might even break my rule of never paying a hundred."

And Raquel would hand him his voucher. "Maybe you'll catch a blue-eyed fish."

"I thought you got fired," Colorado now said, sizing her up. He had rarely seen her standing and had forgotten how tall she was. Not a spinner, not one of these petite things you could toss in the air like a kitten. No, Raquel was a lot of woman, the kind you had to wrestle with, and who might pin you to the mat more often than not.

"I quit," Raquel corrected him.

"Have you been working out?" Colorado Bob asked, squeezing her biceps.

"Hey, what are you doing?" Raquel exclaimed with mild indignation.

"I just can't help admiring female beauty. I'm a connoisseur, you know."

"You're too cheap to be a connoisseur," Raquel remarked. "You're just an addict."

"I always pay a fair price. And in your case I would break my rule and lay out a hundred."

"Okay."

Colorado laughed, thinking she was playing with him. But her expression was serious, even troubled. "What did you say?"

What had she said? What was she doing? If she had to pick from all the men in the bar, Colorado Bob would be at the very bottom of her list. On the other hand, she hadn't been here half an hour and she had a firm offer of a hundred. If she didn't jump at this chance perhaps no one else would approach her and she would go home broke with a box of condoms she would never use. What was an hour with this fat bastard against the continuation of her studies, her car, her room at Laura's house?

"In advance," Raquel whispered. "And no funny business."

"Holy shit! This is my lucky year." Then, noting her distress and wanting to befriend her, he added, "You're really hard up aren't you?"

"We're all hard up," she teased.

"Let me go to the ATM. Don't leave. Don't talk to strangers."

Gloria was busy across the bar. Raquel was glad she hadn't heard. She could have run out, of course. But she didn't. Why should I feel so ashamed and embarrassed? she asked herself. It's just societal conditioning. Look at Laura. She's as good as anyone I know. Look at the other girls here. Are they any worse than the girls on the other side of the wall? I'll take the worst of them over Mr. Escudero's niece any day.

She drank the rest of her beer, no longer sipping.

Colorado had a brainstorm at the ATM, a solution to both of their problems. She needed money and he had his principle to preserve. He didn't have a room at the hotel, of course. But he spent enough money at the bar and restaurant and casino that the management usually comped him one if requested. Tonight he was pleased to hear the Irazu suite was available.

"We're going to break you in in style," he told her back at the bar. "They like me so much here they comped me a suite."

"What makes you think you're breaking me in?"

"I can see the terror in your sweet blue eyes."

"It's loathing. Okay. You're right. So be nice."

He took her hand. He took it like he was grabbing his hat. But for Raquel it was a strange feeling to be holding a strange man's hand. It wasn't something she did often, or lightly. Except for her boyfriend, she couldn't think of the last time she had held a guy's hand. Ticas were known for being affectionate, but Raquel was an exception.

They stopped at the puta registration. She had to sign her name and hand over her national ID card. The young man at the desk recognized her with a stare that said everything.

Raquel lowered her eyes. She could still save her virtue. Say it was a joke, grab her ID and flee. But she merely watched as the clerk filed her card alphabetically in a box filled with other ID cards and foreign passports. Be strong, she told herself. This was paying for her tuition. Who was this clerk to judge her? Rise above the fray.

But as they waited for the freight elevator she felt naked before the world. She resisted the urge to remove her hand from his.

"Let's take the stairs," she said.

"It's on the top floor. Do you want me panting before I even take my shirt off?"

The elevator finally opened and they squeezed inside.

"I've been lusting after you for a long time," Colorado Bob confessed. "So don't hold it against me if I fail to perform with my customary stamina."

"This may be my first time but I'm not a virgin. And I have friends in the business, so I know more than you think. So don't try any tricks."

"I don't know what you're talking about."

"Like telling me girls do it without condoms, or trying to talk me into perversions. I know what goes on here, so if you think you're going to take advantage of me, think again."

"But I don't want to take advantage of you. I just want to take you! In fact I have a proposition for you," he said as he opened the door to the Irazu suite and waved her inside.

Despite having worked at the hotel for nearly a year, Raquel had never set foot inside a guest room, and she looked around like a curious child, almost forgetting why she was here.

The suite consisted of a living room with a plush sofa and chair, a large round table, a wooden computer desk, a phone with two lines, a TV with a DVD player, and a minibar. The large bedroom contained a second TV, another phone, a large dresser and mirror, and a king-sized bed with a jungle pattern comforter. Raquel was admiring the panoramic view from the window when Colorado Bob pinched her ass.

She shrieked and turned to hit him, stopping herself at the last moment, remembering her place. "Hey," she warned him instead. "Be nice."

"I have your welfare in mind, baby. You want to hear my proposition?"

"I don't know."

"I'll call some of my buddies and ask them over. If I can get you four more sessions tonight you'll do me for sixty."

"You want to be my pimp?

"Pimps get a lot more than ten percent. I just want a modest discount."

"Ah, because you never pay a hundred," Raquel realized.

"It's not the money, it's the principle."

"Okay, but you pay in advance and I'll refund the forty dollars if the other guys show. And no monkey business. One on one, no cameras, no guys watching. No seconds. And no one fatter or older than you."

"Next thing you'll tell me I can't smoke a cigar in my own suite."

"Smoke all you want. We psychology students all know cigars smokers are closet homosexuals," she teased him with a brave smile.

But inside her stomach was turning. What was she doing here, alone in the Irazu suite with Colorado Bob of all people, about to get undressed and lie on the king-sized bed with its awful African print comforter and let that enormous slob stick his...

God! She ran into the bathroom, while Colorado Bob slumped on the sofa and began making his calls. She turned on the water and splashed her face. She realized she was hyperventilating and told herself to take deep breaths. She looked at herself in the mirror.

I can't believe anyone would even want me the way I look, she told herself. Men are blind. Then she noticed the jacuzzi tub and opened the door long enough to shout out, "And no jacuzzis!"

But she probably had no right to make such a demand. Colorado Bob was promising the chance to make a windfall. Maybe she was the one who should start being nice. There were a hundred girls down below who would scratch her eyes out for this kind of money.

She sat on the toilet and called Laura on her cell phone. Raquel often appeared older than her eighteen years because of her intelligence and maturity. But she was still very inexperienced in life, and Laura, Carmen and Tita Moon, thought they might act less mature at times, were all several years older.

"How is Tita?" she asked, suddenly recalling the plight of her fellow lodger.

"I think they are going to let her out of the hospital tomorrow," Laura replied. "I visited her earlier and she was very emotional. But I think she was so frightened by last night she will never try to kill herself again."

"Well that's good. Listen. You'll never guess where I am. I'm in the bathroom of the Irazu suite."

There was a moment of silence on the other end. "At the hotel?"

"I decided to start working here."

Laura's confusion was obvious. "You mean back at the travel desk? But then why are you in the Irazu suite?"

"Not the travel desk. You know!"

"Oh my God! I can't believe it. Raquel, you're the last person..."

"I don't want you to talk me out of it."

"But why?"

"You know why. I need money. I've been looking for work for a month and I'm desperate."

"Raquel, that's not a good reason. As far as the rent, I can wait. We can work something out. I would feel too guilty taking money that you earned—"

"But I need money for everything. School, my car, my independence. Why did *you* start working?"

There was another pause. "I had a child."

Raquel was shocked. She had never heard Laura speak of a child. "I didn't know."

"She was born premature and died at four months. I don't talk about it."

"I'm sorry. But then why did you continue? I mean, after the baby..."

"Because I liked the money and I liked the sex and I liked the attention from men all over the world and I was too lazy to go to university. But you are different, Raquel."

"I don't think I am. I think I'm the same as you. I just have less experience with guys. That's why I called. I don't want you to talk me out of it. I want you to advise me how to handle men."

"You mean you haven't done it yet?"

"I'm sitting on the toilet still in my clothes. I have a box of condoms in my purse."

"And what's the guy like? Anyone I might know?"

Now it was Raquel's turn to be silent. She didn't want to say, but then she thought if Laura was going to help her, she had a right to know.

"It's Colorado," she whispered.

"Oh shit! Get out of there now! Jump out the window if you have to!"

"I can deal with him. It's the sex I'm worried about."

"But Colorado is a slob, he does not respect women, and he never pays a hundred."

"He is paying me a hundred. In advance. I am the first one," she said, almost proudly. She decided not to mention the possibility of a rebate.

"One of the things I am worried about," she continued in an embarrassed voice, cupping her hand over the phone, "is what if he lies on top of me? He's so heavy. How do you deal with that?"

"Sharp fingernails. I never slept with him myself. But no, don't worry about that. Most very fat men do not like to do missionary because it takes too much energy. And I know from friends who have been with him that he prefers the woman on top."

"Well that won't be so hard then," Raquel said with a sigh of relief. "What about the condoms? Do I put them on or do they?"

"You put them on. Sometimes they will be hard already. If not give them a hand job or massage until they are. If you like to dance you can do a striptease, turn them on that way. It's up to you. Some of the girls here give blowjobs without condoms and men will often ask for that. But don't give in. And no French kissing. And no anal. Let them get a Colombian if they want that. What else? A lot of guys want to lick you. I say that's up to you. The same with lesbian shows. Just agree on the price and get the money in advance. Of course, I didn't always get the money in advance myself, especially with regulars. But it's a good rule."

"Thanks a lot."

"But these are details anyone can learn in two minutes," Laura went on. "The more important thing, what separates the elite working girl from the puta, is more difficult to learn."

"You mean respect?" Raquel guessed.

"Exactly. You have to be strong and take control. But it's a fine line. For instance, a lot of guys don't like smart women. So you have to let them think they are in control, but actually you are. You know what I mean?"

"I already made a mistake by teasing Colorado," Raquel admitted.

"Don't worry about him. With Colorado I think you can be a little cruel, because he doesn't take himself seriously. That's the one nice thing I can say about him. Some men like cheerleaders who will stroke their ego, some men like geishas, some men like dominatrixes. You have to figure out their personalities and take advantage of their desire for you. You're a psychology student. I don't need to tell you this."

"Yes, but I'm only in my first year."

"Well, after Colorado you'll be ready to graduate. Or you'll be a vegetable in the psyche ward. Good luck."

Raquel washed her face again, brushed her hair and checked her makeup, not for Colorado Bob's benefit as much as for her own. She opened the lubricant and rubbed a generous amount inside her, then smelled her hand, overcome with revulsion and curiosity. It wasn't so bad, but she washed her hands thoroughly anyway. Then she opened the box of condoms and took one out and read the instructions. Here goes, she thought.

Colorado Bob was still on the phone. But there were five crisp twenties on the table. Raquel stashed them in her purse and returned to the bathroom, where she undressed completely and wrapped herself in one of the plush white oversized towels reserved for the suites. Laura's suggestion of a striptease was out of the question, and she suspected Colorado was already sufficiently aroused.

She returned to the living room and hesitantly sat next to him on the couch, as though she were entering a cold swimming pool. Colorado smiled, still talking to one of his friends, and put a huge hairy hand on her knee. Raquel tentatively swept her hand along his shoulder.

"This is your lucky night," he told her, finally finished with his calls. "You'll be able to retire tomorrow."

"So your friend is coming?"

"Friends, my dear. Friends! They wouldn't miss this for the world."

She eyed him skeptically. "No funny business, right?"

"A more sensitive group of seasoned mongers you will not find. Straight fucking. We won't even swear."

"But you just swore."

He set his cigar in the ashtray and put his arm around her. Raquel felt her heart racing. "You want to do it here or in the bedroom."

"How about the floor?"

"The floor!"

"My back, you see." Not surprisingly, Colorado Bob had back problems, and the beds in the suites were softer than those in the standard rooms.

This was good news. It meant he wasn't going to try to get on top of her. He undressed, letting his clothes fall where they may, and grabbed a towel of his own, which he spread on the floor between the couch and table. With a groan of anticipation he lay on his back.

"You know what to do dear, or would you like some help?" he asked, tilting his head up.

To Raquel's relief he was already hard. And if he was volunteering to put the condom on, why refuse?

"Watch and learn," he said, tearing open the wrapper and rolling it on in a smooth motion. "Looks easy, but I've had inexperienced girls who get it going the wrong way and it becomes an ordeal. The best ones put it on with their mouth."

"Do you want a pillow? You don't look very comfortable."

"I'm in heaven. But a pillow will be better to see you with."

Raquel didn't know why she had made the suggestion. She handed him one of the large satin pillows from the couch and then, without thinking, shut her eyes and reached down and grabbed him.

"Ahhh."

She had done this often enough with her boyfriend. She closed her eyes and imagined it was he she was wrapping her lips around. The condom tasted peculiar, but she was grateful for this barrier separating her from Colorado's pallid flesh.

"Open your eyes, baby. Look at me with those blue eyes."

Raquel reluctantly complied. He was breathing heavily and she almost stopped, thinking he might be in pain, perhaps having a heart attack.

"Oh sweet Jesus!"

He made her stop, but for different reasons. He was fast approaching the breaking point and wanted desperately to come inside her. This had been a fantasy of his since he first saw her sitting with her legs crossed behind the travel desk. True, he'd had a lot of women since retiring to Costa Rica with a healthy nest egg from the building supply business. But very few had been beautiful, because he refused to pay a hundred and he was drawn to girls who were not repelled by his size and habits. In fact, for all his swagger and banter, he was somewhat intimidated by pretty women and felt truly relaxed in their company only when he had something to offer them, as in the case with Tita.

Raquel straddled him and rocked back and forth. Colorado closed his eyes, so she closed her eyes as well. She felt his hands squeezing her knees and a couple minutes later he grunted with pleasure and let go.

She rose up and rushed into the bathroom, leaving him to dispose of the condom. She jumped into the shower and turned up the hot water.

"What are you doing in there?" Colorado called after a while. "Your next appointment is on his way up."

He waited for her to emerge before he went in himself, his clothes and towel in a pile in his hands.

Raquel began to dress, then wondered why, since she was only going to have to disrobe again in a few minutes. But the thought of meeting a stranger wrapped in a towel seemed undignified to her.

She had just slipped into her shoes when there was an eager knock on the door. A monger knock. His name was Jerry and he was on the wrong side of fifty, a couple years older than Colorado Bob, but in good enough shape to take the stairs if he had to. Firm and tan, with thinning brown hair and wire-rimmed glasses, he was one of Colorado's poker buddies. He was a semi-retired broker, dividing his time between Chicago and San Jose.

He smiled amiably, introduced himself without trying to kiss her and helped himself to a beer from the minibar.

"I booked a fishing tour with you a few months ago. I guess you don't remember."

Raquel hadn't really wanted to look at him closely, but now she had no choice. "Sorry."

"That's all right. But I remember you," he said with a smirk. "Obviously."

"You naughty boy."

Colorado came out, dressed and washed, though the blood hadn't quite left his cheeks.

"Don't waste the girl's time, Jerry. The bedroom's thataway!"

Raquel led him into the bedroom and locked the door. "Can you please pay me first?"

Jerry gave her the money. "You know I don't normally pay up front. But Colorado vouched for you. Just don't tell the other ladies."

"I'm not going to tell anyone anything."

"I also never pay a hundred for less than two hours. But I won't make an issue of that tonight. But I do expect French kissing."

Raquel frowned. Jerry was obviously a control freak, a negotiator, and she was about to go out and lay down the law to Colorado. But then she decided to see if she could take control of the situation herself.

She took off his glasses and began unbuttoning his shirt. "No kissing on the mouth, French or otherwise," she said quietly but firmly. "Colorado should have told you that. "But you can kiss lower down if you want."

This was obviously acceptable to Jerry, for he remained silent as she undressed him further. Besides, he was blind without his glasses.

Raquel turned the TV on to a music video station in case Colorado tried to listen at the door and drew the curtains over the window.

Jerry did go down on her and he was much better than her boyfriend. Well, he should be, with all his experience. She lay quietly, not enough of an exhibitionist to fake an orgasm. But when he fucked her she did start to moan a little, surprised at the way he made her feel. Despite his age, his body felt strong and he knew how to make love to a woman. He didn't try to kiss her mouth, but he kissed her neck and licked her ear and she thought, what the hell, it doesn't feel half bad.

He came on top of her. When Raquel rolled him over she saw his cock becoming flaccid before her eyes. But what startled her was the semen in the tip. She had never seen semen before. She hadn't looked at Colorado at all, and with her boyfriend he always came inside her.

"The tissues are there," he told her.

"Oh."

She awkwardly unrolled the condom into a handful of tissues and thrust it into the waste basket beside the bed.

She began to dress, even though she was only going to take a couple steps to the bathroom for another shower.

"You must have been with a lot of women," she said.

"That depends who you're comparing me to. Actually I was a virgin till I was twenty."

"Really?"

Then the next twenty years I only had three women, all wives. Now ex-wives. Of course I'm making up for it now."

"Well, you seem to know what you're doing."

He pinched her cheek. "Thanks, sweetie. You're gorgeous."

She let him go into the bathroom first. Then she hurried in and took her shower. She had wanted to ask him what he thought of her as a lover, but she lacked the courage.

When Raquel came back out Colorado and Jerry were sitting on the sofa watching a boxing match. She grabbed a Red Bull from the minibar and walked to the window and peered at the lights of the city. It was a beautiful view, yet what ugly things she had to do to behold it. Still, she had two hundred dollars in her purse. She wouldn't have to let her gas tank run down to empty. She wouldn't have to borrow Laura's food. She wouldn't have to drop out of school. Two hundred dollars was more than some Nicaraguans earned in a month.

The door opened and three boisterous, forty-something men, Bingo, Ian and Stan, stumbled in carrying six-packs, potato chips, poker chips and cards.

"Why'd you bring beer?" Colorado asked. "I have a minibar."

"Yes, but it's a minibar," the one called Bingo pointed out. He was bald, with bushy eyebrows that reminded him of the unfairness of the world. He wore a red Hawaiian shirt, open to reveal a pair of gold chains and a hairy chest. Indeed, hair seemed to grow everywhere but on his scalp.

"And they charge four dollars for a beer in the minibar," Stan remarked. He was a retired dentist from New York, clean shaven, with manicured hands.

"They're comping me the room," Colorado said.

"But not the minibar," Ian chimed in, betraying his roots Down Under with his Australian accent. An expat from Melbourne, he was the youngest and best looking of the group, with long brown hair he wore combed back and faded tattoos covering his biceps.

"Of course the minbar's included," Colorado shot back. "They'll even comp me room service. Who do you bozos think you're dealing with?"

"Well in that case I'll drink the good stuff," Stan said, opening the minibar and removing the miniature bottle of Hennessy.

"What's a chick doing here?" Bingo exclaimed, looking at her for the first time.

Raquel stared at them, her back to the window. She had no idea what was expected of her now. Maybe these three had just come to play poker and it was time for her to go.

"Hi, I'm Bingo," he said, shaking her hand. "Can I book an excursion with you to the bedroom?"

"Not so fast," Stan said. "Seniority rules. That is, unless you haven't gone yet, Colorado."

"The bedroom is thataway, boys," Colorado said. "Cut cards if you like."

"How about rock, paper, scissors?" Bingo joked.

Or was it a joke? As Raquel watched them cut cards for her she stood enthralled at these men, all old enough to be her father, acting like little boys. Then she realized something she had not considered before. They would not only talk about her among themselves, they would talk about her to whomever would listen.

"Hey wait a minute," she said in an urgent voice. "You're not going to write about me on the internet?"

"Of course we are," Bingo replied. "You think we like sex? What really turns us on is posting on message boards. You're just a means to an end, baby."

She stepped in front of Colorado. "You can't write about me!"

"You should use a stage name if you're shy."

She thought for a moment. All right then. Write all you want, but don't describe me too accurately and call me 'Miss Escudero,'" she said, thinking of her former boss's niece.

Stan took her hand, having drawn an ace. He was a gentleman, grateful and easy to please, and she was back in the shower twenty minutes later.

When she came out the boys were playing poker, drinking and smoking. It wasn't even midnight and she had three hundred dollars in her purse, as much as she had made in a month at the travel desk.

She drank an orange juice and grabbed some potato chips from the table.

Ian was next. He was the quietest among the guys, but in the bedroom he liked to talk. Raquel saw him right away for preferring the cheerleader type. He asked for a massage first and she could tell he wanted her to compliment his tattoos and listen to his stories about being in the Royal Navy, about bars and fights and bikes and strippers. But in the end, despite his rough good looks and certified manliness, he was as insecure as any of the others, asking her over and over if she liked it, if she liked him, if she was going to come.

Of course she wasn't going to come. But she might have enjoyed the sex if she weren't so sore and tired. And she still had Bingo waiting in the wings. As it was, she tried her best to give Ian what he wanted, and send him back to his mates.

She had never taken so many showers in her life. She had thought she would be in tears by now, but her fortitude surprised her. She avoided thoughts of shame and self-pity by trying to view the experience from a distance and analyze its meaning. So much was new and strange to her. But what puzzled her most was why Colorado Bob was so eager to let his friends in on the action. The discount could only be part of the story, she realized.

If I were a man and a woman I had been lusting after suddenly became available, I certainly wouldn't call my friends to join in, she thought. I would want her for myself. I would be jealous.

She tried to recall all the occasions she had seen Colorado Bob. At the travel desk, in the bar, the casino, milling around the lobby, at Laura's retirement party. She realized he was rarely alone, and more often in the company of men than women. Maybe that's it, she thought. Women for him were like fish or cigars or beer, something he used to help him bond with other men. Maybe, despite his salacious persona, he cared less for the love of the opposite sex than for the friendship of his own.

Bingo didn't ask for a massage but asked to massage Raquel. She greeted this request with relief, glad to rest for a few minutes, even if Bingo was less than an accomplished masseuse. He took his time, still wearing his boxers, and made small talk about the hotel, local restaurants, the latest movies. He seemed to talk just to talk, not nervous but disengaged. He didn't appear to want a cheerleader or a geisha or a dominatrix. Maybe there were more than three types, Raquel thought.

She lay on her back as he caressed her breasts and wondered what other types there might be.

"You're going to have to stop this soon if you want to have sex," she finally said.

"I don't want to have sex."

She opened her eyes.

"Some nights I just can't, you know."

"Why don't you take a pill?"

"They don't work for me."

Thus far Raquel had been doing her best to cope with men's lechery. She hadn't had to deal with their vulnerability, and she almost felt disappointed.

"Well, is there something you want me to do?"

"Don't post this on the internet," he said with a wink.

She winked back. She reached out to him and he held her in his arms, no longer trying to make conversation. For the first time that night she felt comfortable.

"But if tonight's one of your bad nights, why did you come?"

"Because you'll be gone tomorrow."

"Gone? Where am I going?"

And then Raquel realized what Colorado Bob had assumed and what he told his friends. That explained his excitement, his urgency. Raquel, the good girl who lost her job at the travel desk was hard up. Desperation had driven her to the other side of the wall. But once she had a couple hundred dollars she would pay her debts and disappear behind another desk, respectable again. And there were girls like that. Who tried the life for a night or a weekend or a month and never came back.

But Raquel was coming back. Wasn't she?

She didn't even have to shower this time, but only washed. Ian had been called away for some reason more urgent than an all night poker game, but the other three were enjoying themselves beneath a cloud of smoke, the 24-hour sports channel providing ambiance.

"You must be hungry after burning all those calories," Colorado said, as Raquel grabbed a Sprite to go. "I'll order room service."

"He must really love you," Jerry remarked.

"He said it's comped," Raquel reminded him.

"He didn't ask if *we* wanted anything."

"I could use a club sandwich," Raquel told him.

Colorado lumbered over to the phone and ordered for everybody. After he hung up, Raquel tried to slip him his forty-dollar discount, but he waved it away.

"Put it in the game," he said. "There's an empty chair. We're playing Texas hold 'em. I'll teach you."

"I know how to play," Raquel said, having been around the casino too long not to be familiar with the games. And she had played with her university friends, though never for stakes higher than a few hundred colones.

She sat between Bingo and Colorado, wondering even before she drew her first cards if he was bluffing or not. Was he being uncharacteristically generous or was he trying to win back all the money she'd made with her box of condoms? She didn't know. But she knew herself, and resolved not to lose more than the forty dollars she cashed in for chips, or to drink anything stronger than Sprite. After she ate her club sandwich she would go home with $460 in her purse, as much money as someone with a degree might make in a month.

But her club sandwich was now a mere shred of crust on a plate set outside the suite, and Raquel was still inside, intent on a pair of queens.

Dawn was breaking by the time Colorado Bob rose with a terminating yawn. Rather than losing the forty dollars he had given back to her, Raquel had won sixty more. Five hundred and sixty dollars! That was as much as a professor makes in a... Well, she was too tired to do the math.

CHAPTER 16

THE JUNGLE

For those gringos with romantic sensibilities who visited the Hotel Grand, there were two kinds of women who could spell their ruin. Everyone knew about the first kind. The Gingers. The girls who would lie and steal and betray and yet who were sexy enough and charming enough and young enough that their victims, however intelligent and worldly, were simply lost in their grasp, just like a dextrous insect that crawls too far into the flower of a venus fly trap. No one would deny that the Hotel Grand was a paradise for those amorous men drawn to the natural beauty of Costa Rica and the natural beauty of its women. Yet in the eventful decades of the hotel's existence how many sad tales might one tell of formidable, affluent men reduced to tears and bankruptcy by the Gingers within its walls?

But there was a second type of woman, usually overlooked, whose intimacy posed dangers no less grave. Women such as Laura. The good women, the great women. These women would not ask for anything. They were independent to a fault, too trusting for their own good, the kind of women who, having sold themselves, would give themselves. And that's where the danger lay. Because who could not but fall in love with such creatures? Rare as

303

the resplendent quetzal that drew birders from all over the world
to the forests of Costa Rica for a momentary glimpse of its shimmering plumage. The Laura's would not beg or steal. They did
not have to. Men showered them with gifts, with apartments, with
rings, and whatever money they had left went to pay for the in-
creasingly frequent airline tickets back and forth, until they were
finally swallowed by the jungle.

Laura, of course, lived in total ignorance of this second group,
to which she belonged. How could a sincere woman such as herself,
who never manipulated men the way the Gingers did, cause anyone harm? She didn't see herself as virtuous or better than others.
She just treated people the way she herself wished to be treated.
And if men fell in love with her, well, that happened all the time,
with everyone. You only have to open your front door to fall in love,
she had said more than once. And if men were melancholy or jealous or possessive, well, that was in their nature. She certainly did
nothing to encourage it. After all, her clients knew her profession.
They knew what she would give them, and what she would not.

But of course they didn't really know. They gave her a hundred
dollars and an hour later or a day later or a week later it was as
though there had never been a transaction. It was Laura the friend,
Laura the girlfriend, Laura the future mother of their children.

Laura had not completely appreciated what Dennis was going
through. If she had she never would have agreed to work for him.
But she hadn't been oblivious either. She knew he wanted more
than a business relationship, more than a friendship. She knew
he was jealous and possessive and Quixotic in his pursuit of her.
But she viewed these as normal human passions that would pass in
time as long as she did not encourage them. And she had not encouraged them. Not once had she slept with him since her retirement, or kissed him passionately, or played sexual games with him.
She had not even flirted with him, so careful had she been not to
cross the line. For in many ways the life of a prostitute was like the

life of a spy, and to excel in those professions one had to separate business from pleasure and family. Laura had always been good at compartmentalizing her life. She didn't understand why others couldn't do the same.

So she was puzzled the following Monday morning to find the door to Pan American Web Services locked. Maybe he stepped out, she thought, opening the door with her own key. But the lights were off. Her computer was gone.

She stood in shock, staring at the empty space on the table where the computer had sat. Then she noticed the sheet of paper lodged under the phone.

moved back home
family emergency

And there was a check made out in her name for two weeks' salary.

It took a while for the reality to sink in. Even after she tried his cell and got a recording that the number was not in service, she still did not understand what had happened.

She went to the soda across the street and mused over the situation while sipping a banana milkshake.

It was all the fault of that damned Jaime Primero, she concluded. If he hadn't walked into the Hotel Grand at the very moment she was showing the professor's photo she would be working at her desk right now and not drinking a banana milkshake, suddenly unemployed.

There had been one minor eruption, which she should have heeded as a warning sign that Dennis was about to explode over the Latino idol. But she didn't take notice, and Dennis exploded in the two major eruptions that followed, obliterating his presence in her country and her life.

The minor eruption was truly a small matter blown out of proportion. She had been looking through a magazine last week and saw the Delerio soap ad with Jaime Primero, sparkling clean and smiling seductively with his capped teeth. She tore it out and taped it above her desk, where he smiled down on her.

The next day it was gone. She didn't even notice until the end of the day because she was so busy. It was one of those feelings when you know something is missing, but not quite what. Then she remembered the advertisement.

"I threw it away," Dennis told her, coming upon her as she searched behind the desk.

Laura turned to him indignantly. "You had no right to touch my things!"

"It was on my wall," Dennis pointed out.

"So I cannot decorate my space? I thought you wanted me to feel like a part of this company, not like some immigrant worker with no rights."

"Of course I—"

"You didn't even speak to me about it! I demand you give it back."

She stormed into his office and unwadded papers from his trash basket.

"Where is it?"

"I burned it," Dennis confessed, beginning to feel warm himself.

"You burned it! Look, I thought our relationship was professional? Tell me yes or no? Are you my boss and my friend or a jealous husband?"

Dennis had no choice but to back down. She was right, after all. What else could he do? He even offered to hunt for another copy of the ad, and this mollified Laura.

Which was unfortunate, because rather than heeding this warning sign, she put it out of her mind. So far out that when she saw a color printout of a cock lying of her desk the following morning she peered at it from different sides and held it at arm's length and squinted, not certain what it was, thinking it might be a satellite photo.

When it became obvious that it could be one thing and one thing only she burst into Dennis's office without knocking and thrust the obscene image before his eyes.

"What do you think you're doing?" she screamed. "Do you want to be prosecuted for sexual harassment? If it's your idea of a joke to put an enlarged picture of your penis on my desk for all the world to see—"

"My penis!" Dennis thundered back, in no mood to mollify her this time. "Do they really all look the same to you then?"

Laura was befuddled. She peered at the picture again, shaking her head back and forth.

"It's not my penis!" Dennis clarified for her. And he held up his digital camera.

Laura stared at the camera. "But I..." And she covered her mouth with both hands, the offending image fluttering to the floor between them.

These first two eruptions were stories they might have laughed about with friends years later, but the third eruption was tragic rather than comic and highlighted the divergent dreams of two young people who otherwise might have been destined for partnership in life, whether in friendship, business or love.

Last Thursday had been the two week anniversary of her night with Primero. Every night since then she had dreamt of having his child. And by last Monday she was already late. So her hopes intensified day by day. Her horoscopes confirmed her wishes. She didn't even buy tampons, so strong was her faith. And then Thursday night she bled.

She took a long bath and cried, gazing at the small, framed photograph she normally kept by her bedside. The photo she turned face down whenever she had guests, because until she told Raquel the other night, only her mother knew she'd had a child. She never told the father, who had been a casual boyfriend in any case, and who was no longer in her life by the time she delivered. The photo was taken by her mother a couple days after the baby's birth. Laura looked pale but was smiling, holding her frail daughter in a pink blanket.

She had given birth three months prematurely, and this was the only photo she possessed. The poor creature had spent her brief existence in the hospital, and Laura had watched her struggle and decline with horror.

Life is so unfair, she thought the night of her period. Tita tries to kill herself because she is pregnant, while I, who want nothing more than to have Primero's baby, fail to conceive. It would have been such a beautiful child. Not frail at all but a champion, with my light complexion and his charisma. And he would have taken responsibility as the father. How could he not, once he saw how beautiful his child was? And whether he married me or not, whether he settled in Costa Rica or I followed him around the world or we decided to go our separate ways and only be a family at Christmas and Easter, it would be a fairy tale.

She should not have gone into the office Friday. But after having missed work two weeks ago she was determined not to call in sick.

She could not help sobbing at her desk, however. But when Dennis put a hand on her shoulder and asked what was wrong, she could have lied. She could have said something about Tita Moon, or her mother, or blamed her emotions on the time of month, which was true enough.

But instead she let her guard down. She forgot Dennis the suitor and saw only Dennis the friend. She threw her arms around him and cried that she was not pregnant with Jaime Primero's baby.

Dennis held her for a long time, shedding a few tears of his own, which she did not see. This was an eruption without arguments. The most dangerous of all.

She finished her banana milkshake, finally admitting to herself what she had tried so hard not to acknowledge. That there was no family emergency summoning Dennis back to California. Or rather there was a family emergency. But here. She was his family.

She sat in the dark, gilded bar at the Conquistador later that evening with Porter, drinking a cocktail from a tiki glass. It was happy hour, but he was the only one smiling.

"During your wedding I never would have thought that when we met again you would be the one who was content and I would be depressed," she admitted in a sorrowful voice.

For Ginger had not emptied Porter's bank account and run off with a teenage stud. Not yet anyway. Nor had she been sighted at the Hotel Grand. She even cooked dinner now and again. Porter had never looked happier. Laura had to admit there was even some flesh on his bones.

"I am glad to see you are doing well, of course," she continued. "You deserve to finally be happy, and no one hopes it lasts more than I do. But look at me. I have lost everything. My friend, my business." She decided not to mention Jaime Primero. "I finally achieve my dream to build my own home, away from all the noise and drama of the Hotel Grand, and I end up cleaning blood off the walls because one of my lodgers decides to cut her wrist! It was my rule not to rent to working girls. Not to bring that life within my walls. But no one answered my ads, so I had to rent to Tita. Then Raquel decided to go pro. So now I am renting to two working girls! Everything I have wanted has turned out the other way. And I am so sad for Dennis. I feel so guilty. If I knew how strong his feelings were I never would have agreed to work for him."

"I know," Porter said sympathetically, fingering his glasses. "Is it possible to keep the business alive? Maybe bring in someone else?"

"No. It was all Dennis's idea. Without him there is no Pan American Web Services. You don't know how hard he worked on it."

"You worked hard too, I'm sure. I'm sorry it ended this way. But there will be other opportunities for you. You're a bright women."

"I guess," Laura agreed equivocally.

Porter shook the ice cube in his ginger ale and pointed his finger at her. "Whatever you decide, don't go back to that place."

"What else can I do?" she asked him with pleading eyes. "At least for a while."

"I don't have a lot of discretionary income at the moment, but I can lend you enough to hold you over until you find another job."

Laura stood and put her hand around his bony wrist, much as she had done the first time they had met, in the Irazu suite. "I did not call you to ask for money," she said proudly. "I just wanted to talk to you. I was worried about you. Just as I am worried about Dennis."

"Worry about yourself," Porter advised her, rising as well and kissing her on the cheek. "It's a steep cliff you're walking on."

Laura recalled entertaining a similar concern for him at her retirement party, when he had been drunk and pining for Ginger. That he might try to drive to Limon and plunge from a mountain road.

It was Saturday night at the Hotel Grand. Mr. Escudero's niece had long since finished her shift at the travel desk, but a group of new arrivals were examining the brochures. Another new arrival was checking in, squeezing his suitcase between his legs as if the smirking girls sitting on the wicker sofa behind him had come here with the sole intention of stealing his collection of tropical shirts, his outdated library edition of Lonely Planet's *Costa Rica*, and his SPF 45 sunscreen. A cry of joy erupted from the casino as an aging monger collected his winnings at the craps table. Upstairs at the Canopy Diner all the tables were occupied, and waitresses stepped over outstretched stilettos like trekkers avoiding roots in the rain forest floor.

And in the Red Volcano Jaime Primero was singing his latest music video on the televisions overhead, but his seductive voice was muted by the seductive clamor below. Laura did not notice him. Her eyes were on the door, on a pair of good-looking gringos stepping past the security guard.

She stood with Carmen and Tita Moon, just like old times. But not so old. Just a month ago. Their ranks should have been shrinking, but they were swelling, for Raquel had joined them as well. They stood in the usual spot, squeezed by the crowd, on the raised platform between the bar and the front tables, dressed in tight jeans and tops, smoking cigarettes and gossiping, four wistful soldiers on the front line in the unending battle between women and men.

A shout was raised by Gloria at one of the back tables. Someone was drinking a Red Volcano. Laura cheered with the rest, optimistic despite the cruel fate that had granted a happy ending to Ginger of all people, while leaving her and Tita Moon, Carmen and Raquel hungry and abandoned, to slash their own path out of the jungle.

But several months yet remained until her twenty-fifth birthday. Her horoscope that morning had read:

Do not despair at minor setbacks. Though your romantic and financial fortunes may have recently taken a turn for the worse, be assured these developments are only temporary. Keep your wits about you and your eyes on the stars, which will soon be aligned in your favor.

She was confident she would yet achieve her dream of retirement before she blew out the candles on her next cake.

www.ingramcontent.com/pod-product-compliance
Lightning Source LLC
Chambersburg PA
CBHW071105250626

47159CB00002B/610

9 780997 616712